Don't miss
THE CRUELEST CUT
by Rick Reed

THE COLDEST FEAR

RICK REED

PINNACLE BOOKS
Kensington Publishing Corp.
www.kensingtonbooks.com

for Jennifer

PINNACLE BOOKS are published by

Kensington Publishing Corp.
119 West 40th Street
New York, NY 10018

All Kensington titles, imprints, and distributed lines are available at special quantity discounts for bulk purchases for sales promotions, premiums, fund-raising, educational, or institutional use. Special book excerpts or customized printings can also be created to fit specific needs. For details, write or phone the office of the Kensington special sales manager: Kensington Publishing Corp., 119 West 40th Street, New York, NY 10018, attn: Special Sales Department; phone 1-800-221-2647.

This book is a work of fiction. Names, characters, businesses, organizations, places, events, and incidents either are the product of the author's imagination or are used fictitiously. Any resemblance to actual persons, living or dead, events, or locales is entirely coincidental.

PINNACLE BOOKS and the Pinnacle logo are Reg. U.S. Pat. & TM Off.

ISBN-13: 978-0-7860-2484-1
ISBN-10: 0-7860-2484-4

First printing: September 2011

10 9 8 7 6 5 4 3 2 1

Printed in the United States of America

CHAPTER ONE

Snow hung heavy in the branches of Scotch pine and cedar trees, and where it hadn't turned to slush, the land was covered in a foot of snow. The storm had surprised everyone, and as the tall, dark-haired young man stepped off the bus in the town's center he could hear generators humming in every direction.

The town hadn't changed much, and even with snow, all the old landmarks were still there. Bertha's Diner was still on the corner, across the street from Rambo's, a redneck tavern where violent brawls broke out over imagined remarks or innocent looks. Next to Rambo's was the old five-and-dime where he used to look through the plate-glass windows at the toys and candy and wonder what it would be like to have a whole dollar to spend.

The five-and-dime was now a Dollar General, but the displays in the window could have been from fifteen years ago, as if time had somehow shifted backwards. But it hadn't. He had traveled a great distance to get here. And he was here with a purpose.

The judge had sentenced him to the asylum until such time he was declared fit to stand trial, but that day had never come. He had spent fifteen years inside. Fifteen years of watching, listening, learning what to say and how to say it. Learning how to convince the doctors that he was cured.

Before he had gone to the asylum he had hidden something in this town. Hidden it in the only place that, as an eight-year-old, he knew it would be safe. For fifteen years he had dreamed of this day, when he would finally reclaim what was rightfully his.

He half expected that when he returned to Shawneetown, Illinois, everyone would cast curious looks at him. Would wonder what he was doing home. What he was doing "out." But the town that had seemed so bustling to him as an eight-year-old only looked tired and depleted to him at age twenty-three.

There were just a handful of people on the streets. Like the snow, they looked washed of color, drained of life. He crossed the street, stepping into the ruts left behind by cars, and walked into the narrow gangway between Rambo's and the Dollar General store. The odor in the narrow alleyway reminded him of the burnt-grease smell on his father's clothing when he would come home from a night of drinking and gambling in the back room at the tavern. He remembered his mother being unable to buy food or clothing for them because of his father's affection for blackjack and poker.

The alleyway emptied out into a field behind the buildings and led into the woods. The State Highway Department used the field behind Rambo's to store crushed cinders and bricks for when the roads iced over. The huge pile of grit was gone, but even after fifteen years the cinders crunched under the smooth soles of his brand-new dress shoes. The asylum had given him shoes, slacks, a button-down shirt, and a recycled sport coat whose sleeves were several inches too short. They were his only possessions.

At the edge of the field was a small cut-through that the kids had used to get into the woods. A few hundred yards through the woods to the south were railroad tracks. And less than a mile on the other side of the tracks was the tiny house where he had once lived with his mother, father, and sister.

The house was gone now. The bus had driven past the lot on the way into town. A row of cheap duplexes had been built over his old stomping grounds. He had stared at the wide expanses of snow behind the duplexes and remembered the night he had run out the back of his house, through the fields and into the woods, covered in blood and weaving between the big wild blackberry bushes, which tore at his bare arms and chest. It had been snowing that night, too.

He made his way down the path behind Rambo's, and emerged from the woods into a small clearing where an old cabin stood. Its wood was blackened with age, and the handmade shutters were lying on the ground, smashed into pieces by vandals, everything covered in pristine white snow, but it was still there. When he was a kid, the cabin was rumored to be haunted. The truth was that it was a historical landmark. A Civil War general had lived there.

He didn't care about the historical significance of the cabin. He only wanted the item he had hidden there that night when he had run from the back door of his home covered in blood, some his own, some his father's. He had run in a daze, but with enough sense to know he had to hide it. The bone axe was what had finally set him free and he couldn't let anyone get it. It belonged to him and he to it.

He stopped just inside the sagging doorway of the cabin and closed his eyes to re-create that night. Three steps ahead he heard the floorboard creak. He knelt and found the loose floorboard and pulled at it with his fingers until it came free. Reaching into the small opening, roughly four inches by six inches, his hand closed on what he wanted. The bone axe was much bigger than the opening, but when his hand came back out it was closed around the short wooden handle of the weapon. The blade was handmade, forged from heavy iron, covered in years of rust. It was crafted to slaughter cattle, the blade sharpened and heavy enough to cut through bones.

He hefted the weight in his hand. It had seemed much larger and heavier when he was eight years old.

He'd have to find a place to stay, at least for the night. Somewhere out of town. He'd take the axe with him to give it a proper going-over. The bone axe still had a lot of work to do. Killing his father was only the beginning.

CHAPTER TWO

Five years later, Evansville, Indiana

Jack Murphy stood six foot, with a solid build, and a shock of dark hair he had taken to wearing spiked in the front. His gray eyes could turn dark when he was angry or threatened, or soft as a cloud when he was happy. They were soft gray now as he stood on the front porch of the river cabin he called home and gazed across the Ohio to the Kentucky side.

It was late fall; the trees that lined both shores had already lost most of their color. The early sun cast dizzying lights across the swift-moving water. Less than two hundred yards from his door a small spit of sand protruded from the river that was a favorite party site for the younger boaters. He'd spent many a lazy summer day watching bronzed bikini-clad bodies applying suntan lotion.

Unconsciously he rubbed at the thick white scar that ran from below his right ear, down his jaw and across his chest, ending above the left nipple. The scalding hot shower had started an itch that wouldn't end.

"You want freshened up?" Susan asked from the doorway.

Jack turned and found her holding the coffee decanter and wearing nothing but one of his white dress shirts that she had left unbuttoned. Her long blond hair framed her face, and not for the first time, the sight of her made breathing a conscious effort. The steam that rose from the open decanter could not match the steam he felt rising from within.

As the chief parole officer for the southern region of Indiana, Susan had seen and done things that would make strong men run in panic. Jack had never been able to understand why a woman so smart and beautiful had picked such a dangerous career.

"You must have been reading my mind," he said, and held out his mug for a refill.

"If I was reading your mind we'd be back in the bedroom and you would be late for work, Mr. Detective," she said with a giggle.

"Well, you have the day off for a change and I have at least . . ." he looked at his watch and said, "ten more minutes before I have to leave."

"Behave!" she said, and put her arms around his neck, her face mere inches from his.

Just as their lips touched the police radio that lay on the porch railing beside him crackled to life.

"All available units. One William Four is in foot pursuit of an armed suspect at Southeast Fourth and Main Street."

"Hold that thought," he said and headed for his car.

Seven o'clock in the morning, downtown traffic in Evansville was at its usual frantic pace when Jack Murphy drove his unmarked police car, a silver Crown Vic, up on the curb alongside the tall buildings, stopped at the mouth of the alleyway, rolled the windows down, and then turned off the ignition to listen. The other drivers apparently didn't seem to think this was odd behavior and continued in their dronelike traffic patterns on their way to and from their jobs.

The sound of footfalls was getting closer, the *slap-slap-*

slapping of shoe leather on asphalt. He listened to the quick succession of steps and began counting to himself, *one, two, three . . .*

Jack simultaneously cranked the ignition and stomped the accelerator. The car lurched across the mouth of the alley, blocking it entirely as he slammed on the brakes. The runner, unable to stop in time, struck the side of the car and splayed across the hood, smashing his face on the windshield. From inside the car the man looked like a squashed bug.

Jack Murphy jumped from the Crown Vic, dragged the groaning man onto the ground, and handcuffed him. The Evansville Police Department motto is *In Connection With the Community*. This was as fine a connection as Jack had ever made.

Two uniformed officers—one a rookie who Jack didn't recognize and the other an older cop named Wilson—came running up the alley. Wilson, half a block behind the youngster, was winded and gasping for air. He looked down at the man lying at Jack's feet.

"That's him. He just robbed the pharmacy with a knife," he said.

"He's fast," the younger cop said. He was at least as tall as Jack at around six foot, but was much more lean and baby faced. The younger cop added, "I would've caught him."

Jack and the older cop exchanged a look. They both knew that one day this youngster would be puking his guts up after a foot pursuit and would learn to take his time.

"Well, he's all yours," Jack said. "Just trade my cuffs off and you can have him."

The younger cop's name tag read OFFICER BLOOMBERG. Jack watched as Bloomberg expertly patted the suspect down, put his own handcuffs on him, and took Jack's off.

"Thanks, Detective Murphy," Bloomberg said, handing the cuffs over.

"I need to go to the hospital," the man said from the ground.

* * *

Detective Liddell Blanchard presented an imposing figure in any setting. At a little over six-foot-five and weighing in at "full-grown Yeti," he was the biggest man on the Evansville Police Department. When Jack arrived in the small parking lot behind police headquarters, he spotted Liddell leaning impatiently against the metal railing at the back entrance to the detective's office.

Jack squinted into the sun and glanced at the big man. He and Liddell had been partners for almost six years. Liddell's nickname on the police department was "Cajun" because of his Louisiana upbringing, and his addiction to Cajun cooking. Jack called him Bigfoot for obvious reasons.

"You're late, pod'na," Liddell said. "Sergeant Mattingly's gonna have your butt."

Jack strode up to the door. "He's already got mine and yours, too." Sergeant Mattingly was a short man with a very wide build. He resembled an old Volkswagen van with a bad hairpiece, and had a temperament to match.

Liddell nodded. "You're still late though."

"I ran into someone on the way here," Jack said.

"Yeah, I heard. And I heard the guy's threatening to sue you and the department. I think Internal Affairs was mentioned as well."

"Internal Affairs keeps a seat warm for me," Jack said. "In fact, I think they might give me my own parking spot."

Jack started toward the door, and Liddell stopped him, saying, "We just got a run."

"Can I go to the men's room?"

"Sure. But if you go in there you'll get yelled at," Liddell reminded him.

Jack muttered something, and they headed for the car.

CHAPTER THREE

The call reporting the murder had come from the Marriott on the highway near the airport. The caller had requested that police keep the response to a bare minimum, stating "this sort of thing just doesn't happen at the Marriott."

The police dispatcher didn't like the caller's tone of voice, so she sent four uniform cars, detectives, crime scene, fire and rescue squads, and the coroner. By the time Jack and Liddell arrived, the front entrance of the hotel was blocked with police and emergency vehicles including the coroner's black Suburban. Surprisingly, there were no television crews.

Jack and Liddell nodded at the uniformed officer standing guard at the front entrance and walked past the check-in counter, where a harried-looking woman was talking to an older officer.

They rode the elevator to the third floor. The room they wanted was near the end of the hallway, where five black Pelican hard-side cases lay open in the hallway near the door of the room. Arranged neatly inside the cases were cameras, fingerprinting equipment, and other tools.

"Look at all the goodies," Liddell said, eyeing all the cameras and technical equipment. "Marcie wants me to buy a new camera."

"You mean she doesn't like your state-of-the-art Polaroid?"

The sergeant in charge of the Crime Scene Unit, Tony Walker, stepped out of the room and motioned for Jack and Liddell to come in. "Stay with me," he said.

Sergeant Tony Walker was fifty years old with the physique of a thirty-year-old, and except for his salt-and-pepper hair you would easily mistake him for the latter. They followed Walker into the room and stopped just outside the bathroom door, where Jack could see two crime scene techs in white Tyvek clothing, booties, and hoods. One was taking digital photos. The other was busy taking notes and making a pencil sketch that was better than a computer-generated drawing.

"So what have the techs come up with?" Jack asked. Their backs blocked most of his view of the bathtub, but he could see one slender arm draped over the side of the tub. The arm ended at a bloody wrist. No hand.

Walker shrugged. "She's in pretty bad condition." He tapped the shoulder of the nearest tech. "Give us a minute, guys."

Darkish water trickled over the edge of the tub, running down the side and flooding the tiled floor of the small room. Inside the tub was the body of a white female, submerged, with only the top of her head and right arm above water. Her red hair floated like the bloody spokes of a wheel, radiating away from her skull. Her right arm was draped over the side of the tub. The skin near the wrist glistened with droplets of blood. A little blood had gathered where the arm made contact with the side of the tub, but Jack guessed that most of it had washed away with the water that spilled over the side of the tub.

The red hair floated away from the front enough for Jack to see that her face had been destroyed. He hoped they would find some identification in the hotel room because there would be no easy way to identify this woman. Whoever had killed her had removed her face and her right hand. The left arm was down in the water beneath her.

"The killer smashed her teeth out," Walker commented.

"The other hand?" Jack asked.

Walker shook his head. "We won't know until we move her."

Jack looked more closely at the wounds on top of the victim's head. The red hair was thick, even though it was now soaked with blood where it was pasted against the top of the woman's skull. Several deep gashes crisscrossed the scalp. *Maybe she put up a fight and was struck on top of the head with something, but she wasn't killed in this room,* Jack thought.

The body was turned slightly away from the threshold of the doorway where Jack stood, but he was able to see that the wound to her face started at the top of the forehead and moved downward, slicing through meat, skin, and sinewy muscle. The killer had cut away most of the face, including the nose and lips. It looked as if he had hacked downward with something wide and sharp. Where there should have been a face, only a skeletal mask remained. The eyes were missing, leaving bloody chasms in the orbital sockets.

"Is it okay if I get closer?" Jack asked. Walker nodded.

Jack stepped into the room and felt the water soak into his loafers. He stood directly above the corpse's head and looked down, then quickly retreated out of the room.

"Any weapons yet?" he asked Walker.

Walker turned and spoke to one of the techs, who handed him a plastic bag sealed with red evidence tape. Inside the bag was a long-handled teaspoon. The steel surface was smeared with something dark.

"This was left on top of the sink," Walker said.

"Can you take out someone's eyes with a spoon?" Liddell asked.

Walker shrugged. "It would be pretty hard. Whoever did would have to be incredibly strong to tear the ocular muscles free."

"Did anyone check to see if the hotel has a video system?" Jack asked.

Liddell and Walker looked at each other and shook their heads.

"You're not just another pretty face, pod'na," Liddell said and called downstairs to the uniformed sergeant in the front lobby. He listened for a few beats before saying, "Oh yeah? It figures." Turning to Jack he said, "They don't have a video camera at the entrance. We'll have to do this the old-fashioned way."

"You said the water was still running in the bathtub when the hotel employee found her?" Liddell asked Walker.

"The overflow of water could have carried away quite a bit of blood, but as you can see much of the water has soaked into the carpeting at the threshold," he said, and pointed at the doorway. There was a bright red stain in the dull Berber carpet. "The employee—the manager, I think—had a complaint from the guests on the next floor down that water was leaking through the ceiling into their room. She came up and found the body and turned the water off."

"It was very cost-conscious of her to think of saving water," Liddell said, earning a warning look from his partner.

Walker said, "I think the murder took place in the bedroom. The bedspread is soaked in blood, and the arterial spray we were talking about is all over the room. We found more blood pooling on the floor at the bottom of the bed. Also, there is arterial spray on the ceiling and wall near the side of the bed nearest the door to the room."

He reached a gloved hand into the water and moved the

victim's head only slightly to the side. A swirl of blood issued from an area of the victim's neck about two inches below and forward of the right ear.

"Let me know as soon as you get something, Tony," Jack said.

"Little Casket's here, but she went back downstairs just before you arrived." Walker was referring to the chief deputy coroner, a diminutive woman named Lilly Caskins. "Little Casket" was a nickname that suited her well, because she was evil looking, with large dark eyes staring out of extra-thick lenses, and horn-rimmed frames that had gone out of style during the days of Al Capone.

Jack respected her work for the most part, but she had an annoying habit of being blunt at death scenes. He found it surprising that a woman could have absolutely no compassion for the dead, and no love for the living.

Jack felt a presence nearby and turned to see the squat figure of Detective Larry Jansen standing just inside the entrance to the room. Jansen reminded Jack of a bumbling TV sleuth, with his wrinkled and dirty car coat, worn and scuffed black shoes, and mop of uncombed greasy hair. Jansen was questioning the officer who was keeping the crime scene entry log. He made some notes and then looked up, noticed Jack, and walked over.

"Well, look who's back," Liddell said.

Jansen had just returned to duty after receiving a thirty-day suspension without pay for violating department policy. A less connected detective would have been fired on the spot, but Jansen knew where all the political bodies were buried. The man seemed to be coated in Teflon, and it was a surprise to almost everyone that he had been suspended.

"You gonna take this one, Jansen?" Walker asked jokingly.

"Yeah, I'll take it. I was in the area," Jansen responded.

This was not the kind of case that could be entrusted to a

detective like Jansen, who would undoubtedly shuffle it into a folder and bury it. In truth, any type of case should not be assigned to him. "Too late, Larry. The captain already assigned it to us," Jack lied.

Jansen glared at Jack and Liddell, his mouth a tight line, and then he shrugged and left the room.

Jack pulled out his cell phone and punched in the number for Captain Chuck Franklin, the commander of the Homicide Unit. Franklin would then call the chief. The chief would probably call the mayor and the mayor would call whoever was holding his leash at the moment. Politics was a wonderful thing. No one wanted to get caught with their pants down when the news media got wind of this.

Outside the hotel Jansen was dialing his own cell phone. He could care less about the captain or chief of police. *I'll take care of Murphy and that Cajun partner of his,* Jansen thought.

CHAPTER FOUR

Blake James finished running four miles along the riverfront and was leaning against a marble column of the Four Freedoms Monument to stretch. This morning's run had been shorter than he would have liked, but he had to get to work, and he had not been late a day in the last three years since taking over as the news anchor for Channel Six television. At twenty-six years old he was the youngest anchor in the history of the station. Since he ran religiously he was in the best shape he had ever been in. His muscles sang with the exertion he had just put them through, but he was on a runner's high and when his phone rang it didn't surprise him. He was on call twenty-four hours a day. It was probably the station.

He looked at the display and groaned out loud. Two icons appeared on the screen: DECLINE and ANSWER. His thumb hesitated over the DECLINE icon for a few rings, but then he pressed ANSWER and said, "Hello, Detective Jansen. What can I do for you so early in the morning?"

"Ask not what you can do for Larry Jansen, but what Larry Jansen can do for you," the detective said with a chuckle. His intention was to quote the late, great President

John Fitzgerald Kennedy. It was a game he and Blake played. Blake was somewhat of a historian.

"Friday, January twentieth, 1961, the inaugural speech of John F. Kennedy," Blake said. "Outgoing President Eisenhower was present at the inauguration. In fact, Kennedy had attended Holy Trinity Church earlier and rode to Congress with Eisenhower. Snow had fallen the night before and there were thoughts of cancelling the speech. The elections had been close, but the senator from Massachusetts had beaten the incumbent vice president, Richard Nixon, and was anxious to start the arduous task of gathering support for his agenda. Chief Justice Earl Warren administered the oath of office and a poem was read by none other than Robert Frost." Blake hesitated and then asked, "Do you know what the poem was, Detective?"

As always, Jansen had a short fuse. "Nah. I don't know what the poem was, Blake. But I got something real hot for you. Do you want it or not?"

"The answer is 'The Gift Outright,' Larry. Of course, the handwritten poem he had composed for the presidential occasion was actually 'Dedication,' but no one really knows why he read the shorter poem in place of it. Both poems spoke to the same human conditions—those of power and control and abuse of the lower classes." Blake delivered this narrative as if he had been present during this oration by Robert Frost.

"Okay, Blake. I'm a dumbass! Is that what you want to hear? Well, screw you very much and I'll give my tip to someone else."

Blake James laughed and the sound was infectious. Jansen could no more be mad at this man than he could be mad at himself. It was no wonder someone with the personality of Blake James was the most popular news anchor in Evansville media history. Jansen started laughing, too.

"We still friends, Larry?" Blake asked.

"Yeah. I guess so."

"Then all is well with the world," Blake said, and laughed again.

"I got a murder for ya," Jansen said.

"Oh? Are you the lead investigator?" Blake asked.

The line was silent for a moment; then Jansen said, "No, Blake. I'm not the lead investigator. Why's that matter?"

"Is Murphy the lead?"

The line was silent much longer this time. Blake could imagine Jansen struggling with his anger. It was no secret that he hated Murphy. It was also no secret that Jansen was a horrible detective and could screw up a confession.

"Okay, you're right. It doesn't matter, Larry. Tell me about it. And don't leave anything out." Blake slipped into news-anchor talking-head mode, all business.

Blake had Jansen repeat the whole story twice to be sure he hadn't left anything out, and then ended the call. Blake then punched in the number for the newsroom at Channel Six. His co-anchor, Claudine Setera, answered on the first ring.

Larry Jansen looked at the business card he had kept in his wallet for the best part of a week now. He wondered if he should have called her instead of Blake. But then he thought about his wife and a momentary fit of conscience struck him.

He remembered when his wife was young and beautiful and desirable. Not as desirable as Claudine Setera, but nice. Real nice. Back then the smell of her hair was like fresh flowers, the taste of her lips—and other parts as well—was like a drug that made him shake with need. But since she had become ill she smelled like dried urine and he didn't dare breathe when he gave her a quick peck on the cheek before going to work. He wondered how things had gotten so messed up.

CHAPTER FIVE

Lilly Caskins looked on with consternation as Blake James pulled into the parking lot. He slid his athletic body from his vehicle and smoothed his long dark hair back out of his eyes. He reminded her of Antonio Banderas. She normally didn't like reporters, but Blake was cute. Even an old dame like her could see that he had a cute butt. But she didn't like her name in the news, didn't like seeing herself on television, and absolutely hated the way the cameramen seemed to deliberately catch shots of her when she was standing next to the tallest policemen, thereby making her look like a fussy old dwarf.

"Hello, Lilly," Blake said. Coming up quickly, he gave her a firm hug, enveloping her diminutive form into the folds of his clothing like Count Alucard in the old Dracula movies.

"Hmmpf. Hello yourself," she muttered, but didn't try to extricate herself too strenuously. He smelled of sweat and cologne and man scent. She backed up a step and had to crane her neck to look him in the eye.

"Why, Lilly, you're blushing," he said with a smirk.

She could feel her face flush and looked around the parking lot to be sure that no one else had noticed. Behind her she saw Claudine Setera, a smarmy smile pasted to her face, and a Channel Six cameraman pointing the camera lens her way. *The bitch filmed the whole thing,* Lilly thought as she stormed away and back into the safety of the Marriott.

"What do we need that shot for?" the cameraman asked.

Claudine ignored him and approached Blake. "What was that all about?"

Blake's expression turned to ice. "Just watch me work, little girl," he said and strode away toward the front entrance of the Marriott.

Claudine and the cameraman trotted along behind.

Lilly Caskins entered the hotel room and headed straight for Jack.

"The jackals are at the door," she said.

"Yeah? Well, I guess they were bound to show up sooner or later, eh?" Jack said.

"That damned Jansen," Liddell muttered.

Jack looked at him and shook his head. *Jansen. Which means the "jackal" Lilly is referring to is Blake James. Jansen talks about Blake like he's the best thing since sliced bread,* he thought.

"Blake James's down there," Lilly said, confirming Jack's thoughts. "And he's got that little Italian honey you guys have been ogling."

Liddell straightened his tie, smoothed his hair, and popped a piece of gum into his mouth. "I guess I'd better go talk to her—them, I mean," he said.

"You're married, Bigfoot," Lilly reminded him. "Better send Jack. It's just a matter of time before that parole-officer gal kicks him to the curb."

Jack gave her a severe look. "Her name is Susan. She's not a 'parole-officer gal,' she's the chief parole officer in Evansville, and I didn't get kicked to the curb yet."

Liddell smirked. There was going to be a fight. Six-foot-tall, hard-as-nails Jack Murphy, against four-foot-five, skinny-as-a-rail, and old-as-a-redwood Lilly Caskins. Murphy didn't stand a chance.

"Sorry, Jack," Lilly said, "I didn't mean it that way. Just having a bad day."

Liddell swallowed his gum and choked as it went down the wrong way. Neither Jack nor Lilly made a move to help him, suspecting he was just putting on a show.

Liddell coughed into his hand a few times and excused himself to go and meet the press.

"You need to keep him on a leash," Lilly said, coming as close to a grin as Jack had ever seen.

"He's all right, Lilly. Give him a break." Jack looked back toward the bathroom, where the crime scene techs were lifting the body from the bathtub. A body bag was open on a gurney near the tub. The techs gently lowered the body into the black plastic bag. Jack stopped them before they zipped it shut.

"Just a minute," he said, and both he and Lilly took another look at the victim.

"Destroyed the face," Lilly said, and then added, "She knew her killer."

Jack looked at her. He was thinking the same thing, but he was curious why Lilly thought so. "Have you seen something like this before?"

"Yeah," she said. "When I was in Vegas at a medicolegal death-investigation school. They showed photos of a woman with her face smashed in with a brick. In that case it was an ex-husband that was smashing what he could no longer have. What he couldn't stand to look at."

"But have you ever seen a face removed?" Jack asked. Lilly shook her head.

Jack was still gloved up. He looked down on the grisly thing that was once a human head and carefully moved the face to the side. Long red hair fell across the gaping wound in the slender neck. Her head had almost been severed from her body. *So that explains all the blood in the bedroom,* he thought.

The face was flattened, as if something heavy had been slammed into it, smashing it down and crushing the bones. But when he looked closer he didn't see bone fragments, or the radial fractures that you would expect from a blow that came straight into the face. He wasn't a medical examiner, but Jack could tell the direction of the blow was from above the face and down to the chin.

He lifted the left arm gently by the wrist and could feel the coldness of the flesh even through the gloves. Rigor was beginning to set in, and the muscles were becoming rigid. He wondered why only one had been removed. *Not trying to hide her identity,* Jack thought. *So why cut the face off and smash out the teeth?*

Lilly got a funny look on her face. "Jack. Look at the top of her head."

Jack remembered noticing the cuts on the scalp when he had first viewed the scene. "What about them?"

"What do those cuts look like to you?" she asked, impatiently.

Jack moved the hair to get a better look at the deep cuts, then gave Lilly an inquiring look. The cuts looked like numbers.

"Three seventy-five?" Jack said.

"Yeah," Lilly agreed. "That's what it looks like to me, too."

Little Casket was in charge of the body now. A couple of techs would escort her to the parking lot, where they would load it into the cargo area of the coroner's wagon. And then Lilly, like Charon, the ferryman of Hades, would carry the soul of the newly deceased across the river Styx into the world of the dead.

This is death in all its glory, Jack thought. He stood beside the doorway to the bathroom, where techs were finishing collecting evidence, and pulled his phone from his pocket.

"Hi, handsome," Susan said, answering the call.

"I just wondered what you were doing," he said in a low voice.

"What color panties am I wearing? Is that what you mean, honey?" she said and giggled.

"Well, I was actually going to tell you what I'm not wearing," he said. The crime scene tech in the bathroom yelled, "Get a room."

"What was that?" Susan asked.

"Nothing," Jack said, and pointed a finger at the grinning tech.

"I'm going to have to go into a meeting in a minute," Susan said, and Jack could hear someone calling to her.

"How about meeting at Two-Jakes later for supper?" Jack asked. It was a date he hoped he would be able to keep.

Susan sighed contentedly. "At least you're still asking."

"I promise that I'll try to be there," Jack said, feeling a little defensive. Her birthday was just four days away and he needed to pick her brains about what she wanted. He was thinking of a jogging outfit.

"Then the answer is yes. Gotta go," she said, and they hung up.

For a moment he wondered what it would be like to have a normal life. To not have to get up to his elbows in the messes that anyone in their right mind would run away from. *Is this any kind of life to offer a woman?* he thought.

When he'd married his ex-wife, Katie, he'd been a policeman for a just few years, but he already had a pretty good idea what their life would be like. His father had been a cop, and he, his younger brother, and his younger sister had always felt that the only parent in their lives was their mother. His dad was always unavailable, either sleeping, working, or on some other type of police activity.

Katie's life had been different. Her father was a high school teacher, her mother a stay-at-home mom. Katie only had good family memories. Vacations, holidays, visiting relatives, all the things that a well-adjusted family would experience. But then, she was an only child, and the worst problem her father had to deal with might be an unruly student.

Jack's family life was much different and he had been made to grow up very fast. He still remembered his mother telling him, "I depend on you, Jack. It's your duty to look out for the little ones." And he had been doing that his whole life. His brother and sister were both happily married with families of their own now, but Jack still did his best to protect them. Maybe that was why he had become a cop like his father. He had grown up protecting people who were weaker.

He knew Katie had wanted children, and he wished he could have given her the two-point-three children that every family in the United States boasted. But he had always been held back by the reality of evil in the world. How could he bring children into that, knowing that he might not be home if they needed him?

And that led him to another thought. Did Susan want kids? They'd never talked about it.

He looked at his watch and wondered what was taking Liddell so long. The man had only gone down to the front desk to get a list of employees and guests who were in the hotel last night.

He was absentmindedly leaning in the bathroom doorway when the tech said, "Got something here, Jack."

* * *

The tech used a pair of plastic tweezers to pick something out of the bloody water that remained in the bathtub and held it up. Jack stepped into the small bathroom and shut the door behind them.

Both men looked at the item. It was obviously fleshy and Jack put words to his thoughts, "Is that a tongue?"

The tech nodded, and said, "Yeah. I think so."

Officer Morris had been with Crime Scene Unit for seven years now and had seen some crazy shit in his day, but this was up there in the top five. "I pulled the stopper and when the water wouldn't drain I felt around. This was stuck in the drain under the plug."

"Her tongue?" Jack asked.

Morris shrugged. "I don't know if anyone looked in her mouth."

"Anyone else see this yet?"

Morris shook his head. "I just found it."

Jack knew that something like this wouldn't remain secret long. "*You* collect this," Jack said, "and not a word to anyone outside of Sergeant Walker, Liddell, and me."

With Jansen showing up at the scene like he did, Jack didn't want to take a chance that this would leak before they could even verify that the tongue—if that's what it was—belonged to the victim.

"You, me, Liddell, and Walker," Jack said. "Put nothing in the computer yet."

Morris cocked his head.

Jack said, "I'm going to get Walker. Keep the door shut."

The killer was in the catbird seat. Evansville Police cars were everywhere, and uniformed officers stood at all the entrances to the Marriott. He knew they would be inside as well, guarding all the stairways, asking questions, checking to see if there was video and all the other things that policemen were apt to do. But nothing they did would trip him up. He was too good at this. *Better at my job than they are at theirs*, he mused.

Five years and countless bodies had given him the upper hand. He was like a wind, or a fleeting thought. There one moment, and gone the next. This was the seventh state he had chosen to visit, and he had left a slew of bodies in his trail. In one state he was called The Axe Man. In another he had been dubbed The Handy Man. Yet another, probably more aptly, described him as The Cleaver.

But in all his travels he had never heard his real name. And in that anonymity he felt comfortable and yet disappointed. What had started as a mission to rid the earth of the scum like his father had turned into a killing spree with no purpose other than the killing itself. In fact, it was getting quite boring.

And then he had happened to find a news article online about a detective in Evansville, Indiana, who thought he was some kind of badass. He'd been intrigued. He remembered thinking that it might be fun to go to Evansville. It had been five years since he had been anywhere near his birthplace in Illinois, and Evansville was only a stone's throw away.

There is an old saying that goes, *You can never go home again*. But it's wrong. He did come home. And now the fun was just beginning.

CHAPTER SIX

The weatherman had predicted a warm and sunny day, but Louise Brigham looked up at the darkening sky and recognized the makings of a thunderstorm. The clothes she had washed in the sink that morning still lay in the laundry basket waiting to be hung on the makeshift clothesline she had strung between her apartment and the one behind her.

Project housing allowed for very little in the way of a yard, so the closeness of the buildings was used for other things, such as hanging wash and giving the children a safe place to play under the constant eye of one neighbor or another.

Louise brought the clothes basket back into the kitchen and let out a sigh. The nearest Laundromat was twelve blocks away, and through some of the worst neighborhoods in Evansville. Even the police seemed to avoid those areas unless they were in groups. But from what she had heard on Channel Six news on television this morning, there were other parts of the city that were just as dangerous. Some type of murder investigation was going on at that big hotel out by the airport.

She hadn't always lived like this. At one time she had been married to a good man and had a high-paying job. Back then she still had a good figure and nice features and the world had looked bright and promising. She would never have dreamed it would end up like this a mere five years later.

She looked down at the basket of wet clothes. *They won't dry themselves,* she thought.

She went to the closet to get her Windbreaker—the only jacket that she owned. When she pulled the door open she noticed something wasn't quite right. Then she heard a noise behind her.

CHAPTER SEVEN

They now had a name for the victim at the Marriott. Cordelia Morse. It said so on her Illinois driver's license and on a library card for the Gallatin County Public Library. The address on the driver's license was for a post-office box in Shawneetown, Illinois. Jack had heard of the town, and the things he'd heard weren't flattering.

Her purse was found in the hotel room's closet along with a lightweight jacket. The jacket pockets contained the usual items—a travel pack of Kleenex, some change, and a small scrap of paper with nothing on it. The purse, however, was a gold mine.

Crime scene would be at the Marriott for the rest of the day, but by eight o'clock that morning, Jack and Liddell decided to split up to follow up on the scant information they had extracted from the scene. This case promised to be challenging. Not only because the victim was from another state, but because the amount of violence done to the body indicated so many things.

The killing could be a domestic homicide, a husband or boyfriend thing where he catches her in Evansville seeing someone else and snaps. But she had registered at the Marriott for a week, and there had been no calls to or from her room, so that kind of eliminated the domestic issues.

Of course, the lack of calls could mean that she had used a cell phone, although no cell phone was found at the scene. But why would the killer take the phone and nothing else? *The killer did take something,* Jack reminded himself. *He took her face and her eyes and her hand. The tongue was another matter. What did that mean?*

One of the crime scene techs had also found a set of keys on the floor under the bed—an electronic key that was probably a car key, and two or three well-worn keys. *Maybe dropped by the victim and ended up under the bed during the struggle,* Jack thought. The keys were attached to a faux-diamond-studded letter *C. C for Cordelia, the name on the driver's license?*

Jack stepped out of the back foyer of the hotel and into the parking lot. Black clouds moved to the north and thunder rumbled in the distance. It was unusual to have thunderstorms this late in October. He hoped the rain would hold off at least until he could find the victim's car and have it secured by Crime Scene.

Holding the black plastic key in the air, he pressed the red rectangular button. Twenty or so yards away a car alarm went off. Jack followed the sound until he spotted the red Toyota whose lights were flashing. He silenced the alarm and called Sergeant Walker's cell phone.

"Found her car," he said when Tony came on the phone.

"I heard," Tony said. "I'll send someone."

A few minutes later a female crime scene tech pulled up in a marked car. She was as tall as Jack, strongly built, and he imagined that if her hair wasn't pulled back into a tight ponytail, she would be a knockout. She looked like a bodybuilder, her face angular and sharp but pretty.

"Hello, Detective Murphy," she said, and they shook hands.

Jack had been expecting someone who was already on scene to come out of the hotel and process the vehicle.

She noticed his hesitance and said, "Officer Martin." Her voice was deep and pleasant, almost sultry, but she was all business. When he still didn't speak, she said, "Don't worry, Detective Murphy. I may be new—and a woman—but I'm very competent."

"I have no doubt," Jack said, a little offended by her attitude. Maybe more offended that she was slightly on target about his thought process. "I just wondered how much you know about what is going on here, Officer Martin."

Instead of answering right away she slipped on a pair of gloves and pulled a digital camera from her vehicle. "You'll tell me what I need to know. So what are we looking for, sir?" She offered Jack a pair of gloves, but he declined.

"The car should be fingerprinted first before we open it," he said, and walked a little away and called Sergeant Walker.

"Tony, Officer Martin is here, but I think she may need another pair of hands."

"Sorry, Jack. I'm out of officers. You'll have to be her backup."

Jack put the phone back in his pocket and walked back to the young tech. "It appears that I'm your backup."

She grinned and offered him the gloves again. "Well then, let's get to it."

For the next fifteen minutes Jack alternately watched and/or handed Officer Martin fingerprint brushes, print-lift kits, and her various cameras, until she declared the car securely fingerprinted on the outside and pertinent areas inside. Jack had to admit that she was very competent, and probably more thorough than some of the more experienced crime scene officers that he knew. He had to resist the impulse to tell her that she had done excellent work, for fear that this might be taken as a gender-biased remark.

"What now?" he asked.

She opened the driver's door of the Toyota. "You can look inside, but not get inside. Please don't disturb anything," she said, and then seeing the look on his face, added, "sir."

There was nothing in plain view inside the vehicle, or in the trunk, but in the glove box he found the rental agreement. Otherwise, the car was so clean and tidy it didn't appear to have been driven. Jack doubted the killer had been in it, but it would still be towed to storage for a thorough examination by Walker's crew.

Jack straightened up and stretched his back, and said, "Thanks for the assistance, Officer Martin."

"I'll have it towed to our garage. We'll call you when it's been processed, sir."

Jack slipped off the latex gloves and stuck them in his pocket, then pulled out his notebook and wrote down the description of the car, including license plates and location in the parking lot.

The rental agreement was from Alamo Rent A Car at Evansville Dress Regional Airport, less than a mile away. *Why would she rent a car from there?* he wondered. The answer might be at Alamo. His next stop.

Jack called Liddell from Alamo's rental office inside the airport.

"The red Toyota I found in the parking lot was paid for by a guy named Jonathan Samuels," Jack said. "Same post-office box number in Shawneetown, Illinois, as our victim. Are you back at headquarters?"

"Yeah," Liddell said. "I'm running Cordelia Morse through the system. Whoever killed her wasn't after money. There was almost three thousand dollars in twenty-dollar bills in the purse."

"The injuries weren't to hide her identity," Jack said.

"Yeah," Liddell agreed.

"Check her out with narcotics," Jack said.

"You think she was dealing?" Liddell asked.

"She left her own car behind at Alamo when she picked up the Toyota," Jack said. "There was a small bag of marijuana tucked under the driver's seat."

"But not three grand worth?"

"No," Jack admitted. "But it's possible she was going to buy drugs and use the rental car to transport. That would keep her personal car free from possibly being seized by the government if she were caught."

"So it could be a drug deal gone bad?" Liddell asked.

Jack didn't think someone would go to the extremes that were evident in the death of Cordelia Morse for three thousand dollars. And then not even take the money. Something else was going on here.

"I don't have a clue yet, but when I get it all figured out I'll let you take all the credit as usual, Bigfoot," Jack said with a smile.

"You are so good to me," Liddell said.

"I found something else," Jack said, becoming serious again. "There was a business card for one of the Bange brothers. Lenny Bange. It was on the floor of her rental car."

"Bange, Bange, Bange," Liddell said. He was very familiar with the three brothers. All were attorneys and ran a lucrative practice in the downtown area.

"Run Lenny Bange and Jonathan Samuels of Shawneetown, Illinois, too," Jack said.

"I'm running down the names of people who stayed at the hotel last night and calling them. Is there anything else you'd like me to do? Like maybe solve the world's food-shortage problem, and bring about world peace while I'm not busy?"

"That would be nice, Bigfoot."

"Speaking of food, where we going to eat?" Liddell asked.

Jack felt a little hungry, too, but he wanted to keep going

while he had something to work on. And Lenny Bange was the next lead. "I'll grab a sandwich on my way to Lenny Bange's office."

"I'll order a pizza then," Liddell said.

Jack knew that meant two large kitchen-sink pizzas from Turoni's were about to meet their death at the hands of the Cajun-ator.

They hung up and Jack sat in his car looking at Lenny Bange's card and the small plastic Baggie of marijuana. Room 316 at the Marriott, where Cordelia Morse was found hacked to death, had been paid for by a credit card. That card belonged to Lenny Bange. The car she had at the hotel was paid for by a man named Jonathan Samuels. *Very curious,* he thought. Cordelia Morse seemed to have a knack for getting guys to pay her bills.

He wondered what other talents she had.

CHAPTER EIGHT

Three uniformed officers stood in the hallway, guns drawn, expressions chiseled out of granite, as Jack and another officer stood on each side of the door to room 375. The killer would have to be stupid or suicidal to have left such a clue and then to hang around to be caught. But the fact was that room 316, where Cordelia Morse was found butchered, was at the opposite end of the hall from room 375. And the killer had carved the number 375 into her scalp.

The fact that there was a dead body just down the hall necessitated a quick entry. There was no time to get a search warrant. And no need.

Jack mouthed to his cover officer, "On three."

The officer nodded and Jack soundlessly mouthed, *One, two* . . . On three they both kicked a foot into the door beside the locking mechanism. The door slammed inward.

Jack moved low to the right into the room and the uniformed officer moved to the left, both men's pistols extended, sweeping the room. The blinds to the room were drawn, the only light seeping in from the shattered hallway door.

Jack and the officer checked the obvious places where a

person could lie in wait for an ambush, but the room was empty. Jack was beginning to feel foolish and could feel the stare of the officer who had made entry with him. But then he spotted something on the foot of the bed.

"How about some lights?" he said to the officer.

The lights came on and Jack could see what was on the foot of the bed. It was a newspaper. The front-page story was one Jack recognized. On top of the newspaper was an object that looked like a bloody eyeball.

"Better get crime scene in here," Jack said. Both men retraced their steps, making a careful retreat from the room.

The newspaper was three months old and had a front-page story about one of Jack's previous cases. It was a sensational case and had been on the front page for several days. This particular story was not very supportive of Jack and had in fact hinted that he was a gun-happy cowboy.

The eye was probably from the victim, Cordelia Morse, but that would have to be determined by the medical examiner.

Lilly Caskins told them the autopsy would be sometime after noon, so he had a little time to play with. But not too much.

He took out the business card that he had found in Cordelia's rental car. Lenny Bange, Esquire, of Bange, Bange and Bange, Attorneys at Law. The business card depicted a smiling Lenny Bange wearing a cowboy hat, the brim pushed back with the smoking barrel of a six-gun. The logo read: *Get more Bange for your Buck.*

It was actually quite a catchy advertisement. There were several billboards around town that showed a posed picture of the three brothers, wearing old-west attire complete with gun belts and pistols. The words on one billboard stated, BANGE BANGE BANGE, and below the picture of the three brothers dressed as cowboys the caption read, WE SUE DRUNK DRIVERS.

It should say, "We sue everyone," Jack thought.

CHAPTER NINE

The offices of Bange, Bange and Bange were in the Court Building downtown. It wasn't actually the building where trials were held, but had been named that because it was directly across the street from the old county courthouse once upon a time. When the new court building had been built on property directly behind the Civic Center on Main Street, the Court Building and the Old Courthouse had found use as office space for several companies, but mostly for lawyers.

Jack rode the elevator to the eleventh floor with a young guy in a very expensive suit who was trying hard to look grown up. Jack had seen him around the courthouse before. He was tall and thin, with a scraggly mustache that was more peach fuzz than whisker, but the suit was top shelf. Apparently he was making some pretty good bread.

"How long have you worked for Lenny?" Jack asked, trying to be polite.

"You're Jack Murphy, aren't you?" the young man said.

Jack put his hands up in mock surrender. "You got me."

The man grinned and put out his hand. "How do you know I work for Lenny?"

"You're going to the eleventh floor. That entire floor belongs to the Bange brothers," Jack said, shaking his hand.

The young man nodded. "Name's Manny. Manny Bange."

Jack looked the youngster over more closely. He didn't remotely resemble the Bange brothers. They were all short and squat, with wide heads shoved on top of muscled necks and shoulders.

Manny noticed the look and said, "Lenny is my adoptive father."

"You have my condolences," Jack said, and this brought a smile.

The doors opened on the eleventh floor, and Manny stepped out, motioning for Jack to follow him. "Who are you here for?" he asked, and added, "Not me, I hope."

"Lenny," Jack said.

"I'm heading that way. I'll sneak you past his secretary."

"She's pretty fierce?" Jack asked.

"Gestapo," Manny said with a smile. "We got her after her tour at Guantanamo Bay."

Jack had to laugh.

"You seem like a nice guy," Jack said.

"So why am I an attorney?" Manny finished, and both of them chuckled. "Heard that one a few times."

Cordelia Morse, Liddell thought. He'd run the name through their local system and came up with no record. He'd run her in IDACS, the Indiana Data and Communication System that contained criminal records for all of Indiana and had come up with zilch, also. He'd even run her through NCIC, the National Crime Index Center that was maintained by the FBI, and still nothing. Of course, that didn't mean much. Women legally changed names easier than he changed his underwear, and if they didn't commit a new crime under the new name they could avoid being found in the computer.

He was luckier with the Illinois driver's license, but it

didn't tell him much except for the post-office box number in Shawneetown, Illinois. Jonathan Samuels had nothing in the local database either, and without a date of birth or Social Security number to put with it he could go no further.

It was beginning to look like he and Jack would be taking a trip to Shawneetown. From what some of the other detectives were saying, that town was just a spot in the road. Backwoods. Countrified to the nth degree. And then they had made gestures as if they were picking a banjo.

Liddell himself was born and raised in a little town in Louisiana called Placquemine, and he had spent six years at the Iberville Parish Sheriff Department before meeting his wife, Marcie, and then moving to Evansville so that she could be near her family. The guys in the detective office would undoubtedly consider Liddell's hometown to be a spot in the road, too, but he knew they would never make banjo-picking remarks to his face.

He didn't mind being called "Cajun" because people in Indiana seemed to think that anyone coming from Louisiana was a Cajun. But in fact, his side of the family had been mostly Creole, which was a mix of native Indian and blacks. As cracker white as Liddell's skin looked, no one would ever guess that his great-great grandpa was as black as the ace of spades. Not Negro, not Indian, just Creole.

The autopsy on Cordelia Morse was scheduled for this morning, and he had nothing to show for an hour of work except a driver's license status and a post-office box number in Shawneetown, Illinois.

His cell phone rang. Recognizing the caller's number he answered, saying, "Doctor Love's House of Pain."

Marcie Blanchard was prepared for this. "When's the doctor coming home?" she asked.

"Don't know," Liddell said. "Autopsy's this morning sometime, and Jack's talking to some attorney."

"Oh dear! Is he in trouble again?" she asked.

Liddell laughed. "Nothing that Doctor Love can't get him out of, babykins. What's for supper tonight?"

"Depends on whether Doctor Love gets home before it gets cold." She said this in a whispery voice that made his heart melt.

"Love you, Marcie," he said.

"You keep Doctor Love safe. Call me when you can."

He promised to keep in touch and hung up.

His thoughts turned to his partner. Jack was the best friend Liddell could imagine. They were more like brothers than partners. Liddell had been there when Jack and Katie were married, and he'd been there when they divorced. He'd watched his partner go through hell over the divorce, and still could not understand why they had split up. But it was Jack's life, his own business. Still, he wished that his partner could be as happy as he was with Marcie.

His desk phone rang.

"Evansville Police Department," Liddell said into the receiver, then listened for a moment and hung up. It was time to go to the morgue.

CHAPTER TEN

Jack had concluded his meeting with Lenny Bange and was waiting at the coroner's office entrance when Liddell arrived.

"Any luck?" Jack asked. Liddell shook his head.

"She has no record under the name we have for her," Liddell said. "Nothing local on Samuels. I didn't have time to check with narcotics yet, but I'll get them after the autopsy." Then he asked, "Any luck with the shyster?"

"He said Cordelia made an appointment over the phone, and was supposed to meet with him tomorrow. He said he's never met her and didn't know where she got his business card."

"Maybe she found it in the back of an ambulance," Liddell suggested.

"Anyway," Jack continued, "Lenny specializes in civil law, but he didn't have a clue what she wanted. His secretary took the call and she couldn't—or wouldn't—remember anything about the woman who made the appointment, except that she was sure it was a woman's voice."

"Think she was going to sue someone, and was killed for it?"

Jack just shrugged. "We'll have to wait until we have more questions before we bother Lenny again. He was very defensive considering the simple questions I was asking."

"He is an attorney, Jack. They're used to getting paid for their time," Liddell said with a grin.

"Did you get a street address in Shawneetown?" Jack asked.

"All we have is a post-office box."

"We need someone to identify the body," Jack said. "I think Shawneetown is only about an hour's drive away."

"The way you drive it will be ten minutes, pod'na. We need to call Captain Franklin."

The men looked at each other.

So far they had a dead woman who seemed to have no reason to be in Evansville, much less a reason to be dead. They would have to depend on another police agency, the Shawneetown Police Department, to assist them in getting information. They didn't even know how long she had been in Evansville, just that she had been in the room for two nights and had paid up for the rest of the week. But they did have the name of the person who had rented the car for her. Jonathan Samuels. Maybe he could help them with their inquiries.

"No one at the Marriott remembered her. I talked to guests, maintenance, and management. No one remembers her receiving any visitors," Liddell said.

"Did we check the outgoing phone calls?"

"We did. No calls," Liddell said. "Of course, she could have received calls and they wouldn't have a record because they all come in on a trunk line and no one remembers any."

"And she didn't have a cell phone," Jack said. "What young woman doesn't have a cell phone these days?" *Something else to ask in Shawneetown,* Jack thought.

"She still had four days to go, and an appointment with Lenny Bange scheduled for tomorrow," Liddell said. "If she took a room for a week, it's reasonable to believe that she was here to do something. I mean, Evansville is not exactly a touristy place."

"Yeah," Jack agreed. "Still, I guess we should get uniforms to pass her picture around. Maybe even take it to the security people at the Blue Star," he said, meaning the Blue Star Casino, a local riverboat. "Maybe she was a gambler?"

"Well, let's get this over with and then I'll let you drive me to Shawneetown," Jack said.

"Wow! You mean I can drive?"

"You betcha, Bigfoot. I might even let you buy me some coffee on the way, too."

"By the way, that was a pretty good catch on the stuff in room three seventy-five today, pod'na," Liddell said.

"Crime scene rushed the newspaper to the State Police Crime Lab to see what they can get off it," Jack said. "Maybe we'll get lucky and find some fingerprints."

Liddell laughed. "Yeah, and maybe the killer wrote his name and address on it, too."

"I hear you, Bigfoot," Jack said. He had worked hundreds, if not thousands of cases, and had only found fingerprint evidence meaningful in a handful.

"We need to get Angelina in on this," Liddell said. Angelina Garcia, a civilian employee of the police department, worked in their computer section. She was currently on loan to the vice squad, and was helping break an encrypted computer program from a seized computer. Everyone on the department knew that Angelina was the best when it came to computers or putting data together to make it mean something.

"You think the captain will get her for us?" Liddell asked.

"Maybe if you ask. He doesn't like me."

"He likes you okay," Liddell said. "He just thinks you're a smart-ass."

"Hey. I resemble that remark," Jack said.

"This guy really likes to cut people, don't he?" Liddell offered.

"Seems that way," Jack agreed. "What he did to that poor girl's face . . ."

CHAPTER ELEVEN

The forensic pathologist, Dr. John Carmodi, known simply as Dr. John, had already prepped the body of Cordelia Morse and was dictating his initial observations into the microphone that was suspended by a boom over the stainless-steel autopsy table. Foot pedals located on each side of the table, allowed the pathologist to take hands-free, real-time taped notes during the autopsy.

"Greetings and salutations, my Yeti brother," Dr. John said through his green face mask as Liddell and Jack entered the room.

"I hope that wasn't on the tape," Jack said.

"Is he gonna be a party pooper?" Dr. John asked Liddell.

Jack hurriedly changed the subject. "What can you tell us about the wounds to the face?"

A magnifying lamp on wheels was pulled over and Dr. John examined the victim's face. "The face was cut off with something very sharp or very heavy . . . or both," he said. "The cut starts at the frontal bone and whatever the weapon was, it sliced down along the superciliary ridge, fracturing the supraorbital ridge and taking skin, muscle, cartilage, and part of the nasal bone, continuing down through the anterior nasal spine and almost cutting into the palate and alveolar arch."

"Pretend you're talking to Liddell, Dr. John, and say that in English," Jack said.

"Okay," Dr. John said and made a chopping motion with his hand. "The killer used something heavy and sharp and chopped her face off with one stroke."

"Yeah, that's what I thought," Liddell said.

"Any idea what kind of weapon?" Jack asked.

Dr. John shook his head. "Something big, heavy, and sharp."

"Like a hatchet?" Liddell offered.

"Think bigger. And heavier," Dr. John said.

"You mean like an axe?" Liddell said.

Dr. John threw gloves to the detectives. "Put these on and help me turn her body over," he said.

Jack and Liddell gloved up and helped Dr. John roll the body onto its side. Dr. John pulled the hair away from the back of the neck.

"See that?" Dr. John asked, pointing to some bruising at the base of the neck, and again at a spot in the middle of the back between the scapula. The men nodded.

"I'm betting that the killer put a knee in her back and held her facedown on the floor. With her head tilted back and her chin propped against the floor, her face would be at the right angle for a blow from a heavy hand axe to do the damage."

He pointed to the bruises at the base of the neck. "See how this bruise on the left side of the neck is bigger than the others?" he said and held his left hand out as if he were gripping the victim's neck. "Our killer is left handed. He held her with his right hand and used the left to deliver the blow from the weapon."

Jack felt a knot forming in his stomach. "Was this done before or after she was dead?"

"Definitely after," Dr. John answered. "I can tell you right now that the blow to the face didn't cause her death. Of course I'll have to finish the autopsy to give you the cause of death. But I can tell you off the record that it is probably going to be due to exsanguination."

"Excuse me?" Liddell said.

"Total hypovolemia," Dr. John explained.

"Once again?" Liddell queried.

"She bled to death, Bigfoot," Jack said.

The men rolled the body back onto her back and Dr. John continued his examination. "I'll do a rape kit, but there are no outward signs of a sexual assault."

Jack didn't think the victim would care at this point. *Let's see,* Jack thought. *Do I want to be raped and then have someone cut my face off? Or do I just want to have my throat slashed?* But it would be nice if the killer had left some DNA behind.

Dr. John tilted the victim's head back and to the right and exposed the wound to the bright overhead lamps. The killer had nearly cut her head from her body. "If my theory about the killer is correct, and he is left handed, then this blow was delivered from behind. It could be the same type weapon. Maybe we'll find some trace evidence when I get tissue samples from inside the wound."

Jack looked at the gaping chasm that opened in the neck of the victim. He imagined the scene and could see the killer standing behind Cordelia. She could have been lying with her back to him, or sitting. If she was standing the killer must be extremely tall to have delivered an upward blow without striking her shoulder. It made more sense if she was seated and the killer stood behind her. He could then grab her by the hair and pull her head to the right while driving the blade of the weapon at an upward angle, slicing through muscle, tendons, and arteries on the left side of her neck.

Jack ran that scenario past Dr. John, who nodded and

probed inside the wound. "Carotid is severed cleanly," Dr. John said. "Only one blow." He moved the portable light closer to see deeper inside. "He was either very lucky or knew what he was doing."

Just then, Lilly Caskins and the police crime scene photographer entered the room.

"This isn't a knife wound, Jack," Dr. John said. "If Sergeant Walker is correct about the amount of blood found in the bedroom, and depending on how much blood was washed away . . ." He gently palpated the entry wound before continuing. "This is the most likely cause of death. But at this point we have to rule out everything else, including drowning, aspiration of blood, et cetera. And because she was placed in the tub it washed away some of your clues, didn't it?"

"What about the cuts on top of the head?" Jack asked.

Dr. John moved the hair around the cuts and said, "You mean the number. Three seventy-five?"

Jack nodded.

"Looks like the blade of a knife. Not the same weapon that was used on the face and the neck. Maybe a pocket-knife."

Jack asked, "You'll keep us posted?"

Lilly answered for the doctor. "I'll call when we're through." She then asked a question of her own. "Did you find a next of kin yet?"

"All we have so far is a post-office box number in Shawneetown, Illinois," Liddell told her. "But we're going there as soon as you finish up here. We'll call you when we find a next of kin."

Dr. John advised, "You two have time for a cup of coffee before we get started on the autopsy. There are some pastries in the break room, but you'll have to make your own coffee."

Liddell was already headed for the door when Jack remembered another piece of evidence found at the scene.

"Oh yeah, Dr. John, there was something else found at the scene." He then told Carmodi about the fleshy material the crime scene tech had found in the tub's drain.

"Is she missing hers?" Liddell asked Dr. John.

"Let's have a look," Dr. John said, and he and Little Casket began prying the victim's jaws apart. Rigor was still fixed, and the muscles would have to be forced.

Jack may have imagined it, but he could swear he heard the jawbone cracking as the mouth inched open. Carmodi used a penlight to look into the cavity of the mouth. "The tongue has been excised," he said.

Lilly excused herself from the room and was back in less than a minute carrying a plastic bag containing water and a piece of something fleshy. Officer Morris, the crime scene tech who found the tongue, had collected it along with water from the tub. It was a general rule of evidence collection that something found in water is collected in water.

Dr. John held the bag up to the light and examined the tissue inside. "I'll have to take it out, but it looks like a tongue to me." He pressed the pedal on the floor and activated the mike before opening the bag and spoke the date and time he was opening the bag and where he was told it was found.

Using a large pair of tongs that looked to Jack like the kind used for cooking, he pulled the tissue from the bag. In the amplified light from above the autopsy table, the item looked very much like a tongue, or at least part of one. Carmodi recorded some more notes, but the gist of what he was saying was that this could very well be the victim's tongue.

"He cut her tongue out?" Liddell asked.

Carmodi nodded. "You'll need DNA run to be precise. But yes, I would say this is the victim's tongue."

CHAPTER TWELVE

Jack and Liddell sat in the county morgue break room, sipping coffee and talking. Well, Jack was sipping coffee and Liddell was inhaling chocolate long johns, crème horns, and cake donuts with white icing and sprinkles like a man on a mission.

A young woman came into the room dressed in mint-green scrubs and a mask and gloves and announced that the autopsy was about to begin. This was the forensic patholo-gist's assistant, Ginger Thomas.

They followed Ginger back down the hallway to the au-topsy room, where Dr. John nodded to her. She began prep-ping the victim's head for the incision that would be made laterally around the back of the skull. The skin would then be reflected away from the skull and pulled over the top of the head and face to allow clear access for the bone saw.

This was the part that Jack had never become comfort-able with, and was glad to see that Liddell had turned his face away as well. Although he accepted the science of au-topsies, the procedures reminded Jack of a butcher shop he had once worked in while a teenager. Slicing up things that had once been living would never appeal to him.

By the time Jack zoned back in to the autopsy the skull

cap had been removed and the brain was being examined for abnormalities or any other medical reason that could have caused death. The pathologist's job was to eliminate any other cause of death, except *the* cause of death. For example, if a defense attorney were to find out that the deceased's blood alcohol content was above .25 percent, he could argue that the victim might have died from alcohol poisoning.

Jack had worked such a case. Three men had gotten another man drunk with the intention of robbing him, but hadn't counted on the fact that he might resist. He was beaten unconscious and then carried into an alley and left in the trash, where he aspirated his own vomit and suffocated. The defense successfully argued that the blood alcohol percentage was so high that the amount of alcohol consumed could have killed the man by itself. The jury, not knowing that the normal blood alcohol of the victim was never much lower than toxic, found the defendants not guilty of murder.

"We have a winner," Carmodi announced, shocking Jack out of his reverie.

"What is it, doc?" Liddell asked.

Carmodi had the neck opened, exposing the laryngeal cavity. "The carotid was severed." He pulled the tissue back to show the detectives the flaccid carotid artery.

"He knew what he was doing," Liddell said.

Carmodi shook his head. "Not necessarily, Cajun. He might not have even been trying to hit the carotid."

Jack had a question. "Then why not cut straight across the throat?"

Carmodi looked at him from under the plastic visor and shrugged.

"I mean—and I'm just thinking out loud here—why not cut across the throat? Why did he cut at an upward angle?"

Carmodi had measured with a probe earlier. "It didn't have to be deep to get the carotid, Jack. Only about two inches, maybe less. But you're right about the upward angle. He wouldn't have done this much damage if he had just sliced her throat straight across."

"So, he might have intentionally targeted the major blood vessel in the neck?" Jack asked.

Liddell saw where this was going. "You're the expert here, doc. What's your gut tell you?"

Dr. John appeared to be weighing the evidence. Finally he checked the recorder to be sure it was turned off before saying, "I have to agree that there is some evidence that the carotid artery was the target. Whoever did this made neat work of it. Not medically trained, but knows his way around the body, I'd say."

"Is that just your gut talking, doc?" Jack asked.

"Why is that so important?" Dr. John asked.

Jack shook his head. It just didn't feel right to him. "Why kill her with one precise blow to the neck . . ." Jack began, and stared off into space as if he was visualizing the killing. "And then force her to the floor where he hacks her face off?" Jack saw the confusion on their faces and explained, "The first blow doesn't seem to be consistent with the other damage he did to the body after he killed her. So why? Why not just cut her head off? Why take her face and knock out her teeth? If he was trying to keep us from identifying her, why not take her purse and identification?"

Carmodi lifted the victim's right arm that ended in a bloody stump where the hand should have been. "Notice anything unusual here?"

"You want me to give you a hand?" Liddell offered, and earned a scathing look from Lilly Caskins.

Carmodi pointed to several places on the stump that were shiny. "See this here? And here?" Jack nodded. "Our killer had some skill with a blade to do this." He lay the arm down gently. "The hand wasn't surgically removed. Off the record it looks like the same weapon was used to sever the hand at the wrist. And that's not as easy as they make it look on television."

"Anything else?" Jack asked.

"Well, my unofficial opinion is that cause of death is exsanguination. Loss of blood. The method of death is a wound to the neck severing the carotid artery. The removal of the tongue, eyes, and hand was postmortem. She could have survived any of the other injuries, including the removal of her face, *if* she had found medical care immediately. The wound to the neck dropped her like a stone."

The room became quiet while they digested this.

CHAPTER THIRTEEN

The autopsy was thorough. It lasted two hours and thirty-three minutes, and by the time Jack and Liddell left they were gasping for fresh air. Dead flesh and exposed innards have a particular smell that can never be described to someone not familiar with them. While the long dead make even the strongest stomach roil, freshly dead bodies reek of their own mélange of odors. Jack had taken his sport coat off before entering the autopsy room and was now hesitant to put it back on.

"So we have two scenarios at least," Jack said, facing Liddell. "Okay, since you're bigger you get to be the killer." He stood directly in front of Liddell. "She was cut on the left side of the neck with something sharp and heavy like an axe blade."

Using his right hand, Liddell mocked a swinging motion to the left side of Jack's neck. "That makes our killer right handed."

Jack turned around, his back to Liddell. "Do it again."

Liddell made the swinging motion again with his right hand. This time it appeared that if the killer used his right hand, the knife would have struck the victim in the right side of the neck.

"Dr. John said the blade penetrated at least four inches," Liddell said. "He thought the killer used his left hand. How many people are left handed?"

"Too many," Jack said. "And besides, the wound was made at an upward angle. It would have been hard to get that kind of cut if the victim was standing up unless the killer was extremely tall."

"Cordelia was five foot six inches tall," Liddell said. "The killer would have been at least as tall as me, and even then it would be hard to get the right type of angle with her standing. It makes more sense if she was already on the ground, or on her knees when the blow was struck."

"She could have been struck in the face and then fallen to her knees," Jack offered an opinion. "Then the blow to the neck," he said, making a motion with his left hand as if he was swinging a short axe at an upward angle.

"Looks about right to me," Liddell said. "But of course we don't know any of this for sure."

"Okay. Let's go through what we do know." Jack said. "According to Cordelia's Illinois driver's license she is five-foot-six-inches tall. If she was standing when she was killed there would have been more blood on the ceiling and floor according to Walker. Not to mention that the killer would have had a hard time striking the blow if she was standing."

"So what are you saying, pod'na?"

"Walker thinks she was killed on the bed," Jack said, and then shook his head. "We need to talk to Walker again. Get a better idea about where she might have been when the blow to the neck occurred."

"Want to go now?"

Jack held up the bag of personal items they had recovered from Cordelia Morse's clothing. The bag contained one earring, some change, and a chewing-gum wrapper. "Did you keep the driver's license?"

Liddell pulled it from his pocket.

"Let's go to the station and fill Captain Franklin in. Then we need to go to Shawneetown. Let's get a map and find out who we need to talk to."

"How's about hitting Donut Bank before we go back to headquarters?" Liddell said.

"You go ahead. Inhale a dozen or so for me."

"You cut me to the quick, pod'na," Liddell said, but before they could start toward their cars the coroner's secretary came into the parking lot and told Jack that he had a phone call.

CHAPTER FOURTEEN

Satellite dishes were hoisted from the roofs of the Channel Six and Channel Forty-Four news vans parked just outside the crime scene tape. The news crews were mingling with the crowd of onlookers who were bellied up to the yellow crime scene tape. Small clusters of people stood around, talking excitedly or laughing and slapping each other high-fives. It was party time in the Sweetser Projects.

Detective Ray Chapman was a thirty-four-year veteran detective. He had the gray hair and the lines in his forehead to prove it. He had caught the run and now stood with his hands in his pockets, a dour look on his face, as he waited for Jack Murphy and Liddell Blanchard to make their way through the crowds. He'd called them as soon as he had arrived.

Jack pulled the Crown Vic past the news media vans and felt the familiar tingle of anticipation. He looked around at the crowds of onlookers and newspeople. He knew that the killer might be among them.

In one of these clusters, Jack recognized Channel Six's own Claudine Setera, who was just wrapping up an interview with a dangerous-looking young man wearing pants whose waistband threatened to fall off his bony hips. A dozen or so enthusiastic teens were surrounding the pair, hamming it up for the camera and hoping they would get a glimpse of themselves on television later. Several of the kids were making grabs for the cameraman's equipment belt.

"Jack. Jack Murphy!" Claudine called from the other side of the yellow tape.

Jack hesitated, but then remembered that if you didn't tell the media something—no matter how useless a piece of information—they would report that the police had no comment. "No comment" always came out sounding like *"The police are hiding things from you that you need to know."*

"Miss Setera," Jack said, "I've only just arrived and probably know less than you do."

She gave him a look that said, *Of course you know less than I do.*

"Could I just get a photo of you entering the crime scene again?" she asked. "We didn't see you arrive."

Sergeant Walker had stopped and now smiled at Jack. "You're a movie star," he said. "I'm heading in."

Jack nodded at Walker and then raised his eyebrows at Claudine.

"Oh, just come out here a few feet and then cross under the tape," she said, and shrugged.

"Okay," Jack said, and ducked under the tape and walked a few feet from the cameraman. She didn't care what he had to say, she just wanted some film to play along with her scripted version of events. "Is this okay?" he asked, and she nodded.

When he was finished reentering the crime scene for benefit of the camera he approached his partner. Without even a thank-you, Claudine and her cameraman were loading the Channel Six van, no doubt to make a hasty retreat from the area before the throngs of kids could strip them of valuables.

Detective Chapman walked toward Jack and said, "I think I might have found your missing hand." Chapman ran a hand through his thick gray hair, and then gave Jack a disconcerted look. He put his notebook in his jacket pocket and then stuck both hands back in his pockets, and to Jack he looked like an old coat hanging on a coatrack. His whole manner spoke of someone who was wrung out.

Jack and Walker exchanged a look. Walker nodded, and confirmed, "We found a hand at this scene that doesn't belong here."

Chapman was looking at the crowds of people. He was not a happy man.

"One of their neighbors has been slaughtered, and they act as if this is some sort of entertainment for their benefit."

"You've got your time in, Ray," Jack said. "You've got enough to draw a good retirement. Go fishing whenever you want. Eh?"

Chapman's face hardened. "You think I can't cut it anymore?" he asked, surprising Jack.

"I'm just saying, Ray," Jack began, but then thought better of it.

Chapman seemed to get a grip and pulled his notebook back out, and forced a grin. "Well, maybe I will take retirement, Jack. But it won't be today. We've got a looney tune to catch."

Liddell was talking to an officer who was holding an aluminum clipboard and pointing down the passage at other apartments and then at the area of ground next to them that had been roped off with yellow crime scene tape. Liddell thanked the officer and walked over to meet Jack.

"Give me some good news, Bigfoot."

"I think we're looking at the same killer here," Liddell said.

"The coffee is wearing off," Jack said and wiped a hand across his face.

Liddell pulled out his notebook and recited, "Louise Brigham, black female, age thirty-three, two kids, both at school when this happened. Neighbors say she's stand-up. No drugs. No enemies. No male visitors. Ex-husband in Toledo, Ohio. No problems there. No fights with anyone. She's on Section Eight housing, and doesn't work.

"Her throat is cut. Just like the last one. Little Casket's crew is on the way," Liddell said, meaning that the coroner's office had been officially notified by the police dispatcher and someone would be arriving shortly. Probably Little Casket herself.

"We have a motive yet?" Jack asked.

"No motive. No weapon," Liddell confirmed, and then he leaned close to Jack's ear and said, "The killer left a hand behind."

Jack felt a knot forming in his stomach.

Liddell added, "And he took her face and eyes."

CHAPTER FIFTEEN

Jack stared at Liddell, waiting for the rest of the statement.

Liddell continued. "Yeah! Her face is missing just like the last one. And the hand we found here isn't hers because this victim is black and the hand we found is from a white female."

"This just gets better and better," Jack muttered.

"That's not the best part," Liddell said, and motioned for Jack to follow him.

Corporal Joe Timmons was guarding the crime scene entry and handed the sign-in log to Jack at the doorway. Jack signed his name, the date, and the time he was entering the apartment. Timmons had at least forty years under his belt, and had been a field training officer for the last fifteen years. *Another guy well past retirement,* Jack thought.

"Kooky's guarding the kitchen," Timmons advised.

Jack remembered Officer John "Kooky" Kuhlenschmidt, and he really didn't want to think about it.

"Oh boy. I hope he hasn't thrown up all over the body," Liddell muttered as the two detectives made their way inside.

The apartment building was built in the early 1940s to

house the influx of returning World War II soldiers. Each building held eight two-story apartments with only a few inches of drywalled space to separate them. Each apartment had a front and rear entrance. The front door entered the living room, the other entered the kitchen. There were three of these developments inside the city limits of Evansville and each had its own special name. This one was called the Sweetser Projects.

Jack and Liddell entered the living room.

"Give the kid a chance," Jack said, although he was thinking the same thing as his partner. The last time Kooky had found a dead body he had hurled all over the place, including on Jack's shoes.

One of the crime scene techs met them in the living room and indicated they should follow him to the kitchen. From the kitchen doorway, Jack could see Sergeant Walker kneeling a few feet from a prone figure on the floor. Officer Kooky Kuhlenschmidt was out cold.

Jack and Liddell stood in the kitchen and watched the two white-clad techs who had helped remove Kooky from the floor and were now gathered closely around another prone figure, this one the body of the victim, Louise Brigham.

Jack noticed several things immediately. The victim was lying on her back with both arms folded across her chest. Unless you are planning on being dead, you probably won't lie in this position. So it followed that the killer positioned her like this after death. Her face and both eyes had been removed by the killer as well. She was African American, and a hand from a Caucasian female was propped against the side of her head.

The killer must have thought he was were being cute because he had used children's Band-Aids, the kind with pictures of *Sesame Street* characters, to hold the fingers of the severed hand down, except the middle finger. *A one-finger salute,* Jack thought. *A comedian.*

On the other side of the victim's head was a water-filled glass tumbler in which something was floating. "Is that an eye?" Jack asked. Walker nodded.

The victim was on her back, her head lying in a pool of blood. A darkish smear of blood spread across the floor for a foot or so and ended at another smaller pool right above her head. Someone had written two letters in blood next to her face. J M.

"What's going on, Jack?" Walker asked.

"Looks like Jack has a fan," Liddell said.

"She was moved," Jack said.

Walker nodded. "It looks like her skull was struck with something really sharp. Just look at that! It looks like her head was almost split in two from behind."

"Do you have photos of that?" Jack asked, pointing to the smaller pool of blood where the victim must have been lying facedown at one point.

Walker asked one of the techs, who said they had plenty of shots.

"Let me have one of those long Q-tips," Jack said.

Walker handed him one and Jack using the wooden end of the swab to feel around inside the bloody mess. He was scraping it back and forth until he felt it stick on something.

"There's something under the blood," Jack said.

Walker saw what he was doing and took some paper towels and began wiping at the pool of blood. When it was wiped away there was a line about four inches long and very narrow cut into the linoleum tile.

He looked at Jack and Liddell. "You think this is where he did it?" Walker asked.

Jack shook his head in disgust.

"Just like at the Marriott," Liddell said. "He chopped her face off right here."

"Got something in the sink, Sergeant," one of the techs said.

"He didn't take one of the victim's hands this time," Jack said.

Walker pointed to the skeletal face. "Didn't take the tongue, either."

They all walked over to see what the tech had found in the sink.

There were no dirty dishes, but in the bottom of the stainless steel sink was a large kitchen knife with a serrated blade. The edges and the wooden handle were still crusted with blood.

"You think he used the knife to take her eyes out?" Liddell asked.

Walker looked around the room. On the cigarette-burned countertop next to the sink was a small plate with pieces of bread crust on it. A skillet with a glass lid sat on a burner of the stove. Something thick coated the bottom of the skillet and the room still smelled like fried bacon.

"She was making something to eat when the killer came in," the tech suggested.

Or maybe the killer made something for himself after he killed her, Jack thought. He remembered talking to a detective from Jamestown, North Carolina, a few years back who had worked a crime scene where the killer had butchered a woman—cut her into ten pieces—and then made himself a meal and sat at the victim's table and ate. The detective had later asked the killer why he would do that. The killer had calmly responded, "Cuttin' her up was hard work."

"You'll collect all this stuff?" Jack said.

Walker nodded, saying, "Maybe we'll get some DNA."

"Who found her?" Jack asked.

"A neighbor named Simmons, sir." This came from the crime scene tech who had found the knife and spoon in the sink.

"Go on," Jack said. She was the same tech who had searched the first victim's car at the Marriott, but for the life of him, Jack couldn't remember her name.

She noticed him struggling for a name. "Officer Lucy Martin," she said.

"Go ahead, Officer Martin."

"Ms. Dorothy Simmons lives two apartments down— turn right and it's on the left, sir. She was coming over to borrow some coffee and saw Ms. Brigham's door standing open. She came in and called for Ms. Brigham but didn't get an answer straightaway, sir. She came into the kitchen to help herself to some ground coffee because she didn't think Ms. Brigham would mind. That's when she almost tripped over the body. She was understandably upset and Officer Lynn is talking to her in her apartment. I didn't overhear the exact address. Sorry, sir."

Walker had turned his back and was suppressing a smile.

Jack smiled, slightly surprised at this thorough account.

"Well, you are very observant, Officer Martin," Jack said, and then to Liddell, "Why didn't you know all that, Bigfoot?"

Walker showed the two detectives back to the entrance. "One eye missing, and one left behind," Walker said. "This time a knife was used to excise the eye. The killer uses whatever tool is handy to take the eyes, but always the same weapon to kill."

"He brings it with him. It has significance," Jack said.

"The first body was missing a hand, and that may be the one we have here. Both eyes were taken from both victims.

The one that was left behind here is from a blue-eyed person," Liddell said.

"Couldn't be from this victim," Jack said.

Liddell shook his head.

"What is it, Bigfoot?" Jack asked.

"This guy is targeting you, pod'na," Liddell said. "He left that newspaper article about you in that hotel room with an eye from a blue-eyed person on it. And now your initials turn up next to the body of this victim. Not to mention the way the hand was left behind."

"Maybe it's because of my bubbly personality," Jack said, but he had been thinking exactly the same thing and could feel a twinge in the scar running down his jaw.

Tony looked at Jack and Liddell. "Think the killer's trying to tell you something?"

"I'd be happy to talk to him," Jack said.

CHAPTER SIXTEEN

Arnold Byrum had dreamed of becoming a cop since as far back as he could remember. He ate, breathed, and lived the Evansville Police Department. But his doctor had discovered he had a heart murmur a few years ago, and there was no way the police department would ever hire him. At age twenty-one his dream was over.

Of course, his mother was pleased because Arnold had never been away from her for more than a few hours at a time his whole life. If he had been able to pass the police physical he might have moved out on his own, and away from her. Mother would never have accepted that.

Being a policeman was out, and the only other thing in life that gave him pleasure was writing. It was the drive to write that brought him to his current job as a reporter for the local newspaper. When he'd won a local writing contest sponsored by the newspaper, he was given a chance at some real writing.

Now, after four years of running "copy" and covering meaningless bits of news, twenty-three-year-old Arnold Byrum had wrangled an assignment to the police beat. How he had ever accomplished that was a surprise to everyone, but not to Arnold. It was as close as he could get to doing police work. It was in his blood.

His editor, Bob Robertson, had broken a lot of newspaper traditions by taking a chance on him. Police reporters were traditionally tough, gruff, cigar-smoking, cheap-whiskey-swilling, womanizing, bar-room-brawling types. Arnold stood well over six foot tall, and weighed a solid two hundred-fifty pounds, with wispy brown hair that was already deserting his freckled crown. His ears were large and stuck straight out from his head as if they were air brakes. His eyes were over-large, bright blue, and he had a bad ticker. But if you cut him he would still bleed cop.

There is an idiom in news work, *If it bleeds it leads*. Arnold had learned early in his assignment to the cop beat that if he wanted to keep this position he would have to cover the sensational stories that the public fed on for entertainment. The more blood and mayhem, the more ink his editor would throw at it.

But this morning he wanted nothing to do with the newspaper, nor with the police department. Something besides police work had captured his attention, and her name was Bernice.

She was almost as tall as Arnold, but where he was solid she was shapely, where his hair was thinning hers was long and brown and luxurious. She was his age. His dream girl. And if Mother ever found out that Arnold was looking at this woman in the way that he most definitely was looking, she would scald his hide from his bones.

He knew what he had been doing for the last week was wrong. He knew he was going to Hell, just as Mother had predicted for him so many times in his life. But he couldn't help himself. He would spend the day in his cubicle, which just happened to look directly across to Bernice's desk, and he could see under her desk. See her perfectly tanned long legs under the desk. Sometimes he imagined that he could see more than just her legs.

Work today had been a nightmare, and all he wanted to do was lie across his bed and shove it all out of his mind. All of it except pretty Bernice. He thought about how she had caught him looking at her legs today and had smiled at him. He could feel himself becoming aroused at that thought. *What did that mean?* he wondered.

He lay back and closed his eyes and placed his hand down the front of his khaki pants. Bernice was so beautiful. More than any other woman he had ever seen. He was aching all over. Just wanted to stay under the covers with his eyes closed and think about Bernice.

"Arnold? Are you up? Arnold? I need my medicine!" his mother's shrill voice cut into his thoughts. It was early still. His day off. And she was bleating out demands. She knew she didn't get her medicine until noon. She just wanted company. Well, he wasn't going to answer. He would get her medicine when he was damn good and ready.

"Arnold? I know you're awake. I heard your bed creaking. I need to be turned, Arnold," came the voice again. "Why won't you answer your mother, Arnold? What are you doing down there? Are you defiling yourself?"

He let out a sigh and threw the covers onto the floor. He would have to get up. He would have to go upstairs. All so that he could patiently explain for the millionth time that she couldn't have her medicine for another two hours. He was just putting his feet down to locate his slippers when the phone rang in the living room.

"Arnold, the phone," mother said, unnecessarily.

He sat still, letting the phone continue to ring. Maybe if he didn't answer it would stop? Maybe Mother would shut up as well? And then a thought struck him.

"Arnold?" his mother yelled, startling him out of his thoughts, and he thought he could hear her trying to get out of bed. He jumped up, and forgetting his slippers he ran from his bedroom at the back of the house, down the hallway to the living room, yelling, "I've got it, Mother."

He picked up the receiver and said, "Hello."

"Arnie?" the voice said.

He cleared his throat nervously before saying, "Detective Jansen. You've woken Mother."

Jansen was used to hearing about Arnold Byrum's eccentric mother. He could commiserate with the guy for the task of taking care of an invalid for years on end. His own situation wasn't so different. "Sorry about your mom, buddy, but I've got something hot for you."

"Oh, goody," he said with feigned enthusiasm.

Jansen filled him in on the early-morning murder at the Marriott hotel, and then told him that there was a second murder, this one in the south-side projects. When Jansen finished, Arnold let out a sigh.

"So, we seem to have another spate of murders in Evansville," Arnold remarked. Evansville was a pretty quiet town normally, although they had their share of murders over the last couple of years. *But, then, two murders in one day aren't necessarily a crime spree.*

"Are they connected?" he asked Jansen.

The line was quiet. Then Jansen said, "Well . . . we're not really sure yet." In truth, he didn't know much of anything about the second murder except that the hand from the Marriott murder had been found there. But he wanted to put as much pressure on Murphy and Blanchard as he could. And there was nothing better to pile the pressure on than the news media stirred into a frenzy.

He'd been careful building his news-media contacts, and he only fed them things that they could have gotten from any number of sources. The thought of this new girl, Claudine

Setera, caused him to get a lump in his throat. She was definitely hot. But so far she had not been interested in what Detective Larry Jansen might be able to do for her career. She seemed to think she could make it on her own. Apparently she didn't know how things worked in Evansville.

If he could make the public think there was another serial killer on the loose it would do several things for Larry Jansen. He could zing the politicians again, make himself more desirable to Claudine, and shove the news media right up Murphy's ass. And all the while, he could remain outside the nuclear-blast zone. This was Larry's specialty. It was why he was the king, and had been untouchable.

Nobody screws with Larry Jansen, he thought, and smiled.

Arnold was confused when he hung up the phone. What did Jansen mean, "They're trying to keep it quiet." Jansen wouldn't say who was keeping it quiet, but he hinted broadly that the orders to shut the news media out had come all the way from the top. And how could "they" keep serial killings quiet?

According to Jansen, the first victim was the lady at the Marriott whose body was found early this morning by the desk clerk. Arnold had been unaware of the announcement of the killing on Channel Six news this morning because he had been . . . preoccupied. According to Jansen the woman had been hacked to death and then one of her hands had been cut off. That hand was found six hours later at the scene of the second murder. And that woman had also been hacked to death.

Arnold switched on the small television set in his bedroom, tuned to Channel Six, and watched until the recap of the day's events. A glowering Jack Murphy could be seen crossing under the yellow crime scene tape, heading for the door to an apartment, while a crowd of onlookers clamored nearby.

Arnold felt a twinge of envy. That should have been him

taking charge of a murder scene. Should have been Arnold talking to the news media. *Detective Byrum, what can you tell us?* that cute reporter would say to him. And Arnold would say, *No comment at this time, Claudine.*

And speak of the devil, he thought, just as Claudine Setera's sweet face filled the television screen. Arnold reached over and turned up the volume.

SETERA: Once again, Blake, we've just seen Detective Jack Murphy enter the newest crime scene—the second one since we reported from the Marriott hotel this morning—and take over the murder investigation of a woman who lived here in the Sweetser Housing Development. The police are not releasing the name of the victim as of yet, but sources close to the investigation say that she was murdered in a very similar fashion to the victim who was murdered this morning at the Marriott hotel near the airport.
BLAKE JAMES: Claudine, can you tell us if the name of the first victim has been released by police yet?
SETERA: Blake, the police are being very tight-lipped about any of the facts surrounding these two murders. I have it on good authority that orders have come from high in the ranks of the police department, telling the officers not to release any information as of yet.
BLAKE: Do the police suspect a serial killer, Claudine?
SETERA: Too early to say, Blake. Once again, the police are releasing no information, but we will continue to try and find what we can to warn the public.

Arnold winced at that last remark. Claudine Setera was not playing fair. She knew that the police couldn't release the name of a victim until they had notified the victim's family and made a positive identification. But she was making it sound like the police were holding back information that the public needed to be safe from this killer. He would never write an article like that. Never slam the police unnecessarily.

He flipped the television off and thought about what Jansen had said. It was almost a repeat—word for word—of what Setera had said. Had Jansen called her before he called Arnold?

Regardless, Claudine Setera hadn't mentioned the severed hand found at the Sweetser scene. Nor did she seem to know about the eyes taken from the first and second victim, or that an eye was left behind at the second murder, and that one of the crime scene techs said it was blue, and that the second victim didn't have blue eyes.

It wasn't much, and it was his day off. He really didn't want to go in to work. But then, maybe this was just the right kind of story to get Bernice to notice him more.

Arnold knew a lot of cops, and so he picked up the telephone and began calling. An hour later he was depressed. Getting information was harder than he had imagined, even for him. Both of these were Jack Murphy's cases, and no one wanted to step on the wrong side of him. But at least he had verified a few key pieces of information. Enough that he believed his editor, Bob Robertson, would run with the story in the evening paper.

He picked up the phone one more time and had begun to dial the newspaper when he heard his mother breathing on the extension in her room.

"Mother. Please hang up the phone."

"I need turned, Arnold," came his mother's cracked voice.

I really need to get her a full-time nurse, Arnold thought for the millionth time.

CHAPTER SEVENTEEN

Lilly Caskins had shown up with a deputy coroner who looked like a pro football player. His arms were as big as Jack's thighs. Liddell asked, "Think Lilly hired him in case the Suburban breaks down?"

"He's big enough to carry you around like a sack of potatoes, Bigfoot," Jack said.

The man must have heard the remark because he turned toward the detective and flexed his biceps at them and smiled.

"That's really scary, pod'na," Liddell said.

"What's so scary?"

"Lilly hired someone with a sense of humor. That's not like her," Liddell said. "And earlier she apologized to you," he reminded Jack. "What's going on?"

"Maybe she's just mellowing," Jack suggested. "It comes with age, buddy."

"Nah. As old as Little Casket is, the only thing she could do is petrify."

"I heard that," Lilly's voice came from behind them.

"Sorry, Lilly," Liddell said.

Lilly ignored him and directed the body's preparation to be removed from the scene and taken to the morgue. When she had left the apartment Jack leaned over and whispered to Liddell, "When you die, you should do it in another county."

Liddell nodded agreement.

There was nothing else for the men to do at the scene, so they agreed to meet at police headquarters. They still needed to brief Captain Franklin and the chief on the two murders. Jack knew the news media was breathing down the chief's neck wanting a news update. Jack had also heard that Claudine Setera was calling the second murder "the work of a serial killer." Where she got this information he wasn't sure.

The inside of Chief Marlin Pope's office was tiny compared to the outer office where guests were greeted by his secretary. The Civic Center's Building Authority couldn't believe it when Pope—a newly appointed chief of police at the time—had asked them to *downsize* his personal office space to make more room for visitors.

His naysayers said it showed his lack of understanding of his job as police chief, and even his friends thought it was a mistake to show a weakness. Pope had ignored all the hubbub, electing instead to get on with the business of policing Evansville.

Marlin Pope was used to people questioning his wisdom. The fact that he was one of a handful of black men ever to work for the Evansville Police Department was always the first thing that people noticed about him. The second thing was that he was the first black person ever to attain the rank of deputy chief, and the only one ever appointed by a mayor as chief of police.

Pope was standing at the bank of windows behind his desk, looking out onto SE Seventh Street toward the downtown walkway. He kept his back to them as he said, "Talk to me."

For the next ten minutes, Jack and Liddell told the chief everything they knew about the two murders committed that day—the similarities, the differences, and the glaring connections. When they were finished talking, Pope turned toward them and let out a sigh.

"So. It's happening again," he said.

CHAPTER EIGHTEEN

Arnold Byrum was waiting inside his green 1972 Pontiac Gremlin when Jack and Liddell pulled into the parking lot at the Vanderburgh County Coroner's Office for the second time that day.

"Barney's here," Liddell said.

"Who yanked his chain?" Jack asked.

"Probably the same asshole that called Blake James, ya think?"

Jack shifted the car into park and wondered why Arnold would be waiting for them at the morgue. Even though Channel Six was hinting at a serial killer, no one knew about the connection between the two deaths except for Crime Scene, the chief of detectives, and the chief of police. Well, except for Little Casket, and it was a sure bet that she wasn't telling.

Arnold spotted the detectives and pushed open the door to his car. It made a loud groan as if it was ready to fall off onto the ground, but Arnold didn't seem to notice.

"Hey, guys," Arnold said, his expression somewhere between serious and a smile.

"Gomer says hi, Barney," Liddell said to the little man.

"Be nice, Bigfoot," Jack said out the corner of his mouth.

Arnold genuinely smiled now. "Ah, that's okay. I don't mind being teased. You know I'm one of you."

Jack knew he meant it too. It was hard to be mean to Arnold. He was like family. Always there, and always rooting for the blue team. He had never once written a derogatory article about the police department, and had often written glowing stories about "Jack Murphy—Superhero."

"What can you do for us, Arnold?" Jack asked, causing Arnold to giggle.

"Is that a giggle I hear?" Liddell said, and grabbed Arnold, wrapped him up in a bear hug, and gave him what they used to call a noogie on top of his head. That was when someone would use their middle-finger knuckle to rub the top of your head until it burned your scalp.

Arnold pulled away, still giggling, and Jack just watched in fascination at how grown men, especially his partner, could turn into children at the drop of a hat. He liked Arnold, but business was business, and he was going to have to cut Arnold off at the knees if he was looking into the recent murders.

"You two get a room," Jack said.

"Aw, he ain't hurtin' me," Arnold said.

"We have something to do, Bigfoot," Jack reminded Liddell.

"Yeah?" Arnold asked. "Anything you want to tell me? Something I can write?"

Liddell leaned down and whispered, "Jack is hot for Lilly Caskins. She's going to have his love child."

"I've got work to do," Jack said, and stomped in the front door of the coroner's office. He wasn't mad, he just wanted an excuse to extricate himself from Arnold. He hoped his partner would take the hint and get rid of the reporter.

"Hello, Lilly," Jack said, and waited at the open doorway. You didn't just walk into her office. "Just wanted to let you know that we still don't have a next of kin on the Morse woman. We found a cousin for Brigham. Nancy Marx. She's on her way to pick the victim's kids up from school and will then come here to identify the body."

"Where's the Cajun?" she asked.

"He's out front with Arnold Byrum, the guy from the newspapers."

"I know who he is," she snapped. "Don't you think I know who Barney is? I've been doing this longer than you've been shitting solid."

Jack threw his hands up in surrender and stood. He'd seen this side of Little Casket before. This was about a five-mega-ton attitude, which was mild, but he didn't want to be in the blast radius when she exploded.

When Liddell entered the autopsy room in the back area of the coroner's office Dr. John was examining the hand that had been found at Louise Brigham's crime scene. The body of Cordelia Morse was in an open body bag on a gurney near the autopsy table.

"Captain on deck," the forensic pathologist, Dr. John Carmodi, quipped, and came to mock attention, which earned him a scathing look from Lilly Caskins.

In the next breath Dr. John was in full professional mode and dictating into the microphone that hung above the autopsy table.

"Addendum to the autopsy record on Cordelia Morse from this morning," he said, and then continued to describe the reason for the reexamination of the body.

When he was finished taping he looked at Jack and Liddell. "It's a match. The hand that you found at the second murder scene belongs to this poor girl. Do you have someone comparing fingerprints?"

Jack nodded in the affirmative. "Walker did a cursory look before we came over, and he said it was a good possibility. We wanted to let you look at the hand before we took prints from it."

"I will wait on the fingerprint results before I give my official opinion, if you don't mind."

Liddell grinned at Dr. John. "You mean you're not omnipotent?"

"You mean impotent?" Lilly chimed in.

Dr. John feigned a look of shock, and said, "Why, Lilly. You made a joke."

Lilly kept her head down and marched toward the door to the freezers where they kept the bodies that were either being preserved for autopsy or waiting to go to funeral parlors. "I'll get Brigham," she said.

Ten minutes later, Dr. John had dictated his observations and was preparing the body for the autopsy.

"Her clothing doesn't appear to have been messed with," Liddell said.

"We'll do a rape kit anyway," Dr. John said as he and a crime scene tech began removing the clothing, photographing it, and then bagging each piece separately. It would all be examined more carefully at the crime lab.

With that task completed, Dr. John and the tech performed another cursory examination of the unclad body.

"Look at this," Dr. John said, and pointed to a location almost directly in the middle of the victim's back. Brigham's skin complexion was so dark it was difficult for Jack to see what Dr. John was pointing to. But as the pathologist angled the overhead light he could make out a slightly darker discoloration of the tissue in the center of the back between the scapula.

It was almost a perfect circle, darker than the surrounding tissue, and about four inches in diameter.

"This is just like the injuries on the Morse girl. The killer put a knee in her back and held her head back, chin down hard on the floor, and then chopped her face off."

He pointed to the same bruising at the base of the neck that they had seen on Cordelia Morse. "See how this bruise on the left side of the neck is bigger than the others?"

He held his left hand out as if he were gripping the victim's neck. "Our killer is definitely left handed. He held her with his right hand and used the left to deliver the blow from the weapon."

CHAPTER NINETEEN

The bold headline of the evening newspaper proclaimed, SERIAL KILLER, and the subtitle, in only slightly smaller font, read, POLICE COVER-UP.

Chief Marlin Pope threw the newspaper across the office, and then slammed a meaty hand on the top of his desk. "I'm going to geld him!"

He wasn't referring to Arnold Byrum. No one in the room had to ask who he was referring to.

"I want Jansen in my office in five minutes," Pope demanded of Captain Chuck Franklin.

Captain Franklin was only slightly less angry than the chief of police. What Detective Larry Jansen had done could not be repaired.

"I've already reached out for him," Franklin stated. "He's not answering at home, or on his cell, and his radio must be turned off."

"Is he on duty?" Pope asked.

"Yes."

Pope took a couple of deep breaths. The fact that Jansen was out of touch while on duty was enough for an immediate suspension, but then Pope would have to risk *that fact* getting in the news as well. He promised himself that when this current situation was resolved that he would make a permanent solution of Larry Jansen, no matter what it cost.

"Jack, I want this leak contained," Franklin said to Murphy.

Jack wanted badly to say something like, "You want me to shoot him?" Instead, he said, "What are we doing about the media?"

Jack thought about the current newspaper article. Few people knew that one of the victim's hands was missing from the first crime scene. Even fewer knew that hand had been recovered at the second crime scene. But only a couple of people knew that the hand had been deliberately placed near the body as a message. He could still see the little hand sitting on the floor beside the victim's head. *At least Arnold didn't report about the newspaper left in room 375 at the Marriott, or my initials written in blood by Brigham's body.*

Pope was shaking his head. "I thought Arnold Byrum was one of the good ones."

Jack noticed Liddell looked uncomfortable, and said, "Well, Chief, I guess we'd better get back to work."

Pope seemed preoccupied and didn't look up. The captain just nodded at them and said, "Go ahead. I'll deal with Jansen. You just make sure . . . never mind. Just go."

In the hallway Jack stopped Liddell. "Tell me."

Liddell's face reddened.

Detective Larry Jansen sat in his car on the top level of the casino parking garage. The top deck was always deserted because it was out in the weather, and the gamblers were too lazy to walk the hundred or so yards to get to the elevator banks. It was Jansen's favorite hiding spot when he didn't want to be found.

Captain Franklin was looking for him, and that hadn't figured in to his plans. He'd disabled the police radio in his car by pulling the antennae cable loose in the trunk, but that would only give him an excuse for not answering the radio. He'd been out of communication most of the day now, and had even screened his police-department-issued cell phone calls. Eight attempts already by the chief's secretary, and if she was calling he was in deep shit.

From his vantage point he could look down along the riverfront and across the Ohio River and on into Kentucky on the other side of the river. Off to his right, the festively painted smokestacks of the floating casino rose thirty feet into the air. *Every day's a party,* he thought. That was Blue Star Casino's slogan. *Well, this day has been no damn party.*

On the street below him he could hear the occasional traffic, voices raised in merriment or anger, and the mind-numbing pounding coming from someone's car stereo. In the old days he would have been able to go down there and yank the stereo out of the car and lob it into the river. But these weren't the old days.

Because of all the lawyers and bleeding hearts in this town he wouldn't even get away with writing the noisemaker a ticket for disturbing the peace. It was too bad really. A little ass-kicking by the police had never hurt anyone. And back then, people respected the police.

But all this reminiscing was just delaying the inevitable. He needed to go downtown and face the music. The only thing that would save him now was a heart attack or a stroke or something.

Heart attack, he thought. *No, a stroke.* He started his car and drove down the descending set of concrete ramps to the exit. Welborn Hospital was only six blocks away.

"Sorry, Jack."

Liddell and Jack were in the hallway of the Civic Center as Liddell explained what was bothering him. "I forgot to tell you that Arnold had been asking some strange questions back at the morgue."

"What do you mean, strange?"

"You know? Stuff like, 'Is this a serial killer?' and 'So you and Jack are working both of these?' You know. That kind of stuff." Liddell shrugged. "It didn't seem important at the time. Just questions any reporter might ask."

Jack relaxed. "Well, you can't be a mind reader, you know."

Liddell was still tense and Jack could tell he was angry with himself.

"Forget it, Bigfoot," he said. "You've messed up a lot of things, but this wasn't your fault."

That drew a grin from the big man. "Gee, thanks, pod'na. It's good to know you're in my corner. But in my own defense, I have to tell you that I didn't spill any of that stuff in his story. I didn't give him anything."

They grew serious. Someone had given away their investigation big-time, and they both hoped that it was Jansen. It sure seemed like it had to be him, but there was the worry that maybe someone else was playing the game now. And if that was true they were in for a rough ride.

Just down the block from Louise Brigham's tiny apartment, the killer sat in his car and watched the circus taking place. Cops had taped off a good portion of the block, but the news media were still bellied up to the crime scene barriers, pushing for a sound bite, or to shoot ten minutes of video that would end up as less than two seconds of television time. Even being here was a great waste of his time, but all things considered, it was fun to watch.

The evening edition of the *Evansville Courier* lay unread on the front seat of his SUV. This paper was a definite keeper. The story was flawless. Well, almost flawless, because it didn't tell who the killer was. *But that would be pre-mature*, he thought. *Don't want to ruin the surprise. What fun would that be?*

Right now he had other duties to attend to. His mother had always said, "Idle hands are the devil's playground." And that thought made him chuckle.

What would she think of that saying now? he wondered. His hands hadn't been idle, but the things he'd done in the last twelve hours would surely be considered the "devil's playground."

He lifted a manila folder—the one he'd found in Cordelia Morse's room—from the seat next to him and flipped through the contents. There was an address with a detailed map paper clipped to it. Inside were several photos and newspaper clippings. *Cordelia has been very busy,* he thought. *The prying bitch almost ruined everything.* But, in a way, she should be thanked. She had found someone he had been trying to find for years. The next victim.

But the next target would be a little more difficult than any of the others. Too close to home. If there was such a thing as a serial killer's how-to manual, the first chapter would be called "Never shit in your own nest." It was a crude saying, but still, very to the point.

After he had been released from the asylum he had im-mediately cleared out of the Illinois/Indiana area and moved down south. Within a week he had claimed his first victim. That one was far too close to home, and it hadn't taken the police very long to come knocking. He had thought he'd taken every precaution, but his face was too well known. It had taken all his talent to get the police off his scent, but it had taught him a huge lesson. Since then he'd traveled the country, honing his butchering skills, never killing more than a few in any given locale.

But then he had the misfortune of coming across the arti-cle about Jack Murphy. Call it fate. Call it kismet. Whatever.

He found himself being drawn home. And at the same time his long-lost sister, Cordelia, was close to finding him. She had some connection with a local attorney, Lenny Bange, and he still wasn't sure what Lenny had been able to do for her, but he planned to find out. Maybe she had only asked him to help her track her brother down. Maybe she knew something that she shouldn't. In any case, she could not be allowed to find him. No one could ever know who he really was. So, of course, he had to stop her. But to find out that Cordelia had also found the other . . . well, that was serendipitous.

He would kill the woman, of course, and then he could go back to his tried-and-true methods. Oregon would be a good place for the next kills. Oregon had their fair share of serial killers. One more wouldn't matter one iota.

He looked at the newspaper photo of the woman and reread the twenty-year-old article from the Shawneetown newspaper. She looked old even then, and now she was ancient. It had been many years and a lot of miles since their paths had last crossed.

Another of his mother's sayings came to him, *A lot of water under the bridge.*

He never knew what that meant exactly, but it was appropriate in an ironic fashion in this case, since that saying would directly involve the next murder.

He smiled at the thought of Arnold Byrum finding the note he'd left for him. Arnold had to be in hog heaven, getting all of that information. And if Arnold wasn't as stupid as he looked, he had probably figured out by now that the information was coming from someone directly involved with the slayings. Like maybe the killer.

This is working better than I'd imagined, he thought and started the engine.

CHAPTER TWENTY

Shawneetown, Illinois, covers two and one half miles of Southern Illinois and boasts fourteen hundred residents according to the Internet. Jack looked at the hand-painted billboard as they flew down the highway at nearly twice the speed limit. Written in foot-high white letters on the billboard that marked the city limits were the words, 1,412 CITIZENS AND ONE GROUCHY OLD COOT. Under the words was a painting of a frowning face with shaggy white hair and a scruffy growth of beard.

"They must be talking about you, pod'na," Liddell said, and slowed to twenty-five miles per hour as they entered the town proper. Captain Franklin had called ahead to let the Shawneetown Police Department know the two detectives were coming, but Jack had not heard who would be meeting them.

After driving less than five blocks they were already coming to the other side of town, or at least the end of civilization. The downtown buildings were built close to the road with barely enough room for narrow sidewalks. The sun was just going down, but CLOSED signs hung in the darkened windows and doors.

The town seemed smaller than it looked on the map, and

more unfriendly than you would imagine a small town to be. They turned off Highway 13 onto North Lincoln Avenue and then onto Shawnee Hill Drive heading north. The houses and trailers were scattered outside the city proper. Blinds moved in windows, but no one came outside their homes. In fact, they hadn't seen a single soul outside since they had entered the city. Jack had heard a rumor on the cop grapevine that this town liked to smoke the green giant, and that marijuana consumption was an Olympic sport here.

"It's a perfect night," Liddell said. "Where is everyone? Where are the kids?"

"Maybe the crumb-munchers heard that a full-grown Yeti was coming to eat and pillage," Jack suggested. He'd gotten into one of his quiet moods and had hardly spoken during the forty-minute trip from police headquarters.

"You could be right, pod'na. I thought I spotted some lamb's blood on the doors downtown."

"That only works in the Bible, Bigfoot," Jack said, finally coming out of his reverie.

"You're almost funny," Liddell said. "Did you hear that the last chief of police here was convicted of growing and selling marijuana?"

"Yeah," Jack said. "He's got new charges now."

Liddell glanced over. "I thought he was in prison?"

"He is. But while he was in prison he tried to hire someone to kill the judge and prosecutor that put him away," Jack said.

They passed a small town park with swing sets, teeter-totters, and a merry-go-round, all unoccupied, and drove on in silence, looking out over the landscape. Unlike the Evansville area, the trees here still held a painter's palette of fall foliage with reds, yellows, and greens that were visible in the car's headlights. The area was absolutely beautiful, but devoid of people.

Liddell followed a sharp curve, then headed up a steep

hill that would eventually feed back into Highway 13. The police department was supposed to be at the top of the hill. It was. And suddenly they were there.

Liddell pulled into a gravel parking area just big enough for two vehicles. A marked police car of sorts occupied the other space. The police car looked like an Indy 500 pace car, and on the hood and sides a firebird was painted. The police station was a trailer with wooden steps leading to an open door. Rock music played loudly from inside.

Liddell and Jack mounted the steps and walked into the open door of the Shawneetown Police Department. Standing with his back to them, a younger man in a skintight uniform played the air guitar along with the rock music. He was close to Jack's height of six feet, but he was thin to the point of being bony, and his face was a study of sharp angles with a peach-fuzz mustache. He was about to belt out the chorus when he noticed he had company.

Lieutenant JJ Johnson motioned for them to wait and crossed to his desk to turn the radio off. "That's better," he said when it was quiet, with not the slightest hint of embarrassment showing on his face. He stuck out a callused hand that belied his youth. "Lieutenant Johnson. Call me JJ."

Jack and Liddell shook hands with him and introduced themselves; then JJ motioned for them to find chairs. Luckily there were exactly three chairs inside the small office space.

"Chief said you'd be here this evening sometime," JJ said, and spit into a Styrofoam cup that was stained brown inside. "What he didn't say was *why* you was coming."

Jack noticed that JJ's uniform shirt was half buttoned up and he was not wearing a belt. He guessed that the young cop must have been off duty, but being the junior officer in this two-man department, was stuck with doing the grunt work.

On the wall behind the other desk was a photo of the

chief of police that bore a strong resemblance to JJ. Jack guessed there might be some nepotism at work in the hiring practice of the Shawneetown Police Department.

"I hope we didn't interrupt any important plans, Lieutenant," Jack said, and noticed the young man straighten up slightly with pride at being addressed by his rank.

"Naw, sir," JJ said, and spit into the cup again.

He reminded Jack of most of the young policemen he'd met over the years who were trying desperately to present a tough side. Most of them bought pickup trucks, or muscle cars, and tried very hard to grow mustaches. And then there were the ones who had taken up chewing tobacco, or smoking cigars. And of course the ones that added to the above by hanging out at the Fraternal Order of Police Club and drinking heavily to prove just how "bad" they were.

JJ fit the profile. He was trying to grow a mustache, was chewing and spitting, and even though he didn't have the physique for it, he had his button-up shirt pegged at the sides and arms. Jack knew JJ would have a pair of wraparound shades in his police car somewhere.

"We're investigating a suspicious death," Jack said, and saw a gleam come into JJ's eyes. "The victim used this address as a next of kin," Jack said, and showed JJ the Illinois Bureau of Motor Vehicle printout on Cordelia.

JJ's face turned ashen and the hand that held the paper shook, but only slightly. "Oh my God, it's Cordelia," he said.

"I'm sorry, Lieutenant," Jack said. "I hope she wasn't a relative." He was kicking himself for forgetting that in these small towns everyone knows, or is related to, everyone else. He should have smoothed the way over the telephone, but there was no putting the cat back in the bag now.

JJ went behind a desk and sat down. "She's not a real relative, but we grew up together. Lived in the same house. She lives in an apartment on the other side of town. You guys passed the turnoff for her place on the way in here, I bet."

Liddell took out his notebook. "Address?"

"I know right where it's at," JJ said. "You said a suspicious death? Can you tell me what happened to her?"

Jack pulled up a chair and began. When he was finished, Lieutenant JJ Johnson stood, buttoned his shirt, and said, "I'll take you."

CHAPTER TWENTY-ONE

It was late afternoon when Arnold finally made it through the garage door into his kitchen.

"Arnold, is that you?" came his mother's voice from up the stairs. "Arnold, where have you been?"

"Yes, it's me, Mother," he said with a sigh. He took his jacket off and laid it across the kitchen chair, then slipped out of his shoes. His feet were killing him. They had always been uncomfortable, but his mother had bought them for him many years ago, just before she became ill. He couldn't bring himself to part with them.

He put the kettle on to boil, hoping some chamomile tea would relax him a bit, and opened the door to the fridge to see if there was something to eat when his mother's voice startled him.

"Arnold, you'd better get up here."

She sounded panicked. Arnold ran to the stairs. "Mother? What is it?" She didn't answer, and he ran up the stairs and down the hall to her room. When he opened the door the overpowering odor of urine hit him.

His mother lay on the bed, propped up against the head-board by several large pillows, and everything, bedding, and clothes were soaked in urine.

His excitement at being on the front page of the newspaper had lessened gradually throughout the workday, but the sight of his mother's frail and almost bony figure lying in that filthy mess finished off any thoughts he'd had of himself or his own importance. *I shouldn't have left her alone for so long,* he thought.

"Couldn't you reach the bedpan, Mother?" he asked, and her expression hardened.

"Pah! Why don't *you* use the bedpan?"

She did this deliberately to punish me, he thought.

The doctor had told her to use her walker and go to the bathroom. Lying in bed all day was not good for her. But she was stubborn, and seemed to take pleasure in her self-imposed helplessness. Regardless, she was his mother, and he couldn't bring himself to be cross with her.

With a resigned sigh he said, "Let's get you cleaned up, Mother. Then I'll bring you some sweet tea."

"Hmmpf," she said, and looked down at the floor beside the bed. Arnold followed her gaze and spotted a pile of urine-soaked newspaper. He recognized the front page. His story. His front-page story.

So. I guess that's what she thought of my story, he thought, and dutifully bent to retrieve the wet mess.

In the master bathroom he disposed of the wet newspaper in a plastic bag, tied it shut, and set it by the door. His hands were smeared with black ink from the wet newspapers, so he used his elbow to turn the hot water handle on the sink.

He scrubbed his hands with lilac-scented hand soap under the scalding hot water and counted silently, *One Mississippi, two Mississippi, three Mississippi,* until he reached twenty.

As soon as he turned the water off his mother yelled from her bed, "I didn't hear you count, Arnold!"

"I counted to myself, Mother."

"I said . . . I didn't hear you!" Her voice was sharp. "Don't sass your mother, you ungrateful twit."

Arnold turned the faucet back on, and this time counted loudly so that she would hear, but he didn't put his hands back under the water. The skin on his hands was red and painful from the hot water as it was. This was his little rebellion. A small thing really. A concession. He had been pretending to obey her for such a long time now that it came easily.

He smiled and began filling the tub with water for Mother's bath.

"Are you filling the tub, Arnold?"

"Yes, Mother."

"Well, don't get it so hot this time!'

"I won't, Mother."

"And don't get it too cold!"

"It will be perfect, Mother," Arnold said, his mind filled with the memory of Bernice's smile.

CHAPTER TWENTY-TWO

Liddell had somehow squeezed into the backseat of JJ's souped-up Pontiac Firebird police cruiser, but it was a very tight fit. Jack sat in the front passenger seat, holding on to the hand strap above his window as JJ expertly negotiated a curve. A fiery bird was painted on the hood of the cruiser, and Jack felt that was appropriate as they flew down the hill toward the center of Shawneetown.

When they had explained to Lieutenant Johnson why they were in Shawneetown they weren't surprised that he knew where Cordelia lived. After all, it was a small town. But they were taken aback by the fact that Johnson had grown up with her.

"My parents was killed in a car wreck when I was three. Aunt Elmira took me in like I was her own. Elmira adopted Cordelia about the same time, or maybe Cordelia was left with her as a foster parent. Can't say for sure because it never mattered to us. We was family," JJ said.

"So you probably know more about Cordelia than anyone?" Liddell probed.

"We went through grade school and high school together. Friends are mostly the same. Jon was always her best friend though."

"What can you tell us about Jon Samuels?" Jack asked.

"Well, for one thing, he wasn't Cordelia's boyfriend. He's gay."

"So he was her roommate?" Jack prodded when JJ seemed to have dropped the subject.

"Yeah. Something like that, I guess. We were all friends when we was little and it seemed like a normal enough thing to me for Cordelia and Jon to live together," JJ said.

Something in JJ's tone made Jack feel that the lieutenant was avoiding his questions, so he changed the subject. "So do you still live with your aunt?"

"Oh no! I moved out a long time ago," JJ said. He seemed much happier talking about himself than about Cordelia or Jon. "Got my own place in Old Shawneetown about a year ago." The way he said "Old Shawneetown" made Jack think it must be the garden district of Shawneetown. "And then Cordelia moved on in with Jon."

"So, where does Jon live?" Jack asked.

"Well, that's the thing, Detective Murphy. Jon's sick a lot so he ain't home much. Know what I mean?"

"Pretend I don't know," Jack said.

JJ chuckled at the sarcastic remark. "That's a good 'un. I gotta remember that." He looked over at Jack with a huge grin and said, "Pretend I don't know." He swerved off the side of the road and back on, causing Jack's knuckles to turn white. "I gotta tell Uncle Bob—I mean the chief—that one."

"So, where is Jon's place?" Jack asked again.

"Oh. Yeah." JJ punched down on the accelerator.

Halfway to Jon Samuels's apartment, Lieutenant Johnson said, "Aunt Elmira's in a home right down the street. Couple of Cordelia's friends work there. They were real tight. If anyone besides Jon knew what Cordelia was doing in Evansville, it'd be them. Want to stop there before we go see Jon?"

Jack and Liddell agreed it might be faster to talk to the friends and aunt before going to Samuels, but then they might have agreed to anything to get out of the police/race car and put feet back on safe ground.

JJ pulled into the parking area of an old three-story home that had been converted into a nursing facility and braked hard.

"I guess she must have finally found out," Lieutenant Johnson said, as the men extricated themselves from the low-slung seats.

Jack wanted to shake the young officer, but he forced himself to say calmly, "Found out what, Lieutenant?"

"Who her real family was," JJ said, then grinned. "I know. Pretend you don't know, right?"

Jack nodded. "From the beginning please."

"Cordelia was adopted. We were both adopted. But Elmira is my real aunt. You understand."

Jack had already heard this part, but he waited.

"Okay. Cordelia was about two or three when Elmira adopted her and none of us ever knew where she came from. I know I said it didn't matter to us, because she was family, but it mattered to Cordelia." He could see he had lost the detectives so he started again. "I mean we were never told where Elmira adopted her from. It was always kinda hush-hush. But as soon as Cordelia got old enough to start asking questions, that was always the big one."

"So you don't know if she found out who her parents were?" Jack asked.

"I know she was on to something. A couple of weeks ago she told me she was going to see an attorney."

"Where did she get the idea to see Lenny Bange?" Liddell asked.

"Well, I'm not sure if she brought his name up or if I did," JJ lied. He had suggested Lenny because he wanted an excuse to get to meet the man. Lenny Bange was connected, and not just in Evansville and Shawneetown. He had "businesses" all over the place. A man could get rich working for

Lenny Bange. But he would never tell these two detectives any of this. They were cops, just like him, but they were outsiders.

JJ continued, "He's been around town a little and seems to be doing all right for himself." He made his hand into a gun and pointed it at the ceiling, and said, "Bang, bang, bang."

"Why would she need an attorney?" Liddell asked JJ.

"I don't really know. She seemed to think that she was going to need one." JJ looked at them seriously and said, "Is that important? I mean, is that a clue or something?"

The visit with Aunt Elmira was useless. She was suffering from dementia and couldn't even remember that Jack and Liddell were detectives from Evansville after being told so repeatedly. There must have been a small part of her in there, however, because when they left her alone in her room she was rocking gently in her chair with tears running down her heavily lined cheeks.

When JJ had introduced the two Evansville detectives to his former classmates and told them about Cordelia they both broke down and cried. They were only slightly more helpful.

Lisa had gone to high school with Cordelia but had moved away until she landed the job at the nursing home. She hadn't seen much of Cordelia for the last year, but when Jack broached the subject of Cordelia hiring an attorney there was a light of recognition at the name of Lenny Bange. She denied knowing the man except for the catchy ads, but she confirmed that Cordelia was obsessed with finding out who her parents were, and if she had siblings.

Abby was a hairdresser turned medical assistant who had kept in touch with Cordelia more closely. She said Cordelia was very secretive and had kept it quiet if she was hiring an attorney. It was obvious that she knew the name of Lenny Bange in a more personal way than she let on, but there was no way to force the information out of her.

Jack gave both the women a business card and asked them to let them know if Aunt Elmira had anything else to tell them. Both women seemed to think that was funny, and left the business cards lying on the breakroom table where they had been sitting.

As they exited the house JJ took a can of tobacco out of his back pocket and stuck a pinch under his lip. "Any of that help you guys out?"

Jack shook his head. "I'm not sure, but I think we need to go and see Jonathan Samuels," Jack said.

"No problemo," JJ said, and got up. "Let me tell Abby we're leaving." He hurried back into the nursing home.

"Telling the women to keep their mouths shut about Lenny," Liddell said.

Jack nodded.

The little writing table was butted against the wall under Arnold's bedroom window. On top of the table were a new laptop computer and his spiral reporter's notebook. The notebook was open to the pages where he had written the things the voice had said to him over the telephone. The anonymous source had been dead-bang accurate on both of the murders.

He had considered going to Murphy and telling him about the calls, but he knew that his editor would kill him if he did so. In fact, Mr. Robertson had as much as ordered him to "keep his trap shut." Arnold felt that this went against the ethics of professional journalism, but if he made Robertson mad he might lose his job. If he lost his job he would lose any chance of ever being with Bernice.

The phone rang.

"Hey, Arnie," Larry Jansen said. "Got something for you."

Chapter Twenty-three

The moon was full and high in the cloudless sky, where it was surrounded by a reddish hue. The cornstalks in the fields had already dried to a crackling brown and Halloween was only a week away. *Hunter's moon,* Jack thought as JJ drove slowly through the downtown area and south toward the river through farm fields that smelled of earth and dampness. Except for the throaty roar of the car's big engine, the night was quiet and they had not passed another car along this stretch of road.

"Cordelia and Jon moved out here about a year ago," JJ explained, breaking the silence. Liddell rode in front with the seat pushed all the way back to allow for his long frame. Jack said from the backseat behind JJ, "You say there is an apartment building out here?"

JJ laughed. "Yeah. Barry Dimmett and his brother Larry took over their dad's farm when he died.

Liddell mouthed the words *Barry and Larry* to Jack and grinned.

JJ continued, saying, "And they sold twenty acres to a developer from overseas. I guess they thought an apartment complex was a great idea, but it never caught on and so most of the apartments are still empty. There were supposed to be four buildings, but after the first one didn't rent out I guess they gave up."

Mistaking the other men's silence for interest, he continued. "So Bob Daywalt—he owns Daywalt Pharmacy in town—bought the ground and is going to turn it into a subdivision."

"Does he have a brother?" Liddell asked, and Jack punched the back of his shoulder.

"I mean, how long before we get there?" Liddell said and looked at his watch. It was almost nine o'clock and they were getting nowhere.

"We're there," JJ said, and turned down a gravel drive that ran between withered brown cornstalks.

He drove another hundred yards and the land opened up into a large graveled parking lot that surrounded a two-story wood-sided building. No lights were on, and there were no cars in the parking area.

JJ said, "Cordelia's car ain't here. Jon's car neither."

"Well, we're here. Might as well check," Jack said, relieved for a chance to stretch his legs.

They knocked at the door to Jon Samuels's apartment, and except for a dog barking from somewhere inside, there was no sign of life. They tried several other doors of apartments where lights were burning, but no one answered.

"Jon must've got himself a dog," JJ said, then, "So where to next?" His eyes were wild with anticipation. This was his first big case.

"Well, Lieutenant," Jack began, "we need to get back to Evansville, but we'd appreciate it if you would look at the list of friends that Aunt Elmira gave us to make sure the phones and addresses are correct."

JJ's face dropped like a kid who had just had his puppy taken away. "You don't want me to talk to them for you?"

Jack and Liddell exchanged a look. Neither could think of a reason that JJ couldn't interview other friends, and it would save them another trip back to this weird little town.

"If that wouldn't be imposing?" Jack said, and JJ's face lit up.

"Great! I mean I got lots of things to do n' stuff. But if you need any more help, just call. I'm always happy to help a fellow detective out. I'll call you tomorrow and let you know what I find out."

"Also, let me give you the coroner's number in Evansville," Jack said, and handed JJ a card with Lilly Caskins's number on it. "Give that lady a call. Think you can identify the body?"

"I'll do it."

CHAPTER TWENTY-FOUR

Detective Jansen told him that Detectives Murphy and Blanchard had gone to Shawneetown to check out Cordelia Morse's past. Along with the other information he'd come into possession of, Arnold started thinking that maybe there was a good follow-up story in Shawneetown. He felt a little guilty about benefiting from the death of the unfortunate young woman, but, he thought, *Was it my fault that she was killed? No, it wasn't.* Besides, the story would be a better follow-up than the one he had planned.

Jansen had given him the name of the chief of police and the lieutenant who formed the entirety of the Shawneetown Police Department. Arnold called the police station about nine o'clock that evening and left a voice message. He received a return phone call from Lieutenant JJ Johnson less than thirty minutes later.

An hour after that call Arnold arrived at the Shawnee-town police station. He found Lieutenant J. Johnson, leaning in the doorway of the trailer in full uniform with sunglasses pushed up on top of his head even though it was pitch black outside. Arnold noticed a huge lump under JJ's lower lip, and for a moment thought maybe the man was deformed until he saw JJ spit into a Styrofoam cup.

JJ chauffeured him around, speeding around corners and cutting down alleys until Arnold thought he would wet his pants, but it had paid off. He didn't get to meet Aunt Elmira because of the late hour, but he met someone more valuable . . . Jonathan Samuels.

The killer watched Arnold and the skinny policeman go into the upper apartment. He almost laughed at the idea that Arnold Byrum had unknowingly saved Jonathan Samuels's life. If that damn cop wasn't present he might still go over there and whack the reporter and the queer. But the cop was a different thing. Maybe later.

Jon Samuels was a problem. He shouldn't be allowed to talk to Murphy, but now the reporter got involved and whatever Samuels knew would end up in the newspaper so what purpose would it serve to kill him now?

The lights were on inside, and the door stood open to Jon's place. There were no other cars in the parking lot. No one appeared to be home. The building was hidden from the road by cornstalks and so distant from other neighbors that no one would hear the screams.

This is so tempting, he thought, and smiled. *Only one way to decide.* He took a coin from his pocket. *Heads I kill them all. Tails they live another day*, he thought, and flipped the coin.

CHAPTER TWENTY-FIVE

The moon was full and high in the sky when Jack pulled into the gravel lot behind his cabin. Susan's little Honda del Sol was parked, and with a cop's habit he felt the hood. It was cold so she had been here awhile. *Probably asleep,* he thought. It was late. He hadn't called except once that morning to make a date that he hadn't been able to keep. In fact, he hadn't even called to tell her he wasn't going to be there.

He looked across the river at the intermittent lights marking other small cabins along the banks of the Ohio on the Kentucky side of the river. He'd met some of their residents over the summer, on the sandbars that skirted the shoreline. They were mostly good folks who just wanted to live and have fun. He wondered what kind of person could stalk them like game. Kill and mutilate them without any feeling. And he wondered why this killer was sending these messages to him.

He made a mental note to talk to Susan about this. She had a right to know that some psycho had started communicating with her boyfriend. He wondered how she would feel about that. Would she leave him? Would she help him find this scumbag? He believed she would do the latter. She was beautiful, athletic, and great in bed, but she was as tough as

they came and this killer would not want to mess with her.
Still . . .

Jack trudged up the porch and the moment he entered the cabin he knew something wasn't right. It was too dark. He always left a night light on in the bathroom, and a small electric candle in the kitchen window. One that Susan had bought him.

He drew his Glock .45 and crouched inside the doorway, trying to discern any movement in the cabin. Something made a shushing noise from the bedroom, so he moved that way. As he rounded the corner of the doorway he saw the candle being lit. Susan lay on top of the sheets, wearing one of his T-shirts and panties. On the table next to the bed was a tray of cheese and a bottle of red wine called Ménage à Trois, his favorite.

He started to speak and she put a finger to her lips. "Just come to bed. Even warriors have to relax."

There were at least two things Jack knew about Susan Summers. She was never wrong, and her smile could melt an ice floe.

Jack awoke to the sound of a small engine puttering along the shoreline. He'd drunk too much, and for some reason gone to sleep in the rocking chair on his front porch. The porch was littered with the slaughtered remnants of almost a full case of Guinness, and it must have gotten cold outside because he had pulled a plastic tarp over himself. He pushed the tarp onto the deck and got up, stretching his aching joints.

Where is Susan? he wondered, and then remembered that she had gotten called in to work. He had to smirk at that, because that was what always happened to him, and he was the one that was leaving in the middle of the night.

After she left he had walked out to the porch and had a few beers. *What was it?* he thought. *About two in the morning. Something about a parolee being arrested for breaking up a biker bar hunting for his errant girlfriend.* The parolee had been arrested and of course someone had to prepare a warrant for the "retaking of an offender." Apparently she was still dealing with the detainee.

He tried to remember if he had talked to her about the situation that was developing with the killer and asked for some help on this one. Maybe ask her to get Dr. Don Schull to assist again. Schull was a retired forensic psychologist but still dabbled in the trade from time to time. *Did I even talk to her at all?*

He entered the cabin and spotted a note on the kitchen table. It read: *I've got coffee ready. Also there are some left-over goodies in the fridge. And yes, I'll help you, but I have someone different in mind than Dr. Schull.*

Now it came back to Jack. Susan had said that Dr. Schull was in Thailand with a girlfriend. *What's up with that?* he wondered. *And who was she referring to? Who did she have in mind?*

He poured himself a cup of coffee and then took a quick shower.

Thirty minutes later he was sitting in the chief's office, with a pain in his neck and cramps running down his back from sleeping in the uncomfortable wooden rocker.

"How did he get this?" Chief Pope asked.

The chief was referring to yet another front-page story by Arnold Byrum. This time Lieutenant JJ Johnson was being quoted as *assisting Evansville detectives Jack Murphy and Liddell Blanchard in their serial killer investigations.* Jonathan Samuels had also been interviewed and although he hadn't said much, it was obvious that the police hadn't talked to him first. The end result was egg on the face of the Evansville Police Department.

Captain Franklin stared at the floor, leaving Jack to answer the question. Liddell had escaped this meeting by being needed in Crime Scene to sign for some evidence.

"We have no proof, Chief," Jack said. They all knew that Larry Jansen was the leak in the investigation, but they needed some type of proof before the chief could take any type of disciplinary action. And even with proof, it would be a difficult task to punish Detective Larry Jansen, because he was under the protection of the mayor and was presently in the hospital for medical tests. Supposedly he'd had a mild stroke.

"I called Lieutenant Johnson in Shawneetown this morning," Jack said, "and he told me that Arnold Byrum showed up shortly after we left last night. We probably passed him on our way back to Evansville."

"It's not like it was being kept secret, but no one knew you and Liddell were on your way to Shawneetown," Captain Franklin said. "Have you been turning reports into Central Records?"

Jack nodded in the affirmative.

"Well, there you go," Franklin said. "Anyone with clearance could read the reports, and you probably mentioned somewhere that Cordelia Morse was from Shawneetown and that you had been unable to contact the next of kin."

"So we still can't finger Detective Jansen for the leak?" the chief said to no one in particular. "Okay, so what about this Jonathan Samuels? How did Arnold find him and we didn't?"

"I'll take the blame for that one, Chief," Jack said. "I had his name on the list of people we were going to contact, but it was getting late, and the town was zipped up by the time we finished interviewing the aunt at the hospital. It was my decision to call it a night and return later."

To Jack's surprise the chief smiled at him, and said, "Scooped by Arnold Byrum. You'll never live it down, Jack."

If another officer had said that, Jack would have told them to take a flying leap. But you don't talk to the chief of police that way. "I'll get on it right away, Chief," Jack answered.

Captain Franklin was trying to suppress a grin as he said, "Maybe you should take Arnold with you."

"Will that be all?" Jack asked.

"Get back to work, Detective," Chief Pope said, and as Jack closed the door behind him he could hear them laughing. Outside the chief's conference room Jack looked around to be sure he was alone before muttering, "Bite me. All of you."

Jennifer Mangold looked up and said, "Excuse me?"

"I said, 'Fine by me. How about you?' " Jack lied.

"What's up, pod'na?" Liddell asked, after seeing the look on Jack's face.

Without looking over, Jack said, "I'm going to cook his goose."

"Who are you talking about?"

"And I'm going to skin the one that's leaking to him," Jack added.

Liddell had the morning newspaper on the seat next to him. The headlines this time declared, SERIAL KILLER VICTIM WAS SEARCHING FOR PARENTS.

"So we missed talking to a couple guys? So what?" Liddell asked.

Jack looked over at his partner and seeing the grin on his huge face he could feel his anger slowly draining. "So, I don't like people leaking things involving our case. Especially when we missed it the first time. And how did Arnold find him?"

Liddell laughed out loud. "The great Jack Murphy has been aced by Barney."

"Oh, now don't you start up, too," Jack said.

CHAPTER TWENTY-SIX

An hour later Jack and Liddell pulled into the gravel lot of the Shawneetown Police Department. JJ's souped-up Firebird police cruiser was gone. In its place sat a large black Suburban with smoked windows.

As they exited the car they were hailed from the wooded area across from the trailer. A big man—almost as big as Liddell—was coming from the tree line carrying a roll of toilet paper. He was dressed in the same uniform as Lieutenant Johnson, but where JJ's was pegged skin tight, this man wore his loose and comfortable.

He approached them, twisting his gun belt straight across his massive stomach. "Toilet's fudged up again," he complained and straightened his uniform shirt. "City won't pay to fix this pisshole of a trailer, so I got to go in the woods."

"Chief Johnson?" Jack inquired.

The big man switched the toilet paper to his other hand and shook with Jack and then Liddell, before heading up the metal steps into the trailer. Liddell wiped his hand on his pants and they followed Chief Johnson into the Shawneetown Police Station.

The chief's portion of the trailer was well decorated and took up half of the total space. He looked across the desk at the two detectives and then sighed before saying, "Looky, fellas. This is a quiet little town. Or at least it was up till you guys came here stirring things up. Now my lieutenant is running around like he's some kinda TV detective, and that damn Evansville newspaper of yours has got the media calling every five minutes."

Jack moved his chair closer to the chief's desk, and keeping his voice low, said, "Chief Johnson, it's not our intention to cause any problems for you or your town. We're investigating the death of one of your people."

Before he could add that the murder of Cordelia Morse was tied to a second killing that had happened within hours of hers, the chief cut him off.

"She got herself killed in Evansville, boys. That's your jurisdiction."

Jack shook his head. "It doesn't matter where she was killed. Her roots are here. Her family and friends are here." Then, seeing the stubborn look on Chief Johnson's jowly face, he decided to change tactics. This was Chief Johnson's home ground. Render unto Caesar that which is Caesar's.

"To be honest, our chief of police, Marlin Pope, told us to come and see you personally. He said he met you once, sir, and that you wouldn't steer us wrong," Jack said.

Chief Johnson looked sternly at both men and then his features softened. Jack didn't know if Johnson had ever met Chief Pope.

"Pope, huh?" Chief Johnson said. "Black guy, right?"

Jack relaxed a bit.

"Okay, looky here, fellas," Johnson said. "I'm sorry about JJ talking to that reporter guy. I gave him a good talkin'-to about it, but he's still young. You know?"

Jack and Liddell nodded.

"So what can I do for you?" Johnson asked.

* * *

Jonathan Samuels was home when Chief Bob Johnson arrived at the apartment with the two Evansville detectives in tow. To Jack, the man looked to be barely twenty years old, and except for the multicolored spiky hair, Jon personified the word average. It was apparent from Samuels's icy stare that there was history between himself and the chief of police.

"Nice pedal pushers, Nancy," the chief said to Samuels and then, "This here's some detectives from Evansville. They want to ask you some questions about Cordelia. You be nice and answer them truthfully, you hear me?"

Jack extended a hand and said, "Detective Murphy. Jack."

Samuels shook his hand, but his eyes never left those of the big chief of police.

"Did you know, Detective Murphy, that pedal pushers were all the style in the fifties. Marilyn Monroe, Audrey Hepburn, Annette Funicello, for example, all wore pedal pushers as an alternative to the poodle skirts. But now they are called capri pants, because capris are cut a little tighter, showing a gal's figure off better. So if Uncle Bob here wasn't such a fascist he'd know that no one wears pedal pushers anymore."

Chief Johnson's features stiffened and his hand was moving to his handcuffs, when Jack interrupted the promise of a violent ending to this interview.

"My ex-wife brought a pair of pedal pushers back from a trip to New York City. She said they still call them that out there. So I guess they never go out of style," Jack said, and smiled at Jon. He didn't know if this was true or not, but it could be.

Chief Johnson saw his opportunity. "So I guess you don't know everything, do you?" he said to Samuels.

Liddell began coughing into his hand.

"Can I get you something, Detective?" Samuels offered.

"Water," Liddell answered in a raspy voice.

Jon turned to go back into the apartment for the water. When he was out of earshot Liddell stepped up to Chief Johnson and said, "Thanks for all your help, pod'na, but now that you've played the bad cop, how 'bout letting Jack ask him a few questions in private?"

Liddell was every bit as big as the chief, but where Johnson had gone to fat, Liddell was solidly built. Chief Johnson must have seen the foolishness of angering the bigger man, but his ego was as large as his frame and he had to make one more stab at being in charge.

"Listen, smart-ass, I'm the chief here. I know this little whootchie-koo and he's not the nice little downtrodden mother's son like they show on TV. This'un here'd cut your throat if you turned your back on him. I'll wait in the car like one a them turban-wearin' cab drivers. But don't take all day." With that he turned on his heel and sauntered out of the apartment door.

"Think I made him mad, pod'na," Liddell said.

"You think?" Jack answered.

"My big criminal record is possession of part of a marijuana cigarette," Samuels confided to Jack and Liddell. "The judge threw it out of court. Johnson's hated me ever since. But he hated me even more when Cordelia moved in with me. I think he had his eye on her. You know?"

Jack raised an eyebrow at this information.

"I'm gay, not stupid," Jon said. "And I also figured out that you were trying to keep me and Baldilocks from going at it."

"Baldilocks?" Liddell said.

"Yeah," Jon said, a huge grin spread across his face. He handed the water to Liddell. "What can I do to help? Cordelia was special to me. And, no, she wasn't gay."

"Tell us everything you can about Cordelia," Jack said.

Jon let out a sigh and invited them to sit, and as they did Jack's foot struck something next to the couch. He looked down and saw that he had knocked over a bowl of what looked like dry dog food.

"You have a dog?" Jack asked.

Samuels chuckled. "She's at the groomer's."

"I heard her barking the first time we were out here. What kind of dog is she?" Jack asked out of politeness.

"Oh, just a mutt," Samuels offered. "I just got her. She belonged to a friend who recently passed away. But I'm sure you would rather hear about Cordelia."

He then told the detectives how he and Cordelia had met in grade school, and how they had at first formed an alliance because they were "different" from the other kids. Jon because he was gay, and Cordelia because she was adopted. She had been there for him through his struggle to go straight, and later, his discovery that he was HIV positive.

"Cordelia was a beautiful person, Detective. She was smart, quick-witted, humorous, and loved her aunt and would do anything for her friends. But as soon as they found out she was adopted they taunted her and made up stories."

"What kind of stories?" Liddell asked.

Jon took a sip of his beer. "They called her a killer. Said she killed her family. It was just kids being mean. You know how they are."

Jack and Liddell looked at each other in surprise.

"I didn't tell that newspaper guy any of this. None of his business," Jon said.

A question came into Jack's mind. "How well did Chief Johnson know Cordelia?"

Jon cocked his head, and said, "You noticed."

"Noticed what?"

"That the chief of police doesn't seem interested in solving her murder," Jon said.

Jack hadn't really read that much into it, but he nodded.

"Well, he visited her frequently over the last several years," he said, and paused as if wondering how much to tell.

"He seemed to have a sweet spot for her. More than he should have, what with his nephew being raised with her and all. And he didn't want her living here with me. He even suggested once that he would get her a place in Old Shawnee-town by him and offered to pay for it."

"That's strange?" Jack asked.

"That old penny-pincher? He don't give nothing away. So why is it that he's not doing more himself to find out who killed her?"

CHAPTER TWENTY-SEVEN

Later, as they stood in the parking lot outside, Chief Johnson called the Gallatin County prosecutor for a search warrant of Jon Samuels's apartment. He offered to take the detectives to the best restaurant in Gallatin County. They were buying, of course. And it was just a coincidence that the restaurant was owned by the chief, and managed by his wife and daughter.

Liddell jumped at the chance.

"This guy never eats, Chief," Liddell complained. "He's trying to starve me to death."

Chief Johnson smiled and patted his own stomach. "I know what you mean. Just follow me and we'll be putting down a plate of flapjacks and bacon in ten minutes' time."

"What're we waiting for?" Liddell quipped. "Thanks, Chief Johnson."

"Call me Bob," Johnson said.

Liddell concentrated on the road as Jack made several quick telephone calls. The first to Captain Franklin to tell him about their talk with Jonathan Samuels. Franklin agreed that they needed to search the apartment and said he would send crime scene guys if Jack thought they were needed. They both knew that the Shawneetown PD did not have the resources, man power, or experience to deal with something like this.

Jack hoped that Chief Johnson would see the wisdom in obtaining a search warrant, and would allow the Evansville Police Department to assist in the search. Jack would prefer to have Sergeant Walker bring a few crime scene techs from Evansville to carry out the search.

The next call was to Sergeant Walker. "How fast can you get to Shawneetown, Illinois, Tony?" he asked when Walker came on the line. He filled him in on what he needed and was about to call his own county prosecutor, just to keep them in the loop, when his cell phone rang in his hand. It was his ex-wife.

"Hi, Katie," he said, and cupped his free hand over his ear to hear above the road noise.

"I read the paper this morning. Are you okay?" Katie said, her voice full of concern.

"Yeah, I'm fine," he said. It was always like this. She would call out of the blue, and then he would be left feeling guilty and not even know why.

"Are you at least getting some sleep, Jack?"

"Like a baby," he said, but in fact he hadn't been sleeping well at all. Last night he'd gone to sleep on his front porch covered with a plastic tarp. "And we're getting ready to go to a restaurant and have a sit-down meal."

"Well, I won't keep you," her voice trailed off, waiting for him to say something, but when he didn't, she said, "I'll call Susan and keep her entertained."

Jack didn't know what to say to that. So he said, "Thanks for calling. Take care of yourself and don't worry about me. I'm a big boy."

"Did you remember to buy Susan a birthday present?" she asked.

"I'm thinking of getting her a running outfit." She was silent and he knew that meant she had a better idea.

"Okay, I give up. What should I get her?" he asked.

"I was just thinking that a nice light blue warm-up outfit in size ten would be perfect," Katie said, surprising him.

"Really?"

"Yeah. Susan loves to run, and light blue is her favorite color," Katie said.

"I know," Jack said, although he couldn't remember her ever wearing light blue. "I'm getting it today."

He heard Katie laugh and then she was gone.

"I really am getting it today," he said to the dead line and then punched in one last number.

"Angelina, I need your help again," Jack said.

"Anything, boss," she said, and he could detect a hint of boredom in her voice.

"I need you to go to Hibbett or Dick's Sporting Goods and get a light blue running outfit for me."

"What size are you?" she asked.

"It's for Susan," he said.

"Sorry, boss, but I draw the line at buying gifts for your stable of women." She hung up.

"What stable?" he said to the dead line and closed his phone.

"Garcia's going to get it for you?" Liddell asked.

"She'll get it," Jack said.

"Want me to call Marcie?"

"I'll take care of it!" Jack said. "By the way, I talked to Susan last night and she said she's got someone in mind to help us out. Schull is out of the country, so it's somebody else."

"Couldn't hurt," Liddell agreed.

"Yeah," Jack agreed, but he thought about how Susan and Schull had once been lovers and it still niggled at him. He didn't normally have a jealous bone in his body, but when it came to sharing Susan he found out he had a whole jealous skeleton. He didn't like the feeling, and hated to admit it even more.

Ye Olde Shawneetown Diner was housed in a massive two-story brick building that was built in the early 1800s when the rivers were the primary means of moving both people and consumable goods. Three thousand square feet upstairs and a similar amount down. Johnson had renovated the upstairs into living quarters that he and his wife shared with their only daughter.

The building sat back far enough from the street to allow for outside tables and chairs on three sides of the building, with a covered balcony on the front and both sides as well.

"You own this, Chief?" Jack asked.

Chief Johnson shoved his hands in his pockets and looked at the ground. "Well, me'n the bank. And the place doubles for my home right now until it can generate enough money to pay for itself."

Jack was half owner of the Two-Jakes Restaurant and Marina in Evansville, and was impressed with the restoration work that Chief Johnson had done to the old building. The business part of his mind was already working on a cooperative angle whereby he could link his own waterfront restaurant with the one he stood looking at now. Two-Jakes enjoyed a steady stream of travelers, from both up and down river, who would tie up at his floating docks and come into the restaurant or bar. With just a little cross-advertising he could build both businesses' clientele. But he wasn't here to talk about the restaurant business.

The interior was as magnificent as the exterior, with oak pedestal tables covered with heavy linen tablecloths, heavy wooden chairs, floor-to-ceiling windows that allowed a view of the waterfront, a small raised dance floor next to an expensive-looking bar. The only things missing were customers.

Chief Johnson noticed Jack looking around and said, "We don't do the business I'd hoped yet, but it's early days. We do a better evening and weekend crowd. They always come to drink and dance."

"So what's on the menu?" Liddell said, sniffing the air.

"Gertie!" Chief Johnson called, and a woman came from the kitchen.

"What do you want?" the woman asked. She was wearing a colorless frock with a stained apron tied loosely at the waist. Her dark hair was pulled back tightly in a ponytail that lay across her shoulder, and her skin was smooth and clear. Jack guessed her age at about thirty, but her demeanor suggested someone twice that age.

"Gertie, honey, this here's Jack Murphy. And that tall galoot is Liddell Blanchard. They's homicide detectives from Evansville."

Gertrude Johnson eyed the visitors and a smile came to her eyes. She wiped her hands on the stained apron and said, "Sorry. I was in the back cleaning." She blushed slightly, and then shook hands with both men.

"You should have told me we were having company, Daddy." She excused herself and went back into the kitchen.

"That's my daughter. Her and her momma run the place. I just pay the bills," Johnson said. "She's a looker, ain't she?"

"I'm already married," Liddell said, and Jack nudged him in the ribs.

Johnson didn't seem to hear the remark and offered the men seats at a table near the kitchen. "I'll get her to rustle up some grub," he said, but before he could leave the room his cell phone rang. Johnson looked at the caller ID on his phone and said, "That was quick. Guess we'll have to get the food to go. Your search warrant's ready."

CHAPTER TWENTY-EIGHT

Judge Abner Hudgins, circuit court judge for Gallatin County, had interrupted a fishing trip to come in to work and sign the search warrant. He stood in his office beside hundreds of leather-bound law books, dressed in stained khakis and Keen sandals, with his thick white chest hair showing through the neck of a white button-up shirt. A safari hat was laying on one of the heavy mahogany chairs. Two fly-fishing rods leaned against the wall.

Hudgins was a man of few words, but he had been very interested to read the search warrant for the apartment that Cordelia Morse had shared with Jon Samuels. As he finished the last page and put his sweeping signature to the document he looked up at Jack and Liddell.

"This search warrant doesn't say a lot of things, does it?" he asked.

"It's complete, sir," Jack assured him.

Judge Hudgins made a dismissive motion and said, "Oh, it's complete enough. And you can see that I signed it." His eyes drew into narrow slits as he sized the men up before continuing. "How much do you know about the killing?"

Jack was about to answer when the judge raised a hand to stop him. "I mean the killing of Cordelia's daddy?"

* * *

"Pretend I don't know anything," Jack said to Judge Hudgins. Seeing the sharp look he earned for his remark, he added, "which shouldn't be hard because I know nothing."

The judge gave Chief Johnson a questioning look. Johnson shrugged and said, "I'm afraid that must have been before my time."

"That's right, Bob," the judge said. "I forgot that you moved here from—St. Louis was it?"

"Been here twelve years now, Judge," the chief said.

"Well, sit down. I think you all should know all this, too. It may not have anything to do with what you're investigating, but then again . . ."

Jack, Liddell, and Chief Johnson took seats in front of the judge's desk and waited for him to begin.

"Dennis Alexander Morse," Judge Hudgins said. "The most despicable man I ever had the displeasure of knowing." He picked up the phone on his desk and called his secretary. "Alice, bring us some iced tea, please." He hung up and continued.

"Denny was in the war. The one called Desert Storm. The military discharged him as unfit for duty. But we all knew there was more to it than that. We knew what kind of boy he was when he joined the service, and believe you me, the whole town breathed a sigh of relief when Denny went away in nineteen-ninety. When he came back he was changed. And not for the better."

Alice, a matronly woman with a no-nonsense air, came in with a silver tray containing glasses, teaspoons, an ice bucket, and a large glass pitcher of ice tea. She began fixing one for the judge, but he dismissed her. She looked a little put out, and Jack guessed that she wanted to hear whatever story it was the judge was telling these men.

After Alice left the room Judge Hudgins said loudly, "Alice, quit listening at the keyhole, darlin'," and they heard footsteps walking away.

"Where was I? Oh yeah," he said. "Denny came back and found his wife was pregnant."

Jack and Liddell leaned forward.

"Apparently the wife took in a little comfort while he was gone. Since he was gone more than a year, he knew there was no way that was his kid."

"Cordelia?" Liddell asked.

"Yeah, little Cordelia," the judge confirmed. "We never knew who the father was. But you have to keep in mind that when Denny left her, she had no money, no job, and ended up losing their house to the bank. And she had a little boy to worry about, too."

"There was a brother?" Jack asked.

"Name was Cody Morse. Momma had a thing for names that began with a *C* I guess. Anyway, Cody was about five when Denny went away, maybe six or seven when Denny came back from the war."

He paused while he offered the others a drink. As they fixed their glasses he continued.

"Well, Denny got home and moved the family to Eldorado, Illinois. I thought we were shod of them, but a few months later I got a call from the sheriff that he had Denny in jail for putting the missus in the hospital. Apparently she had tried to run from him and come here to hide out where she thought she had friends. Denny found her and almost beat her to death.

"Back then I was with the prosecutor's office. We tried like hell to keep him in jail, but the wife, she says he didn't do anything to her. She said she fell down. So we had to let him go."

All the men in the room were aware of similar cases. It was a sad fact of life regarding domestic violence cases that more times than not, the truth never came out, and nothing ever changed.

"Well, before the wife—her name was Brenda—before Brenda was released from the hospital she had Cordelia. Sometime during the night, Brenda just got up and left. Without the baby. Just disappeared. Left with just the torn and bloody clothes she'd gone into the hospital with."

"What happened to her?" Johnson asked.

The judge looked at the men and shrugged. "We tried to find her, of course. Thought maybe Denny had killed her. We searched everywhere, but there was nothing to be found. Back then, of course, we didn't have the technology that could have been thrown at such a search in this day and age, but we always figured she'd just had enough. Left here and started a new life somewhere else. At least that's what we all wanted to believe."

Alice came back in with another pitcher of iced tea and this time she had some pastries. Liddell and Johnson both took several and another glass of tea.

With half a scone in his mouth, Liddell asked, "So what happened to Cordelia? Did she get raised by Denny?"

"That's a good question and the answer is yes and no," the judge said, and grabbed the last pastry before Liddell could swipe it. "I tried to keep him from getting the child," Judge Hudgins said, and sighed. "But back then the welfare department didn't really have any teeth. In the end she was given back to Denny, although I didn't know then why he was fighting so hard to keep her."

"What do you mean?" Jack asked. He wasn't sure he wanted to know the answer.

"Well, Denny was about as blackhearted as any man I've ever run across. And we didn't really find out what he was doing to those kids until one day we found Denny, laying in a pool of blood on the kitchen floor. He was so cut up we had to identify him with dental records. Which wasn't easy because his whole face was cut off."

Jack and Liddell exchanged a look but didn't interrupt.

"Cody was found in the woods behind the house a few hours later. Covered in blood. We never found the murder weapon, but as best I can remember, it was something like an axe or a machete maybe. Cody was incoherent, babbling. Poor kid was covered in bruises, and we later found he had been sexually abused as well."

CHAPTER TWENTY-NINE

The judge told a good story, but in the end most of it came down to his memory. The records from that far back had been moved years ago to the basement of the town hall. Back then, nothing was on computer, and if there were hard copies of the case file there was a chance that some of it might be missing because that's just the way it was.

Chief Johnson said he thought there were some police records in the police storage shed, and he promised to find what they had on Denny Morse and the family.

The small police parade made its way from the downtown courthouse toward the apartment complex where Cordelia Morse had lived with her school friend, Jonathan Samuels. Chief Johnson led the procession, with Sergeant Walker in the middle and Jack and Liddell bringing up the rear. The mood in the cars was somber after hearing the story told by Judge Hudgins.

"It's not exactly the same story that Samuels told us, is it?" Jack asked.

"He's the same age as Cordelia. Maybe he just doesn't know all the facts," Liddell suggested.

Jack grunted. "Hell, the chief didn't even know about

this. And why would an twenty-year-old murder have anything to do with what we're looking into right now?"

"You think Alice or the chief will be able to dig out all the records for us?" Liddell asked.

"Too bad it's not on a computer system. We'll be lucky if they can find the paper files."

"You think Cordelia tracked her brother down?" Liddell asked.

"You heard what the judge said. There was no trial. He was committed to a mental institution. It's anyone's guess where he is now. They didn't even take fingerprints because of his age."

"We need Garcia's help with this," Liddell said.

CHAPTER THIRTY

Arnold's follow-up story had been a big hit, but in the newspaper business it was already yesterday's news the minute the paper hit the stands. He knew he was going to have to come up with something even more spectacular for tomorrow or he would be relegated to the back pages again.

After returning home from Shawneetown last night he'd had to address his mother's needs, type out his story, and e-mail it to his editor. He had only managed about two hours' sleep before he had to go back to work. He was sitting in the editor's office now with a cup of cold coffee and a headache, and his eyes felt like they had sand in them.

"Are you awake, Arnold?" Robertson yelled at him.

Arnold straightened in his chair and nodded. His heart was trip-hammering in his chest.

"Reggie, your article's out. Arnold's is in," Robertson said to the reporters that were gathered in the room.

Arnold couldn't believe that the editor was promising him another story. If he was getting Reggie's spot then it would be the front page of section B, but that was still a front page.

He looked across the table at Reggie Washington, the reporter for the society page, and saw the barely controlled anger showing on the older man's face. Arnold could only imagine how Reggie felt, never having had a daily column of his own. In his three years at the newspaper he had worked filler stories and then was assigned to the police beat, but less than half of his articles ever made it to print.

His feelings of sympathy toward Reggie were quickly forgotten when Bernice entered the room with a stack of papers for her boss to sign. She had long tresses of shiny brown hair, and skin so fair it made Arnold ache with the temptation to reach out and touch it. But he'd never been with a woman, never had a girlfriend, and would never have the nerve to speak to any woman, much less Bernice.

His mouth went dry as she leaned over the conference table to pick up the signed papers, and her breast brushed against his hand. His mouth moved like a fish out of water, torn between smiling and the less important task of getting air into his shocked lungs. His face turned a bright red when Bernice looked down at him, smiled, and said, "Good story, Arnold."

He was still staring after her retreating figure when Reggie pinched him on the arm.

"The boss is asking you a question, man," Reggie was saying.

Arnold looked at Mr. Robertson, but the words coming from his boss's mouth weren't making any sense. Something about "another follow-up" and "get your head out of something" and then it all came back into focus.

"What the hell is wrong with you, boy?" Robertson said and threw his arms in the air. "This whole damn place is full of pussy poachers! Why can't I get a real reporter?" He sounded angry, but he was grinning, and in reality he was pleased to see Arnold show some interest in a woman. His smile said, *Maybe that boy will make a reporter someday after all*.

Arnold's face went red again at the mention of the word

"pussy." Mother would never approve of that kind of language. Arnold looked at Reggie Washington and Garry Tisdale for support, but they were both smirking. Garry because he really was a pussy poacher, and Reggie, well, Reggie was a different kind of poacher. He liked men.

"Sorry, Mr. Robertson, sir," Arnold stammered. "I was just thinking about my next follow-up article."

"Cheesus H. Cracker, son. That's what I been asking you for ten minutes. Now do you have anything for a follow-up or am I gonna have to go back to the society news?" He said the latter with no attempt to hide his contempt for such writing.

Arnold knew that, once upon a time, Bob Robertson had been the police beat reporter. Back in the day, as they said. He also knew that Robertson had no time for society stories, gay men, or black reporters, and Reginald Washington had the misfortune of covering all those bases.

He contemplated saying, "No. I don't have a follow-up story yet." He liked Reggie. Reggie was different, and up until today, had always been kind to Arnold. But then he thought of Bernice's smile, and the way she had congratulated him, been proud of him, not to mention that he had actually touched her breast.

"Yes, sir, I'm working on a follow-up story. I've got to talk to one more source first. I can have it by two or three, sir."

"You have until noon," the editor said, and then lifted his bulky frame from his chair and walked out of the meeting without another word.

On the way out of the office, Garry Tisdale slapped Arnold on the back. "Great work, Arnold," he said, and it sounded sincere. "We'll make a reporter out of you yet."

Reggie watched Tisdale strut down the hallway, heading in the direction that Bernice would have gone, and gave Arnold a mocking look.

"You think you got a chance with that?" Reggie said and scoffed. "Tisdale been punching that since she came here."

Arnold didn't care for the way Reggie was speaking of Bernice. "I'd appreciate it if you didn't talk about—" He paused, and realized his fists were clenched. He was actually becoming angry, something he hadn't done in a great while.

"I get it," Reggie said. "Good luck with all that." He stopped just inside the doorway and whispered low enough for only Arnold to hear, "Look at you, and look at Garry. Which way you think she gonna swing?" And with that remark, Reggie sauntered down the hallway.

The clock was ticking. Arnold still had nothing more to add to his story. Robertson would skin him alive. It was almost noon and he was beginning to feel like a character in a movie, waiting for a showdown at high noon. He would be facing off with Reggie Washington. But instead of guns, they would draw notebooks from their back pockets and see who could write the first story. *There can be only one*, Arnold thought, remembering Bernice's smile.

He looked at Reggie walking down the aisle and said, "Hasta la vista, baby."

CHAPTER THIRTY-ONE

It was early afternoon and a drizzling rain was misting down as Jack and Liddell arrived at Samuels's apartment with Sergeant Walker following in the crime scene van. The chief had followed in his own vehicle. Samuels was waiting at the front door of the apartment holding the leash of the ugliest dog Jack had ever seen. Samuels was wearing white pants that were skintight and came down well below his knees. He wore a multicolored pastel top that reminded Jack of one of Susan's blouses. His hair was green tinged now instead of multicolored.

Liddell leaned over to Jack and said, "Must be the mutt he told us about. I've never seen anything like it. What do you think it is?"

Jack looked at the dog and shrugged. She was tall and built like a poodle, but with a pug snout and ears that sat high on her head and rotated like radar dishes. Ugly had a new meaning, but the dog wasn't his problem. Keeping the redneck chief of police from messing with Samuels to the point of losing the focus of this investigation *was* his problem. He looked over at Chief Johnson. The look on the chief's face said he was spoiling for a fight.

The layout of the apartment was typical of any two-bedroom place. The living room was first, separated from the kitchen by a breakfast bar. Behind the kitchen was a small hallway that led to the two bedrooms, which shared a bath.

"The big bedroom is Cordelia's," Samuels said. "It's on the left. And I haven't been in there, in case you want to know." He had directed this last remark to Chief Johnson, who was standing in the doorway with his thumbs hooked into his gun belt.

"Listen up, Nancy," Johnson said to Samuels, "I'm gonna stay out on the porch and have a cigar." He looked at Samuels and ran the cigar in and out of his mouth, and then grinned. "You stay outta these men's way, you hear?" He cast a glance at the dog, which responded with a low growl.

Samuels ignored the insults, and spoke to Jack. "Well, if Boss Hogg's not going to be in here I guess we can wait on the porch. I trust these other men."

"This won't take long," Walker said, and they watched Chief Johnson make his way down the stairs and head toward his police vehicle.

"We can talk on the porch," Jack said, hoping to avoid more hostility. Besides, the apartment was too small for all of them. Liddell and Walker would easily be able to handle it.

Samuels walked to the end of the upper porch and sat in one of his neighbor's white wicker chairs and looked out across the fields. Chief Johnson waddled down the stairway toward his vehicle. As irritating as the man was, Jack wished he would at least stay on the porch so that they could say that he maintained the scene of the search, but you don't tell a chief of police what to do. Jack turned his attention to Samuels.

"Sorry about the chief," Jack said.

"It's okay. I'm used to it," he said, and scrubbed the head of the dog, who was looking Jack over very carefully.

Jack chuckled, and said, "Boss Hogg. That's good."

Samuels looked up at him and grinned. "Don't forget Baldilocks."

Jack reached out a hand toward the dog, palm up. "Seems like a nice dog," Jack said.

Before Samuels could warn him, the dog strained at its leash and snapped at Jack's outstretched hand. Jack was able to pull his hand back just in time.

"Sorry, Detective Murphy," Jon said. "I've only had her a few days and apparently she doesn't like men."

"Yeah, I can tell," Jack said. "I heard her growling at the chief, but I figured that was just because the chief is a dick."

Samuels laughed out loud.

The search of Cordelia's apartment was anticlimactic considering the amount of preparation it had taken to set it up. Liddell came out of the apartment first, and shook his head at Jack's questioning look.

"Not a thing, pod'na," he said, and peeled latex gloves from his hands. He motioned for Jack to follow him back inside, where he led Jack to Cordelia's bedroom. He kept his voice at a low whisper and said, "Take a look in the closet."

Jack opened the folding doors. There were dozens of hangers but only two pairs of jeans and a few cotton tops. On the floor of the closet were two pairs of dirty tennis shoes.

"She only had a few clothes with her at the Marriott, didn't she?" Jack asked.

"What young woman that you know has less than a semi-truckload of clothes and shoes?" Liddell shook his head. "Someone has cleaned out her closet, pod'na. And I didn't find any underclothing in her dresser, either. It's like all of her panties and bras have been taken along with her clothes."

Jack walked to the dresser and opened the drawers. "Let's talk to Samuels," he said.

* * *

Jack and Liddell found Jon Samuels still at the end of the porch with the dog. Chief Johnson was standing at the back of the crime scene SUV talking to Sergeant Walker.

"Jon, would you mind coming in here a minute?" Jack said from the doorway of the apartment.

Jon looked up and a shadow crossed his features. Jack had seen this look on hundreds of witnesses and suspects. The "moment of truth" look. When they realize that you know.

"Does *he* have to know?" Jon asked and nodded toward the chief of police.

"It depends, Jon," Jack answered truthfully.

Samuels tied the dog's leash to the railing and hugged her, commanding her to stay, and trudged down the porch. He entered the apartment and motioned for the two detectives to follow him into the bedroom. He opened the closet and Jack and Liddell saw a wide assortment of Victoria's Secret–type bras, panties, and other lingerie on hangers. There were at least a hundred pieces in all, and on the floor of the closet was an assortment of high-heel shoes and sandals and boots.

"I guess your Sergeant Walker thought all this was mine," Samuels said. A sardonic grin played at the corners of his mouth. "Not really my style. Or my size."

Jack sat on the edge of the bed and said, "What are you not telling us, Jon?"

CHAPTER THIRTY-TWO

The killer stayed in the shadows, leaning against one of the huge metal struts of the abandoned Ohio Street Rail Bridge, and looked down at least thirty feet into the water that flowed below him. He should have come here earlier, but even *he* had to work sometimes.

The Ohio Street Bridge had been abandoned in the late seventies when the new Ohio Street was built less than a hundred yards from the old one. At one time there were two bridges, side by side, one for the trains and one for vehicular traffic, and both spanned the mouth of Pigeon Creek where it emptied into the Ohio River. The railway bridge had been upgraded and painted, but the traffic bridge had fallen into disrepair and was an eyesore in the area.

Just downriver from that spot the Blue Star Casino, the floating riverboat, was anchored. Upriver was the abandoned SIGECO (Southern Indiana Gas & Electric Company) building, which had supplied electricity to the tri-state area before coal stopped being such a big part of the fuel source.

He knew all of this because his grandparents had owned a houseboat that they kept tied up on the water not far from where he now stood. Everything was gone now. His grandparents died while he was still young, and although they had always been good to him, his memories of the houseboat were clearer than those of his grandparents. His life had started inside the cold concrete walls of a mental asylum. He had accepted the fact that he would never see his sister or mother again, and that he had killed his father. He had become The Cleaver.

And now, because of Cordelia, he had found his mother. The woman who had abandoned him. He was grateful to her, because she had caused him to become the man he was today. But he hated her for leaving him with an abusive degenerate who was a father in name only. He had settled up with his old man years ago.

Sometimes, in that dark period between sleep and dreams, reality and "what might be" clashed in his heart. There were nights when he would wake screaming, but there was no sound, and his heart would trip-hammer against his ribs. The medicine the doctors had given him only made it worse. They only numbed the outward expression of disgust and flight he so desperately sought in his dreams. If there was a God, then there was surely a Hell and he had spent most of his life there.

He wished he could make everyone else see what he saw. Feel what he felt. But what he had learned from life is that people tend to ignore others, simply dismiss them, unless there is something life-changing, some catastrophic event, to stamp a memory onto their minds. The thought that people were more forgettable than events both amused and comforted him. Soon there would be another unforgettable event here. In fact, it would be front-page news.

CHAPTER THIRTY-THREE

"Look, Detective Murphy, I don't want to say anything more," Jonathan Samuels said. He sat on the edge of the couch, head propped between his hands.

"Jon, I don't want you to say anything bad about your friend. I just need to know the truth. That's the best way to help her now. To find out who did this to her," Jack said. Liddell had opted to wait outside with Chief Johnson. Jon was gradually opening up, but Jack knew the man was holding something back.

Jon let out a deep sigh, and said, "Cordelia was a call girl." He got up and paced around the room. "Those clothes you found in my room are hers. I hid them from your men because I didn't want anyone to know. But that's all there is. I don't know any more."

"What about her appointment with Lenny Bange? Could Lenny know more than he is telling us?"

Jon sat motionless. If he heard the question he wasn't going to answer. Jack knew this was all he would get from him for now.

"Okay. That's something, I guess." Jack stood and handed Jon a business card. "If you think of something else, please call me." When Jon didn't look up, Jack leaned over him and made eye contact. "No matter how trivial it might seem. Understand?"

Jon gave a half smile. "You're a good man, Detective Murphy."

"I don't know about that, but if I promise you something you can count on it."

He left Jonathan Samuels in his living room. The dog barked at him as he walked to the stairway, and continued to do so as he made his way to the car where Liddell waited for him.

Chief Johnson joined Jack and Liddell in the parking lot.

"Give you anything new?" Liddell asked.

Jack looked at the chief. He was uneasy talking about the case in front of the man. But he *was* the chief of police here and had a right to know what was going on.

"The Victoria's Secret stuff we found in Jon's room belonged to Cordelia," Jack said, and he noticed that Liddell was surprised but Chief Johnson didn't react. He remembered what Jon had said about the chief's unwarranted attention to Cordelia. *This little town is just full of secrets,* Jack thought.

"It makes me think we need to dig harder into Louise Brigham's past. Maybe there's something we didn't find there," Jack said.

"You think she might have been a call girl, too?" Liddell asked.

"So Cordelia's death probably has nothing to do with her living here," Chief Johnson said, a little too quickly for Jack's taste. "I guess you boys have been barking up the wrong tree."

The chief hitched his gun belt up and made for Jon's apartment. "I'll tell the judge what you found," he said over his shoulder, "but first I got some words with Mr. Jonathan Samuels."

"Did we say that her death had anything to do with living here?" Liddell asked.

"Let me tell you what Jon told me about the chief," Jack said, and from upstairs they could hear the booming voice of the chief yelling over the strained voice of the younger man.

On the drive back to Evansville the two detectives drove in silence for a few miles before Liddell broke the silence, saying, "Chief Johnson didn't seem surprised that Cordelia was in the flesh business."

"You noticed that, too, huh?" Jack had an unpleasant image come to mind of a red-faced, sweating Chief Johnson lying on top of the petite young woman, and he shuddered.

"She worked a part-time job at the Dollar General in town," Liddell said. "Think we should talk to them?"

"The chief said she only worked there during the holiday seasons. And Samuels said she hadn't worked there for months. I doubt it will be anything."

"I don't think Louise Brigham was a hooker, Jack," Liddell said.

"Me either," Jack admitted. "I think she was just what she appeared to be, a single mom trying to get by." He was quiet, thinking, and then said, "I think Cordelia was the real target. Brigham was a cover-up."

"Yeah," Liddell agreed. "Look at what the killer did to Cordelia. You don't do that kind of violence unless you have a personal grudge. Cordelia was definitely a person of interest to the killer."

"Samuels knows more than he's telling," Jack added. "He had time to hide things in the apartment before we came back with a search warrant."

"How much do you think the chief is involved?" Liddell asked.

"The judge said the chief came here about ten years ago. Cordelia's problems started way before that. Her mother left just after her birth and was never seen again. Her father was murdered by her brother when she was two years old. And according to Samuels and Lieutenant Johnson and others, she has never stopped looking for her mother and brother," Jack said.

"Which brings us back to her appointment with Lenny Bange," Liddell added. "But what could Lenny do for her?"

Neither man knew the answer to that question.

"Well, at least we now know how she was going to be able to support herself," Jack said. "That is something we need to know more about." He looked out the window and saw golden cornfields glowing in the afternoon sun. "Needle in a haystack," he said.

CHAPTER THIRTY-FOUR

Shawneetown Police Lieutenant JJ Johnson put the binoculars on the seat beside him and started the engine of his police cruiser. He'd watched the Evansville police officers and Uncle Bob going in and out of Cordelia and Jon's apartment. They had come away empty-handed.

Then he watched Uncle Bob reading the riot act to Jon, and the whole time Jon just kept his eyes on the ground with his fists clenching and unclenching. JJ had hoped to see Jon haul off and pop Uncle Bob in the kisser, but he'd known Jon since grade school and there was no way he would do something like that.

JJ then parked on a side lane and waited for everyone to leave. Uncle Bob and the Evansville guys left, but Samuels was still in his apartment. JJ hoped Jon would be pissed and take off just to get away, and he was right. A few minutes after Uncle Bob had driven by, he spotted Jon Samuels's little purple Pontiac Vibe pull out onto the road that ran back into Old Shawneetown. The dog was riding shotgun with its head stuck as far out the window as possible.

He didn't know how long Jon would be gone, but he would have to make the best of it if he was going to get a chance to look around that apartment on his own.

He parked in front and hurried up the stairs to Jon's door. He'd been here many times as a friend and even if someone did see his car outside it wouldn't mean anything. The key was under the mat like it always was and he used it to open the door, then put the key back.

JJ stepped inside and shut the door behind him. He knew Cordelia's bedroom was on the left and Jon's on the right, but what he was looking for wouldn't be in a bedroom. Cordelia was too smart for that. And she was too smart to tell Jon everything she was up to.

Those Evansville detectives seemed pretty sharp, but then Jon knew a thing or two about searching, too. He knew because he was good at hiding things of his own, and had been doing so since he was a youngster. For example, there was an ounce of weed hidden in the police station that Uncle Bob had never found. JJ was careful to smoke it outside, and only then when he knew where his uncle was located, but the fact that his fat-ass uncle had never sniffed it out told JJ that he was a better cop than Bob would ever be. *You gotta think like 'em to catch 'em,* he always said. *So now, if Cordelia had something important, where would she have hid it?* he asked himself.

He looked under the throw rug in the living room and found some old rolling papers. Pocketing these, he checked the bathroom. He reached his hand into the toilet trap, but there wasn't anything hidden there. He looked inside the toilet tank and again nothing. He checked under the sink, shook out all the towels and washrags and even dumped the talcum powder. Nothing.

He went back to the living room and was about to leave when he noticed it was awfully cold in the apartment. The air conditioner was on high and it was only seventy degrees outside.

The air conditioner, he thought, and went to the a/c unit that was fitted into the wall under the living-room windows.

He looked at the frame and saw that it wasn't stuck down too tight. JJ pulled out a penknife and pried at one side of the frame until it popped off the wall.

At first he didn't see anything but the air conditioner unit and the metal housing that held it in place. He took a small powerful flashlight from his pocket and shone it around the edges of the unit. There was something underneath that looked like a piece of cloth.

JJ used the penknife to snag the cloth and pull it free from the housing. The material was wrapped around something and when he pulled it free, a small paperback book fell to the floor. He picked it up and looked at it more closely and realized it wasn't a novel. He opened it and looked at the first page of handwriting.

"Hot damn!" he said.

CHAPTER THIRTY-FIVE

The clock on the wall over the detective sergeant's desk said it was three-thirty in the afternoon. Only a few of the second-shift detectives were still in the office. Most had reported in at three and then got the hell out before Sergeant Mattingly could assign them more work. The ones that were left in the office had been conscripted into helping with the telephones and they were none too happy with Jack and Liddell.

Not that they blamed Jack and Liddell for the onslaught of telephone calls since the news release of the murders, but they did think that Jack and Liddell should answer their own phones. Jack didn't blame them. Answering calls from every crackpot in the city definitely sucked.

Jack made it to the back of the room, where he expected to find a foot-tall stack of messages regarding the murders, but was surprised to find his desk had been cleaned off.

"You're stuff's been taken by Homeland Security," Sergeant Mattingly yelled at him from across the room. "Something about it being considered toxic waste and declared an issue of national security."

"Where am I supposed to work, Sarge?" Jack asked.

"You have a new office in the basement, Jack. The old 'training' office," Mattingly said, a grin plastered on his face.

"Yeah, the toilet-training office!" one of the detectives said loudly, and everyone laughed.

Jack knew where the old training office was located. He also knew it had been vacated by the training unit because it was considered a health hazard. The police department was housed in the Civic Center, on the same branch of the building as the sheriff's department. The police department had most of the first floor and basement, while the sheriff's department and jail were housed on the second and third floors.

The inmates had figured this out and would routinely stuff clothing or sheets into their toilets to cause them to back up into the walls and plumbing chases. The waste would eventually find its way through the ceiling of the police department.

"Better take a raincoat," someone yelled at Jack as he left the office.

JJ sat at the breakfast bar in Jon Samuels's apartment. The little book he'd found hidden in the air-conditioning unit lay open on the cigarette-burned Formica countertop. There was no name or other identifying marks on the covers of the book, but he was pretty sure it had belonged to Cordelia. It was a combination diary, address book, and appointment book.

He recognized several of the names listed in that little book, and they belonged to some pretty important people. He was pretty sure the other names were fat cats as well.

So this was Cordelia's client book, he thought. *I never would've believed she was doing all these guys.* The Cordelia who JJ remembered while growing up was very quiet and kept to herself. She was a looker for sure, but because he had grown up in the same house with her, he had never thought of her as a woman. But after reading some of the entries here he had a whole new view of who Cordelia had been.

He had always wondered why she had taken the apartment with Jon, and way out in the cornfields away from everyone. But now it kind of made sense. She and Jon both had things about their lives they didn't want to parade in front of the public. Everyone knew Jon was as gay as a Care Bear, but outside of the local names in this notebook, probably no one in Shawneetown had any idea that Cordelia was a hooker.

Uncle Bob had taken a chunk out of his ass after those Evansville detectives complained about him talking to that reporter. But now JJ had something that would eliminate that from ever happening again. *Uncle Bob and Cordelia!* he mused. *Who'da ever thunk it?*

CHAPTER THIRTY-SIX

"Hey, Garcia?" Liddell said from his desk in their temporary office. There was room for exactly three desks in the cramped quarters that used to be the "training office" in the basement of the police station. It smelled of wet dog and more unpleasant things. The concrete walls were covered with cracked and peeling puke-green paint and stains.

Garcia was removing laptops, extra monitors, and other electrical equipment from three banker's boxes stacked on a large table that ran across the back of the room. "What is it, Cajun?" she replied. She didn't bother to look up. She knew that Blanchard was up to some stupid joke. *He probably has pencils sticking out of his nose or something,* she thought, and then couldn't help but smile at the thought. *He's just a big kid.*

Liddell's mouth was full of the Styrofoam peanuts that some of Garcia's equipment had been packed with, and he couldn't call her name again, so he just grunted.

Garcia sighed and looked up.

Liddell began shooting the Styrofoam peanuts out of his mouth, just as Jack came into the office.

"If we don't look, will he quit?" she asked, and Jack shrugged.

"Nah. He's not out of peanuts," Jack said. "Which desk is mine?"

Garcia pointed to the remaining desks and said, "Take your pick. Your stuff is in the little storage room over there." She hooked a thumb behind her at another door. The storage room was actually a tiny closet that held a stack of boxes.

Liddell was now cleaning the top of his desk with Lysol and a rag.

"I didn't know you were such a good housekeeper," Garcia said.

"That's because you haven't been here long enough to know the history of this office," Liddell said to her. He then filled her in on the flooding and pestilence that could come from above at any time, and she stopped unpacking and began putting things back in the boxes.

"Jesus," she said, and crossed herself.

"Won't help," Liddell quipped. "Only Lysol helps." He tossed the can to her.

"Am I interrupting anything?" said a voice from the doorway.

Jack looked up to see Susan Summers standing in the open doorway, holding a box of pastries from Donut Bank Bakery. She looked very smart in her navy pantsuit. It fit so well that he wondered where she was carrying her gun.

Liddell was up and relieving Susan of her burden before Jack could even say hello.

"So this is the new digs?" Susan asked, looking around at the World War II–era desks, the stained concrete floor, and the open ceiling showing plumbing and rusty vent pipes.

"Jack's moving down in the world," Liddell said around half a powdered-sugar donut that crusted the outside of his mouth.

"Sergeant Mattingly was kind enough to show me the way," she said. "He laughed the whole way here. Now I think I understand what was so funny."

"It's temporary," Jack said, and walked over to embrace her.

"I thought Chief Pope liked you?" Susan said.

Jack looked defeated, and said, "Deputy Chief Dick is in charge of office-space assignment."

Susan nodded. There was a long-standing feud between Jack and Deputy Chief Richard Dick. Somehow the deputy chief had been nicknamed "Double Dick" and his ego had demanded retribution.

"I'm glad you came," Jack said.

"I called my friend and he said he would be contacting you," she said.

"Apparently Don Juan is out of the country with a new girlfriend," Jack said to Garcia. To Susan, he asked, "So who is the friend?"

"It's a surprise, but you'll be glad to hear from him," Susan said. "What else can I do to help?"

"Here's a list of names involved in the case so far," Garcia said, and handed a printout to Susan. "Can you see if they come up on any of the parole or prison databases?"

Susan glanced down the list and looked at Jack. "I had an idea last night."

"I'll bet Jack did, too," Liddell said, grinning.

Susan laughed and said, "I wondered if I could call a friend of mine with the Illinois Department of Child Welfare Services."

Jack hadn't thought of that. It would be easy for that department to trace records of Dennis Morse and his family. They might even have information on Cordelia's brother, Cody.

"That's a great idea, Susan," Garcia said. "Wish I'd have thought of that."

Jack gave Susan a hug. "I knew there was a reason I kept you around."

"So now you love me for my mind?"

"Hell no!" Jack said. "I mean, there's lots of reasons."

"Might as well shut up, boss," Garcia said.

"Okay," Jack said. "So when can you crank up your computer?" he asked Susan.

"I'll call my secretary and get her started," she said and picked up one of the desk phones.

"Smart, sexy, and she carries a gun," Liddell whispered to Jack.

"It's the last part that scares me, buddy," Jack said.

She noticed him watching her as she spoke on the telephone and gave him a wink. She hung up the phone and said, "Ms. Heddings is running the list. I should have something for you in a day or so. Maybe sooner."

She caught Jack's eye again and smiled at the undisguised look of affection he gave her. "Well, I have to get back to work. See you tonight then?"

Jack smiled sheepishly and shrugged.

She stood on tiptoes and planted a lingering kiss on his cheek. "There's more where that came from," she said, and then hurried down the hallway toward the stairs.

CHAPTER THIRTY-SEVEN

Angelina was used to putting in long hours, but she had never been in the basement of the police station so late. With its concrete walls and floors it felt like a tomb, and didn't smell much better. Jack and Liddell had gone to a meeting with Captain Franklin and Chief Pope, leaving her to do what she did best—analyze data.

She punched a key on her keyboard and was pleased when the video projector came to life and displayed a map on the wall. It would have looked better if she'd had some type of screen for a background, but the green-painted cinderblock wall would have to do. *Note to self: Bring a bedsheet to work tomorrow.*

She had set up their communications links with police dispatch and the detectives' office. Two telephones with dedicated phone lines had been run into the little room that Angelina had come to think of as the "war room." The name was appropriate because this was where the battle against the bad guys was planned. She had taken a piece of A4 printer paper and a Magic Marker and printed WAR ROOM in big block letters, then taped this to the outside of the door. She knew the guys would get a kick out of it.

The next thing she did was to create a chart on her computer. She had taken some computer classes recently at the FBI Training Center in Quantico, Virginia, and what she was creating now was called "profile charting." The idea was to dissect each case down into manageable events and then have a method of visually comparing the data.

As a computer analyst the idea was not new to her. She had been doing the same thing for the last five years without calling it profile charting, but after hearing it from the big boys, the FBI, the data gained credibility when she had to sell the value of the information to her bosses.

She entered the information from both of the murders into the chart and then punched a button to display the results on the wall. The only thing that jumped out at her was the fact that nothing jumped out at her.

The last thing she would do tonight was to run the victims' and witnesses' information through the computer to see what popped up. All she needed was a little luck, and that thought reminded her of a quotation attributed to Thomas Jefferson: "I'm a great believer in luck, and I find the harder I work the more I have of it."

She got down to work.

On the maternity ward the staff smiled at the killer as he carried the bouquet of flowers down the hallway. How ironic that his mother had taken a job at Deaconess Hospital in Evansville—less than an hour away from where she had abandoned her own children. Basically right under his nose, and on a maternity ward, of all things! The thought that the woman who didn't want her own children was responsible for bringing babies into the world was sickening.

She had shocked him when she tapped him on the shoulder and asked who he was looking for. At first, because of her huge smile, he thought she recognized him. Knew he was her son. But it was evident that she had no clue.

He had played this scene through his mind his whole life. He would walk up to her and without saying a word she would know him. She would wrap him in her arms and cry and apologize for leaving him. Of course he wouldn't forgive her, but that was what a mother was expected to do. Wasn't it?

He spotted her in the room with the newborns, but when she looked up and smiled there was no light of recognition in her eyes. She knew him from somewhere, but she had no idea he was her son. He was a stranger to his own mother. He handed the flowers to one of the men standing beside the viewing window and left.

So that was it, he thought. *The grand and wonderful meeting with my mother.* But it didn't matter. Nothing would have changed what would happen now. As he followed her yellow Hummer down the dark streets he knew that there could be only one outcome. The bone axe would end another life.

He drove north on Browning Road, feeling a sense of comfort envelop him as he crossed Highway 57 and drove into the county, where a blanket of stars replaced the sodium-vapor streetlights' unnatural glow. It was quiet, as it should be an hour before midnight.

The yellow Hummer drove slowly. With so little traffic he was forced to remain at a distance, barely keeping the huge vehicle's taillights in view. Soon the narrow county lane widened at a gated community. He slowed and watched the Hummer pull up to a guard shack. Light shone out through an opening door and a man wearing a dark blue uniform stepped outside to greet the resident. No gun belt, no weapons. The guard was in his seventies and walked with a limp.

This will be easy, the killer thought, and pulled into Oak Meadow Country Club Estates and up to the guard shack. He motioned to the guard that he was with the vehicle that had just gone through. Without even walking outside, the guard waved him through. He smiled as he followed the Hummer's lights.

Oak Meadow was a golf community. He wondered what she would be doing living here, and hoped that she wasn't married. That would complicate matters. When he had met her at the hospital he didn't see a wedding band, but that didn't mean much these days.

The big yellow SUV slowed near the driveway to an enormous house, a garage door rolled up, and the Hummer disappeared inside. Before the door shut again he was able to see that there was only room in the garage for one car. A moment later lights came on in a downstairs room, and then another one upstairs. The sounds of dogs came from inside the house. From their frantic barking he could tell they were small. A sign for an alarm company was stuck in the lawn beside the front door, but that wouldn't be a problem. He was sure he could get her to open the door.

As he sat on the street watching her house, his thoughts turned to Cordelia. After all, she was the one who had led him to their mother. In a way, he was sad that there was no social recognition when they had met at the Marriott. Cordelia's voice was soft and slightly husky like he had always imagined their mother's voice would be, but beyond that there was nothing familiar. He had looked in her eyes and seen nothing of himself there before he struck her in the face with his gloved fist. The blow had knocked her to her knees. He then stood behind her and swung the bone axe upward, driving the sharp instrument behind her jaw and up into her skull. Though the axe had a short handle, the blade was heavy and sharp and cut through her neck like soft butter.

He hadn't actually gone to the Marriott with murder in mind, but when she had called him at work that day and identified herself as his sister there was no hint of pleasantness in her voice. She was all business. And when he had agreed to meet her, she had threatened to go to an attorney and have DNA samples taken. He could never allow that to happen. There were databases available to law enforcement that would match his DNA and bring the posse to his door.

Cordelia had not only found him, but she had done what he had been unable to do all these years. She'd found their real mother. She even had newspaper clippings and a photo, and something that looked like police records. He wondered what she thought would happen when she finally found him, confronted him with her existence as his only sibling. Did she think he would be ecstatic? Could she have imagined what he would really do? He didn't think so.

He had killed Cordelia impulsively and it had been sloppy. He cleaned up as much as possible but knew he had left a lot of evidence behind. He was very knowledgeable about the practices of serial killers. So he was well aware of the problems with personal killings. When you kill someone you know, there is always a connection. Something that will eventually identify you as the killer. When you kill a stranger, there is no connection. Nothing to lead the police to your doorstep. The most prolific serial killers targeted prostitutes, the homeless, hitchhikers. The stupid ones target children.

That was why he had been so careful over the last decade to plan his killings, but also to vary the style and method. No pattern, no connection. Police profilers in eight states were looking for twelve different killers, when in fact, he was the one responsible for all of those killings.

But even with all of that knowledge, he had fallen into the trap of killing someone connected to him. Now it was just a matter of time before the police realized that the person responsible for killing Cordelia was someone close to her. All he could hope for was to make this process as long as possible. Gain some time to clear out of the area and establish yet a new identity.

He had been following the police investigation closely in the newspapers and on television. So far they had nothing. They were paying so much attention to the taking of body parts that they were missing the point. Serial killers take souvenirs for a reason. They don't leave their souvenirs behind for the police to find. Besides, taking body parts was not his style. He took their faces. That was where the true self resided. That was what he was taking from them. Their true selves.

He had spent too much time sitting on the street. It was time to go. But as he drove away from his mother's house he came up with a plan and turned around in a driveway.

He would do it tonight.

CHAPTER THIRTY-EIGHT

Jack and Liddell spent the better part of two hours meeting with Chief Pope, Deputy Chief Richard Dick, and Captain Franklin to work out the details of the statement that would be delivered to the media in the morning. The television stations were angry that Arnold Byrum, an unknown newspaper reporter, had scooped them on the recent murders. They were accusing Chief Pope of playing favorites and deliberately cutting the other journalists out of the loop. Pope didn't want the media to find out that they had an inside leak, and while he didn't want to release anything that would be detrimental to the investigations, he knew that he had to throw them a bone.

Detective Jansen was still in the hospital "undergoing tests" and was not expected back to work for a few days. So far, doctors had found nothing wrong with him.

After the meeting they met Garcia in the new war room. Her hair was mussed and it looked like she had been sleeping, face-first, on the top of her desk.

"It's after midnight, Angelina. Don't you have a home to go to?" Liddell asked.

"Your wife called," Angelina said. "And she asked if you

could find your way home. She said it would be worth your while."

Liddell grinned. "Guess I'd better go."

"Don't worry about us," Jack said. "We'll muddle through somehow."

"What do you mean 'us'?" Garcia said. "You got a mouse in your pocket?" And with that she clicked off her computer and picked up her purse.

"Nice one," Liddell said, and put his arm out. Garcia looped her arm in his and they exited the war room together.

Jack spent a few minutes going over the printouts on Garcia's desk, but he knew it was a waste of time. He was tired, mentally and physically. What he needed was some junk food and a Guinness or two. Maybe then he could sleep. Or maybe just skip the food.

He flipped the lights off in their new office and locked the door.

Jack drove slowly down Lynn Road to the cutoff dirt lane that led to his cabin and pulled into the gravel lot behind his cabin. Two cars were already parked there. One was Susan's blue Honda del Sol. The second car was a black Mazda SUV. He didn't recognize it.

He switched his headlights off and rolled to a stop. Getting out, he drew his .45 semiauto Glock and walked silently down the side of his cabin in the darkness. He could hear soft voices on the porch and as he rounded the side of the cabin he was shocked to see Susan sitting on the front porch with Blake James, the anchorman from Channel Six.

Jack stepped into the halo of light coming from the kitchen window and Blake James jumped up from the porch swing, where he had been sitting very close to Susan.

"Hold on, Detective Murphy," Blake said, holding a hand

out in front of him and the other on his chest. "It's not what it looks like."

"What does it look like?" Jack asked, still holding his pistol, although he had lowered the barrel toward the ground.

Blake let out a nervous laugh, and looked at Susan.

"Blake is a friend," she said, and gave Jack an angry look.

Jack slid the pistol back into its holster and walked up onto the porch. "It's late. I think you should be leaving, Mr. James," he said.

Blake's television smile was back in place when he said, "I only came to see if I could get a quote. Your chief is dodging us in favor of that newspaper guy."

Jack looked at Blake, and the way the man held himself—every hair in place, polished white teeth—only a halo was missing. "You know I can't talk to you on the record or off without permission of the chief of police, Mr. James."

Blake James stood his ground, and Jack muscled his way past the man, surprised at how strong he was. He'd always thought reporters were soft and timid. Blake reminded him of one of those guys who hangs out at the gym waiting to pick up women. Not quite a muscle-head, and just smart enough to be a problem.

"It's late. I'm going to bed. No comment."

"Jack, that's rude," Susan said.

Blake strode off the porch and turned, saying, "It's okay, Susan. We'll see each other at the gym."

Aha, Jack thought.

"And Detective Murphy," Blake added. "You'll never catch your man by sleeping the time away. Time is a precious commodity." When he said this he winked at Susan.

Jack stepped to the edge of the porch, only restrained by Susan's arm blocking his way. "We could step around to your car and discuss this some more, Blake," Jack said. He knew his face was getting red and he didn't understand why Susan was taking up for this polished freak show.

Blake James held his hands up in submission. "I didn't mean to offend you, Detective. I report the news, I don't make it." And with that he laughed and Jack heard the crunching sound his shoes made as he walked to his vehicle behind the cabin.

He heard a door open and then shut, then an engine start before he turned to Susan and said, "How could you bring him here?"

"I didn't invite him," she said. "He just showed up."

"Yeah, right," Jack said, and immediately regretted the tone in his voice. "Look, Susan, I'm sorry," he said, but she was already picking up her purse and fishing for her car keys.

As he watched her disappear around the side of the cabin he wondered if he should go after her. But it was too late. He knew that they would work this out better if they both had a good night's sleep.

Just then Susan came back around the side of the cabin. There was no longer a look of anger on her face, but what was there was worse. Jack saw pity in her eyes.

"You're a good man, Jack," Susan said. "But I'm afraid for you." She retreated the way she had come and he heard her car drive away.

CHAPTER THIRTY-NINE

"Gina Sampson. Events coordinator for Evansville Beautiful," the pretty young woman said aloud to her reflection in her cars inside mirror. *Not bad for a twenty-three-year-old with a brand-new master's degree in business administration,* she thought.

She looked around the empty parking lot, but it was early yet. People would show up in droves to help celebrate the opening of the new Greenway Walkway. The city had advertised the event for months, not to mention spent millions of dollars to develop the bicycle and pedestrian path that ran from the mouth of the Pigeon Creek entrance at the Ohio River, along the Howell Wetlands, and on to Garvin Park, seven miles away. It had taken city workers and volunteers the best part of six months to clean up the debris along the banks of the Pigeon Creek. Next year they would build the wooden bridges that would allow visitors to cross the water at various points. Then would come the planting of perennials and shrubs and other decorative landscaping.

In the next few hours tents and chairs would be set out by volunteers at both ends of the Greenway. Tables would be laid with T-shirts bearing the logo I RAMBLED THE GREENWAY.

She looked around the gravel lot and looked at her watch. It was still early. *But where the hell are the volunteers?*

And then she saw a small parade of vehicles coming down Ohio Street, and the lead vehicle, an old Chevy truck carrying a load of canoes, flashed its lights at her.

"Hurray! The troops have arrived," Gina said out loud.

The sun was just rising as Jack stood on the porch of his river cabin. He sipped coffee and watched his floating dock as it rose and fell with the swells created by a passing boat. He wished he was fishing, or out on his boat before the weather became too cold to risk it. But today was a workday and he had to get in early enough to try and pry a clue loose from this mess. He had tried calling Susan twice and got her answering machine, opting not to leave a message.

He couldn't help but wonder how well Susan knew Blake James. She had never mentioned the man before, but it was obvious that they knew each other well enough for her to be comfortable with him at Jack's cabin.

I'm not jealous. Just curious, he thought. And then he remembered it was Susan's birthday in two more days, and he still hadn't bought her a present.

"I'm not jealous," he said out loud and headed for his car to go to the chief of police's news conference.

Louie Parson had worked for the city of Evansville for thirteen years, and before that he'd been a delivery driver for the school corporation for twelve years. *Another two years of this crap and I can retire with a full city pension,* he thought. *Fifty percent pay and cheap life insurance for the rest of my life.*

That was what he was working for, trading the next two years of misery for the rest of his life. Not a bad deal. And all he had to do today was deliver a trailer load of banged-up kayaks and canoes to the put-in area so some environmental types could paddle down the Pigeon Creek. Personally, he would rather swim in a sewer than go near that creek.

When'll these idiots quit throwing good money after bad? he wondered. But, of course, he knew the politicians would never stop spending the public's dollars as long as the news media was favorable. And so far, a lot of people seemed to think that taking water excursions on the toxic waste that filled the Pigeon Creek was a good idea.

He pulled off Ohio Street into the gravel lot that led down to the ramp and that was when he heard the first scream.

Louie Parson had spent six months in Vietnam as an eighteen-year-old, so he had heard screaming before. And the scream he'd just heard sent a message directly into his brain and triggered the fight-or-flight reflex that had been honed all those years ago.

He jumped from the truck and prone'd out in the gravel, all senses on alert. He could hear sounds of feet coming fast, crunching on gravel, excited voices being raised but talking fast and over each other until they were unintelligible. *Some bad shit is going down,* he thought, just as two young women came rushing past his truck.

He grunted as he pushed up to his knees and reached out for them yelling, "Hey. What's going on?" But they ran without looking back.

Louie got to his feet and wiped his hands on his jeans. He looked around to see if anyone had seen him jump out of his truck and splay out on the gravel, but not a soul was in sight. He felt a little embarrassed that he had dropped to the ground like he had.

He shut the door to his truck and walked in the direction the women had come running from. There was a young lady standing in the water, perfectly still. The stagnant water had turned the bottom of her white dress a nasty shade of green.

Louie waded into the water, feeling the creek mud suck at his work boots. When he reached her he thought she looked familiar. *What's her name? Sam, or Sammy. No, it's Sampson, like the strong guy from the Bible stories.*

"Miss Sampson," he said softly. She didn't seem to notice him so he said a little louder, "You got to get outta this stinkin' water, hon."

She turned her head and he could see that the lights were on in her eyes, but no one was home. Then her mouth opened wide and the scream that emanated was so shrill the nesting birds from both sides of the creek took flight.

Louie picked her up in a fireman's carry and began slogging out of the water. He could hear her making little puckering noises with her mouth and hoped she wouldn't let loose that big cannon mouth of hers again, at least until he could get her to the truck. And suddenly he was being beaten across the back and shoulders by a very alert Gina Sampson, who was yelling every obscenity she had probably ever heard in her short life.

Louie was so stunned that he lost his grip and both of them went tumbling in the filthy water of Pigeon Creek.

"Stop that shit, lady. Dammit, stop hitting me," he said.

The tumble into the cold water must have snapped her out of whatever had taken hold of her. She grabbed Louie by the front of his shirt and yelled into his face, "Call 9-1-1!" She pointed to a place on the water just past where she had been standing.

Louie turned, feeling the mud squishing through his fingers where he was trying to keep upright, and saw what she was pointing at, what had been blocked from his view before. Something was suspended several feet over the water, hanging from a thin rope that was tied to one of the struts of the bridge. He would deny later that he had screamed like a girl until Gina Sampson slapped him very soundly across the face.

CHAPTER FORTY

The police department classroom served several purposes. During in-service training it was used to satisfy the twice-yearly requirements of police training in updated constitutional law and recertification in things like CPR and Hazardous Material procedures. The classroom was also equipped with a fancy backdrop and podium when it was necessary to release news to the media.

This morning the classroom was filled to bursting with reporters from television stations, local newspapers, and local radio stations. The huge blue podium that bore the EVANSVILLE POLICE DEPARTMENT logo was almost hidden by camera tripods and microphones. Captain Franklin and Deputy Chief of Police Richard Dick stood to one side of the podium, detectives Jack Murphy and Liddell Blanchard on the other. Behind the podium, Chief Marlin Pope waited for the noise to lower so he could be heard.

"Let's get started," Pope said, raising his voice above the racket. When everyone had quieted he looked around the room and began.

"The Evansville Police Department is currently investigating the deaths of Cordelia Morse and Louise Brigham," he said.

Before he could continue, a man from the back of the room said, "Is it confirmed that the murders are the work of a serial killer?"

Pope didn't recognize the man and asked, "Who are you with, sir?"

The man cleared his throat. He was tall and thin, with a sun-darkened complexion and weathered features. "I'm with the *Shawneetown Democrat*," he said.

Pope looked over and noticed Jack was writing in his notebook. This was someone they should talk to. "I'll answer some questions after I'm finished with this statement. So please hold your questions," Pope said, and continued with his prepared release. The information he gave the reporters was nothing that hadn't already been released, but most of them didn't seem to care as long as they had something to report.

Pope finished by saying, "Are there any questions?"

"Do you have any leads as to who the killer is?" a voice came from the back of the room.

"I think I've already addressed that," Pope said, and called on another reporter when Blake James stood up in the back of the room. Blake towered over the nearest reporters, his blue suit pressed smartly.

As he moved toward the podium the throng of reporters seemed to clear a path for him. He stopped in front of the chief of police and said in a clear voice, "What we all want to know is how much longer the city will be at the mercy of this sadistic killer. How close are you to making an arrest? What are you doing about this?"

The looks on the other reporters' faces mirrored the questions that Blake had asked. It was obvious that they respected Blake, and also that they agreed with him. After all, they had a duty to inform the public. And Blake was challenging the chief of police to give them some facts. They could smell blood in the water.

"We are doing everything possible to bring this investigation to a successful conclusion," Pope said.

Blake smiled and looked at Jack, saying, "So in other words, the investigation is stalled." He turned to face the other reporters and said, "Perhaps we should ask Arnold Byrum. He seems to know everything."

It took all of Jack's willpower to keep quiet. Just then a uniformed sergeant named Taylor came into the back of the room. His face was a mask of control, but Jack could tell that the man could barely contain himself. He nodded at Jack and then motioned for him to come out in the hallway.

Jack was glad of the excuse to walk away from his confrontation with Blake, and left the room. Sergeant Taylor was waiting a short distance down the hallway.

"Jack, we have another one!" Taylor said.

CHAPTER FORTY-ONE

The killer stood near a television camera crew that was busy filming the police activity under the Ohio Street Bridge. Police were positioned on both banks of the Pigeon Creek and the parking areas had been cordoned off with yellow crime scene tape. He wondered how the police thought they could control a scene like this. For all they knew, valuable evidence could right now be washing down the creek and into the river.

Both Channel Six and Channel Nineteen had turned out with their live-reporting vans, their antennae dishes towering above them, broadcasting into homes everywhere. He couldn't resist taking some video with his iPhone. After all, this was a momentous occasion for him. *Ding-dong the witch is dead,* he thought.

Liddell piloted the blue and white watercraft with police markings down Pigeon Creek, approaching the scene of the most recently discovered body. Sergeant Tony Walker and another crime scene tech knelt in the bow.

Liddell had been part of the Iberville Parish Sheriff Department's Water Patrol and Rescue Team when he was with that department in Plaquemine, Louisiana. Most of his time was spent performing rescues of small fishing craft from the numerous waterways that branch from the Mississippi River. The Atchafalaya Basin is partially located in Iberville Parish as well, and the other part of his Water Patrol duties included assisting the Law Enforcement Against Drugs, or L.E.A.D. Task Force, in intercepting drugs that would come into the parish from across the Mississippi.

As a result of these duties, Liddell Blanchard had accumulated more hours on the water than any other deputy in the history of the Water Patrol. Added to that was the fact that he was an accomplished diver. Because there was not as much need for water patrol in Evansville, Jack had almost forgotten about his partner's skill on the water.

Sergeant Tony Walker leaned over the side of the rescue boat and examined the body that twisted in the slight current of Pigeon Creek. A white nylon rope was stretched taut between the neck of the dead body and the bridge strut overhead. Walker looked at the victim's upper torso and yelled to Jack, who was standing on the creek bank.

"Looks like a woman. Her arms have been secured behind her." Walker shook his head.

The victim's body was above the water, the head canted to one side, tongue swollen and protruding past where the lips would have been if they weren't missing. Someone had cut the face away, peeling it from the bone. Lips, cheeks, and nose were gone, leaving the swollen tongue to protrude from the mask of death.

Liddell looked around cautiously, wanting to yell something to Jack, but then saw the news media vans and onlookers gathered less than a few hundred yards away. He pointed to his cell phone.

Jack called Liddell. "Is it our guy?"

"Looks like it," Liddell said. "The entire face is missing."

"Did he take her eyes?" Jack asked.

Liddell asked Walker and then came back on the line. "I don't think so, pod'na. But it's hard to say with the damage that was done this time. Looks to me like the whole skull has been crushed."

Jack heard Walker ask if Little Casket was on her way, and responded, "She's been called. Should be here in a few minutes, but I think we need to get this body out of here."

Liddell shook his big head up and down. "Will do, pod'na."

Jack watched as Sergeant Walker and the crime scene tech prepared to recover the body, and he busied himself making phone calls to his chain of command. They would need this information quickly.

He pulled a laminated Evansville city map from the glove box of his police car and secured it to the hood with four large magnets. He used a grease pencil to circle the locations of the other two bodies and then marked a spot in the middle of the creek. The obvious thing that stood out was that this was the first body that was transported from a death scene. Not to say that she couldn't have been killed right on top of the bridge and then strung up and dumped over the side. But it just didn't feel right.

Who is she? Why her? he thought. *And why bring her here?*

"Hey Jack," Walker called to him, interrupting his thoughts.

Jack looked up and Walker was holding up a set of keys that were attached to what appeared to be laminated plastic cards. He shook out a plastic bag and put the items inside.

"I found her identification," Walker said, and handed the bag to Liddell.

Liddell moved the items around inside the bag and took out his cell phone again, indicating Jack to do the same.

"Set of keys attached to some plastic identification cards for Brenda Lincoln," Liddell said, when Jack answered the phone. "Deaconess Hospital employee named Brenda Lincoln," he added.

The photo on the ID was of a somber-looking woman in her mid-fifties with tight-permed hair and a sallow complexion. The eyes, deep set and brooding, were those of someone who had witnessed much pain in life.

"She works the maternity ward at Deaconess," Liddell said. "I'll call Garcia and get her started on this."

"I'll meet you at the dock," Jack said to Liddell and flipped his phone shut.

Arnold Byrum was waiting for Jack and Liddell outside the yellow caution tape.

"Hey, fellas. Can you spare a minute?" he asked, but the men walked past him without a word. Arnold scurried behind them.

"Don't be mad, guys. You know that someone would have written those stories if I didn't."

Jack paused. Arnold was right, of course. And Jack also knew that if someone besides Arnold had written the stories that person would have been even more sensationalized and more contemptuous of the police.

Jack turned toward Arnold. "Ask your question."

Arnold got his notebook out.

"Let's see . . ." he said and looked over his notes from the scene. "I know you can't give me the victim's name, but can you verify that it's a woman? Maybe give me an approximate age?"

"Yes, it's a woman. And, no, we can't give you an age. You should never ask a woman's age," Liddell said, and batted his eyes at Arnold.

Arnold laughed and it sounded like a donkey with hiccups.

"You can say middle-aged, white female," Jack said. "Any other questions? We have some things to do."

Arnold scribbled furiously, then looked up and said, "No. Nothing that you would answer." He smiled and walked away.

"Well, it won't be long before our leak calls Arnold and fills in all the blanks," Liddell said.

"Maybe we don't have a leak," Jack said.

"Jansen's the leak," Liddell said. "We both know he's been selling us out since this began."

"But what if it isn't Jansen?" Jack persisted. "What if someone else was talking to Arnold? How is he getting that kind of accurate information so quickly?"

Liddell gave him a curious look. "Well, he had been dead-on with his reporting. But are you suggesting that Arnold is in contact with the killer?"

Both men thought about this for a moment. "Nah! Can't be," Jack said.

"Arnold could never keep that kind of a secret," Liddell agreed.

CHAPTER FORTY-TWO

Brenda Lincoln's body had been found at nine o'clock that morning, but it had taken almost five hours to recover the body and get a search warrant for her house. If Sergeant Walker was correct about the time her body was suspended from the bridge, it meant the killer had a substantial head start on them.

Captain Franklin had made arrangements to have the witnesses from the creek brought to police headquarters to be interviewed by other detectives while Jack and Liddell continued to work the scene.

Liddell was directing the team of rescue divers in their search of the creek around where the body was recovered, in particular the mouth of the creek where it fed into the Ohio River. Garcia had discovered that Brenda Lincoln owned a new Big Bird–yellow Hummer, and a quick check of the victim's residence by Vanderburgh County officers had determined the vehicle was not at her house.

Jack was coordinating the uniformed officers who had been pulled in to secure the scene and help search a wide area around both sides of the creek when one of the divers yelled, "I got something."

* * *

Steel cables creaked and sang, and the Hummer made a sucking noise as it was winched from the mud at the mouth of the creek. Jack and Liddell stood beside the wrecker driver watching as the vehicle was pulled onto dry land.

"Hold it," Jack said to the wrecker driver, and the man flipped a lever that stopped the winch.

"What is it, pod'na?" Liddell asked.

"Something's in the front seat," Jack said.

According to the manager at Case Security Agency where Charlie Birger had worked as a security guard for the last five years, Charlie had just turned seventy-three and was planning on driving to Sarasota, Florida, to visit fishing buddies that weekend. But he had agreed to fill in for another employee who had called in sick, and that was how he came to be working the gate at Oak Meadow Country Club. Liddell had interviewed the manager over the telephone and was reading from his notes to Jack and Lilly Caskins as they watched the body of the man being taken from the front seat of the Hummer and placed on a gurney. Moving the man had been tricky because his head had almost been severed from his body.

"Any family?" Little Casket asked Liddell.

Liddell looked at his notes. "A son, daughter-in-law, and two grandkids in Alabama," he said. "Wife died three years ago from cancer. The son is on his way to your office."

"Well, let's get him down to the office then," Lilly said and turned away.

"We have to go to the other victim's house and serve a search warrant," Jack said to her retreating figure.

Without looking back, she said, "I'll call you with the results."

Liddell watched her walk away and said, "I already know the results. Someone cut his head off his body."

"Yeah," Jack said. "But why?"

Liddell was watching the two rescue boats still on the water, their dive teams busily searching grids along the bottom of the creek. "If there's a weapon out there I don't think we'll ever find it."

"He didn't throw the axe away, Bigfoot," Jack said. "He likes it too much."

Garcia had given them the address and vehicle information for Brenda Lincoln within minutes of Jack's telephone call. A bright yellow H3 Hummer would have been fairly easy to spot, and so Jack could understand the killer dumping the vehicle in the creek, wanting to ditch the vehicle in a way that it wouldn't be found. What he couldn't understand was why the killer had taken the victim's vehicle in the first place.

The reason became clear as he and Liddell drove up to the guard shack at the gated entrance of Oak Meadow Country Club. A video camera was mounted directly over the top of the door, pointing out toward the entrance from Browning Road. One of Sergeant Walker's crime scene techs was just coming out of the shack with a balding man right on his heels. The man's mouth was drawn into a tight line and his forehead was pale, but his cheeks were bright red.

Jack stopped the car far enough to the side of the entrance to allow traffic to pass. He and Liddell walked over to where the tech and the man were engaged in a heated conversation.

"You have no right to come into this property," the man was saying to the tech, who looked relieved to see Jack approaching.

"I explained to the gentleman that we have a search warrant," the tech said to Jack and rolled his eyes.

"Now who is this?" the man asked, unable to keep the anger out of his voice.

"I'm Detective Murphy," Jack said, and showed the man his police credentials.

The man examined them longer than necessary, and Jack was sure he was doing so in order to give himself a moment to defuse. Jack sized him up as the security manager for Case Security Company. He looked fit, although a little ragged around the edges as if he drank too much. *Ex-cop. But not a local,* Jack thought.

"Sorry," the man said and handed Jack's badge case to him. "Tom Shettle," he said and extended his hand. Jack took it. "I'm the owner of the security company here."

"Where were you a cop?" Jack asked.

"Still shows, huh?" Shettle said with a grin. "I was a detective with Detroit PD."

Shettle pulled business cards from his wallet and handed them to Jack and Liddell. "I've been doing this for thirteen years and never had any shit like this happen."

"How much do you know?" Jack asked.

Shettle shook his head. "No one has told me squat. Just came in and started taking things and asking questions. I don't suppose you can fill me in?"

Jack laughed at the man's directness. "I can tell you that we are investigating four murders that may or may not be related. Your guard is one of them."

"Christ!" Shettle said and leaned against the wall of the guard shack.

"So we'd appreciate any help you can give us," Liddell said.

"Sure. Of course," Shettle said. "Will this be in the paper? I don't need any negative publicity."

"What do you think?" Jack said.

Shettle looked at the sky and muttered an expletive.

"Any chance that video camera works?" Jack asked.

Now Shettle laughed. "What do you think?" he said.

CHAPTER FORTY-THREE

So far all of the victims had come from addresses close to downtown. This one was in a gated community ten miles north of city limits. It was still in Vanderburgh County, but out here in God's country, Jack and Liddell were outside their jurisdiction.

County mounties had secured the front and back of the victim's house, and marked sheriff's cars were sitting at both ends of the street, only allowing the residents through. A Vanderburgh County Sheriff's Department detective had been called to the scene, and now walked up to Jack and Liddell. Jack had spoken to the man on the telephone numerous times, but this was the first time he'd met him. He was trying to remember if the phone conversations were pleasant or if he'd been an asshole.

"I heard'a you," VCS Detective Robbins said, shaking Jack's hand.

Jack looked at Robbins. The man was probably less than five and a half feet tall, thin running on skeletal, with a face so craggy that he could make commercials for Marlboro cigarettes, a pack of which was sticking out of the detective's shirt pocket.

"I heard'a you too," Jack said. "Tim Robbins's kid, right?"

"Oh, ha-ha. I never heard that one before," Robbins said sarcastically. "I heard you was a handful."

"Two hands full," Liddell added.

"And this big drink a water must be the Cajun," Robbins said and shook hands with Liddell.

Robbins leaned in close to Liddell and Jack and said, "Look, you and I both know that this should be your investigation," and he paused while the men nodded. "So, if you tell me what you need from me, I'll try to stay outta your way."

Jack grinned. Liddell said, "You could have one of your guys get us some donuts."

Robbins chuckled. "You want coffee too?"

"Yeah," both Jack and Liddell said in unison, and Robbins walked away shaking his head.

"Hey, Tommy," Robbins said to one of the deputies, "go down to Honey Fluff on the highway and pick up three coffees and a half dozen glazed." He turned and saw the hurt look on Liddell's face and added, "Make it a couple dozen."

The deputy called Tommy was wearing wraparound Oakley sunglasses so it was impossible to read his eyes, but Jack could read the expression. Tommy got in his car and peeled out on a Code-Three donut run.

"You get a warrant?" Robbins asked.

"Got it right here," Liddell said, lifting his right foot and showing his size-thirteen-triple-E shoe.

"He's not house-trained yet," Jack said, and handed the real search warrant to Detective Robbins.

Robbins flipped through to the pages that explained the probable cause for searching the residence. "Looks good to me. Good to be careful," he said, "but you could'a saved yourself some time and paper if you'd called me first."

"Why's that?" Jack asked.

"'Cause I live right there," he said, and pointed to a two-story brick home with a thirty-foot day cruiser sitting on a trailer in the long driveway. "I know this lady has no family or children, unless you want to count her two Yorkies. So no one will be giving you any shit about going in there."

"You got a key?" Liddell asked.

Robbins had been holding the key in his hand during the entire conversation. He handed it to Liddell. "I'll go in with you to corral the animals. Those little Yorkies will eat your shit up."

"Okay, you go first," Liddell said to Robbins, and handed the key back to him.

CHAPTER FORTY-FOUR

The information Garcia found on the Indiana Bureau of Motor Vehicles database showed that Brenda Lincoln owned only the one vehicle, the yellow Hummer. The information that Detective Robbins gave them was that Brenda lived alone with two dogs. She had very little social life.

"I don't think she ever had visitors," Robbins explained as they walked through the living room behind Sergeant Walker. "She didn't say so, but I had the feeling she was never married. Never talked about a man at any rate."

The inside of the house was spotless. The dogs put up a good defense, but Robbins soon herded them into the soft-side carrier that Brenda must have used for transporting them. He excused himself and took them across the street to be taken care of by his wife.

When Robbins returned they resumed the walk-through of Brenda Lincoln's home. Even though he had given the investigation over to Jack and Liddell, in the eyes of the law, Robbins was still the jurisdictional officer.

"Sorry it took me so long," Robbins said, though in fact he had only been gone about three minutes. "The wife is pretty upset about Brenda. They weren't close, but Nita, my wife, used to come over and take care of the animals when Brenda was out of town."

"Was she out of town much?" Liddell asked.

Walker passed out latex gloves to the three men and donned a pair of his own. "Don't touch anything," he reminded them.

"You mean I shouldn't have taken the guns away from the Yorkies?" Robbins said, and Liddell chuckled. Walker and Jack gave each other a knowing look.

"To answer your question, my very large friend," Robbins said to Liddell, "no, she didn't take many trips. But once a year she went to Mexico. Probably would have been going again in a few weeks. She fancied a place called Aventura Spa Palace. Maybe we should all go down there and see if it has anything to do with this case," Robbins said, and winked at them.

"Yeah," Jack said. "I'm sure my chief and your sheriff would pay for a few days at a resort in Mexico."

"Just a thought," Robbins said.

They moved down a hallway, where Walker opened each closed door. They discovered a walk-in closet on the left, a bedroom with adjoining bath on the right that Robbins said was the victim's, another bedroom on the left that had numerous tattered stuffed animals and bowls of dry dog food on the floor, and the last door led to the garage.

When Walker opened the garage door all four men let out a gasp. The scene before them was shocking even to seasoned detectives. A bloody carpenter's claw hammer had been driven into the drywall directly across and at eye level to the doorway where they stood. Hanging from it was a grotesque mask that must have been the face of Brenda Lincoln. Blood sprays and pools of red covered the concrete floor, and throw-off droplets of blood ran in all directions across the ceiling and walls. The attack had been both savage and prolonged.

* * *

Detective Jackie Robbins stood in the middle of the street, outside the yellow tape, and lit a cigarette from the remains of the last one. He looked up at Murphy with red-rimmed eyes and sucked the smoke deep into his lungs.

"You okay?" Jack asked.

Robbins looked around at the hustle of white-clad men moving back and forth with cameras and plastic cases, and then down the street at the tiny cluster of people—his neighbors—who had gathered into a curious knot near his own front yard, some of them pointing.

"I been a deputy sheriff for twenty-three years. And I was in Iraq for two tours." He paused and took another pull from the cigarette, holding the smoke in his lungs for what seemed an impossible time before expelling the gas and continuing in a weak voice. "I seen some shit. Lots of dead people. Guys blown to bits from IEDs. Babies with their guts on the outside. Civilians castrated and beheaded by religious zealots. But this . . ."

Jack didn't know what to say. He was never good at this part. Consoling people was Liddell's forte. The big man had a way about him that made people feel better. Jack only knew one thing. Get in, get the bastard, get out. He tried not to carry the details around with him any longer than necessary.

"We'll get him," Jack said in a voice so quiet and calm that Robbins looked up at him again.

"I seen your kind before, too," Robbins said. He dropped his cigarette onto the concrete and crushed it out. He was thinking about the special ops teams who had cleared buildings in Baghdad before the ground grunts were allowed to enter. The stories he had heard about Jack Murphy were similar. "Don't take this wrong, Jack. We need guys like you. But you scare the shit out of me."

Jack turned his head away. He knew what Robbins meant. He scared himself sometimes.

CHAPTER FORTY-FIVE

Arnold rushed home and slammed his bedroom door, shutting out his mother's incessant complaining. The note that had been stuck in his hand in the crush of bodies in the hallway at the police station was from the same person who had been leaving messages for him since this all began. There were just too many people crammed into the small space for him to see where the note came from.

At first he'd thought it was Detective Jansen who was giving him the information, but then Jansen had gone in the hospital and there was no way he could have left some of the messages.

His skin crawled with electric excitement, fear and exhilaration fighting for control of his thoughts. Somewhere in the back of his mind he still believed that someone at the newspaper was merely playing a joke on him. *After all, why would someone be sending me notes like this?* he wondered, and looked down at the note that lay on top of his small writing desk.

The first note had come just after Arnold's headline story about the death of Cordelia Morse. He'd found it stuck under the windshield wiper of his Gremlin in the parking lot by the newspaper offices and had almost wadded it up and thrown it away thinking it was an advertising flyer. He hated it when he found things stuck to his windshield.

But he hadn't thrown it away for some reason. He unfolded the sheet of typing paper and read the typed message. The writer was very complimentary of Arnold's story and was suggesting that Arnold had all the talent he needed to "write a book about the murders to come."

Those were the exact words the note used, continuing, *You are in a unique position. You have the talent—and I will supply the information.*

And then the second note had appeared. This time it had turned up in his in-box on his desk at work. Like the first, this one was also typed on a computer so there was no way of tracing it. This note instructed Arnold to see Jon Samuels for an exclusive story. And that had turned out to be a great story. Jon had given him what he needed for yet another front-page news article, and if it wasn't for those tips Arnold would never have made the front page of the newspaper.

After the second note he had followed the instructions of the mystery man and started to write the book. He reasoned that even if the notes were from some jokester at work, it wouldn't matter if he put all of this sensational material down into a fictionalized story. He wouldn't use real names, or addresses, or anything that would embarrass the families of the deceased. It was just for fun. He enjoyed writing. He never intended to show it to anyone or have it published, so what was the harm?

And then, today, Sergeant Taylor had come into the room to speak to Murphy and all hell broke loose. No one had to say anything. It was obvious that there had been another murder. All the reporters had tried to get out of the little classroom at the same time, and Arnold had been caught in the stampede. He had been pushed this way and that until he came to rest against a wall near the men's restroom, and sometime during the melee someone had shoved the folded note into his hands.

He had looked up and down the halls at the retreating figures of the newsmen and uniformed officers, but he didn't know where the slip of paper had come from. It had to be one of the people who had been in the media conference, but there were several uniformed and plainclothes officers in the area, too.

Arnold had gone into the men's room and shut himself into a stall before unfolding the sheet of typing paper with great trepidation. This note was telling him what the police were going to find under the Ohio Street Bridge. It gave him the name of the victim, Brenda Lincoln. It told him where she worked, and what the police were going to discover when they went to her house. It even mentioned that she owned two Yorkies and said, *It was all I could do to keep from wringing their necks.*

Arnold felt like he was standing on high heels when he was able to get up from the toilet seat. Why had the killer picked him? And what was he supposed to do now?

He had decided to go to the location that the note instructed. See if the letter was true. When he drove down Ohio Street, the smell of the river filled his car. He saw the flashing lights, the ambulance, and the blue-clad figures rushing around in the area of the old bridge.

He had almost given the note to Liddell Blanchard on the Ohio Street Bridge today, but it seemed so surreal. And besides, how would he explain any of this? How would he admit that he had two other notes that he had failed to turn over to the police? And even worse, how would he tell his boss, Bob Robertson, that he was sitting on top of a gold mine and had just given the deed to the cops without a fight? A good newsman never gave away his sources.

It could still be a joke, and then he, Arnold, would look

like a fool to the one man who ever took him anywhere near serious. Liddell was his friend. Liddell never made fun of him. And of course there was Bernice to consider.

If it proves to be real, I'll give it to Liddell, he thought. Right now there was a story to be written.

Jon Samuels watched the television with fascination. Another murder in Evansville. This time it was an older woman. A nurse.

Jon nuzzled the dog, which seemed to like laying its thirty pounds of weight across his meager lap. "What's the world coming to, Cinderella?" he asked the dog. Cinderella cocked her shaggy head in that way that animals do when they seem to want to answer your question, but then they consider humans beneath them.

He'd found his apartment in a complete mess when he'd come back to it. He didn't remember the police doing that, but maybe they had. Having all those people in his apartment had been very upsetting. He didn't like being around large groups of people. That was one of the reasons that he had moved into the country.

After the police left, he had to get out of the apartment for a while. He went to see friends and had a couple of margaritas. He could remember the looks on the police officers' faces when they found all those Victoria's Secret items in his closet. The snickering that was just below the surface rankled him.

Jon had discovered he was gay at an early age, but it still bothered him when people looked down at him. He wasn't "damaged" or "mental." He was just who he was.

Now, sitting in his living room, on the same couch where he and Cordelia had so often sat and talked, it all seemed so unreal. Cordelia was dead and he was taking a cocktail of medications to combat a deadly illness. He didn't feel safe anymore. And for some reason he thought about calling JJ. He would feel safe with JJ around. After all, they had been friends since they were children.

But since JJ had taken the job with the police department things had changed. JJ's uncle was the police chief, and there was never a more homophobic individual born than Bob Johnson. JJ was a different person when he was in the presence of his uncle. Lately he had been less friendly even when the chief wasn't around.

"Oh, Cordelia," Jon said softly and began to cry. Cinderella laid her head on his leg.

CHAPTER FORTY-SIX

"I've got the stories on Dennis Morse's death," Garcia announced, and placed a stack of Xerox copies on top of Jack's desk.

Liddell got up and they all gathered around as she summarized what she had found.

"Some of this was on the Internet," she said. "You guys should really make use of this site. It's called Browning Genealogy, but there's a lot of stuff in here going all the way back to the late 1800s in some cases. Plus they have some pictures of people that the newspaper morgue doesn't have. I don't know where they got all this stuff, but it's amazing."

Jack looked at Liddell and said, "Take a note, Bigfoot. Sign us up for Browning Genealogy." Then he turned to Garcia and said, "Now can we have the information?"

"Okay, smart-ass," she said with a smirk, "But one day you'll thank me for that."

She spread the papers across the desktop where they could all see and continued, "Dennis Morse was a union pipefitter. No police record outside a minor drug-possession charge when he was eighteen, but he was in plenty of local punch-ups in the bars around Shawneetown, Illinois. I found his name mentioned in at least three news articles in the *Democrat* back in that time. Usually part of a bar brawl, but no arrests."

"According to the Gallatin County Clerk's Office, he was married to a Brenda Bockstege on January third, nineteen eighty-six." She flipped through a few pages on the desk and laid two documents on top.

"These are the copies of birth certificates for Cordelia Morse and Cody Morse."

Jack and Liddell looked at the records. Both children had been born at the hospital in Eldorado, Illinois.

Garcia sorted through the pages and put two more papers on top of the others, saying, "Here is the first story about Dennis Morse. It's a short article about his unit being deployed to Desert Storm. The other sheet is the one where his unit came home. He was gone a little over a year."

Jack looked at the dates of the articles and the date that Dennis Morse had returned home from Desert Storm. There was no way that he could have fathered Cordelia. Unless of course he was given a leave and came home for a few days during that time. But that was unlikely from what Jack knew of those days.

"And there's more," Garcia went on. She pointed to a Xerox copy of a newspaper story from the Evansville newspaper.

The headline read, MAN MURDERED BY SON. The story got their attention.

When they were finished reading the article Liddell looked at them and said, "You thinking what I'm thinking?"

Jack raised his eyebrows and Garcia held up a hand.

"Wait, there's more. One last juicy piece," she said, and laid another sheet of paper on the desktop.

Jack and Liddell stared at the document. Liddell said, "So

Brenda Bockstege is actually Brenda Lincoln. Our last victim?"

"Bingo," Garcia said, barely able to contain her excitement.

"We'd better call Captain Franklin," Jack said.

CHAPTER FORTY-SEVEN

Lying across the bed in his apartment, Lieutenant Johnson closed the diary and let out a deep tequila-enhanced sigh. *This stuff is dynamite,* he thought. *I never really knew Cordelia at all. Could she really have been tumbling in the hay with all these guys?*

He'd stayed up most of the night reading the diary and looking at the list of names that Cordelia had carefully penned into the last ten pages of the book. One thing all the men had in common was their social status. There wasn't a single name in the book that didn't hold some significance. Doctors, lawyers, judges, a congressman, the fire department chief of the neighboring county, and of course, Uncle Bob. That was the most surprising of all because JJ knew how Bob felt about prostitutes—and truthfully, that's what Cordelia was—and so he was stunned that Uncle Bob would be on that list.

JJ thought maybe Bob was just on the list because he was someone who she may have had designs on, but then on the last couple of pages of the diary he found an entry Cordelia had written that made it clear that Bob was more than a possibility. She had said, *Like laying with a pig.*

JJ laughed every time he thought about that remark.

"Like doing a pig," he said out loud and laughed again. Cordelia had a sense of humor, he'd give her that.

There were thirty-two names on Cordelia's list. Most of them had been mentioned in her diary in a way that would make them unmistakable if their little secret were ever to see daylight. *Was she planning on blackmailing them?* he wondered. *Had she already started?* He looked at the book again, and had noticed that there were checkmarks by some of the names. Including Uncle Bob. *What does that checkmark mean?*

One name in particular had really caught his attention. He had never met this man, but was very familiar with his work. He was a fan, so to speak, and would have loved meeting this guy even if the book hadn't come into his hands. But now, given the fact that his name was so prominent in the book, JJ felt that he had no choice but to contact him. The thought of talking to someone so famous made him tingle with excitement.

JJ stood up and drew up to his full height. He was going to be an important man. Cordelia had made that possible for him. And he wasn't going to waste the opportunity she had given him.

Another thought struck him. The book was the only piece of evidence he had that linked Cordelia to these men. It might be enough to threaten some of them with exposure by just telling them what was in her diary, but there were others who would demand something more. Some proof that they were anything more than fertile soil for a young girl's imagination. What he needed were tapes or video or pictures. Something solid.

He had to go back to Jon's and search again. He didn't cherish the idea of doing that, but it had to be done. He'd have to find a way to get in without confronting Jon. Besides, he didn't want Jon to know anything about this little part of what Cordelia had been up to. Jon obviously didn't know or he would have spilled the beans when he gave up all the Victoria's Secret clothes. If Jon found out now, he might tell that damn nosy detective from Evansville, and that would put an end to JJ's plans to blackmail the people on the list. The end of JJ's chance to get out of this dump of a town and become someone important. He couldn't let that happen.

There might be a better person to begin with, he thought. *Lenny Bange was apparently more than just Cordelia's attorney. Maybe he can give me some information. Hell, maybe he's in on this with Cordelia? Maybe one of the people on this list killed her to keep her quiet about something?*

Making himself think like a cop, he put together a possible scenario. Cordelia is blackmailing people on her list when one of them takes offense. Maybe the guy has something more to hide than the fact that he was getting a little hoochie on the side. Maybe Cordelia starts feeling pressure from the guy, or he starts threatening her and so she goes to see Lenny Bange.

JJ wasn't sure what Jack Murphy knew about Lenny Bange, but in Shawneetown the man had a reputation of being a big-time gambler and drug user. JJ had picked him up in bar fights more than once and was ready to throw the book at him until Uncle Bob stepped in and treated the guy like he was visiting royalty.

Now that JJ thought about it, that kind of made sense. Maybe Lenny was in on this game with Cordelia. Maybe he knew about Cordelia doing the naked cha-cha with Uncle Bob. It was obvious now that Bange had something on the chief. Something that was big enough to bring the chief running anytime Bange got his tit in a wringer.

Yeah, better think this through, JJ, he thought. *There's no hurry. No hurry t'all.*

* * *

Captain Franklin sat and listened until Jack and Liddell were finished. Then he leaned forward and said, "So we have two members of a family murdered. The guard was coincidental?"

Jack nodded. "He saw the killer."

Franklin continued. "The woman from the projects doesn't fit the pattern. What's the motive for that one?"

"Louise Brigham has no connection to any of this, except for the chain of body parts the killer is swapping," Jack said. "I guess it's possible that the mother-daughter connection between Cordelia and Brenda Lincoln could be coincidental, but I don't believe in coincidence."

Franklin leaned back in his chair, trying to solve that part of the puzzle. He hated loose ends. "There has to be some reason that he picked Louise Brigham," he said.

"That's what we have, Captain," Jack said. "The question now is, did the killer know they were mother and daughter? It seems that Cordelia was in the process of trying to find her real mother and brother. We know that she had an appointment with Lenny Bange, and I've assumed that it may have had something to do with her search for family."

Franklin said, "So did she find her mother? Did she already know who she was before she made the appointment with Lenny? What exactly did she want Lenny to do for her? And of course, what does any of this have to do with her being killed?"

Liddell stood and paced the room. "What if the murder of Louise Brigham is just to make us think we have a serial killer?" Liddell said. "What if the targets were always Cordelia and Brenda? What if the murder of Brigham was just a feint? The killer is trying to throw us off?"

"Why would he want to kill Cordelia and her mother?" Jack asked, picking up the thread.

"Whatever the reason," Liddell said, "you can tell he

really had it in for them. I mean, he destroyed their faces. Now that's hatred!"

Jack thought about what Liddell said. It made sense. The killer had a personal reason for killing those two women.

"The violence done to Louise Brigham was all wrong," Jack said, giving voice to his thoughts. "It didn't feel like the same rage the killer displayed at the other two scenes."

"She had her eyes cut out, Jack! That's not enough rage?" Franklin said, but Liddell was picking up what his partner was getting at.

"I think he's right, Captain," Liddell said. "For one thing, look at the damage done to the faces of Cordelia and Brenda. It was like the killer was focusing on their faces— trying to destroy them. Louise Brigham's face was removed, and he took her eyes, but it felt antiseptic." He could see he wasn't explaining himself very well.

"Maybe he destroys what offends him? Or threatens him," Jack added. "Something Louise Brigham saw. Maybe she knew the killer."

Captain Franklin scoffed. "You two are scaring me. You're starting to sound like television detectives. Just get out there and catch this bastard before he kills again."

When they got outside Jack turned to his partner. "That was pretty good reasoning for a Yeti."

"That really hurts," Liddell said.

Lenny Bange cracked his door and yelled, "Lucy, hold all my calls."

"Okay," she yelled back.

Lenny sat at his desk, willing the prepaid cell phone that he had purchased during lunch to ring. It was only his instincts as an attorney that saved him from calling Las Vegas on his desk phone.

He planted his feet firmly on each side of his twenty-two-hundred-dollar desk chair, as if in preparation for headlong flight. *How in the hell did this all go bad?* he thought.

First, Cordelia gets it in her head to try and find her long-lost mother and brother. Then she tries to recruit Lenny to use his resources in her search. She had no idea how much that would cost him. In time and in money, and those were two things that Lenny never gave away.

Then Cordelia decides that she will blackmail Lenny if he won't help her. That was unforgivable. He'd worked hard over the last ten years building up his lucrative flesh business. Cordelia had been a favorite of his rich clients. Not only was she beautiful, young, and sexy, but she was smart. He should have known better than to bring a smart girl in on the business.

And now she was dead. Murdered! But that wasn't the worst of it. He had always suspected that Cordelia kept a diary, but the phone call he'd received today confirmed it. The male caller had even read some excerpts from the diary, and given Lenny dates, names, and times.

The man seemed to think that Lenny was just one of Cordelia's clients, though, so he must not have been a confidant of Cordelia's. Still, the man had possession of her diary.

Lenny had offered to buy the diary, but the caller was too slick for that. He counter-offered to keep his mouth shut about Lenny's "side activities" if Lenny would cough up some serious bread.

He has no idea what he's gotten into, Lenny thought.

The call he was waiting for would take care of this problem. Cubby was connected. Lenny had first met him during a trip to Las Vegas a few years back and had held on to the telephone number. When Lenny called and told Cubby about the predicament he was in, the man had actually laughed.

The payment for his services was phenomenal, but Lenny had reluctantly agreed. What else could he do? You didn't call a guy like this and ask for help and then dicker with him. Whatever it was the man wanted, Lenny would just have to bite the bullet and produce. Or he could bite a real bullet.

Lenny pulled up a file on his computer titled *CM Client*. Cubby had requested the names. It would mean that Lenny may not be able to do business with these men again, but there was no alternative.

CHAPTER FORTY-EIGHT

The early-morning call had taken the killer by surprise.

"I have possession of some information that you might like to know about," the male voice said.

The killer pegged the voice as that of a male, probably in his twenties or thirties, very confident like he was used to telling people what to do. The accent was that of a shit-kicker, but the caller had been careful to block the call so he wasn't *that* stupid.

"I don't know what you're talking about, buddy," the killer said.

The caller chuckled, then the voice grew serious. "I have her diary. Cordelia's diary. She names you in the book—buddy."

"What is it that you want?" the killer asked.

"Why, money of course."

"Why don't you meet me and I'll pay you for the diary," the killer suggested.

"You think I'm stupid, don't you?" the voice asked.

Yes. I think you are dangerously stupid, the killer thought, but he said, "Of course I don't think you're stupid. But how do I know you really have a diary? What proof can you give me?"

"You want proof?" Loud laughter came over the telephone line. "Okay. I'll give you proof," he said. "You betcha I will. You betcha."

"Okay. Okay," the killer said. "What do you want and how do I deliver?"

"Well, that's better," the caller said.

As the killer hung up the phone he became thoughtful. This was something new for him. Maybe it would be fun.

A nurse brought them both a cup of hospital coffee while they waited. Liddell took a sip and made a face. "I think they gave me cyanide by mistake."

Jack poured his coffee into a potted plant and left the empty cup on top of the doctor's desk. Doctors tended to piss him off. The ones he'd met had no sense of humor and expected to be treated like gods.

"I guess our time isn't as valuable as his," Jack remarked, just as the door opened and in walked a short man in a stiffly starched white lab coat.

"Your time's valuable, Detective," the doctor said, and held out a hand in greeting.

"Busted big-time!" Liddell said, and Jack's face turned red.

The detectives shook hands with Dr. Virgil Phipps.

"Can I ask what this is about?" Phipps asked.

"What can you tell us about Brenda Lincoln?" Jack asked.

Dr. Phipps's face stiffened, and he said, "I'm sorry. I didn't realize you were here about Bren." The color drained from his cheeks.

"I'm sorry, sir," Jack said. "We have been asking all of her colleagues and friends about her today. I just assumed you knew why we were here."

Dr. Phipps stood and went to a window that looked out over the front parking lot of the hospital, lost in thought.

"Sir?" Jack said, and Phipps flinched.

"In answer to your last remark, Detective, no one around here would have come to me with any news about Brenda." He returned to his desk and sat again. "I met Brenda after I had just come here from Toledo, Ohio. One of my friends tried to fix me up with her. They didn't realize that she preferred to be alone. I guess they thought that since Brenda was unattached and I was unattached, we would hit it off."

"You didn't?" Jack asked.

"We had coffee in the downstairs lounge sometimes," he said, and looked down at the top of his desk as if he were embarrassed. "We never really got beyond that."

"But you would have liked it to be more?" Jack said.

Phipps's eyes met Jack's and in them Jack saw the truth and felt sorry for the man. Katie had loved Jack once upon a time, and he had loved her, but he knew that was ancient history now. The thing was, that love was like an appendage. Even when it was removed, you could still feel it, just as real as if it was still there.

"We really need some help on this, Doctor. Can you tell us anything? Did she ever confide anything personal to you?" Jack asked.

Phipps shook his head. "It was like she was always afraid. I had the feeling she had been treated very badly by someone at one time. I think she was afraid to let anyone get close to her again. If she ever told anyone anything personal, I don't know who that would be."

Jack and Liddell stood to leave, but Dr. Phipps remained seated. His prior enthusiasm and humor seemed to have deserted him. "I'll call you if I hear anything," he said.

* * *

"You handled that well," Liddell said when they reached the parking lot.

Jack turned back toward the building and looked up at the fourth floor, where he could see Dr. Phipps once again at his office window. Phipps raised a hand and Jack nodded at him.

"Another victim," Jack said.

Liddell nodded. "The dead ones aren't the only victims. Taking someone's life affects so many other people."

"Brenda Lincoln must have been something to have affected him like that," Jack said.

They walked to their car without speaking and were heading to the war room before Jack broke the silence.

"We need to talk to Lenny Bange again," Jack said.

"You think he might have remembered something he didn't tell you?"

"No. I think he was lying the first time around," Jack said.

"An attorney telling a lie," Liddell said, putting a hand over his mouth in shock. "That's not something you see every day."

"You should have been a comedian."

"Mr. Bange will see you now," the young woman said, and motioned for Jack and Liddell to follow her.

"You know why they bury attorneys twelve feet deep instead of six?" Jack asked.

Liddell shook his head, playing along.

"Because, way down deep, attorneys are really good people," Jack said.

"Never heard that one before," Liddell said with a straight face.

"Well, did you hear the one about the rabbi, the priest, and the attorney?" Jack said and then they were at the door of Lenny Bange's office and were led inside.

Bange came around his desk to shake hands. Jack had forgotten how strong the man's grip was. Lenny was short but powerfully built. Jack wondered if the man was on steroids. He was slim in the waist and thick in chest and arms and legs. His head was square, smoothly shaved, and seemed to rest directly on his shoulders with no neck. His features were swollen and even his jaws looked muscled. The overall effect was that of a diminutive strongman in a circus show. All that was missing was a leopard-skin thong and handlebar mustache.

"So this is the one they call Cajun," Lenny said good-naturedly, and shook hands with Liddell.

"Yeah," Jack said. "He's a man ahead of his mind."

Everyone grinned and Jack couldn't help but notice how jolly everyone was. If Bange was being that friendly there was a lubricated penis somewhere in the picture. Bange was being a little too cooperative, which meant that he was ready for them. His lies had been prepared, been rehearsed, and already won an Oscar.

"Did you know Cordelia Morse was a call girl?" Jack asked, and for just a microsecond, Lenny Bange's expression slipped.

The questioning was brief due to Bange's reluctance to answer. As they left the offices of Bange, Bange and Bange, Liddell said, "When you told him Cordelia Morse was a hooker, I thought he was going to swallow his tongue."

"Yeah. It was definitely an 'awww, shit' moment," Jack said.

CHAPTER FORTY-NINE

Officer John "Kooky" Kuhlenschmidt blew the foam from the top of his beer mug onto his training partner, Corporal Timmons.

"Don't get too big for your britches, rookie," Timmons said, and wiped at the stain spreading across the front of his shirt.

"Ex-rookie," Kooky reminded Timmons. "This is my day to celebrate." He hefted his mug and offered a toast. "Here's to the end of my probation," he said, and the four or five other officers gathered for the occasion sloshed their mugs together before downing the entire contents.

"Tell 'em the rest, partner," Timmons said.

Instead of answering, Kooky dug into his jeans pocket and produced a small gray velvet-covered box.

"Oh my God," one of the officers yelled. "You and Timmons are getting married! Well, congratulations."

Timmons slapped the officer across the back of the head, and said to Kooky, "Come on, kid. Tell 'em the rest."

Kooky opened the lid of the box. Inside was a diamond solitaire the size of New York City. "Me 'n Ellen are getting hitched," he said, and his eyes became misty.

"When are you popping the question, hotshot?" one of the men asked.

"Kooky's still a virgin, fellas," Timmons said. "He woulda gotten married today if it wasn't so damn close to Halloween."

Kooky's face turned red, unable to hide the truth in his partner's remarks. He'd tried getting intimate with Ellen dozens of times over the years, but, as they were both Catholic, she had rebuffed him.

"I'm asking her, officially, tomorrow evening. We been talking about this for a long time," Kooky said.

"It's bad luck to ask on Halloween, buddy," Timmons said.

"Well, I got plans for that day. We're going to a hayride and a party, and then I'm going to ask the question."

"Okay, so when's the wedding? We're all invited, right?" one of the men asked.

"I'm hoping it's around Christmas," Kooky said. "We haven't really set a date 'cause I haven't asked yet."

"Christmas isn't a good time, buddy," Timmons said.

"Why do you keep being negative?" Kooky asked, a little annoyed.

"I'm just saying," Timmons said and called for another pitcher of beer for the table.

"Tying the knot at Christmas is very romantic, Romeo," one man said.

"At least he'll be tied in a knot," one of the men chuckled, and another laughed so hard he blew beer out of his nose.

"Quit laughing, assholes," Kooky said. "This is the rest of my life we're talking about."

"You poor clueless baby," Timmins said.

Kooky stared into his empty glass and frowned.

"Okay, we're sorry," one of the men said, pouring more beer from a pitcher into Kooky's mug. "So are we all gonna receive invitations?"

Kooky's face turned beet red. "I'm saving money for the wedding. You have any idea how much those things cost?"

"Well, what do ya think being married is gonna cost?"

"You're married," Kooky said to the man.

Timmons interrupted, saying, "Three times if I'm not mistaken."

"Screw you, Timmons, and the cheap beer you drink, too," the chastised officer said.

Kooky laughed and the mood was once again more about drinking and less about him. He didn't like being the center of attention. The fact that he was the mayor's nephew had not been an easy thing to overcome, and the further fact that he had almost no toleration for the sight of blood or death had pretty much put an end to the career he had dreamed of his entire life.

But Ellen always saw the good in everything. Instead of looking at his compulsion to vomit at the sight of blood as a weakness, she had pointed out to him that he had a good heart and would make an excellent D.A.R.E. officer or a school liaison officer. Plus he was smart. He could remember almost anything he ever read or saw. He would be a shoo-in for taking tests and making rank. Higher-ranking officers hardly ever had to work with dead bodies.

Kooky was pulled out of his reverie by Corporal Timmons. "Who's playing the pipes?" Timmons asked.

"Pipes?" Kooky asked.

"If he plays his cards right, his wife will play his pipes," one of the men joked, but was shouted down by Timmons.

"If we're gonna give the boy a proper police wedding he's got to have a color guard and a bagpiper."

The men agreed. Not because they cared whether Kooky had a proper wedding, but because a "proper police wedding" with a bagpiper meant lots of drinking.

Timmons slapped Kooky's shoulder. "You gotta ask Murphy."

"Jack Murphy?" Kooky asked in bewilderment.

The others all chimed in. "Yeah. Murphy, ya dumb rookie. Didn't you know he played bagpipes?"

"Are you telling me that Jack Murphy wears one of those skirts?" Kooky said, eyes wide.

Timmons squeezed Kooky's arm so tight it hurt. "Don't ever let him hear you call his kilt a skirt."

"Unless you want to be wearing a couple of black eyes on your honeymoon," another chimed in.

Kooky seemed to draw back. "Me'n Ellen hadn't really talked about having a bagpiper or any of this police stuff. We were just going to have a simple wedding at St. Anthony's Church with some family over afterward."

One of the men looked at him seriously and said, "Listen to me, Kooky. This is just the beginning. You let her decide all the wedding plans and it will be the last thing you ever get to decide. This is your wedding too, right? You put your foot down now, or next thing you know you'll be wearing high heels and maxi pads."

"We'll supply the kegs and scotch," Timmons added.

"All you gotta do is ask Murphy," another said.

"Yeah, he oughta love you, bro. You threw up on him a few months ago, and then passed out at one of his recent crime scenes. So he owes you, right?" the man said, and everyone laughed.

How am I ever gonna ask him to play bagpipes for me? Kooky wondered.

CHAPTER FIFTY

The black Ford Fusion rolled slowly down U.S. Highway 41. The driver, a bullet-headed man with a bouncer's physique, was looking for the entrance to the Drury Inn. Cubby Crispino had heard an interesting story about the motel that made him decide to stay there for the next night or so, until his work was done. According to local legend, a few years ago, a military cargo plane had been doing a routine takeoff/landing from nearby Fort Campbell. The plane went down unexpectedly and crashed into the Drury Inn. Lots of deaths. Lots of cops and firemen hurt, too. And then the Drury Inn was rebuilt in exactly the same spot and life went on as usual.

The story was special to him. He liked places that were steeped in blood.

He turned into the back parking lot of the Drury and pulled his environmentally friendly vehicle into a slot. He checked himself out in the mirror. He had to put his game face on. While he was in Evansville, he was Jimmy Campbell, union representative for over-the-road truckers.

The identification he was carrying was legit—all except the photo—and would pass the scrutiny of any law enforcement agent. *It should,* he thought. *It belonged to the asshole*

I killed yesterday and he's still sucking down sand in the desert outside of Vegas.

Cubby Crispino left the car and headed inside. Lenny Bange had given him all the information he needed to get this thing started, but he needed some cash. That was supposed to be delivered via hooker later at the Drury. He was looking forward to the meeting.

Officer Kooky Kuhlenschmidt drank more than he could remember. The bartender at the FOP Club had cut him off and none of his buddies had stuck around to make sure he got home. He was also a little ticked off that he'd paid for all the alcohol drunk that evening, but it was part of the bonding experience among police officers. The new guy always got stuck with the bill.

He left the bar and made it to his red Ford pickup intending to go home. The love of his life, Ellen, was spending the evening with her girlfriends.

As he left the club's parking lot, he remembered Timmons and the guys teasing him about getting Jack Murphy to play bagpipes for his wedding. They didn't think he had the balls to ask Murphy. *I'll show them,* he thought, and turned south toward the river. He knew where Jack lived, and he also knew that Jack kept late hours. He'd just go to his house and ask him. How hard could it be?

Lynn Road was a straight stretch that ran east from Highway 41 South along the Ohio River. The area was underwater much of the rainy season, but the road had never been washed out. There were several cabins along it, all built on poles that kept them high and dry. Murphy lived in one of these.

The killer drove exactly two and a half miles according to

his GPS, but didn't spot the gravel access road until he had almost driven past it. Murphy's cabin was hundreds of yards from his nearest neighbor. It was also the only cabin that could be reached on that access road.

He turned right onto the gravel and slowed. The crunch of stones under his tires was louder than he had counted on. But then, Murphy had a reputation for putting away large amounts of single-malt scotch and Guinness. He felt confident that at this hour of the night, he would not be detected.

He drove south toward the river until he spotted the single muted light that came from somewhere down below. He pulled to the side, into the cornfield, and turned his ignition and lights off. The axe lay on the passenger seat. The dull iron color didn't reflect the bright full moon, but the shape of the blade was distinct.

He decided to watch for a few minutes, and then he would approach on foot. If Murphy was asleep, he planned on leaving him in that permanent condition. *Lights out, Jack,* he thought.

CHAPTER FIFTY-ONE

Kooky saw the taillights of the SUV turn down the gravel drive that led to Jack Murphy's cabin. He smiled at the thought of Jack Murphy driving an SUV instead of a pickup truck like most policemen. That's why he'd chosen his red Ford pickup. *Jack would make a good soccer mom,* Kooky thought and laughed at his own joke.

Up ahead the taillights went out and he saw a brief flash of brake lights.

He thought about turning around and going home, but then the thought of having a police wedding had seemed like a really good idea, and Ellen would surely go along with it.

He continued down the gravel for a hundred yards or so until he noticed a black SUV pulled to the side of the gravel, off into the cornfield. The driver's door was cracked open, but there were no interior lights on. Kooky turned his headlights back on and flipped them to bright. Someone was broke down and it was his job as a duly sworn law officer to render assistance.

"Hey. You need a hand?" Kooky yelled at the man who emerged from the SUV.

"Among other things," the man said and hefted the bone axe high over his head as he ran toward the red pickup.

CHAPTER FIFTY-TWO

Jack Murphy heard the screams while sitting in his hot tub. He grabbed his gun and sprinted down the driveway behind his cabin in a pair of flip-flops and nothing else.

The night air was cooling on his wet skin, the heavy white rock digging into the soles of his feet as he ran toward the screams in the blackness ahead of him. He couldn't tell the exact distance, but they were coming from down the gravel drive toward Lynn Road. The sound of the screams had changed from loud and strong to the unmistakable whine of someone close to death. It was a sound Jack was very familiar with.

The screams stopped. Jack slowed and listened, trying to get a bearing on their location. He heard a door slam less than a hundred yards from him, and then an engine struggling. He picked up his pace. As he rounded a bend in the drive, he spotted taillights in the distance, moving away, and the headlights of what looked like a new pickup truck pointing into the cornfield. Lying in the bright beams of the truck lay the body of a man, his head smashed, bits of brain and a pool of blood spread around it.

* * *

The black SUV turned south toward Kentucky, and then jigged across a field and onto a side road that paralleled Lynn Road, but on the opposite side of the Ohio River.

The killer slowed to a crawl and watched the opposite bank. He couldn't sit there long, but he wanted to see the curling snake of emergency lights as the police cars and medical crews headed toward Jack's place. From his position he would be able to see them coming down Highway 41 in plenty of time to allow him to run the back county roads in Kentucky and come back out on the main stretch that runs through the middle of Henderson.

Murphy is one lucky man, he thought as he watched the first of the flashing emergency lights speeding south on Highway 41. *Well, he didn't get the axe tonight, but someone else did.* He chuckled at his own humor. Besides, he had another place to go tonight. He'd planned on two killings tonight. He would still meet that goal. Murphy just wouldn't be one of them.

He didn't know who the young man who had come across him on the gravel road was, but he seemed to be someone in authority. The way he handled himself, the way he tried to take cover behind his truck door, the weak attempt at defending himself. *Probably a cop,* he thought.

As he watched, a procession of vehicles with rotating beacons headed in the direction from which he had just come. Time to go visit the next one.

Jon Samuels was conflicted. *Should I wear the Calvin Klein jeans and the ribbed T-shirt or the white capri-style pants with the white linen shirt with a thin blue vertical stripe?* Not that it really mattered since this wasn't a date. It was just that the man's voice on the telephone had sounded so . . . suggestive.

He had almost not answered the telephone when he saw

that the number had been blocked by the caller, but it was something he might do himself if he was dialing a telephone number and wasn't sure of the reception he would get. It sure as hell wouldn't be the police.

The man had sounded hesitant at first, but then his tone became warmer and more enthusiastic as he spoke of his relationship with Cordelia. It had surprised Jon that one of Cordelia's old boyfriends would call to give condolences. He warmed to the stranger's thoughtfulness.

By the end of the conversation, he had asked the man to come by and have coffee. *Or did he ask me?* he thought. It didn't matter now because the man would be arriving any minute and he still had to decide on an outfit. He didn't want to look uninterested, but he didn't want to look like a skank either. It had been a long time since he'd felt excited by the prospect of friendship and companionship.

He looked at the clothes lying on the bed. He'd split the difference and wear one of each piece. The Calvin Kleins and the linen shirt. The white shirt would hide his paleness.

Cinderella lay on her side on the bed giving him a look of indifference.

CHAPTER FIFTY-THREE

It was early Friday morning. The day before Halloween. The administrative areas of the police department looked like a ghost town. A few uniformed officers roamed the halls carrying out routines that were much like assembly line work in a factory. Pick up this form, carry it to that office; get this signature, time-stamp that sheet, write a note or two; and then carry the form back to another office where it would go into a basket and slide off into the black hole of the computer system called PAMIS, which stood for Police Automated Management Information Systems. Jack knew that most of the cops called the computer system PENIS for obvious reasons.

Jack left Sergeant Walker at the coroner's office, where the autopsy of John "Kooky" Kuhlenschmidt was being delayed until his parents and would-be fiancée could be notified. He came in the back door of police headquarters and walked down a flight of stairs to the basement. The quiet was tangible.

Only four o'clock in the morning, but word had gotten out quickly of Kooky's murder. Officers who had not been requested to come in early were out in their own cars looking for the killer. Jack felt the same shock and anger as the others, but the person they were looking for would not be standing on a street corner with a sign saying WILL KILL FOR FUN.

He couldn't get the sight of Kooky's mangled face out of his mind. And what was Kooky doing on the drive that led only to Jack's cabin? Was he coming to see Jack? Did he know something about the killer that got him killed?

He had to trace Kooky's last movements that led him to his death. Although they hadn't officially determined this, Officer Kooky Kuhlenschmidt, just hours after completing his probationary period, had become the fifth victim of the killer. Jack was as certain of this as he was of his own name.

Entering the war room, Jack noticed his partner was look-ing very rumpled and sleepy from being roused from bed after only two hours' sleep in the last twenty-four. He'd made the death notification to Kuhlenschmidt's parents. Legally, one of them would have had the duty to formally identify the body, but there wasn't enough left of the young officer's face to identify. He didn't have any scars or other marks, but Jack had found a pay stub in his shirt pocket along with a small gray velvet box containing an engagement ring.

"The engagement ring you found was going to be given to Ellen DeSoto tomorrow night," Liddell said.

"That's horrible," Garcia said.

"The parents said they would notify the fiancée, but I went with them or I would have been back here sooner."

"Did they have any idea why he was on the drive to my cabin?" Jack asked.

"Not a clue," Liddell answered. "But I talked to Timmons and he said they'd been drinking at the FOP Club, celebrat-ing Kooky's getting off probation, and he up and told them about the engagement. According to Timmons, some of the guys tried to talk Kooky into having a police wedding and he was supposed to ask you to play bagpipes for him."

.

"At two o'clock in the morning?" Jack said.

"Timmons said they left the club about that time and he didn't think Kooky was that drunk, but he figured Kooky was coming to see you."

"Awww, Christ!" Jack said.

"Hey, boss, it's not your fault," Garcia said and put a hand on Jack's shoulder.

Jack knew there was nothing he could have done to stop what happened, but he also knew that Kooky had been killed because he was just in the wrong place at the wrong time. The killer had been there for him, not Kooky.

"I know what you're thinking, pod'na," Liddell said, "But just let it go. It wasn't your fault. Don't make this personal."

"What are you saying?" Jack said through clenched teeth. "I'm not making it personal. That's already been done."

Detective Larry Jansen sat in a corner of Duffy's Tavern where the lights were dim and the women were even dimmer. The bar had closed an hour ago, but the regulars were allowed to stay and finish their drinks. He had nowhere else to go so he continued to watch the woman wipe the foamy suds from her lips after she took a gallon-sized drag from a fishbowl of beer.

She wasn't exactly pretty, but her tits were the size of watermelons and he was in the mood for some very casual sex. He figured he would wait until she finished the beer she was drinking and he would offer to buy the next round. She was already getting that rubbery inebriated laughter and talking way too loud.

But even watching the drunken woman's melons jiggle was losing his interest. For some reason he kept thinking about the murders that Murphy was investigating. There was something that he had seen, or been told by someone that he could feel was important. He was tempted to go back to headquarters and have some coffee—clear his head and see if he could resolve whatever it was that was in the back of his mind. But just then the woman spilled half a fishbowl down her thin blouse and Larry's mind was made up for him.

CHAPTER FIFTY-FOUR

Jon Samuels opened the door and a smile spread across his face.

"Come in," he said, and held Cinderella's collar so she wouldn't turn aggressive like she always did when a straight guy came into the apartment. He didn't know how the dog knew the difference. It was uncanny.

"Behave yourself, Cinderella," he managed to say before the visitor's foot came up hard in the dog's ribs, driving her across the floor and into the wall next to the sofa where she lay still.

Jon looked up, no longer smiling.

Lenny Bange had given Cubby Crispino a list of possible suspects when he had called Las Vegas. Cubby wasn't interested in Lenny's list. He hated attorneys. But he decided that to save time he would run down some of the names for himself to see if any of them could be the one that was trying to blackmail the scumbag lawyer.

The first name on the list was Jonathan Samuels, who lived just across the Indiana state line in a shithole of a town called Shawneetown. The only reason it got his attention was because, number one, it sounded like some kind of Indian name, and number two, Jon Samuels was a fag and used to live with the little hooker who had started all this trouble in the first place. Maybe he'd pay a visit and rough the little noodle dick up and see what he could find out.

He smiled at the thought. It would at least fill up some of his time, and there sure wasn't anything else to do in Evansville, Indiana. Even their casino was a disappointment. Now, Vegas—there was where the action was.

He looked the directions up on his laptop. Almost two hours to get there, twenty minutes of kicking ass, then another two hours back to the Drury Inn. There was a HBO movie on that evening that he didn't want to miss. The timing worked perfect.

He pulled his jacket back on to hide his pistol and checked himself out in the mirror. "Hello, Jon," he said to himself. "I'm Mr. Wackadoodle, and I'm here to whack your noodle." This might be fun.

CHAPTER FIFTY-FIVE

Cubby made his way silently up the stairs and down to the door of Jonathan Samuels's apartment. He turned the handle and found the door was unlocked. *This'll be easier than I thought.* When Lenny Bange had called him and asked him to find out who was blackmailing him, he had almost turned down the job because he didn't like to do what he considered grunt work. He wasn't a private eye. He was muscle.

But he could hear the fear in Lenny Bange's voice on the telephone, and that made him feel good. Besides, he wasn't doing much and could use the five large he had intimidated Bange into paying. Five grand to slap some sense into this little prick was easy money.

He looked around the apartment grounds. No other lights were on and there were only two other vehicles in the parking lot. One of them was probably Jon Samuels's car, and Cubby guessed it would be the bright purple Pontiac Vibe. The other, an SUV, might have belonged to the chick that Jon used to share the apartment with. The newspapers were saying she was whacked by a serial killer, but Cubby knew that the girl was hustling for Lenny, so he figured it was more likely one of her clients was pissed off over something she'd done.

Maybe Bange did her himself, he thought, but dismissed the idea, remembering how scared the lawyer was when he'd called. And even if it was Bange, it was nothing to him. He was being paid to find the blackmailer and shut him up. The rest was someone else's problem.

He pushed the door open just a crack and listened. It was silent. Almost too silent. A finger of apprehension bore into his spine, but he quickly dismissed the feeling. Cubby Crispino, six foot two with a hundred ninety-five pounds of muscle, against a fag. What could possibly go wrong? He pushed the door open and then stood wide-eyed at the scene in front of him.

Murphy had too much information. And he was tenacious. The killer's plans to eliminate Murphy were thwarted by the untimely arrival of that young dude in the truck, and for a few moments he had considered cutting his losses and leaving town. He already had excuses ready for his boss and anyone else who might question the timing of his departure, but then the memory of the naked Murphy coming busting ass down that gravel drive, gun in hand, ready to kill him, had made him want to stay and finish what he had started.

When he made the decision not to leave town it had been like being freed from chains. Almost as freeing as the feeling he'd had the day they had released him from the mental asylum. *All better now, Mr. Morse,* the shrink had assured him. All better. It had taken him twelve years to learn exactly what to say, how to act, to create the illusion that the doctors wanted to see.

He'd learned the hard way. But he was always a smart kid. The shrinks weren't stupid. They'd caught him a couple of times when he'd tried too hard to convince them he was "all better." But eventually he'd gotten so good at pretending, that he began to believe his own bullshit. *In a way, it was those doctors who created me. Always pushing, questioning, wanting me to understand why I killed my father.*

The doctors believed that if he could confront the part of him that had killed his father, his other self—the gentle side of him—would once again gain control. In fact, what happened was that when the rational side of Cody Morse met the feral personality that dwelled inside him—the one that newspapers all over the country had come to call The Cleaver—the reality of what he'd done to his father destroyed the good boy. All that was left was The Cleaver.

But the introspection those doctors had forced him through had made something else very clear to him. He hated bullies. Hated anyone who used his position, size, or perceived authority to make other people humble themselves. Hated anyone who pushed him. And these types of people had become the victims that The Cleaver sought out. Men or women . . . it was all the same to him.

He stood, now, just down at the end of the second-floor porch where only yesterday Jack Murphy and Jon Samuels had been sitting in chairs and having a nice little chat. He watched the big man push open the door to Samuels's apartment and freeze in the doorway. He didn't know who the man was, but he was as big as Cody himself, and looked every bit as strong.

Cody wondered if this man could shed any light on the telephone call he had received. Samuels had known nothing. He'd made sure Samuels had no information for him before he ended the poor little man's existence. He had even been surprised to feel a little hesitation before he had swung the bone axe into Samuels's throat. Maybe it was because—once again—this wasn't the type of victim he would normally seek out. Samuels was no bully. If anything he was a victim.

But somewhere out there was a blackmailer who had his name in a diary. His name was there because she had discovered he was her brother and not because he was one of her clients. Eventually the truth would come out. And that would tie him to Cordelia, and then to the others, and then he would be locked up again.

The Cleaver would never go back inside again. Young Cody Morse had felt relief being inside the hospital. He felt safe, and cared for, and had even begun to like some of the staff and patients. The Cleaver had felt rage. The Cleaver wanted out. He hated everyone who stood in the way of his freedom. If he could have gotten to his bone axe back then he would have gotten out of the hospital much sooner. But, he was "all better now."

He felt the weight of the short-handled axe in his hand and it calmed him. He'd used it to cleave most of the meat from his father's face and skull after delivering the killing blow to the man's neck. When he was eight years old the axe had required all of the strength of both of his arms to chop his father's head free from his neck.

During the years that he had been regularly beaten by the bully that he called his father, he had endured verbal and psychological abuse that was nothing near the quick death he had given the man. The old saying about "sticks and stones" was bullshit. He had almost forgotten his real name as a child because the only one he heard come from his father's mouth was "bastard" or "you worthless piece of shit" or his all-time favorite, "faggot son of a bitch."

These words had damaged his self-worth, according to the doctors at St. Francis Institution where he had been "admitted" and kept prisoner all those years. But the words didn't damage his self-worth. They only changed his soul, piece by piece, from a child, into someone who laughed at the doctors and their ignorance of who they really had before them.

The first thing he'd done upon release from St. Francis was to go back to Shawneetown and find the axe. He wasn't surprised that it was still in its hiding place. If he had believed in God he would have believed that God had kept it safe for him. But he believed in something bigger than God. He believed in vengeance.

The axe empowered him. It was like waking from a long sleep. He felt no fear, no pain, and no guilt at being left behind by his mother. It was as if his sister didn't exist in all of this. The only bond he had to her was that they had both been abandoned. He had no earlier memories of her. Couldn't remember one event, a birthday, a conversation, or a game. One day she'd been a skinny two-year-old and the next time he saw her he killed her.

That one act had led to all of this unplanned bloodshed, and this was not to his liking. He picked his victims for a reason. He stalked them like game, and then he put them down like the animals they were. But killing his sister had set off a storm that didn't seem to have an end.

He knew he could have packed up and walked away from Evansville. Still didn't know exactly why he had taken a job so close to Shawneetown in the first place. But he knew he would not leave until he'd finished his mission.

He clutched the bone axe to his side and moved silently down the porch toward Jon Samuels's doorway. Maybe the visitor there had some information. If he did, he would give it to The Cleaver. There was no alternative.

CHAPTER FIFTY-SIX

Detective Jansen sat in his car in the back parking lot of Duffy's Tavern in a disappointed and angry state. The woman with the casaba-melon breasts had turned down his advances and left the bar, being half carried by a little guy with no front teeth. He was glad now that he hadn't wasted two bucks buying her another damn beer.

He blew his breath into his hand and sniffed it. *Hell, it's almost three in the morning. What am I worrying about?* He decided to go into the detective squad room. It should be deserted this time of night and he could sit for a spell. The only thing he had to go home to was a sick wife, and her bitching and nagging. He hoped that whatever he was trying to pull out of his mind would come to him.

In the back parking lot at police headquarters, Jansen pulled into one of the city-council spots that were almost always deserted and parked his take-home car. He was walking toward the back entrance to the squad room when he noticed a couple of cars that didn't belong in the parking lot. One was Captain Franklin's personal vehicle. Franklin was never at work this early and especially not in his own personal car.

The other car was a newer royal-blue Buick that just screamed FBI. That meant something big was going on. Whatever it was, Jansen was going to find out. Information was better than currency in his line of work.

He walked up to the back of headquarters and peered through the heavy glass panes. There was no one in the hallway, but the lights were on in the captain's office. He used his key fob and winced at the electric click as the lock disengaged. He hated these locks that were linked to a security system. There would be a record of his entering through that blasted door at an exact time and date. It took all the sneak out of "sneaky bastard," and he was rather proud of his reputation.

As soon as he was through the door, he entered the detective squad room and looked to be sure he was alone. He logged onto his computer and moved a couple of pending files into the record-room basket icon, and left his computer logged onto the system. It would automatically log him out after an hour and thus it would look like he had worked for an hour and gone home. *What a hardworking man I am,* he thought.

Now that he had created a fake reason for being in the building, he peeked back into the hallway and found it empty and quiet except for the sound of soft voices coming from Captain Franklin's office.

He moved like a shadow down the hall and stood just outside the office, where he could hear the voices much better. He wished he had his digital recorder with him because he could enhance the volume on his computer later. His hearing wasn't as sharp as it was when he was younger.

"Well, I guess this is all supposition until we verify with the coroner," Captain Franklin was saying.

A voice that Jansen didn't recognize said, "It'll be our guy, Captain. If I didn't believe it, I wouldn't be here."

"I hope to God you're wrong, Agent Tunney," Franklin said.

"Call me Frank, Captain," the voice said, and Jansen felt a shock of recognition at the name.

Special Agent Frank Tunney. Serial killer hunter, Jansen thought. And Tunney had said something about it being "our guy." Jansen wondered what he was talking about, and then it came to him. The murders they were working were supposed to be by a serial killer. Obviously this was of interest to the FBI or they wouldn't have sent someone as important as Tunney in the middle of the night. Now he really missed his digital recorder. It would be great to have this on tape.

"So this guy—The Cleaver—has been in your gun sights for some time?" Captain Franklin said.

"Twenty-four known kills so far," Tunney said. "Twenty-five if Brenda Lincoln is another."

"Then Detective Murphy is correct about these cases all being related," Franklin said.

"That's the troubling part," Tunney admitted. "The Cleaver is a very methodical killer. He has always followed a pattern and selected his kill sites inside homes. The killing you have at the motel, and the one in the kitchen—Louise Brigham, I think you said—don't fit with that pattern."

"Brenda Lincoln was killed in her garage," Franklin reminded him. "And she was very publicly displayed."

"He took her face off with a hand axe. The rest of the damage was just to confuse you . . . and me. That's why I thought it worth a trip in the middle of the night. There is something very personal about these killings. Not like the other ones. I think he's just made his first mistake, Captain."

"I hope you're right," Franklin said. "But we're still no closer to catching him than you have been."

"Oh. I think you might be surprised. This Jack Murphy of yours is quite a pistol if I remember correctly."

"It's okay, Agent Tunney. You can call him a smart-ass. Everyone else does."

Tunney chuckled, and to Jansen that was shocking. FBI agents were not known for their sense of humor. To Jansen's trained bullshit meter, Tunney was holding something back.

"I've called Jack and his team to meet us at the morgue," Franklin said. "I'll drive."

Franklin and Tunney were just stepping into the hallway as the back door to headquarters clicked.

CHAPTER FIFTY-SEVEN

A tall man advanced toward him carrying an axe. Behind the man, flames danced into the sky. But the man was a mere black figure set against the inferno. Jack tried to pull his pistol, but it wasn't in his holster where it belonged. He reached to his ankle for the backup pistol he carried, but it too was missing. He steeled himself for the attack.

The ringing phone was like a piece of metal skewering a raw nerve. Jack started awake and then remembered he was still in the office. He had gone to sleep with his head resting on his desk. It was just a bad dream.

Liddell and Garcia had gone to run down information and he had been looking through the folders of the murders. They had worked through the late night and early morning with no success and the autopsy of Kooky was scheduled for this morning. He quickly glanced at the clock. Four-thirty in the morning.

"What?" he said into the receiver. It was Captain Franklin.

"Get down to the morgue. Bigfoot will meet you there," Franklin said, and the line went dead.

Jack hung up and wondered if there had been another murder. *One hell of a way to start Halloween,* Jack thought.

He made a quick bathroom stop and caught a glimpse of himself in the mirror over the sink. He looked like hammered shit. Not bad for four-thirty in the morning with about fifteen minutes of hard sleep.

A half dozen cars sat in the morgue parking lot. Jack recognized Liddell's unmarked tan-colored Crown Vic. Little Casket's Suburban was also in the lot but not near the garage doors where it would have been if there had been a recent delivery of a cadaver. That was a good sign.

Jack buzzed his way in and proceeded down the hall toward the autopsy room. A voice hailed him from Lilly Caskins's office.

"You look terrible, pod'na," Liddell said, as Jack entered the small office. He saw the room was packed.

Lilly was almost hidden behind her desk with Captain Franklin sitting in one of the two chairs in front of Lilly's desk, and Liddell somehow squeezed into the other. Off to the side Angelina Garcia stood twisting the ends of her hair.

He wondered why they were all there, at the morgue, and not in some other capacious location where they could spread out and have lattes and half-caf-cappucinos with sprigs of mint. He didn't have to wait long for the answer.

"We were waiting for you, Detective Murphy," came a voice from behind him. Jack turned and looked into the light gray eyes of FBI profiler Frank Tunney.

Tunney was tall and lean but had an athlete's aura. He was dressed in the traditional blue suit that must be the school uniform for FBI agents. Jack thought it would have been better if they had all been made to wear kilts and then they would look like ancient warriors with serious cross-dressing issues. He kept this observation to himself and said, "Agent Tunney," and shook hands.

He'd met Tunney at several schools where the police department had sent him to learn the art of criminal profiling. Tunney was considered the preeminent authority on the topic and had a reputation among the troops as a serial-killer hunter.

Frank Tunney had earned a PhD in psychology from Harvard at the age of twenty and had spent almost ten years teaching before being recruited into the FBI's famous Behavioral Analysis Unit. He had not only assisted in high-profile cases in the United States, but also been requested and loaned out to several other countries. For someone in his early forties he'd had a full life.

Murphy wondered if the chief had decided to call in the big guns since they—meaning Jack and his team—were at a standstill. His question was answered when Tunney said, "Susan called and explained what you've been working on. It seems we have a mutual interest."

"So you're the friend Susan was talking about?" Jack asked.

"Yeah," Tunney said with a boyish grin. "We go way back, Susie and I."

Jack wanted to ask just how far back they went, but he forced himself to focus on the case. Tunney was exactly the guy they needed on this.

Since Captain Franklin was the ranking man in the room, Tunney addressed him, saying, "Captain, can we all move to the autopsy room please?" The FBI is big on protocol. But Jack thought if Tunney was so smart he would realize that the only one in the room whom he should fear was Little Casket.

As if he read Jack's mind, Tunney said, "But this is your facility, Miss Caskins. Would you do us the honor?"

Caskins turned to Agent Tunney and her face looked like a Dalí painting, because her jaw dropped almost to the floor. She had probably not been called "Miss" Caskins for about eight hundred or so years.

Tunney turned and smiled at Jack, letting him know he had read the power structure in the room correctly. Jack quietly gave him the thumbs-up.

Liddell walked next to Jack down the corridor and leaned over to whisper, "What's going on?"

"Hell if I know," Jack answered. "You mean you've all been just sitting around waiting for me and no one has talked about what Tunney is doing here?"

Liddell got a semi-serious look on his face and said, "Little Casket was in the room and we were all afraid to move much less speak."

Up ahead of them everyone was moving into the autopsy room. Jack could see that Dr. John was inside, stooped over what seemed to be the remains of Brenda Lincoln.

Dr. John was in full scrubs with a mask and gloves. The corpse on the steel table was unclothed and shimmering from the number of cuts that covered every inch of skin. Even the bottoms of the feet were crisscrossed with deep slices, some going into the bone.

Jack noticed a look pass between Dr. John and Tunney, and then Dr. John said, "You were right, Agent Tunney."

"Anyone going to let us in on what's going on?" Liddell said, causing everyone to look at him.

"Are you sure about the results, John?" Captain Franklin asked the pathologist.

"As sure as I can be without sending the tissue samples off for microscopic examination," Carmodi answered. "Which, of course, I was going to do." He looked slightly embarrassed and Jack was more confused than ever.

CHAPTER FIFTY-EIGHT

Claudine Setera rubbed at her eyes and squinted at the red-numbered display of the clock beside her bed. Her cell phone was vibrating and she had to squint to read the little display window. It was that creepy little detective who was always talking to her chest.

She thought about shutting the phone off, but then decided that maybe he had something for her besides a drunken booty call. If he propositioned her one more time she was going to the chief of police and filing a complaint.

She answered the phone. "What?"

"You're gonna want to wake up for this," Jansen said.

Claudine set up in bed at the tone of his voice.

They had moved from the autopsy room to the larger conference room, and were spread out in chairs around the large table, all except Liddell, who was methodically working his way through the room, opening a drawer here, a cabinet door there, foraging for any unguarded snacks.

"So what can you tell us about this Cleaver guy?" Jack asked.

Tunney looked at Jack and answered, "Not what you want

to know, Detective Murphy. We don't know who he is and
that is the thing, isn't it?"

"Well, that would sure help," Liddell said.

Franklin shot Liddell a cautioning look and asked, "Do
you have any forensic evidence, witnesses, descriptions?"

Tunney shook his head. "One of the Seattle papers ran a
composite one time, but it turned out the witness was lying,
and we wasted a lot of time and man power." He got up and
walked around the room. Jack could remember seeing him
do this at the seminars he'd attended. Tunney was in profes-
sor mode, Jack thought.

"The Cleaver has been successful because he never stays
in one place too long. He has never been known to go back
to a location once he has finished his spree of murders. He
always uses the same weapon, a hand axe of some type—
hence the media-given name, The Cleaver—and he always
kills his victims in their homes. We believe he uses the same
weapon because we have been able to forensically obtain
some trace elements of iron from several of the victims'
skulls. His M.O. is to stalk his victim until he becomes familiar enough with them to know when they are home alone,
and then he enters the house—no forced entries—and . . ."

Liddell interrupted him, asking, "You say he has *never*
forced an entry?"

Tunney stopped pacing and placed both hands on the
conference tabletop. "Twenty-four confirmed kills and he
has never once forced his way into a house."

"Well, I'm not as educated as your guys in Quantico,"
Liddell said, "but doesn't that kind of indicate that all of his
victims let him in. That they may have known him?"

Tunney looked like he had anticipated that question. "We
thought of that. And it's a possibility. But when you look at
the scope of his travels, it would be highly unlikely that he
actually 'knew' all of his victims. He has killed people in
eight states from east to west and north to south."

"That's an average of three victims in each state," Dr. John piped in.

"You're not just another pretty face, Doc," Liddell said and blew a kiss at him.

Dr. John looked embarrassed.

"Sorry, Captain," Liddell said, and finally pulled up a chair and sat at the table. "Sorry, Agent Tunney."

Tunney smiled and said, "No apology needed, Detective. Despite what you've heard, FBI agents sometimes do possess a sense of humor."

Liddell leaned toward Jack and whispered, "It's like he can read your mind. That's creepy."

"Focus," Jack whispered back at him.

"Et tu, Brute?" Liddell said.

Tunney apparently was listening and broke out in laughter at this exchange. "You guys are good," he said, and even Captain Franklin was smiling.

"They do pretty good work when they're not screwing around," Franklin admitted. "I just wish they would be more serious when we have a guest from an outside agency," he said, directing this remark at Jack.

Little Casket spoke up. "If your guy is the same as our guy, he's not following the pattern. He's already killed five here and one of them a policeman."

The room became quiet, until Tunney said, "He seems to be straying from his usual pattern, but it's possible that we don't know about all of his murders. Sometimes these killers change their entire style. There are no guarantees in profiling." He looked around the room at each face. "One thing I can predict though. He isn't finished with you."

The front-door buzzer sounded. Lilly stood up and said, "I'll see who it is," and she left the conference room. Before the others could go back to their discussion they heard voices raised. Jack recognized one of them as the domineering voice of Lilly Caskins. The other sounded female and just as determined, which was not a good thing.

Lilly came back in the room and said, "Okay, which one of you idiots told the news media about this?" She explained, saying, "Channel Six. That Italian broad, Claudine Setera. She's at the door. She wants to speak to FBI Special Agent Frank Tunney about The Cleaver."

Standing at the front door of the morgue under a dark and moonless October sky, Claudine felt little, insignificant. But after she scooped all the other stations with this story she would never have to feel that way again. She smiled at the thought of Blake James sleeping through the story of the century. *Well, at least it's the story of the year in this little town,* she thought.

Then she had a more unpleasant thought. She had promised to meet with Detective Jansen at a place of his choosing to "pay him back" for this lead. The thought of that slimeball touching her made her feel sick. But, then, she had no plan to ever hold up her end of the bargain, so he could go play with himself. And she couldn't help thinking that he was probably doing so while he was talking with her this morning. Her stomach clenched.

Where is that little troll of a medical examiner? Claudine thought, looking at the door that had been closed in her face. *There's no way they can ignore me when I drop a bomb like this on them. Should have brought a cameraman,* she thought, but then that would have tipped someone at the station that she was on this story, and she hadn't been at Channel Six long enough to know whom she could trust. Well, after she got the interview with Agent Tunney this morning all of that crap at the station would end. She had reason to believe that Jack Murphy and his team were inside as well.

She pulled out her notebook and wrote down the license

plates of all the cars in the morgue parking lot. The door to the morgue opened and Jack Murphy came out. He was talking on a portable radio as he came out.

"Yes. Please have the vehicle towed to impound," he said into the radio.

Claudine Setera looked out in the lot to the point where Murphy had been gazing. The only vehicle in that part of the lot was the car she had come in. Her personal car. *He wouldn't dare,* she thought.

A marked police car pulled into the parking lot and a police officer who was at least as big as her little car stepped from his vehicle.

"Is this the offender's car, Detective?" the officer asked.

"Tow-away zone, Officer. Unless it has a Coroner's Department sticker in the window—which I doubt that it does—have it taken to impound." The officer turned and walked toward Claudine's car, ticket book in hand.

"You can't get away with this, Murphy," was all Claudine Setera could think of to say, before Jack turned and reentered the morgue, leaving her to argue with the uniformed officer. While she was doing so, Agent Tunney and Captain Franklin were being spirited out the back door of the coroner's office to an unmarked vehicle that Murphy had quietly instructed them to take.

Jack and Franklin had agreed that this was only a temporary reprieve, but there was no way they could allow the news media to catch them all at the morgue. It was obvious that someone had given Setera some very private information. But if she couldn't verify any of it, she was dead in the water until she could.

Jack smiled as he came back in the conference room.

Lilly Caskins's face was unreadable as she asked, "You really gonna tow that reporter's car?"

Liddell was grinning too. "Nah, he just wants to shake her up a little. The officer's been told to give her a stern warning in about ten minutes and let her leave. That'll give Captain Franklin time to find somewhere safe to stash Agent Tunney."

Lilly cracked a grin, and on her it looked like a caricature of an evil pumpkin. "You guys are da bomb," she said and bumped knuckles with Liddell. Lilly was thinking of her earlier encounter in front of the Marriott with Blake James, who was wrapping her in an embrace while this bimbo filmed it all. "I owe you one, Murphy," she said.

"Don't have a clue what you're talking about, Lilly," Jack answered.

CHAPTER FIFTY-NINE

During the hastily arranged exit from the morgue, Captain Franklin had made an executive decision to hide Agent Tunney. Franklin and Tunney were headed to Two-Jakes Marina for a clandestine meeting with Jack and Liddell.

"Sorry for the media reception, Agent Tunney," Captain Franklin said. He was embarrassed that his department's information leaks had been exposed.

"Not a problem, Captain," Tunney assured him. "This isn't the first time I've had to hide."

"Jack and Liddell will meet us there and we'll find a suitable place for you to stay while you're here," Franklin added.

"Murphy thinks on the fly, doesn't he?" Tunney observed.

"That can be a problem sometimes," Franklin said. "But, yes, he is quick on his feet. It's not the first time he's butted heads with the media. Sometimes it doesn't go so well for him, but he's the man I'd want working this case. He never gives up."

"I can see that," Tunney said.

Arnold looked at the typed note. It was from the same person, he was sure of that. But there was something different about it. It frightened him. He was sure that another murder was taking place. And this time, it was happening to someone who Arnold was familiar with. Jonathan Samuels was as good as dead.

Cubby stepped into the apartment and stared at what had been a human being not long ago. The body was probably Jon Samuels according to the description he'd gotten from Lenny Bange, but even his own mother wouldn't have recognized him now. For one thing, the face and part of the scalp had been removed from the body, and a skull now stared at Cubby with sightless eyes.

Had Lenny Bange also hired someone else to take care of his problem? No—he was sure that the gutless attorney wouldn't dare to disrespect him that way. That meant that Jon Samuels must have pissed someone else off enough to get hacked up and scalped. And that probably meant that Samuels was the guy, the one who was blackmailing Bange.

Whoever had done this had saved Cubby some trouble, but now there was the issue of his fee. He could claim to Lenny that he was the one who had taken care of Samuels, but this was not Cubby's style of taking care of things. Cubby was a mean son of a bitch, and he was not to be messed with. He would break bones, maybe kneecap someone, but he left them alive if it was possible, dead if it suited him. In his whole life he had never done anything like what he was seeing here. Whoever did this was in a league of his own.

He had brought a small pry bar with him that served two purposes. He had planned to use it to force entry into the apartment if necessary, and then it doubled as a negotiating tool in case Samuels wasn't forthcoming with information. He slipped the twelve-inch tool into the waistband at the back of his pants since the situation had not called for the tool's use.

He took one more look at the hacked-up corpse that was propped up on the couch and said, "Well, you got lucky it wasn't me that got to you first." He laughed at his own witticism and turned to get out of there when he noticed something running down into his eyes. Cubby put his hand to his face and felt the substance. It was definitely blood, but where was it coming from? Then as if in answer to his unspoken question the bone axe came crashing down into the back of his skull.

The man the FBI had dubbed The Cleaver was slightly surprised by the ability of the large man not only to turn around with the blade of the bone axe buried deep in the back of his head, but also to lift his arm and touch the blood that was flowing down the side of his face. The puzzled look was almost entertaining.

Now he had two bodies to deal with and that wasn't in the plan. *This whole thing has been a disaster since the beginning,* he thought. First Cordelia tracks him down, and then someone tries to blackmail him.

He had thought about not killing this man, but the guy was large and looked powerful. The first rule of killing is "don't lose the fight." He had watched the man put a metal bar in his back waistband. It was likely that he had other more deadly weapons on his person.

He pulled Cubby's body into the apartment and shut the door behind them. *No more company tonight please,* he thought, and searched Cubby's clothing for identification.

The guy was wearing a black leather jacket, black jeans, and a black shirt. "Oh my God!" he said softly. "I've killed Johnny Cash." He chuckled and reached inside the jacket pocket of the dead man, finding a business card.

Lenny Bange, Esq., the card read. And under that was printed, *Get more Bange for your buck.*

"Well, you certainly did," the killer said to the body at his feet. "And now . . . so have I."

Also in the pocket was a small leather business card holder. The killer opened it and found several credit cards and a Nevada driver's license for a man named Crispino out of Las Vegas. Cody checked the man's jeans pockets and in the right pocket found a money clip holding three thousand dollars in large bills.

He patted the body down and felt a hard object in the middle of the back waistband. He reached under the jacket and removed a nine-millimeter Beretta pistol that had been tucked away. It was massive, but the man was able to cover it with his bulk. He laid the pistol on the floor. Not his weapon of choice. He liked to be up close when doing business.

The pry bar was sticking out of the man's back pocket. He slid it out and saw that it had been well used. So the man had come prepared to break into the apartment. He was carrying a lot of cash and carrying a loose business card for an Evansville attorney. He looked like a tough guy. A leg breaker. Was Lenny Bange trying to recover money from Samuels? It didn't make sense. Samuels had nothing. Why would an attorney be sending a hired thug to the apartment of some small-town gay guy?

Bange is being blackmailed, too, he thought. But Samuels wasn't the blackmailer. Now he wished he could have kept the big man alive. There were probably a lot of questions he could have answered. But the big man might have gone for the gun and it would have been even messier.

So that left Lenny Bange. He would have to pay Lenny a visit. What a surprise the attorney would get when he found out that Samuels had been slaughtered, and that the body of another man, an unidentified body of course, was found in the apartment.

He went to the kitchen area of the apartment and retrieved some plastic trash bags. He would need something to put the hands and head in. He stuffed the bags in his back pocket and went back to the body of Cubby Crispino and knelt next to the upper torso. Hefting the bone axe high over his head, he swung down and with one expert blow severed the head from the body. Then came the hands.

He tossed the severed body parts in the plastic trash bag and dropped the pistol in after it. He tied it shut with the handy drawstring top. He would take all the money and identification, but leave the clothes. He didn't want to make it impossible for the police to identify this guy, just tie them up awhile and get them off their pace.

He looked around to be sure he'd left nothing of his own behind when he spotted the pry bar on the floor. He decided to leave it. Maybe one little present for Jack. This was getting to be fun.

CHAPTER SIXTY

Arnold had spent a luxurious twenty minutes in the shower, the water as hot as he could stand it, and now put the finishing touches on his story. It was a good piece. Sure to be front page. He'd stayed up all night working on it.

Arnold called Bob Robertson, his editor, at home. It was a little after five o'clock in the morning, but Robertson answered on the first ring.

"This had better be damned important," Robertson said.

"Sir, this is Arnold Byrum," Arnold said in a weak voice. Mr. Robertson could be a very intimidating man.

"I know who it is, idiot! What have you got?"

"I have a story, sir."

"Tell me," Robertson demanded.

Jack was on his way to Two-Jakes Marina to meet with Captain Franklin and Agent Tunney when he received the telephone call from Chief Bob Johnson in Shawneetown.

"Murphy," he said into his cell phone.

The chief was so upset he was slurring his words like a drunk. The gist of what he had to say was that Jon Samuels was dead.

"Chief Johnson," Jack said, "I can't help but wonder why you're calling me about this?"

"Because of the other dead sucker laying in Jon's front room," Johnson said, as if that should clear everything up nicely.

"Slow down a little, Chief, and tell me what you need me for."

"I don't give a fudgesicle in hell what you're doing, Murphy. You get your ass over here and help me sort this out. I swear to God, boy, I ain't never seen nothing like this. Jon's face is gone and the other guy ain't got no head or hands."

Jack could hear Chief Johnson take a deep breath and let it out shakily. "None of this shit happened before you came over here asking your damn questions."

Jack said, "I have to pick up my partner, but I'll be there in less than an hour." The line went dead, and Jack said to no one, "Don't bother thanking me."

He called Liddell and arranged to meet in the parking lot of the museum downtown near the river. He then called Captain Franklin and explained what was going on.

"I'll call him and see if I can get any more information from him," Franklin said, and Jack gave the captain the cell phone number for Chief Johnson. "Come by and pick up Agent Tunney. He wants to go and see this one for himself. You say he told you that Samuels's face had been taken off?"

"Yeah. And don't forget the headless guy."

"I'll see if he has an identification on the other guy."

Jack didn't think the killer took the head and hands to make it that easy and he said so.

"May not be related," Franklin said, "but Tunney wants to see it, and I agree."

"Be there in five," Jack said, and swung his Jeep into the parking lot of the museum near the levee.

Liddell was sitting on the hood of his unmarked car sip-

ping something from a Styrofoam cup. "Am I driving?" he
asked.

Jack nodded. "Follow me to Two-Jakes. We're picking
Tunney up. I'll leave my car there."

CHAPTER SIXTY-ONE

Chief Bob Johnson stood on the porch outside Samuels's apartment and took gulping breaths of air. He had called JJ ten minutes ago and the numb-nuts still hadn't shown up in that fancied-up Firebird he called a police car.

His chest hurt and he could feel pain settling into his shoulders. He hoped Murphy stepped on the gas and got there quick. This was his kind of stuff, not an old man's job at all. Especially one with a bad ticker and a hundred extra pounds on him.

He walked unsteadily to the stairs. He needed to get some yellow crime scene tape out of his trunk and then block the entrance to the gravel drive leading to the apartments. If that idiot nephew of his would get out here, he had things for him to do as well.

County coroner's office is taking their time, Johnson thought, just as he saw a cloud of dust rising at the entrance of the drive out near the main road. *Better be you, JJ!*

JJ could see all the lights on in Samuels's apartment. He knew his uncle was going to be pissed at him, but he couldn't get there any quicker. He was over in Kentucky with a "friend" and had broken every speed limit to get here, all the while praying that one of the Kentucky state troopers wouldn't spot him.

Pulling up to his uncle's police cruiser, he shut down his engine, but his mind was in overdrive. He sincerely hoped this had nothing to do with his breaking into Samuels's place. Or with the two phone calls he'd made to people over in Evansville. Surely neither of those guys would have anything to do with a murder. But the thought that Samuels had been killed within a day of his making those calls caused a finger of fear to shoot up JJ's spine.

"Sorry, Uncle Bob," JJ said, getting out of the car. "What do you want me to do?"

Chief Johnson was sitting against the back trunk of his marked police car. When he stood up the car's rear end lifted a good four inches.

"Listen here, son," Johnson said, putting a meaty arm around the younger man's shoulders. "When I gave you this job I went to bat for you with the city council. I told them you'd do the job."

JJ had heard this speech before. It was best just to keep quiet and let his uncle vent, but he wanted to know what happened here. Wanted to see it for himself. See if it had anything to do with Cordelia's diary or the phone calls he'd made.

"Can I go up and look?" he asked.

His uncle looked at him for a long time, then shook his head as if he was battling a lost cause and said, "Go on up, then get down here and help me secure this scene."

JJ looked around and wondered what they were securing an empty parking lot for, but he kept his mouth shut and headed up the stairs. He was about halfway up when his uncle called to him.

"Don't go inside, JJ. You can see all you need to from the doorway."

JJ took two more steps before his uncle called out again, saying, "And don't touch the door or anything. I got a call in to the coroner and the state police. I don't want the scene compromised."

JJ ran up the remaining stairs. He already knew that his fingerprints were going to be all over the door and inside of the apartment. He could explain them, except for the ones he might have left on the inside of the air-conditioning unit's casing. But then, the police team from Evansville had already searched the apartment once and didn't look in the a/c unit that time. Maybe the state cops wouldn't look, either.

He stopped inside the doorway like his uncle had told him, but that warning was needless. JJ couldn't have gone in that apartment if his pants were on fire and there was a bucket of water inside the door. The sight before him left him paralyzed.

CHAPTER SIXTY-TWO

Agent Tunney sat in the back passenger side of Liddell Blanchard's unmarked unit behind Jack Murphy. Murphy had offered him the front seat, but this seating arrangement was the only way he could get legroom for his six-foot-three frame. Liddell wasn't wasting any time and, at five o'clock in the morning, was only slowing at the toll bridge to pay the fee. There was little traffic on the road anyway. At the point where Highway 62 becomes Illinois Highway 141, Liddell took a hard left onto Big Hill Road.

An Illinois state trooper passed Liddell going south and Liddell looked at his speedometer. "He's doing over a hundred, Jack," Liddell observed.

"You drive like a girl," Jack said.

"Do not."

"C'mon, Bigfoot. Catch that mother," Jack said.

"Are you going to pay the ticket?" Liddell asked.

"I'll pay the ticket," Tunney said from the backseat.

Liddell stomped the gas pedal down and the car rocketed forward. "Oh well, I can't ignore an order from the FBI," Liddell said.

Jack said to Liddell, "And you always say that FBI agents don't have any balls."

"I never say that," Liddell protested. Jack sat quietly. Liddell looked back at Agent Tunney and said, "I never say that."

"Eyes on the road please," Tunney said. "I don't want my balls splattered all over some cow pasture."

"Where did you get this information?" Bob Robertson was sitting behind his desk, with Arnold squirming in a seat across the room.

"I have a source," Arnold said.

"What?" Robertson shouted. "You have a source. You think that's all I'm going to have to explain when we run with a story that the police just now got involved with?"

Arnold didn't know what to say. He couldn't reveal his source.

"I called Chief Johnson and he confirmed they're working a homicide involving Jon Samuels as the victim, but he didn't want to go on record," Robertson said, but he wasn't really talking to Arnold. He was trying to come up with an angle to use the story. It was a great one, and they would once again have the scoop on the television stations. He didn't really give a damn who Arnold's source was.

"But we have a problem, Arnold," Robertson said, and chewed on his thumbnail. "They got two dead bodies. No identification on the second victim yet."

Arnold saw that Robertson wasn't even looking his direction. He might as well not be in the room. "I can write that into the story if you want, sir," Arnold offered.

"Get back to your source first. See what the score is on this. Then do a quick rewrite," Robertson said. "You have ten minutes and then we're running with whatever you have."

Arnold got up and left the editor's office. He was tired of being a go-between for the killer and the newspaper. They were both using him. He was not going to keep getting pushed around like this. But then he remembered the book he was working on and the thought of having a bestseller made him forget his resentment.

Ten minutes would be more than he would need since he couldn't call his source. Arnold never contacted his source. It was the other way around. He would just use his writing skills to put the second dead body in the story. He picked up the phone on his desk and called a number from his notebook.

JJ returned to his car and drove through the tunnel created by the dark cornfields to the driveway leading to the apartments. His job was to block the road and only let authorized vehicles in. He heard an engine gunning hard before he even saw the headlights as one of the Illinois State Police marked units came into view. JJ pulled out his Maglite flashlight and flicked it off and on to make sure the trooper saw the driveway. The state trooper turned into the drive and didn't even slow to acknowledge JJ as he sped past him, kicking up a choking cloud of dust.

"State troopers," JJ muttered and swiped at his eyes. He could hear another big engine in the distance somewhere, but it was blotted out by the sound of his cell phone ringing.

"Lieutenant Johnson," he said into the phone.

"Arnold Byrum here, Lieutenant."

JJ swallowed. *Not that guy again,* he thought. "What can I do ya for, Arnold?"

Arnold tried to assimilate what JJ had just said. Then he realized that JJ was just being facetious, making a play on words. "Well, for starters you can tell me if Jonathan Samuels was murdered."

JJ thought about it. Uncle Bob would be furious that he was talking to the news media again. But then he thought about the Illinois state trooper leaving him in a cloud of dust, and treating him like he was a school crossing guard and not a lieutenant in the Shawneetown police force. In a short while the cameras would be there and they would all be focused on the state police.

"What do you want to know?" JJ asked.

CHAPTER SIXTY-THREE

JJ watched the tan Crown Vic pull up next to his car and stop. The driver's window came down and JJ recognized Liddell Blanchard.

"The chief told me you'd be coming," JJ said.

"Not even breathing hard yet," Liddell said.

JJ looked stymied for a second; then a grin spread across his face. "Oh, I get it." And he made motions with his right hand as if he were masturbating. "I gotta remember that 'un."

Jack leaned across the seat and said, "Looks like we're the last ones at the party. Anything for us here, Lieutenant?"

JJ stood straight at the mention of his rank.

"I'd take you up there myself," he said, trying hard to look like he was in charge. "But the chief called the state police and he wants me to stay down here and direct them in. I'll call the chief and tell him you're on your way up." JJ took his cell phone out, and Liddell reached out and stopped him from dialing.

"Might be better if we just go on up," Liddell suggested.

JJ caught on. "Okay. I hope them boys don't give you too much trouble about being out of your jurisdiction."

"Hell, we're practically neighbors," Jack said and forced a laugh.

JJ laughed and motioned them to go ahead.

As they drove slowly down the gravel road to avoid kicking up a cloud of dust, Agent Tunney said from the backseat, "You two should sell cars. You'd make a fortune."

"It's a Jedi mind-control thing," Liddell said.

"Only works on weak minds. Like Liddell's," Jack said.

"You're the weak-minded one," Liddell protested.

"Watch this," Jack said to Agent Tunney, and then to Liddell said, "Keep driving forward."

"You a funny man, pod'na," Liddell said with a grin on his face.

I may be down, but I'm definitely not out, Claudine Setera thought.

She had been arguing on the telephone with her station manager for the best part of twenty minutes to no avail. The problem was the murder was not only in another city, it was in another state. She maintained that the murders in Shawneetown might be connected to the three murders in Evansville. He wasn't convinced and didn't want to "commit the station's resources" to a murder in Illinois when they didn't have a definite tie-in with their audience.

"Let me make my appeal in person, Elliott?" she pleaded in a sexy voice. The implications were clear.

"Sorry, Claudine. No can do," he said.

She couldn't keep the anger out of her voice. "That's bullshit, Elliott, and you know it."

He could hear her taking deep breaths, and the thought of what he had just turned down almost made him give in.

"If I was one of your drinking buddies you wouldn't have a problem with any of this," she said. "It's just because I'm a woman. That's discrimination and I plan to talk to the station owners about it. I don't think they'll be too happy that you let something this big go by you because you aren't man enough to meet with me and let me plead my case."

She was really pushing the envelope by talking to the station manager this way. He may be the new guy, but he wasn't a pushover.

Elliott Turner, who had only recently been hired as station manager for Channel Six television station, remained quiet for almost a minute, and then he made his decision. She was right. This was too good to pass up. And she was also right when she said that he would have already committed the station's full resources to any of the male reporters. But not because he was discriminating against women. It was because he had already had a chance to meet with them on an individual basis and knew which he could trust, and even how far that trust could go. With Claudine he knew little. She had not interacted with him since his hiring, at least not on a personal level, and that was probably as much his fault as it was hers.

What he did know of Claudine was that she was very aggressive and a damn good reporter.

"Okay, take one of the satellite vans. I'll get a team in place and we'll do this live at five-thirty." He could hear Claudine take in a deep, surprised breath. "Do you think you can be ready by then?" he asked.

"Yes, sir," Claudine said, her voice tight and controlled. "I won't let you down."

CHAPTER SIXTY-FOUR

There were five Illinois State Police cruisers in the parking area of the apartment building. The crime scene had been taped off and the troopers had been generous in the proportions of the perimeter, which covered almost the entire parking lot and building.

Chief of Police Bob Johnson was standing in the parking lot talking to one of the troopers and another man who was wearing tan slacks and a dark blue knit top. Jack assumed this would be the state police detective in charge. After they showed their credentials to the trooper who guarded the scene entrance, the yellow tape was lifted and they were directed to a parking spot inside the perimeter. The trooper who let them in got on his cell phone and Jack saw the plainclothes guy answer his phone.

"We've been made, pod'na," Liddell said, also noticing this exchange between troopers.

"I thought troopers were like an ant colony and didn't need telephones." Jack said, and Tunney chuckled.

"No jokes around these guys," Tunney remarked. "I've dealt with them a few times in the past and if you think the FBI doesn't have a sense of humor . . ." He left the rest unsaid.

Jack wanted to assure him that they had dealt with Illinois before, but then he remembered that Liddell could use the extra warning. In the past, Liddell had given his best lines to the troopers and no one had even cracked a smile.

The plainclothes guy saw them approaching and looked at them suspiciously. Agent Tunney walked up to the man, and instead of showing his FBI credentials, he extended a hand and said, "Roger. It's been a long time."

The state trooper took the proffered hand and smiled. "Hi, Frank. What brings you out in the sticks?"

Illinois State Police Detective Roger Zimmer was a sturdy man of average size with dark hair and piercing black eyes. Jack guessed his age as being close to his own. It was easy for Jack to imagine himself on the other side of this equation—being the lead detective on a murder case, with two out-of-town detectives and an FBI profiler falling into his lap. He would not be happy.

"I appreciate you allowing us to be here," Jack said, shaking hands with Zimmer.

"Are you kidding? I've heard good things about you two." He nodded toward Jack and Liddell. "And this guy here"— he put a hand on Tunney's arm—"is the best there is at crime scenes."

Tunney looked like he was going to blush. "You give me way too much credit, but I'll take the compliment and return one of my own. I'm glad that Roger is the one working this case. He's like you, Jack. Bites down on a case and won't let go."

Jack and Roger eyed each other. It felt like two alpha dogs meeting and deciding without bloodshed how to divide the spoils. *Grrrr!*

"My guys will be done taking the preliminary photos in a

few minutes and I'll take you through the scene," Detective Zimmer said.

Chief Johnson came up and said, "Don't mind me. I'll just stick my thumb up my ass and pretend I'm Little Jack Horner."

Agent Tunney laughed and reached out a hand. "I'm Frank Tunney," he said to the chief of the Shawneetown Police Department.

"Bob Johnson," the chief said, feeling that the circle of stars on his shirt collar was enough to introduce him as the chief of police, and he'd known this guy was FBI before he got two steps from the car he'd come in.

Zimmer looked at the chief and said, "Sorry, Chief. You don't need an invite from me because this is your jurisdiction. I have to commend you and your lieutenant for the work you did before we got here to help you."

Chief Johnson hitched his gun belt up and looked up toward the second-floor apartment where two bodies lay butchered. Truth was he was glad to be shed of this damned problem, and the state police were welcome to take the case.

"Well, I been up there once already so I don't need to crowd you guys, but I'd like to hear the FBI's take on the scene when you get done up there. You too, Murphy. I'd like to know if this is the same guy that done Cordelia."

Jack nodded understanding. A state trooper at the foot of the stairway yelled at Zimmer, "You ready to go through the scene, Roger?"

Zimmer looked at the group of lawmen and said, "Let's do it."

Arnold typed the last few words in the copy and sent the electronic file to his editor. JJ had really come through. This one had front page all over it.

In less than a minute his phone rang on his desk.

"Arnold Byrum, *Evansville Courier* newsroom," he said into the phone.

"Get in here," Robertson's voice blared from the phone receiver and the line went dead.

Arnold's heart skipped a beat. *Now what's the matter?* he thought, and got up from his desk. He trudged down the empty hallway to the editor's office and was about to knock when the door was yanked open.

"You have a solid source on this, Arnold?" Robertson asked. His face looked pale and shiny and he seemed to be having trouble getting his breath.

"Yes, sir," Arnold answered. "Someone at the scene." He didn't want to give up JJ's name if he didn't have to.

"Well, damn!" Robertson said, and the door slammed in Arnold's face. From the other side of the door he could hear the editor barking orders into his phone, ordering an extra run on production. He heard the words "special edition" and "priority," and then he went back to his own desk to wait for more orders. A part of him was excited, but the other part was frightened. He was in over his head. He'd been doing all this to get the attention of a woman who would never notice him. He would always be an office joke.

Then he cheered. He would have a bestseller when the book was finished. The story of a serial killer as told by the serial killer himself. How could it fail?

CHAPTER SIXTY-FIVE

The killer was listening to the police scanner he had se-creted in his SUV. A few modifications allowed him to hear the side channels as well as the main one. The side channels were the ones that had all the really important information. They were where the cops felt comfortable saying things they didn't want the general public or the news media to pick up. One thing he'd heard had made him angry and afraid at the same time. Agent Frank Tunney was in town. That was bad news.

Tunney was a serial-killer hunter. One of the best in the world. Tunney had been after him for several years now. This was the first time they'd been in the same state, much less the same city, at the same time. Being this close to the man made him uneasy, but at the same time it was exhilarating. Maybe this was his chance to stop the man from pursuing him. Maybe "The Cleaver" would pay a visit to Agent Frank Tunney.

If he left town now, Tunney was bound to be suspicious. He wasn't sure how Tunney had found out about the killings in Evansville, but then, his giving the stories to that little simpleton at the newspaper was like sending Tunney an invi-tation. He wondered if that wasn't what he subconsciously wanted. A showdown. Tunney's brain against Cody's bone axe.

He wiped some spots of blood from the bone axe and dipped it again in the mixture of bleach and peroxide he had prepared in a plastic bucket and thought about the night he'd found his mother.

She had looked at him in horror as he stood face-to-face with her inside her garage. *Horror, not recognition*, he thought. Even when he told her who he was she didn't seem to comprehend. All she did was whimper and stare at the axe in his hand.

He had dreamed of the day he would find her and she would cry and tell him how sorry she was that she had abandoned him. She would try to give him excuses. Try to make him understand why she had left him behind. But in the end it all came down to the same scenario. The axe would kill her just like it had killed his father. The axe had the power of life or death. It always chose death.

Those it killed had deserved it. His mother had deserved it. His father had deserved it. But Cordelia was different. She shouldn't have had to die.

If she had given him time to think none of this would have happened. But, after it was over, after he had killed her, he realized that it was the way it had to be. He had to wipe out the entire bloodline.

Nothing for it now, except to keep going. Move the pace up a bit. Give them less time to investigate, thus giving himself more time to plan how and when and where he would put an end to Frank Tunney and Jack Murphy.

He wiped the axe dry and wrapped it in a lightly oiled cloth before putting it in the canvas bag. It was time to go see the lawyer.

There was little room inside Samuels's apartment even when it wasn't littered with the butchered remains of two bodies. Chief Johnson rubbed at his neck and looked pallid.

"I think I'll wait outside," he said and left the room.

"He doesn't look good," Zimmer said.

Jack nodded toward the body of Jon Samuels. "He looks better than Samuels."

"Let's get out of here," Liddell said. "I think we're in the way." The three lawmen exited the apartment, stood outside the doorway, and watched the crime scene techs work their magic.

"The chief said his office received an anonymous call of a disturbance out here. The call came into their dispatch at three-oh-four this morning. The caller disconnected before the dispatcher could get any further information. I've spoken to the dispatcher, and all she could tell me was that it was a man's voice. They don't have a recorded telephone line because the city council hasn't approved funding," Trooper Zimmer explained.

They were all aware of how even the bigger departments were being killed by budget crunches. The wonder was that a town this small still had a working police department.

"Anyway," Zimmer continued, "Chief Johnson tried to call Lieutenant Johnson to make the run but couldn't reach him. So he got dressed and came out here himself." He looked at Jack and said in a low tone, "Apparently the chief has had some personal issues with one of the deceased men. Is that right?"

"He's homophobic, if that's what you're asking," Liddell answered for Jack. "But I don't think you are looking at the chief for this, are you?"

Zimmer smiled. "No. I don't think he did this. But it may color some of his information about the deceased."

Liddell said, "Looks like someone turned the place upside down. We didn't leave it like this when we served the search warrant."

"The beds have been stripped, mattresses upturned, curtains pulled all the way down, and even the front cover of the a/c unit was kicked in and broken," Tunney observed.

"Temper tantrum? Or were they looking for something?" Liddell ventured.

Jack thought it looked more like someone was searching and got angry when he didn't find what he wanted. Signs of unleashed anger were everywhere, including the overkill committed on the bodies.

"Signs of control and loss of it," Jack said. "What do you say, Agent Tunney? Organized or disorganized killer? Or both?"

Tunney shrugged and said, "I'm going to check on the chief." He walked off the porch and down the stairs to where Chief Johnson was leaning against one of the cars.

"That's it?" Detective Zimmer asked.

Jack shrugged. He couldn't answer for Agent Tunney, but he had no doubt that this killing and the previous ones were connected. Looking at the faceless skull that had once been the smiling face of Jonathan Samuels told him everything he really needed to know. Another thought struck him.

"Where's the dog?" Jack asked.

"Dog?" Zimmer repeated.

"Yeah," Jack said. "Samuels had a dog. Did anyone find it?"

The same crime scene tech who had given them the short tour through the crime scene butted in. "I took the dog outside when we got here." He held out his arm and showed them a few small tears in his white Tyvek coveralls. "It was crouched on the floor between the guy on the couch and the one on the floor and growling. It looked hurt, and there was blood around its mouth, but I didn't see any bite marks on these two bodies. Damn thing bit me when I took it outside."

Jack and Detective Zimmer exchanged a look. Jack asked, "Where's the dog now?"

CHAPTER SIXTY-SIX

As soon as the three detectives stepped outside they heard a commotion brewing near the side of the building. Jack ran down the steps, taking them two and three at a time. When he hit the bottom he saw that Chief Johnson had his pistol out of its holster and was arguing with one of the uniformed state troopers.

Jack approached the altercation and could hear the trooper warning the chief.

"Listen, Chief, I know you have some jurisdiction here, but you have no right to shoot an animal inside this crime scene. Put your gun away, sir."

Chief Johnson's face was full of fire.

"I'll tell you what, son," Johnson said. "I was a cop when the best part of you ran down your momma's leg. This is my crime scene. My city. You are here to assist me. Not the other way around. You understand that, or did you screw your hat on too tight, son?"

The trooper's face was getting red as well when Jack stepped between the men.

"The dog is part of the crime scene, Chief Johnson," Jack said in a calm voice.

"You stay outta this," the chief yelled, and tried once

again to point his pistol at the cowering dog that was partially hidden by the trooper's legs. It was giving a low menacing growl, but Jack could tell the animal was in pain, and
there was blood around its snout.

"Look there, Chief," Jack said. "It's got blood on it. That
blood could be from the killer. The dog might have bitten
him."

"Well," Johnson said, lowering the barrel of the gun
slightly, then raising it again. "All the more reason to put the
mangy mutt down. Easier to get blood samples that way."

Jack got close to the chief's ear and grabbed the hand that
held the weapon, pushing the barrel toward the ground. "If
you so much as touch that dog I'll take your head off," Jack
hissed.

The men locked eyes long enough for Chief Johnson to
realize that Murphy was serious. As he looked up he saw
that other big Evansville detective—the one they called the
Cajun—striding toward him with a determined look on his
face.

"Well, shit!" Chief Johnson said, putting his gun back in
his holster and walking away. "Get that dog out of here."

The trooper gave Jack a grateful smile, then looked embarrassed. "Couldn't let that old redneck shoot the dog, sir,"
he explained. "I got a dog at home and my kids think it's one
of us."

"You did the right thing," Jack assured him.

The dog tried to stand and gave a yelp, sitting back down
on the gravel. Then it looked toward the entrance of the drive
and howled loudly.

The men looked that direction and saw that a Channel Six
news van with an antennae tower partially raised was parked
at the mouth of the drive and a cameraman was busy filming
them.

The trooper straightened his hat and tie and wiped his

shiny shoes on the back legs of his trousers. The guy wasn't old enough to realize that the news media was no one's friend.

Jack recognized Claudine Setera standing off to the side taking notes. The Illinois troopers were standing back as if a goddess had descended from heaven. Jack knew that it was more likely an angel of death straight from hell. But it wasn't his crime scene and he couldn't tell the Illinois cops how to do their jobs. He noticed Lieutenant JJ Johnson lurking on the other side of the news van, checking his teeth out in the back window and running a hand over his shaved head.

Detective Zimmer had been standing on the porch watching the events in the parking lot. When he saw Claudine Setera spot Jack and head in his direction, he hurried down the steps to try and head her off. She was on a collision course with Jack Murphy.

"You really think the dog has DNA from the killer?" the young trooper asked.

Jack said, "Not really. But I wasn't going to stand around and watch that asshole kill it. And speaking of assholes . . ." Jack said, watching Claudine Setera coming his way.

"Be nice, Jack," Liddell cautioned. Claudine Setera walked up to them.

"No comment," Jack said, beating her to the punch.

"I haven't asked a question yet, Detective Murphy," she said in her perfect television-mode diction.

"And you won't be asking Detective Murphy any questions about my crime scene, Miss Setera," Zimmer said from behind her.

She turned in surprise and looked him up and down before putting a hand out. "Claudine Setera, Channel Six news, Evansville," she said.

Detective Zimmer took her hand and said, "Illinois State Police, Miss Setera. I'm in charge of this scene, so I'd appreciate it if you would direct any questions to me. Not that I will be able to answer all of them, but I'll tell you what I can."

Jack was relieved, but before he could extricate himself, Claudine leaned down and patted the dog on the head.

"What a . . . cute . . . doggy," she said. To everyone's surprise the dog licked her hand and allowed her to rub its ears.

Jack looked across the lot to see Chief Johnson coming their way. *Not going to miss his Kodak moment*, Jack thought. Seeing a way to mend fences, he said for the benefit of the chief, "And Chief Johnson here pointed out to us that the dog should be taken somewhere to be examined to see if there might be evidence present that would be instrumental in identifying the perpetrator here. I was just about to take the dog to get examined."

Chief Johnson's mouth tightened until Setera looked up at him and smiled, saying "You're a real humanitarian, Chief. A lot of lesser men would have tried to put the dog down."

Johnson wasn't sure if she was having him on, but he was a politician at heart and knew how to turn the events to his benefit. "I agreed to let Detective Murphy take the animal, and I hope that he will also take it to a veterinarian to be sure it's not injured too badly." Now he smiled at Jack, teeth gleaming like a shark.

Jack could sense that Claudine had seen the entire incident and knew that the chief was trying to kill the dog. She had to also know there was no way the dog would produce any evidence or the Illinois State Police wouldn't let Evansville detectives take the dog out of their jurisdiction. The fact that she'd kept her yap shut and turned the tables on the chief gave her a couple of points.

"You're a nice guy, Chief. Not the kind who would leave a lady stranded in a parking lot of a morgue in the middle of the night," she added.

Scratch the points, bitch, Jack thought.

Zimmer led Setera toward her news van, where they could get their thirty seconds of film for the afternoon news spot, leaving Jack and the others to make their getaway.

Chief Johnson spat on the gravel near the dog and said, "This don't change nothing, Murphy." As he stomped away Jack could hear him mumbling to himself, and he wondered what would become of JJ once the news media had vacated the scene. Surely Chief Johnson had to know that it was his idiot nephew who had brought the news media to the feast.

The trooper watched Claudine Setera's every move. Without taking his eyes from her, he said to Jack, "You really gonna take that mutt to a vet?"

Jack looked at the dog and she bared her teeth at him. "Anybody got a muzzle?" Jack said.

Liddell laughed. "You gonna put it on Setera or yourself?"

Jack didn't feel like smiling. He'd put his foot in his mouth and now he was stuck with a dog who kept looking at him like he was a steak.

"You're not as tough as you want people to think, Murphy," the trooper said.

"He's just a cuddly teddy bear," Liddell added. "So. What are we going to do with the dog?" Liddell asked. "I heard the Chief tell you to get it out of here or he'd shoot it."

Jack looked at Liddell and grinned.

"You aren't putting that mangy injured animal in my clean car!" Liddell said.

Twenty minutes later they were going over the top of the big hill on Big Hill Road and heading back toward Evansville. Liddell was driving, Tunney in front, leaving Jack and the dog in the backseat in an uneasy truce. If Jack even shifted in his seat the dog would emit a menacing growl and bare her teeth.

"Hey, Jack. Don't you always say that no good deed will go unpunished?"

"It's not a good deed, Bigfoot. The dog might hold a clue to the killer's identity," Jack responded, and looked at the dog, who was glaring at Jack suspiciously.

"What are you going to do with that animal, Jack? We're in the middle of a murder case," Liddell reminded him.

"I'm going to put it in a suit and make it my new partner if you don't stuff a sock in it."

"Touchy, touchy," Liddell said. "Didn't Samuels say the dog hated straight men?"

Jack didn't respond. He was just thinking the same thing. And thinking how stupid he was for getting involved in this. He was just about ready to tell Liddell to pull over where they could turn the dog loose when Tunney, who until now had been silent, seemed to sense his thoughts once again and said, "Probably turning it loose out here by one of these farms would be the kindest thing to do."

What the hell would the FBI know? Jack thought. "I'm going to take it to a vet and then I'm keeping it."

The car swerved across the center line as Liddell twisted in the front seat. "You're going to do what? You can't take care of a dog, pod'na."

"Why not?" Jack said.

Liddell straightened the car out and slowed down. "Well, 'cause you live by yourself and you're never home and the dog would destroy your cabin, for starters. And you barely remember to feed yourself, much less give the dog that type of care."

"And it hates you," Tunney added.

Jack ignored Tunney's remark. "I don't live by myself all the time. Susan's there a lot, and the dog likes women."

"Yeah, well, have you asked Susan if you can have a pet?"

Liddell retorted. "And did I mention that we're in the middle of several homicide investigations and you won't be home much?"

"I think, Jack, that you are attaching yourself to the dog as a way to gain some control over these cases," Tunney said. "It's not unusual for someone, especially someone such as yourself who is used to being in control, to try and regain a toehold."

"Please, Agent Tunney. Save your profile for the killer."

"He's right, Jack. The last thing in the world you need is a pet," Liddell said.

Jack reached out a hand, palm up, toward the dog, and had to pull back before he lost some fingers. The snap of the dog's jaws was audible and Liddell said from the front of the car, "Told you so."

"Listen," Jack said starting to get angry. "This dog was the only friend that Jon Samuels had in his life, and it had enough guts to attack a serial killer. It deserves something for that. I'm going to make sure it gets a good home. I'm not keeping it. Okay? So drop it."

"Just a reminder, pod'na," Liddell said. "You had to get Claudine to put the dog in the car. How you planning on getting it out?"

CHAPTER SIXTY-SEVEN

Lenny Bange came awake and shifted his eyes to the red glowing letters of the bedside alarm clock. It was only five-thirty. The alarm was set for six o'clock and he planned on doing some personal errands today. To hell with the office. His secretary could reschedule all of his appointments and he didn't have court. Besides, he needed the day off. The visit from Cubby had unnerved him, and he was still angry over the fleecing he'd taken from the big man. When he'd called Cubby to "take care of his problem" he had agreed on a thousand bucks to just rough the guy up, get any documents, and make sure the blackmailer wouldn't return. But Cubby had taken him for three grand.

He buried his face in his pillow and tried to go back to sleep, but he was angry and a little embarrassed that he'd let Cubby intimidate him. If it had been anyone else, Lenny would have told them to stuff it and taken care of the problem himself. Lenny Bange was a dangerous man in his own right. But he didn't physically rough people up, and in this case he knew that it was physical toughness that was called for. Besides, he didn't have the talent to find the blackmailer. Cubby would easily beat that information out of someone on the list he had provided to the muscle-headed jerk. That was what Cubby was good at.

He rolled over to get up and felt a weight next to him as if someone had just sat on the edge of the bed.

"What the hell?" Lenny said and started to get out of bed when something hard struck him in the face. He fell back against the headboard, striking his head, and a fist came down hard on his solar plexus, driving the air from his lungs. Another blow landed on his face, and another and another until he was dizzy and feeling nauseous and gagging on his own blood. The beating stopped as quickly as it had started.

The first thought that entered his mind was *Cubby.* But the voice that came out of the dark wasn't Cubby's.

"Lenny Bange. Bange, Bange, Bange," the man's voice said, and then he chuckled.

"Who are you?" Lenny heard himself saying though split lips. His voice was so weak he barely recognized it as his own.

"Who am I?" the voice asked.

Lenny felt the man's weight lift from the mattress next to him. His head spun and he thought he was going to black out. Then something moved in the shadow in the corner of the room and a man wearing dark clothing materialized. "I'm death, Lenny."

Lenny felt a gloved hand crush his mouth and nose. He struggled to free his face from the man's grip, but the hand was too strong. A blow landed on his groin, sending lightning bolts of pain throughout his body and taking the remaining air from his lungs.

The worst of the pain subsided, and Lenny sucked in huge gulps of air before another blow landed across the side of his face and another fist hammered into his chest. Lights danced behind the attorney's eyes. He felt sure he would pass out this time, but the man's face leaned close to his ear and a whispering voice warned him, "Don't scream. And . . ." The man paused long enough to grip Lenny's face again, as if in a vice. "Don't lie to me. Nod yes if you understand, Mr. Bange."

Jack, Liddell, and Frank Tunney decided to go back to the Evansville Police Department and meet with Captain Franklin and Chief Marlin Pope and update them on their trip to Illinois. They had spent the best part of the early morning dealing with Shawneetown's case, and had picked up an injured dog in the process. Now it was nearing seven o'clock. Jack was anxious to get back to headquarters and talk to Garcia to see if she had gleaned any more information. After that he planned to pay another visit to the attorney, Lenny Bange.

As they walked through the back entrance to the detectives' office, Jack saw that his plans might have to be postponed.

"Have you read it yet?" one of the detectives said to Jack and handed him the front page of the newspaper.

Liddell and Agent Tunney leaned close to Jack to see the headlines. SERIAL-KILLER HUNTER IN EVANSVILLE: NATIONWIDE MANHUNT BEGINS. Jack looked at the byline. "Arnold Byrum again," he said out loud. "How is he getting this stuff?"

Liddell, who had been reading further down the page, said, "He even has the information from Shawneetown. We just got back and haven't told anyone yet."

"I think your chief might be upset to see all this before we've talked to him," Tunney added.

Jack folded the paper tightly in his fist. "Shit!"

Captain Franklin came up in the hallway and motioned for them to follow him. He headed for the front of the building where the chief of police's complex was located.

"Think we'll get a spanking?" Liddell whispered to Jack.

"You'd like it," Jack said.

"Nothing wrong with a little foreplay," Agent Tunney added.

"Quit it," Liddell said. "You're going to make me like you."

"I already like him," Jack said as they followed Captain Franklin through the locked doors that led into the main public corridor of the police department. Jack noticed the usual crowd of discontented citizens mixed in with law clerks and insurance agents who regularly visited the police department records section.

"Excuse me," a voice came from the hallway that led from the police station to the Civic Center Complex.

Liddell turned and put a hand on Jack's shoulder just as bright lights came on from the direction of the voice. As they turned they were staring into a bright light of the Channel Six cameraman. Next to him was anchorman Blake James.

Liddell turned his back to James and looked at Jack, saying, "We should have brought the dog in with us." Jack tried to hide a smile.

Captain Franklin stepped forward, blocking the camera view of Agent Tunney, and said, "I'm sorry, Mr. James, but we are late for a meeting." Franklin motioned for the others to continue to the chief's office while he stayed behind and dealt with the media.

Jack was more than happy to get out of there, but Agent Tunney seemed hesitant. "We have to go, Agent Tunney," he said and took the man's arm.

They entered the chief's complex waiting room and were buzzed through a connecting door to the inner sanctum. Chief Marlin Pope was holding a copy of the morning newspaper.

"Looks like you're getting that spanking after all, Bigfoot," Jack said to Liddell, but no one smiled.

"Why me? Why not you?" Liddell asked.

Jack shrugged. "Bigger butt, bigger target."

CHAPTER SIXTY-EIGHT

Cody Morse stood in the front lobby of the Civic Center, watching people come and go through metal detectors, and wondered how America had become so screwed up. What did it say for the people of a small town in the Midwest that they had to be so security conscious that they couldn't even pay their water bills or property taxes without having to be subjected to pat-downs and screening by law enforcement?

I've killed more people than they could ever imagine, and yet I can come and go as I please. He looked at the archway of the metal detector and watched as sheriff's deputies made people empty their pockets before allowing them to come inside. A few moments earlier someone had tried to bring a knife inside and it had caused quite a stir. The offender was a construction worker who routinely carried a Buck knife on his belt. It was almost comical seeing the looks on faces as the poor guy was taken aside and searched. *What would they think if I brought my axe?* he wondered.

And now there was something else going on in the police chief's complex, with reporters roaming the halls, foraging for tidbits and scraps of information to feed to their audiences. They didn't know that the star of all this excitement was within an arm's length of most of them. He was just another face in the crowd.

Lenny Bange had proved to be useless. No matter how much skin Cody sliced away with the axe, the man just kept crying and denying that he knew who it was that was calling him. But, Lenny had clarified a few things. Cordelia was a call girl. She was working for Lenny. And she had apparently kept some kind of diary of all the clients and had been threatening Lenny with this before her death. He had also admitted to hiring the hapless clown from Las Vegas, Cubby Crispino, to do some dirty work for him.

He smiled at the memory of Lenny's moaning when he learned of Cubby's fate. It was obvious that he thought Cubby was a tough guy. *I wonder how I compared?*

But eventually he had run out of things to cut off Lenny Bange, and Lenny had gone past his expiration date. Cody still didn't have a clue who the blackmailer was. He didn't know where the diary was. And he had to find that diary. His name was in it. If the police found it first it would raise all kinds of red flags. *That won't do at all.*

Then he had another thought. Arnold had proved very helpful so far in keeping the police in a defensive position. Maybe it was time to move Arnold to a new position on the chessboard. He remembered visiting an antique store in New Harmony, about twenty minutes' drive from Evansville. In that store he had found the general junk that people thought of as antiques. But he had also found a section of the store where old tools were displayed. One of these tools was a small hand axe that was smaller than the one he used, but still would suffice for what he had in mind.

If he left now, he could make it to New Harmony and get back before his absence was noticed. Then he would stop by Arnold's house again. This would be the third time he had been inside Arnold's house without anyone being the wiser. He had to keep an eye on the progress of Arnold's book.

* * *

Missing persons detective Larry Jansen was thinking the same thing as the chief of police. Where in the hell was Arnold getting all this stuff from? It pissed him off. Mostly because Larry was normally in possession of all the information. And he liked being the one who dispensed that information for a price. He didn't like the idea of someone invading his turf.

He had been hiding most of the morning, but he knew he couldn't dodge the chief for much longer. His stint in the hospital hadn't been long enough and when he'd been released the chief had Internal Affairs waiting at his home. There had been questions. Lots of questions. And now this. He remembered an old saying that goes, "Where there's smoke, there's fire." He knew they suspected him of all of these leaks, and what really pissed him off was that for once in his life he was innocent. *Well, mostly innocent,* he thought.

CHAPTER SIXTY-NINE

Chief Marlin Pope sat at the head of the conference table with the newspaper open in front of him. His face was a mask of calm, but Jack knew that inside the man was a volcano of emotion just waiting to bury the person responsible for the leaks in a mountain of choking ash.

"Agent Tunney, I want to apologize for the shortsightedness of some of my men," Pope said. "We know who our leak to the news media is and will have this problem corrected shortly."

Tunney waved the apology away. "Chief, I'm used to this. Believe me, you have not seen 'leakage' yet. I could tell you stories . . ." he began, but then changed directions. "I still have to file a report, but I think I can promise you the full co-operation of the FBI on these cases."

Liddell looked at him and had a sudden insight. "Your boss doesn't know you're here, does he?"

Tunney stared at Liddell, his face giving nothing away, before he answered, "No. He doesn't."

Captain Franklin and the chief turned toward the profiler. He looked sheepish and continued, "Frankly, when I told my boss that I suspected the killings here were the work of The Cleaver, he wasn't very supportive."

Jack watched Tunney with renewed respect. Frank Tunney was a rebel, like him. But the thought of a bunch of suits mixing it up in his investigation didn't make him feel more confident that they would solve these slayings.

"Some psycho killed one of my officers," Chief Pope said. "Your assistance would be greatly appreciated. What can you tell me about the Shawneetown case?"

For the next fifteen minutes Jack filled the chief and captain in on the details from Shawneetown, only leaving out the full-blown confrontation with Chief Johnson over the dog. When he was finished he looked at Liddell and Tunney for any additions or corrections to his account.

Liddell said, "I'd like to hear Agent Tunney's take on this one." And all attention was focused on Agent Tunney, who had been listening intently, arms folded across his chest.

Tunney cleared his throat and said, "Well, let me first say that these killings—with the exception of Jon Samuels in Shawneetown—have been different in several ways from other killings that we have attributed to The Cleaver."

"Do you think Jon Samuels matches the pattern?" Captain Franklin interrupted.

Tunney nodded. "Samuels is right for this killer." He stood and paced behind the seated men. "The other man in Samuels's apartment was beheaded and his hands and head were removed from the scene. That's a troubling deviation from the pattern, but it doesn't mean it wasn't done by our killer."

Tunney turned his attention on Marlin Pope. "I don't know how much you have been told about this killer, Chief, so I'll go back to the beginning. We first noticed the pattern of murders when we received a request from a small West Virginia town for identification of a body found in a wooded area. We had that police department enter the victim information and partial case information into VICAP"—he was referring to the Violent Offender Criminal Apprehension Program—"and received a hit with three other entries. One of those cases was in Pennsylvania, the other two were in California." He waited a beat to let this sink in.

"We now have twenty-four murders in eight states over a ten-year period. This isn't including the murders here yet. The last murders that we know of were in Atlanta, Georgia, and that was over two years ago. Nothing until your stories showed up on my Internet newsfeeds. If he's been other places we haven't received word yet. But the time interval between killings was increasing until Atlanta. There are usually two to three murders in each state. If The Cleaver is responsible for the killings here—and he is—then he is on a rampage.

"In each case he has carefully chosen his victim, maybe watched them for some time, and then killed them at home in the kitchen."

Captain Franklin interrupted again. "But you said the first case you had was a body found in a wooded area?"

"We were concerned about that too, but found that the victim had been attacked in her home—in the kitchen—but had managed to get out of the house and flee. Apparently the killer caught up to her in the wooded area and finished the job," Tunney explained.

"In each of these cases the victims' faces were sheared off with a sharp metal instrument that left traces of iron behind in the wounds. The faces were the only things taken from the scenes. The FBI lab thinks the weapon he uses is a handmade bone axe, the type that was once used to slaughter cattle and cut through bones. It's heavy enough to cleave through skulls, which is the general method of causing death in each case. He kills them with a blow to the head, then cuts their faces off. Sometimes he cuts them other places as well, but only takes the faces."

The men looked at each other, trying to find a way to fit this in with what they knew of the Evansville and Shawneetown cases. Liddell was the first to put words to his thoughts.

"I'm not a psychologist or whatever, but it seems to me that our murders have involved a lot of overkill. And obviously he didn't want us to identify the headless, handless guy in Jon Samuels's apartment."

"I would have to agree with Liddell," Chief Pope said.

Tunney sat back down and clasped his hands on top of the table. "I have to admit that his actions here are confusing. The Brenda Lincoln case is the only tie-in with our set of murders, but if he killed Ms. Lincoln he is our killer, too. And from other evidence you have, I guess you have firmly tied him to your other cases. I would like to examine those cases before I give you a firm decision, okay, Chief?"

Chief Pope nodded at Captain Franklin. Franklin then said, "I'll make sure you have everything you need, Agent Tunney."

Tunney's face took on a look of great concern. "The killer is evolving, gentlemen," he said. "I don't know why. But I can guarantee you he is not finished killing. He's just getting started."

"Jack?" Chief Pope asked. "Do you have a plan?"

Jack wanted to say that his plan was to go home and slog down a half dozen cans of Guinness, and sit in his hot tub until his skin grew scales, but he said, "I have a dog to see to, sir."

Chief Pope chuckled. "You have a dog?"

"Yeah, you should have seen him go all Rambo when Chief Johnson tried to shoot the dog," Liddell said, then saw the look Jack was giving him. "I mean, yeah, Jack brought Jon Samuels's dog back with him. They were going to put it down."

Chief Pope said, "Do I want to know any of this?"

"No, you don't, sir," Jack replied and stared at Liddell.

"Anything else, gentlemen?" Pope asked.

No one spoke.

"I'll let you get on with it then," Pope said. "And we will keep you involved as much as you like, Agent Tunney."

The chief and Agent Tunney shook hands, and Captain Franklin stayed behind when the three, Tunney, Liddell, and Jack, headed back to the war room.

"I wonder what kind of high-level things they're discussing?" Liddell quipped.

Tunney shook his head. "Maybe their golf plans?" he suggested.

CHAPTER SEVENTY

The dog was still in Liddell's car. With keys in hand, Jack exited the back doors of the detective's office. The plan was to have the dog examined by a vet, but now that he thought of it, maybe he should have someone from crime scene on hand to collect evidence. He had only mentioned the possibility of DNA to get Chief Johnson to let the dog live, but the more he thought of it on the way to Evansville, the more it sounded plausible that the dog may have bitten the killer.

He thumbed his cell phone to the listing for Sergeant Tony Walker.

Walker answered on the first ring. "Where do you want me to meet you?" Walker said before Jack could say anything.

"What makes you think I want you to meet me?" Jack asked.

"Well, because you have a dog that you took from the crime scene in Shawneetown, and I am surmising you want me to be present while you have a vet examine the dog."

"Sherlock Holmes has nothing on you," Jack said. "Okay, I'm going to Branson's Vet Clinic over by Fendrich Golf Course. You know it?"

"I'm close. I'll meet you there," Walker answered, and Jack disconnected.

He took the keys he'd borrowed from Liddell and unlocked the door to Liddell's unmarked car. The dog was spread across the backseat and appeared to be asleep but came alive when the door lock clicked, and was now emitting a menacing growl.

"What was I thinking?" Jack said out loud. But *in for a penny, in for a pound,* as his father used to say. He opened the door and climbed into the driver's seat. By the time he straightened up from putting the keys in the ignition, he could feel a warm breath beside his right ear.

"Sit!" he ordered, and to his surprise the dog obeyed. He risked a glance back and saw the dog sitting behind him. Her nose was covered with something crusty and dark, and her eyes looked clouded and unfocused. He felt a stab of pity for the poor animal, knowing she must have tried to defend her master.

"Let's get you to the vet and see what he thinks," he said to the dog, and looking in the rearview mirror saw the dog's ears lift and her head cock to the side. "I'm not keeping you so don't start acting cute," he added. The dog lay down and let out a soft yelp.

Jack reversed out of the parking spot and turned onto Sycamore Street heading south to the Lloyd Expressway. He pulled his cell phone out again and found the listing for Branson's Veterinary Clinic.

A pleasant female voice answered. "Branson's Clinic, Julie speaking."

Jack asked for Brent. He and Brent Branson had known each other since high school. Where Branson was a straight-A student, Jack was always in some kind of trouble. He always knew that Branson would make something of himself. Just as he knew that he would become a cop someday, like his father. In high school Jack had always been the jock, whereas Branson had been a skinny six-foot teen with a shock of unruly red hair. After high school Branson had gone on to Purdue to become a veterinarian. When he came home he had grown another inch and put on about a hundred pounds of pure muscle. *Must've been something in the water at Purdue,* Jack thought as he waited for his friend to come on the line.

"No. I don't want to buy any policeman's balls tickets," Branson's voice came over the phone.

Jack chuckled. "You know policemen don't have balls," he responded as he was supposed to.

"Glad to hear you admit it, buddy," Branson said.

"You coming here?"

"I'll be there in just a couple of minutes. I have an animal I need you to look at."

"Dead or alive?" Branson said.

Jack looked at the dog, who had raised her head and bared her teeth at him. "That's up to the dog," he said, and heard Branson chuckling.

He broke the connection and concentrated on his driving. Only a mile or so to the vet's office, but he felt he needed to hurry. The killer wasn't on a clock. He stepped down hard on the gas.

Larry Jansen left his back door and walked three blocks to where he had parked his unmarked car. The Internal Affairs sergeant had been knocking on his door about every half hour this morning. *Bastard,* he thought. *Who would work for IA?*

He had never known Kooky Kuhlenschmidt, but the fact that one of their own had been killed changed things. Jansen knew the department would pull out all the stops now, and that also meant that they would be coming after him. He knew his own reputation as a news snitch, and that was not what you wanted to be at this particular juncture.

Why did he have to go and get himself killed? Jansen thought.

He hurried down the alley and then down a cross alley to the next block. The reporter's house was on the other side of town, but he could make it if he stayed off the major thoroughfares and away from the convenience stores and hamburger joints where cops tended to hang out.

Time to pay Arnold a visit.

CHAPTER SEVENTY-ONE

"Need some help with the dog?" Walker said. He had come up beside Jack's car door stealthily. The dog twisted toward him and tried to bark but yelped in pain.

Jack rolled his window down, and said, "Could you go in and see if one of the girls will come out and get the dog?" Walker looked at him questioningly, and Jack added, "The dog hates straight men."

Walker grinned and headed toward the gray wood-sided structure that used to be a two-story home and was now the Branson Veterinary Clinic. As he reached the front door, it opened and one of the doctor's assistants named Julie came out with a leash.

"Thought you might need this, Jack," she said and opened the back door of his car.

The dog began a keening noise and put her shaggy head down between her paws, dark eyes locked on Julie.

"Oh, you poor baby," she said, and connected the leash to the dog's collar. She felt around the collar and located the tags. Reading the tags she said, "Cinderella. That's your name, isn't it, sweetie pie?"

The dog came alive at the sound of her name and crawled

across the backseat toward Julie. "Come on, Cinderella," Julie coaxed, and helped the dog out onto the ground.

"The doctor will fix you up, baby," she cooed, and led the limping dog across the lot toward the front doors.

Jack got out of the car and stood with Walker, admiring the ease with which Julie had taken control.

"She's single," Walker said.

Jack, who was tired of his friends trying to fix him up, said, "Who, Julie or Cinderella?"

"C'mon, Jack. She's cute, and she likes you."

Jack shut his door and turned his back on Walker, saying, "Get your kit."

Inside the building, the men were directed to a treatment room, where Brent Branson was examining Cinderella.

"What'd you do to this dog?" Branson said to Jack.

"I didn't do anything."

"Well, she probably has some broken ribs and has a small cut on her head," Branson said, and he sounded a little testy.

Before Jack could protest further, Walker stepped in with his camera. "Mind if I get a few shots of the cut?"

Branson held the dog's head while Julie stroked its back, and Walker snapped several digital close-ups of the wound. He then handed Branson some collection swabs and envelopes and Branson collected blood and hair samples from the area of the wound and more from the muzzle.

"Looking for DNA?" Branson asked.

"Fingers crossed," Walker said.

Cinderella looked at Jack and bared her teeth.

"Why am I the only one she doesn't like?" Jack said, noticing the dog hadn't growled at either Brent or Walker.

"Dogs have a keen sense of goodness," Walker offered.

"And a keen sense of smell," Brent added.

"Why do I bother?" Jack said and sat on the only chair in the small examining room.

* * *

Cody stood in his bathroom, right leg propped on the side of the antique claw-foot tub, and dabbed at the wound on his lower calf—four jagged tears in a pattern about three inches square—that were now bright red with the skin swollen and oozing a reddish fluid. The dog had come out of nowhere and latched on to his leg just as he was raising his axe to finish the job on Jon Samuels.

He'd swung wide and missed the dog's head by less than an inch, and the damn mangy mutt had released his leg and lunged at his nuts. Cody was barely able to turn sideways to avoid being neutered by the beast. He had kicked the dog so hard when he first entered the small apartment he thought it would stay away from him. But the ugly mutt had rallied like an angry hornet and come at him again. He had aimed a kick at the dog's head, but connected with its chest, flipping it into the air. He had swung the axe again, but the dog was too fast.

The bite wounds on his leg didn't hurt until now. *Should have killed the damn dog,* he thought. He poured hydrogen peroxide over the torn skin and watched the liquid turn frothy as it came into contact with his bloody tissue. The sight was fascinating. He had seen a lot of blood over the years, but never his own.

A doctor was out because Murphy might go sniffing around about someone being treated for dog bites and then he would have some explaining to do. He could always drive to another city and go to a MEC Center, pay cash, and make up a name and story to go with it. But right now he had another job to do.

CHAPTER SEVENTY-TWO

Jack talked Branson into putting Cinderella in one of the kennel spaces, but was ticked off that he had to pay for the dog's upkeep. *Twenty dollars a day for a dog that hates me,* he thought as he pulled into the back parking lot of the detectives' squad room. But then, he had also agreed to pay for the dog's medical care, which looked like it was going to be several hundred dollars. Branson said the dog had several broken ribs and would need stitches in the wound on top of her head. He would give Jack some pain pills and antibiotics for Cinderella.

Branson's assistant, Julie, suggested that Jack use chunky peanut butter to hide the pills when he gave them to Cinderella.

He made his way downstairs to the war room and was surprised to see Captain Franklin in the room with Garcia and Liddell.

" 'Bout time you got back," Liddell said.

"Any news with the dog?" Captain Franklin asked.

"There was blood. Walker took some swabbings, but you know how that goes. It could be from Jon Samuels," Jack said. He decided not to tell them that he was having the dog treated by the veterinarian.

"And speaking of blood," Liddell said, and then looked at Garcia. "Go ahead, Angelina. You got the news. You tell him."

"Tell me what?" Jack asked, and Angelina Garcia looked like she was about to burst with excitement.

"We have a DNA match, Jack!" she said.

"Mitochondrial DNA is what gave them the match," Garcia said. "It is a better indicator in females because there are one hundred thousand to one million markers in a woman's egg, where there are only one hundred to one thousand in a man's sperm."

"Let's not get personal," Liddell said.

Garcia ignored his attempt at humor. "Let's put it this way. Sometimes there is not enough of a DNA sample for a comparison, but by looking at only the mitochondrial part of the DNA they can get a maternal match. It basically eliminates the male part of the DNA sample and tests only for the female DNA."

"I'm dying here," Jack said. "What's the punch line? What did you get a match on?"

Garcia took a deep breath before saying, "We have a DNA match from the blood found on Cinderella."

Jack felt a shiver run through him. "So you're saying . . . what?"

"The match was with Brenda Lincoln. Whoever the dog bit is a relative of Brenda's."

Jack got off the phone with Sergeant Walker in CSU and asked Garcia for the file photos of Brenda Lincoln and Cordelia Morse.

"There is a slight resemblance," he said, looking at the two black-and-white photos. "Where's Tunney?"

Liddell spoke up. "He's in the chief's office. He has gotten the go-ahead of the FBI to assist us on this case."

Jack smirked and asked, "So are we going to be submerged in little FBI guys now?"

Liddell laughed. "He promised they would only 'assist' us."

"At least until we solve the case," Garcia said sarcastically, causing both men to look at her. "I mean until you guys solve the case," she added. "Us girls don't count."

Liddell was about to say something, but she beat him to the punch, saying, "And no, it's not my time of month. And yes, Mark and I have a full sex life."

Liddell's mouth clamped shut and Jack laughed.

"It's worth a month's pay to see someone shut him up," Jack said.

"I feel violated," Liddell quipped, and bumped knuckles with Garcia. "You go, girl."

"Let's go see the chief," Captain Franklin suggested.

CHAPTER SEVENTY-THREE

Jansen drove down alleys the last two blocks before reaching Arnold's house. A few minutes ago he'd seen a marked police car, and knew that he was on borrowed time. The chief would have every reason to believe that Jansen was the leak to the news media, and he was probably going to be taking a forced vacation if they caught up to him.

He didn't know what he expected to find at Arnold's, but he knew the reporter was hiding stuff from him. The direct approach hadn't worked, so now it was time to do it his way. A little breaking and entering wasn't against his principles.

He parked in a gravel pull-off in the alley a couple of houses down from Arnold's backyard and reached in the glove box, retrieving the little leather case he kept there. Sticking this in his pocket, he did what he had known so many others shouldn't do. He looked around to be sure no one was watching. The cop in him knew that doing so was tantamount to saying, "Watch this. I'm about to commit a crime."

Satisfied that he wasn't being observed by nosy neighbors, Jansen walked to Arnold's back door. He would have knocked first, but he knew that Arnold's mother was upstairs somewhere—sleeping, he hoped—and he didn't want to get into a shouting match with the old bag. She might call 911 and the shit would really hit the fan. *No, this is a covert operation,* he thought and smiled at the idea. There was something cool about being on the sly.

The back door had the regular locks on it. One on the door handle, and a dead bolt. He prayed Arnold hadn't locked the dead bolt. He pulled the leather case from his pocket and retrieved his lock pick, a plastic card that resembled a credit card, but was more pliable. He had been given the plastic card while he was in the Army. He had been Army CID, counterintelligence, in his younger days. CID Officer Larry Jansen had been a pro with lock picks, but he had found that the plastic card had gotten him through most locked doors.

He slid the plastic edge of the card at an upward angle just below the door handle and was relieved when the door slid open. He stood with his ear to the crack, listening, but the inside of the house was eerily quiet.

Jansen slipped inside, and quietly pulled the door shut behind himself. *What are you hiding, Arnold?* he thought.

Chief Marlin Pope sat on the sill of his office window and rubbed at his forehead. Outside the window people walked with purpose along the wide sidewalks, and across the busy four-lane Martin Luther King Boulevard heading for destinations unknown but seemingly more important than the drama that was playing itself out inside this room. Jack couldn't help but wonder how they could be so impervious to the fact that a serial killer was among them. It could be anyone. The guy in the wild plaid-checkered shorts with the stained and tattered wifebeater. The woman in the gray pleated skirt with matching top and leggings who was gripping her purse so tightly to her chest he hoped there was nothing sharp inside it. Or maybe it was the shriveled homeless creature, sexless and ageless, begging for dimes or dollars, and spitting a viscous black matter into a white Styrofoam cup.

"You think the killer is out there, Jack?" Tunney said.

Jack looked at Tunney and wondered if the man's mind was ever in the off position. Tunney appeared so calm and relaxed, even when he was talking about someone's face being removed with an axe. But Jack could sense the hum of the gears grinding inside the man's mind, could almost see the pulse in his neck. Tunney lived for this. He was always on the scent. *I'm not much different,* he admitted to himself.

"Are you married, Agent Tunney?" Jack asked.

There was a slight tic at the corner of Tunney's eye before he answered. "No," Tunney said.

The two men locked eyes. They both had monsters in the closets. Both had minds hardwired to seek and destroy. Both knew that this life would never be conducive to a lasting relationship, and so they had chosen to be the wolves instead of the sheep. Protecting the flock from predators, but earning a reluctant gratitude that masked fear instead of respect or love. Everyone knew that wolves were only good for one thing. And in that way they both shared something in common with the monsters they hunted.

The Evansville police chief brought the conversation back on track. "The Illinois trooper who's investigating the Samuels case called and said the autopsy is scheduled for this afternoon in Gallatin County," Chief Pope said to those gathered. Liddell was slumped in a large leather chair near the door. Captain Franklin sat near Angelina Garcia in front of the chief's large desk. Jack and Tunney were standing, looking out the window by which the chief still sat.

"Do you want one of us to attend?" Jack asked. He was thinking that it might be a good idea, but he knew that Zimmer was a very competent investigator. Armed with what

Tunney and Jack had provided, Zimmer should be able to handle the autopsy without their presence.

"I need you here, Jack," Franklin said. "From what you said, the Illinois trooper is pretty sharp."

Liddell grinned. "He's a little Jack."

"Okay, I think it's time to get back to work," Pope said, shooing them out.

As they were leaving the chief's outer office his secretary stopped them.

"I have a call for you, Jack," she said and handed the receiver to him.

"Murphy," Jack said. He listened and then handed the receiver back to Jennifer and turned to face Liddell and Tunney.

"What is it, pod'na?" Liddell asked.

"Lenny Bange is dead."

CHAPTER SEVENTY-FOUR

Lenny Bange, like a lot of Americans, lived well above his means. Or at least it appeared so to Jack as he arrived at the crime scene. Johnson Place was an area of Evansville that could have been another part of the country, like maybe the mansions in Santa Monica, or the million-dollar chateaus in Palm Beach. What was missing in acreage was more than made up in the beautiful and expensive materials used to build the massive structures that were considered single-family dwellings in Johnson Place.

Lenny's house sat on a one-hundred-by-one-hundred-foot lot with no grass except a small strip across the front the size of a stripper's panties. Every inch of parking was taken by police emergency and crime scene vehicles. Yellow and black crime scene tape was strung around the periphery. Jack and Liddell ducked under this as they approached Sergeant Walker at the front entrance.

"Notice anything, pod'na?" Liddell said to Jack.

Jack looked around. You didn't have to smell the money to know it was everywhere.

"If we were anywhere else there would be a crowd gathered. I haven't even seen a curtain twitch," Liddell explained.

"Maybe they're all at work," Jack suggested.

"You think these people work?"

"Lenny Bange lived here," Jack pointed out. "He worked."

"He was an attorney, pod'na. That ain't working."

Jack looked around at the drawn curtains of the surrounding houses. "Well, one thing's for sure. We probably won't have any witnesses."

Liddell nodded. "Let's see what Walker has for us," he said.

As they approached the door Jack noticed someone sitting on a small bench, bent over with his head cradled in his hands. A uniformed officer was nearby and said, "Lenny's son."

Jack barely recognized the pale-faced young man whom he had met in the elevator in Lenny Bange's building.

"Manny, right?" Jack asked and extended a hand.

The young man tried to smile, but his lips quivered and he just nodded as tears streamed from his eyes. He buried his face in his hands again and moaned.

"He found the old man . . . I mean Mr. Bange," the uniformed officer explained.

"I'll talk to Manny," Liddell said and took out his notebook.

Jack turned to continue to the house when Manny called out to him.

"You find the monster that did this, Jack," he said through clenched teeth.

"I will," Jack assured him.

"You find him and kill him!" Manny said, and then broke down into sobs.

Walker met Jack and Liddell at the door. He was wearing white cloth booties, blue nylon gloves, and a surgeon's mask pulled down under his chin.

"This is the worst yet," Walker said.

They entered, staying close behind the crime scene sergeant as they were led to a bathroom in the back of the home. They were led through the front foyer, and off to the left, Jack could see a room that must be a library. It held more books than Jack had ever read in his life. All hard-cover. Most leather-bound editions. *Law library at home,* Jack thought.

The living room had an immaculately clean white carpet. Jack noticed that there was very little sign of foot traffic on it. He guessed that what was there had been trampled down by the first-responding officers.

Walker noticed Jack looking at the carpet and said, "I spoke to the officers that arrived first. They came in the front door and walked across this carpet, but they swear there were no footprints in it when they came in. Their impression was that the rug had been vacuumed recently and no one had walked on it."

Jack nodded.

The living room led to a hallway. To the left was a mas-sive dining area with a table larger than the conference table in the chief's complex at police headquarters. To the right was a bathroom. Sergeant Walker stopped and said, "His son found him in here this morning a little after seven o'clock."

Looking through the doorway at the congealing mess that had once been Lenny Bange, Jack understood why Manny had been so upset.

The bathroom was as large as the living room and kitchen of Jack's cabin combined. In one corner was a whirlpool tub that would accommodate two adults. Above the tub was a bank of opaque windows and a shelf full of sex toys. Next to this was a shower stall that was comprised of free-standing glass walls. Jack could see Lenny Bange's body, his back to Jack, propped in a seated position against the glass. The inside of the glass was covered with streaks and smears of something dark.

"The killer finished him off in the shower," Walker said.

Jack and Liddell looked questioningly at him, and Walker continued, "It looks like the initial assault was in the bedroom down the hallway, and he was forced or dragged into the bathroom shower. All the blood is contained inside the shower."

Jack looked back down the hallway, but didn't see any signs of a struggle. Several paintings on the walls depicted colorful outdoor and wildlife scenes. Nothing was askew or on the floor. There were no smears or traces of blood on the walls. At least not that he could see.

"You think he was forced into the shower?" Liddell asked the question that Jack was thinking.

"His pajamas are on the floor of the shower. Looks like they were cut or torn from his body after he was hacked to death," Walker explained.

"Oh," Liddell said. "Continue, oh wise one."

"You won't be talking so cute after you see the body," Walker said.

"Which is when?" Jack asked.

"We've already processed the pathway," Walker said, meaning that they had examined the area that detectives would need to cross to look closer. He led them inside the bathroom and then asked the tech who was still photographing the body to step out.

Jansen crossed the kitchen, stepping lightly, listening for any sound that might tell him if Arnold's mother was awake, or worse yet, downstairs. The house was small and had an odd smell to it, like stale fish. *Probably just old-lady smell,* Jansen thought. He had to give Arnold credit for taking care of a sick mother and keeping a halfway clean house. He wasn't doing such a good job with his own sick wife.

He had only been in Arnold's bedroom one time, and that was because Arnold had asked for his help to mount a large corkboard on the bedroom wall. He knew there was an upstairs, and a basement, but he had never been outside the kitchen except for that one time, almost two years ago. He had never even met Arnold's mother, just heard Arnold refer to her. And from what Arnold had said, she was quite the bitch.

Jansen's wife had been diagnosed with lupus four years ago, and she had been fighting an uphill battle against the symptoms. Two years ago she had given up and stayed in bed almost all the time. He'd hired a housekeeper at first, but when it was obvious that she needed more help than that he had hired a sitter to come in and take care of the wife and the house. It was costly, but in his own way, he still loved her. Sure he was cheating on her, but a man had needs.

Satisfied that he was alone downstairs, he made his way toward the kitchen door that he knew led to the living room. Before he left the kitchen he saw it. On the edge of a wooden chair next to the spick-and-span kitchen table, a small hand axe with a gleaming sharp blade lay on a dishtowel.

"What the—" Jansen said, as he heard a sharp sound.

CHAPTER SEVENTY-FIVE

The killer watched the morning edition of Channel Six news. It was a rehash of last night's stand-up spot with Claudine Setera. *"Reporting live from Shawneetown, Illinois,"* Claudine was saying into the microphone. The camera panned to a man in a police uniform. *It's that shit-kicker lieutenant from the Shawneetown PD,* the killer thought as he turned up the volume.

"Can you tell us the names of the victims, Lieutenant Johnson?" Claudine cooed.

The cop leaned into the camera, a serious look on his smooth, young face, and said, "I'm sorry, Ms. Setera. I'm not at liberty to release the names yet, pending notification of the next of kin." He delivered this line as if he had rehearsed it all morning. Like it was his case and not the bailiwick of the Illinois State Police. *What a self-important little jerk,* the killer thought. But there was something familiar about the man's voice.

"Will you be working with the Illinois State Police on this investigation, Lieutenant?" Claudine asked.

"You betcha," JJ said, and smiled proudly.

The killer felt a tingle of excitement. *Didn't the black-*

mailer use those words? "You betcha," the killer said out loud, and a satisfied smile crossed his lips. He'd killed three men to find this man and here he was on television. The news media is a wonderful thing.

CHAPTER SEVENTY-SIX

Jack left Liddell at the house in Johnson Place, where Lenny Bange had gone out with a nightmarish splash. The attorney had suffered dozens of lacerations from the top of his head to the bottoms of his feet and several broken bones, and his face had been removed and was missing.

The crime lab had called and said there were at least two blood types in the samples that Sergeant Walker had taken from the dog at the veterinarian clinic. Both were human blood, but it was possible that the dog had somehow gotten blood on him from Jon Samuels and the other victim at that scene. It was too early to get excited until that blood was compared by the Illinois State Police with samples from the two victims.

It was a Friday afternoon, and Halloween had turned out to be the nightmare Jack was afraid it would be. The vet's office called to remind him that he had to pick up Cinderella before the office closed for the day.

Driving down Lincoln Avenue toward downtown, Jack punched the speed dial for Susan's cell phone. It rang several times and he was about to disconnect when her voice came over the line.

"Hello, stranger. I thought you had forgotten me," she said.

Jack smiled. "How could I forget you?" he said.

"So what kind of favor do you need?" she asked.

"I'm hurt that you would think I only call you to ask for a favor, Suze."

"So you don't want a favor?" she asked.

"I do need something, now that you ask," he admitted. "But, I'm still hurt that you jumped to that conclusion. What kind of man do you think I am?"

"You're a man. Enough said," she chided.

"Thank you for noticing. Now, about the favor," he said, and explained what he wanted. After she agreed, he punched the off button and concentrated on the next task. This one would not be so easy. It was time to lock himself in the war room and try to make sense of this case.

He would like to have Liddell involved in this, but someone had to stay with the Bange case and no one was better qualified to do that than his partner. An idea struck him and he dialed a number on his cell phone.

"Agent Tunney," said the voice from the other end.

Jack explained his idea and then stepped down hard on the accelerator.

Jack made one more call before arriving at police headquarters, this one to Captain Franklin to update him on the new twist in events. Franklin had offered to move the war room to Two-Jakes Marina for more privacy, but things had happened so fast that never took place. The basement of police headquarters was a pain in the backside, but it was what they had.

Jack made his way to the basement of police headquarters, but this time he used a little-known entrance near the traffic meter maids' office. At the end of a long hallway he used a key he had begged from one of the maintenance crew and entered an unmarked door. On the other side he was in the main hallway of the basement near the department class-room that was used for press conferences. He cracked the door and listened to be sure he was alone before he entered. Only he and Liddell knew of this entrance, and he planned on keeping it that way.

He rounded a corner and almost ran into Special Agent Frank Tunney, who was waiting for him.

"Agent Tunney," Jack said. "Thanks for getting here so quick."

"Jack," Tunney said, "I think we need to talk."

Jack reached for the handle to the war-room door and Tunney blocked his hand. "I mean 'we' need to talk. Alone."

Jack saw something was bothering the man. "Okay. We can use the department classroom. There was no one in it when I came by there."

Tunney followed Jack down the hall. They entered the de-partment classroom and made sure they were alone, then shut the door behind them. "Okay. You go first," Jack said, and sat on the edge of one of the tables.

Tunney paced in that distracted way he had when he was thinking of the appropriate words to use. Finally he said, "I wanted to tell you this, but I don't want it to influence your investigation."

"Well," Jack said. "Tell me."

Tunney paced again, and this time Jack reached out and stopped him. "Come on, Frank," Jack said, skipping the for-malities. "Say what's on your mind. You're killing me with suspense."

"I think I know who the killer is," Tunney said.

CHAPTER SEVENTY-SEVEN

Detective Larry Jansen stood perfectly still. The noise had come from upstairs somewhere. It could have been the creaking of a bedspring, but he wasn't sure. He glanced at the hand axe that was lying on the chair in front of him. It was partially wrapped in a white dish towel that had reddish stains on it.

He listened for the noise to come again. It might be the old lady. Maybe she had heard him come in and had gotten up to investigate? Maybe it was Arnold? Maybe he was still in the house somewhere and had hidden when he heard Jansen making noise at the back door?

He peeked around the corner and looked down the hallway that led to the stairs and up to the second floor and the old lady's bedroom. Arnold's bedroom was past the stairs on the first floor. He could see that the door was shut to that room. There was a bathroom and a storage closet off that hallway, and both those doors were shut as well.

Larry craned his head around the other direction and saw the living room and entryway. Nothing. The house was surprisingly neat. Arnold had even kept the plastic covers on the couch, loveseat, and chair in the living room. The throw rug looked freshly vacuumed. No dirty dishes, no discarded food wrappers, no magazines or newspapers or any of the detritus that you would expect to find in a single man's house. *I got a housekeeper and my place ain't this clean,* Jansen thought.

The noise didn't come again, so he decided to continue his little walk-through of Arnold's house. He would leave the axe where it was for now. He knew the murders Murphy and Blanchard were looking into involved something like a hand axe. But Arnold? No way!

The hallway was devoid of any photos, paintings, wall sconces, any type of decoration. Jansen could see square outlines on the walls, indicating that at one time the walls had been decorated.

When he reached the door of Arnold's bedroom he was surprised to find there was a Schlage lock on the door knob. *Why would Arnold put a lock on his bedroom?* Jansen wondered. He tried the knob. It was locked. *People don't lock interior doors unless there's something inside they don't want you to find,* he thought.

He pulled out the leather wallet that contained his lock picks. The celluloid wouldn't work on this door. He would need the metal picks, and it had been a while since he'd used them.

Jansen inserted the longer pick that ended with a small curve at the end and felt gently along the inside. There were five tumblers in this lock. He located each one and then inserted a second tool in the lock opening. This one was straight and stiff and was only needed to keep tension on the plate that would allow him to turn the barrel that contained the tumblers.

Keeping pressure on the tension bar, and twisting it to the right, he again dragged the other pick across the tumblers. He was rewarded with a soft *snick* as the barrel turned to the right. The door popped open.

He was about to enter the bedroom when the noise came

from upstairs again. He braced himself, expecting Arnold's mother to call out. But nothing happened. As much as he hated to, he decided that he needed to go up the stairs.

He pulled Arnold's bedroom door almost closed. He had never been upstairs before, but he knew that Arnold always talked about his mother being on the second floor.

He took the steps, carefully at first, and then realizing that he was not making any noise on the thick carpet, he quickened his pace. At the top, a small landing led to two doorways. The one on the left was shut, but the one on the right led to a pink-tiled bathroom.

Jansen stepped into the bathroom and noticed the smell of something burnt. He looked in the sink and saw wet ashes and bits and scraps of paper. The faucet had been left dripping. He turned the water off without thinking. Then he heard the sound again. This time it was coming from across the landing. From the other room. The one that must belong to Arnold's mother.

I know I'm gonna regret this, he thought, and walked to the closed door.

"You've got to be kidding me," Jack said. "How do you figure Blake James for the killer?"

"Think it through, Jack," Tunney said. "How long has he been in Evansville? And what do you really know about him? Where did he come from? Family? Friends? There are a lot of questions, but I know in my gut it's him."

"You have a hunch is what you're saying?" Jack asked. "And what am I supposed to do with your hunch?"

"I'm just saying we need to check it out," Tunney said.

"Agent Tunney. I'm in the middle of an investigation, and I don't have shit for evidence. If I start looking into this guy's background and he finds out, a shit storm will come down on this department that even the FBI wouldn't be able to save us from."

"So you won't check it out," Tunney said.

"No. I'll check it out. So happens I don't like the jerk anyway. But I'll have to run it by the captain and the chief first."

Tunney scoffed. "You think they will let you make calls on a media darling's background?" He shook his head. "And I thought the FBI was supposed to be the weak ninnies."

Jack knew that Tunney was right. The chief of police needed to be left out of this. Plausible deniability and all that horse rot.

Tunney read Jack's silence for agreement. "So who do you trust?" Tunney asked.

"Let's go see Garcia."

CHAPTER SEVENTY-EIGHT

JJ looked around his office at the police department and wondered how he had allowed himself to get involved in all this trouble. *It's all Cordelia's fault,* he thought. But he knew that he had made the choice to pursue the people in her diary. It had seemed like a good idea.

He flipped through the single police report that had come in that week—a domestic violence—and not even all that violent. A woman slapped her drunk husband around a little. JJ knew the guy and he deserved more than a slapping. *What kind of guy files charges against his wife?*

His thoughts turned to the two murders at the apartment complex. The sight of Jon Samuels's nearly decapitated body had made him nauseous. But the headless, handless corpse just inside the front door was even more of a gut-wrenching sight. Still, it was exciting. He couldn't wait to get on with another police department. A big one, where he could make detective.

That cute little female reporter Claudine had interviewed him and then she had given him her private telephone number. *Man, I'd like to bite me a piece of that off,* he thought, remembering how her blouse had swelled to overflowing. If he was a big-city detective he'd have more of that stuff than he could handle.

But he still had a problem to deal with. Jon's murder couldn't have been coincidental, no matter what his Uncle Bob said. Bob had been a cop almost all of his life, and he thought that he knew everything.

Uncle Bob had decided that Jon was killed because he was a homosexual. When JJ tried to argue that no one had ever been killed for something like that—at least not in Shawneetown, Illinois—the chief had argued that it was because of Cordelia living a life of sin and that with the additional negative influence of Samuels being a "homo" that it was "bound to happen."

Such a hypocrite, JJ thought. *Uncle Bob's name is in Cordelia's diary, too. So I guess the Lord will smite him eventually.* But he didn't think that a serial killer would be doing God's bidding, and then there was the fact that Uncle Bob didn't know about Cordelia's diary. He also didn't have a clue that JJ had been making calls to people that were in it.

When JJ saw Jon Samuels carved up on the couch, his face missing, and the man on the floor, a jolt had shaken him like a lightning strike. Those were not random murders. He didn't understand what the big man was doing at Jon's place, but maybe the chief was right about that part of it. Maybe that guy was just one of Jon's friends? Or maybe it was someone looking for Cordelia who didn't know she was dead? But it didn't feel that way to him. It felt like some big badass killer had come to Shawneetown to seek vengeance.

JJ wondered if he was next in line because of the calls he had made, but he had been very careful to make the calls from pay phones, and only when he was out of town. There was no way anyone would connect these deaths back to him. No way that the killer would know about JJ Johnson. He was safe as long as he kept his head down and quit making phone calls.

He wadded up the domestic-violence police report and tossed it, one handed, across the trailer, where it swished through the plastic basketball hoop he had affixed to the wall. He jumped from his seat and raised his arms overhead doing a little victory dance, when the phone rang on his desk.

"Lieutenant JJ Johnson, Shawneetown Police Department," he said into the receiver.

"We need to meet," the voice said.

JJ felt his knees go weak.

CHAPTER SEVENTY-NINE

Garcia was just getting off the telephone when Jack and Tunney entered the war room. Before either man could speak she said, "I think I know who we're looking for."

Jack and Tunney exchanged a look. Jack said, "Tell us about it."

Garcia leaned back in her chair and read from a spiral notebook on her lap. "When we found out that Cordelia and Brenda were mother and daughter, it made me think that we needed more information from the old case involving the father and brother."

Jack nodded. Tunney looked stunned but said nothing, so Garcia continued.

"Well, I called Gallatin County Circuit Court to talk to Judge Abner Hudgins to see if he had found the case file on the death of Dennis Morse but got his secretary on the line. Alice said she had some information for us and that she was hoping we would call back."

Jack remembered the secretary trying to listen at the keyhole while they talked to the judge. He doubted that she would have much to add besides rumor or gossip. But on the other hand, sometimes the gossip and rumor made for the best leads.

"Did she have something?" Jack asked.

Garcia's brows furrowed. "I was getting to it." Jack held his hands up in surrender.

"Okay. She said that she found the Morse file, and that she is sending that over to us. But she also found something else she thought we should know about." Garcia paused to flip a few pages on her notebook. "Dennis Morse was named in a paternity suit the year before his wife walked out on him."

Jack remembered the judge saying that Dennis Morse was in the military and had returned home to find his wife pregnant by another man. He had beaten her almost to death and caused the early birth of the child, Cordelia. The wife, Brenda, had delivered the baby in the hospital and then fled never to be heard from again.

"I wonder if Brenda knew about her husband's indiscretion?" Jack said. "Maybe she had an affair to pay him back. She gets pregnant and gets more than she bargained for."

Garcia smiled. "Well, Mr. Detective, I asked that question of Alice. She said that there was a lot of talk back in those days about Dennis and Brenda. I'd been under the assumption that Brenda was a good mother who'd had enough of the physical violence of a nut-job husband and just packed up and moved away. But according to Alice—who said several other women there have the same opinion—Brenda was a 'trollop.' She said that it was possible that Dennis wasn't the father of the boy, either."

Both Jack and Tunney were interested now. This was new information to both men.

"So, anyway, Alice said that the mother was just as abusive to the little boy as the father." Garcia turned to the last page she had written on and said, "So she is sending the case documents of the death of Dennis Morse, and also the paternity suit information. She hoped this would help us."

"Did she have any idea where Cody Morse might be now?" Jack asked. Garcia shook her head.

"I know where he is," Tunney said, and he and Jack exchanged a knowing look.

Jansen stood paralyzed by the sight in front of him. Arnold's mother—if that's who the body belonged to—lay on the bed with the covers pulled up to her chest. Her head was propped against a large pillow, her arms down at her sides. Her graying hair, which had once been carefully brushed out, was matted with blood. The entire top of the bed was covered in blood. Her face was gone, and the skeletal remains peered at him with sightless eyes.

He stared wide-eyed at the thing that had been making the noise that had drawn him to the room. The window next to the bed had been left open and a large black crow was perched beside her head. Its pecking beak, making contact with the face of the corpse, went snick-snick-snick.

Trancelike, he moved forward to shoo the crow away, but it didn't seem to want to leave its meal. Instead, the crow turned one dark eye toward Jansen that seemed to say, "Hey, pal, there's plenty to go around."

Outside the window, Jansen noticed a car on the street below. It was rusted and green and Jansen recognized it at the same moment that he heard a high-pitched keening coming from behind him.

Jansen turned from the window, toward the new noise, blinked, and his life went into slow motion.

Standing in the open doorway was someone familiar, except the face was twisted into a grimace of rage, and one hand was holding the hand axe that had been downstairs by the kitchen table. The man was screaming something as he advanced, but the sound was muffled by the roar in Jansen's ears from his pounding heart. All he could see were the twisted lips, the spittle flying from them, and the axe raising into the air.

Jansen's semiautomatic .45-caliber pistol appeared in his hand, and his finger squeezed the trigger. Jansen barely noticed the blowback as the pistol discharged, but he did feel the sharp pain that seemed to grow outwardly from his eyes and down his shoulders and chest into his arms.

From five feet away, Jansen watched as Arnold Byrum stopped his approach, one hand clamped over the rose-red color blooming on his shirt, the other hand dropping the hand axe to the floor. Jansen clutched at his own chest at the sharp pain that thundered there. His last conscious thought was that he heard sirens.

CHAPTER EIGHTY

Captain Franklin stood on the street and tried to keep his face turned away from the news media that had gathered behind the yellow cordons. Jack spoke on the phone and then, putting it away, approached the captain.

"I filled Garcia in on what we've got here," Jack said, then, "Where's Liddell?"

Captain Franklin nodded toward the house. "He's still in there. It'll take us a week to sort this mess out."

Jack understood what he meant. The hand axe, Jansen's shooting of Arnold, Jansen's heart attack, the mother's face being removed just like the other cases.

"How is Jansen doing?" Liddell asked.

"He won't be answering questions for a while," Franklin said. "I don't believe any of this."

"I agree. There is no way that Arnold is the serial killer—The Cleaver."

Franklin shook his head. "This is all too easy."

Jack was thinking the same thing. Plus, he was sure there was no way Jansen would have been smart enough, or even lucky enough, to have stumbled upon the real killer. From what he and Tunney had discovered with the help of Garcia, they were very sure who the real killer was, and both he and

Captain Franklin had been scanning the crowd since their arrival at the scene. *If the killer doesn't know his cover is
blown, he'll show up here. How could he not?* Jack thought.

Franklin said, "Have you heard anything on Arnold's condition?"

"Ambulance driver didn't give him good odds," Jack said,
"but he made it to St. Mary's Hospital. They have good sur-
geons there." As he said this his hand unconsciously moved
to the scar that traversed a large area of his chest and neck.

"About time," Franklin said, as a black Crown Vic was
admitted under the yellow crime scene tape.

"Who is it?" Jack asked.

"It had better be our search warrant," Franklin said angrily. They had been waiting for almost an hour for one of
the detectives to get a legal description of Arnold's house
and then hot-foot it back to the prosecutor's office and get a
search warrant prepared. Up until this point the only entry
they had been able to make was based on a 911 call made by
Arnold Byrum to police dispatch stating that someone was
breaking into his house. A second call, less than a minute
later, came from a neighbor who heard a gunshot come from
inside the house.

The cops were only allowed to enter parts of the house
where someone could be lying dying or dead, or hiding. To
Jack, this was infuriating. But it was the law.

Jack hadn't told the captain or anyone else yet about the
telephone call he had received from the uniformed officer
who accompanied Detective Jansen in the ambulance to the
hospital. The officer had called Jack's personal cell phone
and told him that while a nurse at St. Mary's hospital was
bagging Jansen's personal property, a small leather case had
fallen out of his jacket pocket. The officer had looked in the
case and found it contained what he described as "burglary
tools."

Jack had told the officer to keep the leather kit, and keep

his mouth shut. Now he was sorry he hadn't shared this with Franklin. He would tell Liddell as soon as he caught up with the Cajun. Then he would decide what to do about it.

It looked like Jansen had been doing a little unauthorized B and E. Which led to the question of why? Jansen was a sneak, but mostly he was such a worthless detective that Jack had to question what could have gotten under his skin to cause him to break into Arnold's house. Jansen would normally walk by a mugging without a backward glance. *Could Arnold have called him to the house? But then why would Arnold call in a burglary to the police? And if Arnold had something to hide, why would he want the police at his house? None of it made sense.*

Liddell stepped out of the front door and said, "Pod'na. You gotta see this," and then he disappeared back in the house.

CHAPTER EIGHTY-ONE

Cody drove south from Old Shawneetown, keeping his car at a distance from the Firebird being driven by Lieutenant Johnson. When he had called JJ to offer to buy the diary, he was surprised that JJ didn't know who he was talking to. JJ was so shocked, he hung up twice before finally agreeing to talk to him.

JJ's denial of any knowledge of the diary ceased when Cody reminded him that JJ had called Cody trying to blackmail him. Then he offered to leave the diary in a secluded spot and then call and tell him where it was, but Cody had silenced him.

"Stop," he had told JJ. And JJ had shut up immediately.

And now JJ was doing everything but going to the meeting place as agreed to. *Tch tch tch,* Cody thought. *Shame on you, JJ. You little liar.*

Cody shadowed Lieutenant JJ Johnson for another hour before he realized the young officer was driving aimlessly and would probably never go to roost anywhere. He had already followed JJ's car across the Wabash River from Illinois into Kentucky and then back again. Now the lieutenant was driving like a bat out of hell down the main highway that led back to Shawneetown from a small town in Kentucky called "The Rocks." Cody didn't want to let him reach home.

He was working against the clock. Every minute the cop was alive was another minute that the cop might realize that the only chance he had to live was to go to the Evansville police and confess what he had been doing. Cody prayed that the cop's pride and fear wouldn't let him do so, but he knew that eventually, self-preservation would take over.

He had hoped to catch JJ alone, but the roads that he was traveling on didn't lend themselves to a covert tailing. If JJ didn't stop soon he planned to catch up to the souped-up Pontiac Firebird and find a way to run him off the road. Looking at the twin exhaust pipes and the low-slung carriage of the Pontiac, Cody thought this might prove a daunting task. His own Honda SUV might not even be able to catch the Pontiac on a straight stretch of road.

CHAPTER EIGHTY-TWO

Jack followed Liddell through the house and upstairs to the bathroom, where a crime scene tech was working over the sink with a plastic bag and tweezers, picking up some dark material.

"Smell that?" Liddell asked.

"Something burnt in here?" Jack asked.

"Not completely," the tech answered, and showed the detectives what she had been collecting. Inside the clear plastic Baggie were several scraps of paper with burnt edges.

The tech was the same one who had worked the Brenda Lincoln scene at Pigeon Creek. She seemed to turn up everywhere.

"What is it?" Jack asked her.

"Printer paper," she said. "Let me show you something." She led the men downstairs to a small bedroom. There was a twin-size bed with a well-worn and almost colorless comforter and a worn-flat pillow, a cheap dresser, and a writing table with a rickety chair. On top of the table sat a laptop. On the table next to it was a stack of printed paper.

"Apparently Mr. Byrum is writing a book," the tech remarked.

"Can we look at what he wrote?" Jack asked.

Sergeant Walker answered from the doorway. "Yes, you can look, but use gloves and don't touch anything else."

"Don't sneak up on a guy like that," Liddell complained.

Walker handed Jack and Liddell latex gloves.

Jack scanned down the first page and then handed it to Liddell and read the second page. "I'll be damned," he said and skipped to the last page.

Jack gave the manuscript to Sergeant Walker, saying, "Show this to Captain Franklin right now, Tony. We have to go."

"What?" Liddell said, but handed the sheet he'd been reading to Walker.

"Just come on," Jack said over his shoulder on his way out of the bedroom.

Liddell moved fast for a man his size, but Jack was already in the car and putting it in gear by the time Liddell slid into the passenger seat. Jack gritted his teeth as he eased the unmarked car out of the crime scene, waiting impatiently for reporters and gawkers to move out of the way so that he could pick up some speed.

Jack almost drove over a television cameraman who stepped in front of their car to get a close-up shot of the two detectives. The man jumped out of the way at the last moment and yelled, "Hey, watch it!"

"You gonna fill me in or am I just a witness to the mayhem you're planning out here?" Liddell said. "Jesus, Jack, you almost hit that guy."

"Yeah, I did," Jack said, and picked up speed as the way cleared before them. Once out of the side streets and on a good four-lane he opened the Crown Vic up, gripping the wheel.

Liddell leaned over and turned on the siren and emergency lights. In less than five minutes they had crossed from the east side of Evansville to the far west and were leaving Vanderburgh County. Jack set the cruise control and the muscles in his jaw eased. He took out his cell phone and then put it down. "What's JJ's cell phone number?"

Liddell flipped through his notes and asked, "What's up with JJ?"

"The page I was reading from Arnold's story back there—" Jack said.

"What about it?" Liddell asked. He had read some of the manuscript, too, but it was a description of the landscape around Shawneetown.

"The page I read described the murder of the next victim," Jack said. "He's going to kill JJ." Jack waited to let this soak in and then added, "He is planning on killing Lieutenant Johnson because Johnson has something the killer wants. He didn't say what it was that JJ had, but no matter what JJ does, he's a dead man. Call him!"

"How do you know that from reading one page, pod'na?" Liddell asked. He dialed JJ's cell number with one hand and held on to the dash with the other as Jack rounded a corner high speed.

Jack said, "Damn! I wish we had that manuscript."

"You mean this manuscript," Liddell said.

Jack took his eyes from the road for a split second to see that Liddell had the pile of papers on his lap and was still wearing his latex gloves.

Jack grinned and said, "You know Walker is going to kill you, Bigfoot."

"Yeah?" Liddell said with a grin. "But you love me . . . don't you, pod'na?"

The Firebird's throaty exhaust bounced back from the trees on both sides of the road as JJ gripped the wheel and tried to hold the car steady in the winding curves. The SUV was only inches from his bumper but struggling to keep up with the Firebird's lower center of gravity and handling ability. The driver of the SUV was a pro, there was no doubt about that. JJ had been through EVOC, Emergency Vehicle Operator's Course, and completed the one hundred hours required with flying colors.

JJ glanced in his mirror and was shocked to see the driver was Blake James, the reporter. A sense of dread ran through him. JJ had called Blake under the impression that this was one of Cordelia's customers. He had obviously been mistaken. Blake must be the killer.

JJ's car should have smoked the little SUV, but James was a damn good driver. JJ knew that in a mile or so the road would straighten out and it would be a flat-out race that the Firebird would win hands down.

But then what? Was the crazy bastard going to follow him into Old Shawneetown? Was he armed? He felt a chill run through him at the remembrance of Jon Samuels sitting upright on the couch, his face missing, the top of his skull caved in. And the body of the other man—a big man, too—on the floor without a head or hands.

CHAPTER EIGHTY-THREE

Liddell flipped back to the beginning of Arnold's manuscript and read out loud. *"She sat on the edge of the bed, while I stood in front of her. Her eyes pleaded with me to understand why she had to find me. Why she needed to know who I was. What she hadn't understood was that it didn't matter who I was—only who I had become. And the only ones that know who I have become are no longer able to tell anyone."*

"What the hell does that mean?" Liddell said, then flipped forward a few pages, and continued reading aloud.

"I could feel the axe handle sticking through the belt in back of my pants. I'm not sure why I brought it. Maybe it was just the idea of having something familiar with me when I had to confront my long-lost sister."

"Is this about Cordelia?" Liddell asked.

Jack was concentrating on driving, but he nodded. "That's what it sounds like to me." They reached St. Phillips Road, the extreme edge of Vanderburgh County, and Jack turned off the unmarked vehicle's siren and dash lights. There was no traffic out here. "Read the last page," he said to his partner.

Liddell rustled the pages and read the last page to himself. "Holy shit!" he said, and read the page again. "Is this where we're headed?"

In response, Jack stepped down even harder on the accelerator. Liddell picked up the radio microphone and called in to dispatch. "One-David-Seven," Liddell said.

"One-David-Seven," the voice on the radio answered.

"Please contact Indiana State Police, Posey County Sheriff Department, and the Illinois State Police. Advise them that One-David-Seven is traveling Code-Three west on State Route Sixty-Two en route to Shawneetown, Illinois. We are requesting Illinois State Police intercept and escort us into town. One-David-Six is with me," Liddell said, telling dispatch that Jack was also in the car.

The dispatcher's voice remained calm, as if Liddell had just ordered a cup of coffee. "Understood, One-David-Seven. I have a message from One-David-One."

One-David-One was Captain Franklin's radio call sign. "Go ahead for One-David-Seven," Liddell said.

The dispatcher relayed the message. "One-David-One advises to call as soon as possible."

"Understood, One-David-Seven out," Liddell said and slipped the microphone back into the dash-mounted holder.

"Hey, Bigfoot," Jack said.

"Yeah, pod'na."

"Did I ever tell you how hot you make me when you talk on the radio, all police-like?"

Liddell laughed and tightened his seat belt. "Did I ever tell you how bad of a driver you are?"

Liddell was still reading Arnold Byrum's manuscript as their car neared Mount Vernon, Indiana. They had picked up an Indiana State Police escort two miles back near the Mead Johnson Pharmaceutical factory and hadn't even stopped for the light at Highway 62 and Highway 69.

The driver of the state police unit looked to be seventeen years old and had a death grip on the steering wheel of his cruiser as he blew Jack's doors in. Jack was doing over one hundred miles per hour at the time and wasn't comforted by anyone that drove more recklessly than did he. He just hoped the kid wouldn't get them killed driving through Mount Vernon, but to the trooper's credit he cleared the path ahead without creating too much chaos on the narrow downtown streets.

On the other side of town Jack stomped the accelerator and flew past his escort without a backward glance. In a few miles he would pass the toll booth that separates Indiana and Illinois. Apparently the Evansville radio dispatcher had called ahead because as Jack's car approached the tollbooth, the operator was standing outside it and waving them through. Jack politely slowed to eighty miles per hour as he flew through the narrow opening.

Jack heard Liddell chuckling. "What are you so happy about?" he asked his partner, unable to take his eyes off the road ahead.

"I've always wanted to do that," Liddell said.

Back at police headquarters, Angelina Garcia was putting through a telephone call to Judge Abner Hudgins's office at the Circuit Court in Gallatin County. The phone rang only once before a woman's voice came on the line.

"Gallatin County Circuit Court. Judge Hudgins's Office. May I help you?"

"Yes. This is Angelina Garcia with the Evansville Police Department. Who am I speaking with?"

"You're the computer lady with those two detectives?" the voice said, not quite a question.

"Yes, ma'am. Can I have your name, please?" Garcia asked again. She hoped she wouldn't have to drag every piece of information from the woman. She knew what little Captain Franklin had been able to tell her about Jack and Liddell's hasty departure from Arnold Byrum's house, and an idea had occurred to her. She wanted to check it out before she said anything to the captain.

Ten minutes and a very sore ear later, she was off the phone and waiting by the fax machine. Though her voice sounded young, Alice Drummond had been secretary to Judge Abner Hudgins for almost forty years. During that time she had kept all of his records, made his appointments, picked up his dry cleaning, and knew where all the skeletons were hidden. Angelina was excited about the information that would soon be coming over the ancient fax machine. She was pleased with herself that she had found information that Jack and Liddell had missed on their visit to the courthouse. But she didn't blame them too badly. After all, they were men and didn't know that if you want the real scoop, you should always ask the secretary.

CHAPTER EIGHTY-FOUR

Indiana State Highway 62 crested a hill just before it turned into Illinois 141 at New Haven, Illinois. Liddell had the phone crammed into his ear to try and hear the captain over the noise of the road and the high-powered engine that Jack was torturing to death.

"Yes, sir. We'll keep you informed as soon as we get something," Liddell said, and put the phone away.

He turned to Jack and said, "We should be meeting Detective Zimmer in a mile or so."

Liddell had filled the captain in on the pertinent parts of the manuscript they had taken from Arnold's house, and had received permission to proceed with their trip. Not that Jack would have turned back even if the captain said to call it off.

"Captain Franklin has been on the phone with the Illinois State Police and they have promised full cooperation," Liddell said.

Jack saw a sharp curve coming up and slowed. "Has anyone been able to raise JJ on his radio?"

"Chief Johnson said he has been trying to find him since this morning," Liddell answered. "Not a peep, and none of the county or state officers have seen or heard from him. The chief said he is seeing a girl over in Kentucky, just across the river. The chief went by there but didn't see JJ's car."

"Did you get an address for her?" Jack asked.

Liddell looked at the notebook propped on one huge leg. "Her name's Eunice and she lives in a little town called The Rocks, Kentucky. It's about five miles on the other side of the Wabash River. I have the address, but I'll have to get directions if you want to go there."

Jack slowed for another sharp curve. "Let's see if Detective Zimmer can get us there," he said.

Liddell shook his head. "How hard can it be to find a police car that looks like an Indy Five Hundred pace car?"

Lieutenant JJ Johnson was testing the limits of his Firebird and finding that it was built for looks, not stamina. He could feel the steering getting sloppy. The hundred-plus-miles-per-hour speeds were taking a toll on his unsteady nerves.

Just as the SUV closed on his rear bumper, the road straightened out and JJ floored the big engine. He pulled away from the SUV slower than he would have believed was possible. *What the hell has he got in that thing?* JJ wondered. Just then he heard a loud pop, and smoke poured out from under his hood.

"Jack," Detective Zimmer said into the phone, "your captain filled me in, but what makes you think the killer's target is Lieutenant Johnson?"

Jack had slowed to a manageable speed now that he was within a few miles of Shawneetown. Detective Zimmer advised that he had driven the stretch of road that Jack was currently on and there was no sign of JJ. Instead of waiting for

Jack and Liddell to arrive in town, he had gone to JJ's trailer. He had found nothing and JJ didn't have neighbors, so there was no one for him to ask about JJ's whereabouts. He was now on his way to Jon Samuels's old apartment to eliminate it from the list of places to search.

"I wondered if you could direct us to a place just the other side of the Wabash River called The Rocks?" Jack asked.

"You talking about Eunice Fetcho's place?"

Jack looked at Liddell and motioned for the notebook. Liddell held it up for him to read. "You know JJ's girl-friend?" Jack asked.

"Ha. That's a good one," Zimmer said. "She's not any-one's girlfriend, Jack. She's a police groupie. Her nickname is Eunice on the Rocks."

"Can you give us directions to her place?" Jack asked.

Minutes later they were following the black unmarked vehicle of Detective Zimmer as he wound he way through Old Shawneetown and past the restaurant owned by Chief Johnson.

Liddell nudged Jack as they drove past the restaurant and pointed out the marked unit on the curb. Apparently Chief Johnson wasn't looking too hard for his nephew. "Think we should stop and see what the chief has found out?" Liddell asked.

Jack didn't really give a rat's ass about the chief. "Too bad the killer isn't going after his lard-butt."

They followed Zimmer down Garfield Street in Old Shawneetown until it turned into Route 56 at the bridge where it crossed into Kentucky. On the bridge Zimmer picked up speed and soon they were cruising southeast down a road that cut through farm fields thick with dry cornstalks.

CHAPTER EIGHTY-FIVE

Lieutenant JJ Johnson of the Shawneetown Police Department had done everything possible to lose his pursuer, but now his engine was smoking and he was losing power. Soon he knew he would have no choice but to pull over and then he would be dead.

There was another popping sound. A thick black cloud of smoke belched out from under his hood and restricted his view through the windshield. The car lost power and slowed. But that didn't stop the SUV from executing a perfect maneuver that would put JJ out of action.

Cody stood on the gas pedal for most of the pursuit, gambling that the policeman wouldn't call for help. But he had given up hope of catching the faster Firebird when they hit the straightaway on Kentucky 56 going northwest toward Shawneetown. In another five miles he would be unable to stop JJ from drawing attention that Cody wanted to avoid.

And then, as if fate had interceded on his behalf, smoke billowed from underneath the Firebird and then blew like a smudge pot with such a thick black cloud that Cody had to back off.

He eased back a few feet and noticed that the Firebird was slowing. Seeing his chance, Cody pulled into the left lane, close to the center line, and lined his right front bumper up with the left rear quarter-panel of the Firebird. Cody cut the wheel hard to the right and executed a perfect maneuver he had watched police perform countless times on television.

The SUV pushed the car into a sideways spin at nearly seventy miles an hour. When the Firebird was perpendicular to the SUV, Cody stomped the gas and rammed the Firebird broadside, driving it down the road sideways.

JJ barely had time to register that he had been struck when he was struck again and was now sliding sideways down the highway, his tires squealing. A new smell entered the passenger compartment from the burning rubber. The side air bag deployed, but it only served to blind JJ to what was coming. Then he was rolling, a sound like thunder in his ears, as the passenger compartment bent at odd angles toward and then away from his. The Firebird tumbled end over end across the road and off into a field.

Cody slammed on his brakes and watched with fascination as the smoking Firebird lifted onto its side and then began a death roll across the tarmac. He came to a rest on the side of the road and watched as the body inside the vehicle was tossed around like a rag doll. The Firebird rolled at least a dozen times before bouncing into the field and then going end over end until it teetered on its front end and fell with a great thud onto its top, coming to rest a hundred feet off the roadway and tearing a jagged path through the brown cornstalks.

Cody listened for a full minute until he was satisfied that no help was coming. He would have to hurry. The Firebird was still sending up a thick cloud of smoke and Cody didn't want any company while he finished his work.

He pulled on a thin pair of leather gloves, picked the bone axe up from the passenger seat next to him, and popped the back hatch of the SUV. He retrieved a small container of gasoline.

CHAPTER EIGHTY-SIX

Jack could see smoke in the distance and wondered what was burning. Then Detective Zimmer put his emergency lights and siren in operation and they were off and running toward the fire.

It took about four minutes to cover the distance. As they came over the top of a hill they could see acres of dry cornfield burning, and in the center of the conflagration a flaming car lay upside down.

"That's JJ's car," Jack said, jumping from his car. He grabbed a fire extinguisher from the trunk and sprayed a path through the burning stalks.

Zimmer came up beside him. "I've called fire and rescue," he said, and deployed his own extinguisher in a sweeping motion as the two men moved forward to the burning vehicle.

"I can see him," Jack said.

Ignoring the flames he reached into the wreck and pulled its driver away from the vehicle and onto the scorched ground. Detective Zimmer used the remains of his extinguisher to create a path away from the fire and onto the road. He then helped Jack drag the smoking body the rest of the way out of the fire.

By the time the men reached the roadway they could hear sirens coming from both the east and the west. Jack looked down at the prone figure he had dragged out of the flames and thought that JJ—if it was JJ—was surely dead. No one could have lived through the inferno that had been made of the Firebird.

The victim's clothing was charred but looked almost silvery, and then Jack realized that he had wrapped himself in a fire blanket. A retching noise came from under the blanket. Lieutenant JJ Johnson threw the blanket open and gulped in lungs full of fresh air.

JJ tried to get up, but Jack knelt and helped him into a sitting position as the sirens came closer. Liddell retrieved a blanket from the trunk of the car and put it around JJ, who was now shivering. Liddell looked at the man's feet and knew they were beyond saving. The fire blanket had protected his upper body from most of the flames, but his boots had melted along with most of the flesh and muscles of his feet.

CHAPTER EIGHTY-SEVEN

At police headquarters Angelina, Captain Franklin and Agent Tunney were in the war room, reading through the files that Judge Hudgins's secretary had faxed. They were excited. All the pieces of the puzzle were coming together.

When Captain Franklin put the file down, Angelina asked, "How is Detective Jansen?" It wasn't that she was really concerned for his health, because Jansen was an insufferable jerk, and he had hit on her a couple of times, but it was the polite thing to do.

"He'll live," Franklin said. "Arnold might be another matter."

"Arnold was shot twice in the face and lived through it," Tunney said, shaking his head in disbelief.

"One bullet entered his sinus cavity on the right side and went out the neck without any damage," Franklin explained to Garcia, "but the other one must have nicked an artery or something and Arnold's brain was oxygen deprived for quite some time. He's in a coma and the doctors don't expect him to be able to talk when—or if—he comes around."

"Did Jansen have an embedded news crew in his hospital room?" Garcia asked sarcastically, causing Franklin to laugh out loud.

"Let's put it this way," Franklin said. "He thinks he caught the serial killer."

"Looks to me like Garcia will get the credit on this one," Tunney said.

Franklin looked at her seriously and said, "You did some great work on this, Angelina. What made you think of it?"

She felt her face redden, although it was nice to be praised for her work. "I didn't do much, Captain," she said. "I just checked out some things that we had all talked about and got lucky. And Susan came up with some tidbits from her sources with the Illinois Welfare Department."

"Listen to her, Frank," Captain Franklin said. "Brilliant, and modest."

"Well, Miss Garcia," Frank Tunney said, "thanks to you I think we will be able to put a face and name on The Cleaver, and make it stick."

The telephone rang and Garcia picked up the receiver.

"Angelina, this is Jack."

He sounded stressed, and she said, "Jack, is everything okay?"

"I know who the killer is," Jack said, and she could hear someone coughing in the background.

"Jack, who is that? Is Bigfoot okay?" She felt a sudden heaviness in her chest.

"Bigfoot is fine. We're with Detective Zimmer in Kentucky. Lieutenant Johnson has been hurt badly and we're assisting. But listen, I need you to dig up everything you can on Blake James. The news guy at Channel Six."

Garcia held the phone away from her face and stared at it. *He's psychic.*

"Jack, that's what I was going to tell you. Blake James is really Cody Fenton Morse. He's Cordelia's brother."

CHAPTER EIGHTY-EIGHT

Jack told Liddell and Zimmer what Garcia had found.

"Let me get this straight," Zimmer said. "This Cody Morse guy came to Evansville just after a string of murders in Atlanta. And those murders were the suspected work of the guy the feds are calling The Cleaver?"

Jack nodded.

Zimmer said, "Then the same type of murders started in Evansville recently and that's what brought Special Agent Tunney to our neighborhood? And now you think that this Blake James, a Channel Six anchorman, is actually the serial killer known as The Cleaver. AND"—he drew the word out before continuing—"you think he is the one that just tried to toast Lieutenant Johnson?"

Jack and Liddell looked at each other and both nodded.

Zimmer put his hands in his pockets and said, "Okay. Sounds good to me. So how do we catch him?"

They were all looking at the ground, until Jack said, "I have an idea."

* * *

Claudine Setera couldn't believe her ears when Elliott Turner, the station manager at Channel Six, called her into his office.

"Look, Elliott, about the remarks I made last time—" she began.

"Shut up," he said. "If you were in trouble the station attorney would be here. As you can see, we're alone."

It dawned on her that he was probably going to try to make her perform some disgusting sexual act in return for keeping her job. She was tired of men thinking that was the only thing she was good at. She was a fine journalist and if that was his idea, she *would* get an attorney and *sue*.

"Jack Murphy just called. Grab a 'live' van and get out there. Here's the GPS coordinates," Elliott said and handed her a piece of scrap paper.

"What is this?" she asked, not able to change gears so quickly.

"It's your big break, Claudine," he said and his smile seemed genuine. "Now hurry over there before the fire department puts the fire out. If you hurry you might be able to catch up with Lieutenant Johnson and get a live interview."

She snatched the paper from his hand and ran for the back parking lot, yelling for her driver and cameraman.

"If he's still alive when you get there," Elliott said under his breath to her retreating figure. He thought about how quickly Claudine had come up at the station. She had the looks and the talent, and people tended to trust and like her. If this worked out for her she would probably get Blake's spot as lead anchor.

He shook his head at the idea of Claudine upstaging Blake and thought, *Blake will be one pissed-off guy*. But, Murphy had asked specifically for Claudine. What was a manager to do?

* * *

At the Alpine Motel the clientele were as anonymous as the homeless. Sitting on wooded acreage on the northwestern outskirts of Evansville, it was frequented by those who could only afford daily rates. Cody had read a book about a serial killer named Joseph Weldon Brown who had stayed at this very same motel for a week while on a seven-state killing spree about ten years ago. In his job as Blake James, he'd found the stories in the news archives at the television station. The idea that another of his kind had been here gave him comfort.

Cody had always thought of himself as more of an avenging angel rather than a serial killer. Definitely not as the man the FBI had dubbed "The Cleaver." *How unimaginative,* he thought, not for the first time. *After all, I only took what rightly belonged to me.*

The people he had killed each had two faces. The one they showed to the public. The kind, hardworking, caring type of face. And then there was the other face. The one that was their true nature. Evil, degenerate, violent child abusers, child molesters, bullies. Like his father. And so, he had taken those untrue faces away from them to let the world see their true ugliness—see them for what they really were.

He wrapped the cloth around the bone axe he had used as a child to kill the man who started all this. The axe had served him well over the last several years—had taken the faces of more than fifty two-faced liars. Wielded by a righteous man of conviction, it had the power to strip even the most powerful enemies of their disguise.

He sat on the edge of the sprung mattress in the twelve-foot-by-twelve-foot room at the Alpine Motel and leaned his head against the streaked wall. The room didn't bother him. He'd been in much worse. The years he'd spent in that asylum after killing his father had taught him to appreciate the present and not worry what comforts he no longer had. Not that he'd had much in the way of comforts before killing his father.

Those years were the only real memories he had. The memories of threats and verbal abuse followed by beatings that left him lying in his own urine, unable to move, afraid to cry. Worse than that, the certainty that he was a coward because he was unable to protect his little sister from even worse abuse at the hands of the man who was supposed to love them, care for them. It didn't matter that he was only six years old at the time. It was his job to protect his sister. And he had failed.

When Cordelia was born, their mother had abandoned them both. From that day it had been just him and Cordelia, locked in a bond of fear and abuse. The beatings had come almost daily by the time he had turned six. Cordelia, although she was barely walking, was no less a target of their deranged father. He had thought back then that his father had blamed them for his mother's disappearance, but now he knew the truth. She, too, had been the subject of the abuse, and she had in turn abused Cody, until Cordelia was born and she saw her chance at escape. Cody didn't blame her for leaving, but he hated her for not taking him with her.

He had lain on the small bed in the room that he shared with his little sister and listened to the moans of his father and the screams of pain from the little girl. He didn't understand what his father was doing until much later in his life. All he knew was that man was somehow hurting his sister and that he, Cody, should be standing up for her. But he was too scared to even look, because if his father thought he was awake and listening he would be beaten again.

He remembered one night, sneaking out of bed, going to the kitchen and eating a slice of dry bread to try and quell the grumbling of his little stomach. The next morning he had awakened to the sound of his father screaming, "You little bastard. I'll kill you." Somehow his father knew he had eaten the bread. The beating that ensued had caused his bowels to loosen and he had defecated on the floor, causing a renewed rage in his still drunken father, who had then dragged him to the bathroom and threatened to "cut his head off" for stealing from him.

Cody closed his eyes. *The sound of his father's work boots on the tiled floor of the bathroom. The sound of a tap being turned on in the old claw-foot tub, steam rising from the scalding water. The hand gripping the back of his neck, bringing tears to his eyes and making his nose run. Then the pain in his side and stomach as the heavy boot came down on him, again and again, finally kicking him almost completely under the old cast-iron tub. The rage that came from some part of him that had been awakened. To his surprise, he scrambled to a crouched position and leaped into the man's chest and face, hands in front of him twisted into claws.*

He remembered his father going down on his back and striking his head on the side of the sink. The man lay on the white tile flooring, dazed, unable to do more than moan, and in that moan came the memories of nights in his room when his little sister had screamed.

Cody had run to the kitchen and pulled open the cabinets under the sink, grabbing the thing that would make all of this go away forever. A voice within him said, DO *it. The weight of the bone axe was almost too much for his skinny arms, but he carried it to the bathroom and stood over the man who had caused all of the pain in his short life. Somehow he found the strength to raise it over his head and drive it down in the center of his father's forehead with enough force to bury the axe blade in the skull. He had to work the handle back and forth to free the blade. When he pulled it loose, he raised it again and again, until there was little left of the man's head, the face completely destroyed.*

The voice that told him to do it had saved him. It had protected him when he was taken into police custody and had nourished him during his long stay in the asylum. Pretty soon Cody the victim was gone. All that remained was the voice.

When he was little his mother had told him that angels looked over him. Guardian angels, she had called them. The voice that spoke to him had given him the strength to live.

He had become an angel. And it was time for Murphy to meet the angel.

CHAPTER EIGHTY-NINE

Claudine Setera was in the Channel Six news van and on her way to a location they could only find with a GPS, somewhere in Kentucky near the Illinois border. Before her boss, Elliott, had given her this assignment, she had been ready to go to Mary's Hospital to interview detective Larry Jansen, who had called and told her he had caught the serial killer.

During that telephone call she had also heard Jansen tell his nurse, "I like my coffee the way I like my women—weak and needy." She had not gotten excited because she knew that the only thing Jansen had ever caught in his degenerate life was probably the clap. But she couldn't pass up the interview and take a chance that maybe he had actually gotten lucky.

Then Elliott Turner had sent her on this story with no details. In a way she was glad not to have to go to the hospital because her gut told her that Jansen's story was going to be bullshit, but she hated driving back toward Shawneetown without a clue what the hell she was supposed to be covering because it would take them most of an hour to get there. All Elliott had told her was that there was an accident, a vehicle fire, and that Lieutenant Johnson had been injured severely.

She smirked at the memory of JJ, the backwoods cop,

coming on to her the last time she was there. Sure, he was kind of cute, but he was just another cop with only one thing on his mind.

At least this time that creep, Arnold Byrum, from the local newspaper couldn't scoop her. As far as she was concerned the best story going on today was Jansen shooting Byrum. She was pissed at the station manager that she wasn't covering that situation. She'd heard through the grapevine that Arnold's mother had been found murdered and her face had been cut off and taken just like the other murder victims.

As the news van crossed the bridge from Shawneetown into Kentucky, Claudine could make out smoke hanging in the air in the distance.

"Hell of a fire," her cameraman/driver noted.

"No shit, Sherlock," she said, ignoring his frown. "What was your first clue?"

A few minutes later Claudine leaned forward against her seat belt and said, "Look at that!"

The news van edged up to the yellow and black crime scene tape that one of the responding troopers had strung along the side of the road. On the other side of the tape were fire and rescue and a pumper truck, plus a half dozen police vehicles, mostly Kentucky State Police, and there were two vehicles that had to be unmarked police cars. One of them looked familiar. Then she saw Jack Murphy inside the ring of uniformed officers. Murphy looked up, saw her, and smiled.

Murphy spoke to a tall Kentucky state trooper and seemed to be arguing with him. Then the trooper nodded and Murphy waved her over.

"Let her and the cameraman through," Murphy yelled at the trooper guarding the entry. The trooper shot a glance at the tall trooper, who shrugged and motioned to let them in.

"Let the games begin," Liddell said to Jack in a whisper.

* * *

Chief Marlin Pope, Captain Franklin, and Agent Frank Tunney sat in the chief's office and watched the live feed from the scene.

"Detective Murphy," Claudine Setera said in her practiced sensual voice, "Can you tell us what happened, and why the Evansville Police Department would be interested in a car fire in this remote part of western Kentucky?"

Jack had given her the question that she had just asked, and told her to repeat it exactly. To his surprise she was playing ball. He looked into the camera, his face unreadable, and said, "The car you see burning behind me"—and he pointed toward the smoking wreck that had once been the prized possession of JJ Johnson—"belonged to a lieutenant with the Shawneetown Police Department in Illinois. His name was JJ Johnson."

Jack hoped that talking about JJ in the past tense would be believable to the public, although he knew the killer would see right through this ploy. "As you can see, Claudine, there is no ambulance here."

He swept his hand around the area and Claudine was surprised that she hadn't noticed the absence of the ambulance before.

"But why are *you* here?" Claudine interrupted. "And where is Lieutenant Johnson?"

This wasn't in the script, but Jack took advantage of the questions to cut to the chase. "Lieutenant Johnson is no longer with us, Miss Setera," Jack said this solemnly, and it was the truth. JJ had been whisked away five minutes earlier by a Life Flight helicopter and was on his way to Wishard Memorial Hospital in Indianapolis, the site of one of the best burn centers in the world.

Jack's face hardened and he moved closer to the camera. "I'm here because the coward that poured gasoline over my friend JJ is watching this program. I want him to know that I'm coming for him. I want him to know that I know who he is."

"Detective Murphy," Claudine said breathlessly, "who is the killer?"

"I have work to do," Jack said and pushed the camera out of his face. "Let's go, Bigfoot." Jack and Liddell shook hands with the tall Kentucky trooper and headed toward the cars.

Claudine Setera, cameraman in tow, followed the two detectives toward their unmarked car, shouting questions. "Detective Murphy, is this the work of the serial killer? Did The Cleaver strike again? Detective Murphy, the public has a right to know who the killer among them is. Detective Murphy?"

Jack and Liddell got into their car and slowly drove out of the scene and back onto the blacktop heading west toward Shawneetown, where they had agreed to call Detective Zimmer before completing the second act of this little play.

Marlin Pope turned the television off and sat on the ledge of the windowsill overlooking the front of the Civic Center.

Frank Tunney folded his hands on his lap and said, "Your man is a good actor."

Franklin shook his head. "Problem is, he's not acting. He means every word."

CHAPTER NINETY

Jack insisted on driving. His hands gripped the steering wheel like the jaws of an alligator as the car hurtled along Kentucky Highway 56 going west into the sunset. Daylight savings time was both a blessing and a curse, giving an extra hour of sunlight in the morning but taking it away too early in the evening. The sun was almost down and Jack was a terrible driver at night.

Liddell was about to suggest that he and Jack swap positions when Jack swerved off the road and slid fifty feet in the soft shoulder.

The car had barely stopped before Jack was out and walking to the other side of the car. He slammed a closed fist on the side of the roof and let out a string of expletives.

Liddell slid out of the passenger seat and leaned against the side of the car until Jack's temper subsided. "Feel better, pod'na?" Liddell asked with a grin.

"No!" Jack spat the word out.

"You shouldn't let it get to you, pod'na," Liddell said. He recognized the signs here. Jack was working himself up into a rage, whereby he would strike out on his own to even the score with Blake.

For some reason that Liddell would never understand,

Jack had this need to right all the wrongs of the world. Of course, it was impossible to do that. When Jack found that he'd chopped off one evil head of the Hydra only to find that two more had grown in its place, he would go off to his cabin and mope and drink massive quantities of Guinness and play his bagpipes until he was too exhausted to do anything but sleep. Then he would come back to work and it would start all over again.

"What happened to JJ wasn't your fault, pod'na," Liddell said, but Jack waved his comment away and got in the passenger side of the car and closed the door.

Liddell slid behind the wheel and drove. Neither man spoke until they had arrived back in Old Shawneetown. Down the street from Chief Johnson's café, Liddell pulled to the side of the road.

"You think JJ really gave the diary to his cousin Gertie?" Liddell said.

"We won't find out sitting out here," Jack said.

Liddell gave him a long look and pulled out on the street again, saying, "Boy, I hate it when you get like this. If you were a woman I'd say it was your time of month, pod'na."

Without looking at his partner, Jack said, "His feet were burned off. The burns on his face will make him a freak. Did we do the right thing by not letting him die?"

"Don't do this to yourself, pod'na," Liddell said. "You're a good man, Jack. You saved JJ's life."

"Yeah," Jack said.

Liddell pulled to the curb in front of the Ye Olde Shawneetown Diner and noticed that there were no cars in the lot or nearby on the street. He wondered where Chief Johnson was.

"You think the chief is going to see JJ in the hospital in Indianapolis?" Liddell asked.

Jack shrugged. "I doubt he could leave the area right now

with what is going on. But maybe we should talk to Zimmer and see if some of the state troopers can take over the duties here for a while?" Seeing Liddell grinning at him, Jack said, "What?"

"Nothing. It's just that you don't ever recognize your own good qualities. You need a wife, buddy. Someone to remind you now and then that you're a human being and not Michael the Archangel."

Jack thought about that. He'd had a wife and blew it. And even when he was happily married, the only times he'd felt human were when someone had died and he hadn't been able to prevent it. So he did what he was best at. He would even the score a little. Make the bad guys pay.

They entered the double French-style doors of the restaurant and found the dining area deserted as usual. From the back of the room they could hear some noise that sounded like someone was torturing a cat, and the sound was getting closer. Then Gertie, or someone who had killed Gertie and taken over her body, emerged from the kitchen, singing at the top of her lungs. The sound was disturbingly ugly, but Gertie, on the other hand, was not.

Gertie was dressed in a soft blue skirt with a white peasant blouse, sensible high heels, and the dirty brown hair the men had seen on their last meeting was now worn down around her shoulders and face. She was wearing a touch of makeup and the result was astounding. Jack found himself wondering how a redneck jackbooter like Chief Johnson could have such a beautiful daughter.

She looked up at the detectives with a shocked look that turned to embarrassment.

"Busted," she said, her face a light shade of red.

"I thought it was quite a good rendition. That was the song from that movie *Practical Magic*, right?" Liddell said. "With Sandra Bullock and Nicole Kidman?"

"You've seen that movie?" Gertie said to Liddell.

Jack gave her a smile he didn't really feel and asked her to come and sit with them for a few minutes.

"Let me bring some coffee first," she said, and headed back into the kitchen, then turned and said to Jack, "You take cream, right?"

"Please sit down a minute, Gertie," Jack said.

"It's really Gertrude," she said, "but I answer to almost anything." She smiled as if this was a joke, but the smile faltered when she saw the serious look on Jack's face. "What is it? What's wrong? Has there been another death?"

Jack could see where she was going with this and hurriedly explained, "We're here because JJ said he gave you something to safeguard for him."

Gertie looked shocked and then nervous. "Is he all right?" she asked.

Jack and Liddell traded a look. Jack was surprised that her father hadn't already filled her in. Jack had called Chief Johnson from the scene of the fire and told him everything that had happened. Why hadn't he been here with his daughter? Why hadn't he told her whether her cousin was alive or dead? It was obvious to Jack that she cared about JJ. And JJ wouldn't have trusted the diary to her if he didn't trust her.

"Where is the diary?" Jack asked. He thought he knew the answer.

CHAPTER NINETY-ONE

Jack and Liddell saw the smoke from the fire before they spotted Chief Johnson tearing the pages from a book and feeding them into the burn barrel. The chief was so intent on his task that he didn't seem to hear the detectives' car tires crunching in the gravel drive where they pulled in behind his cruiser.

"Is that the diary?" Jack asked Chief Johnson as he got out of the passenger seat.

The sky had turned dark and the single bulb on the side of the police trailer had not been turned on. The only light was given off by the fire burning in the barrel. Chief Johnson tossed another handful of pages on top of the flames and sparks shot into the sky.

"I don't know what you're talking about, Detective Murphy," Johnson said without turning.

"That may be the only evidence we would have to convict the man that tried to kill your nephew," Jack said.

"I still don't know what you mean. This is city property and you're no longer needed here," Johnson said. This time there was steel in his voice. Jack moved closer and could see streaks on the big man's face where he had been crying.

"You'll have to live with this," Jack said to Chief Johnson's back, and he and Liddell walked back to their car and left. There were things to do in Evansville. And Jack was sure that Evansville was where Cody Morse would be.

Cody turned on the tiny television in his room, hoping to catch some of the news. Claudine Setera was doing a live spot. It was not her face that caught his attention, but the location. Behind her the smoking remnants of the policeman's Firebird were still being sprayed by firefighters. Cody could see Claudine trying to blink the smoke from her eyes. He turned the volume up.

"Once again, live from a location just south of Shawnee-town, Illinois, we are at the scene of yet another disaster involving one of Shawneetown's residents. The car you can see behind me belonged to Lieutenant JJ Johnson, a ranking member of the Shawneetown Police Department. Police at the scene are unable to say why he was in a police car this far from his jurisdiction or what happened to cause this tragedy. We are several miles across the Illinois border into Kentucky. What Lieutenant Johnson was doing here is a mystery to law enforcement."

The station cut back to Lynn Applewhite, who, to Cody's disgust, was working the evening anchor spot. Lynn was a terrible choice for an anchor position, and if she wasn't sleeping with the station manager, she would have never made it in front of a camera.

Lynn had a believable look of concern on her face when she asked, "Claudine, are the police saying what Lieutenant Johnson's condition is?"

"Lynn, Lieutenant Johnson had already been taken from the scene when we arrived. As you saw in the earlier live feed, Detective Jack Murphy could give us no solid information," Claudine said.

The camera cut back to Lynn in the Channel Six newsroom. She looked into the camera and said, "Claudine, we're going to show that footage to our viewers again."

The television filled with the image of Detective Jack Murphy, his face dark, rage in his eyes. Claudine asked a question and Murphy approached the camera like a gorilla charging a tourist.

"Lieutenant Johnson is no longer with us, Miss Setera," Jack said solemnly. His face hardened and he moved even closer to the camera. "I'm here because the coward that poured the gasoline over my friend JJ is watching this program. I want him to know that I'm coming for him. I want him to know that I know who he is."

"Detective Murphy," Claudine asked, "who is the killer?"

"I have work to do," Jack said and pushed the camera out of his face. "Let's go, Bigfoot."

The cameraman followed Claudine Setera as she pursued the retreating detectives, shouting questions. "Detective Murphy, is this the work of the serial killer? Is this the work of The Cleaver? Detective Murphy, the public has a right to know who the killer among them is. Detective Murphy?"

Cody turned the television off. His hand was trembling, but not from fear. He lifted the bone axe from the bed and felt its comforting weight.

"*You're* coming for *me*?" he said to the blank television screen. "Well, Detective Murphy, your friend and his Thunderbird will never rise from those ashes."

He wrapped the axe in a soft towel and put it in the gym bag he always kept in the car with him. "*I'm* coming for *you*, Jack."

CHAPTER NINETY-TWO

Inside police headquarters in Evansville, Jack and Liddell sat at the large conference table in the chief's outer office. Halloween night, the hour was late. Even the television stations had quit calling for information. Chief Pope sat at the end of the table, arms crossing his chest, listening to Jack and his team as they told the story of Cody Morse and how he came to be back in Evansville.

"Walker and Tunney are rushing the DNA through the system now to see if we can match what we have to the cases the FBI have been working over the past five years," Garcia said. "Tunney flew to Quantico, but said he'll be back tomorrow."

Liddell leaned back in his chair until he heard the wood creak. Captain Franklin shot him a dirty look and Liddell sat up straight. He recovered his balance and said, "I think we may still have a problem in Shawneetown." He looked at Jack for support of his idea.

"Bigfoot's right," Jack said. "The chief over there has created an issue with destroying the diary."

"I thought Zimmer was looking into filing charges on Chief Johnson for that?" Garcia asked.

"He's the chief of police of a two-man department who

just had half the department put out of action," Jack explained. "Even if they could prove that it was *the* diary of Cordelia that he burnt, they would still have to prove that it was evidence of a crime, and without the diary that can never be determined."

Garcia slapped a hand on the tabletop. "You men make things so complicated," she said, and Liddell chuckled.

"Life's complicated," he said.

"So where does that leave us as far as proving that Blake is the killer? Here in Evansville, I mean?" she asked.

"So far, we can only prove that he used a bogus résumé and date of birth to obtain employment at Channel Six," Jack answered. "But Tunney is checking his employment and trying to tie him to the crimes in the other states. The problem is that Cody may have used other identities there."

Liddell added, "And he may not have worked as a reporter in the other places."

Chief Pope spoke up. "Well, at least we have Garcia to thank for getting the court records from the death of Denny Morse and the subsequent commitment of young Cody to the asylum."

"Yeah, that was good work, Angelina," Franklin said, and Jack and Liddell pretended to clap.

Franklin stood up and said, "That's enough for now. Go get some work done."

Jack headed for the war room, but Liddell stopped him in the hallway.

"Where you going?" he asked.

"I'm going to look over the files again," Jack said.

"Isn't Susan waiting for you at your place?"

"Oh shit!" Jack said and changed directions, heading for the back parking lot. He'd completely forgotten that Susan was cooking for him tonight. Well, her version of cooking anyway. Chinese takeout. His favorite. Susan always drank a little wine, got a little frisky, and things got very exciting.

"Isn't tomorrow her birthday?" Garcia asked.

"She's going to be real happy with you, pod'na," Liddell added.

"I'll call her," Jack said, and trotted down the hall.

"Pace yourself, Jack," Garcia said.

"Yeah. You might sprain something," Liddell added.

Jack stopped at the back door, key in hand, when his cell phone beeped at him, indicating an incoming text message. He looked at the display screen and saw a telephone number. He had expected it to be Susan contacting him, but the number wasn't hers. It was the private telephone number for the war room. Since it was a text it could only mean that he was supposed to call that number, but there would be no one in the war room. They were all still in the hallway.

"Look at this," Jack said, and walked back down the hall to show Garcia and Liddell the display on his phone.

They looked at each other and turned down the hallway that led to the basement. Only a handful of people had that number, and due to the lateness of the hour, that was limited to police dispatch, Captain Franklin, or the chief.

Liddell said, "Could be dispatch. Maybe someone's spotted Cody."

Jack only knew that it couldn't be Susan. Therefore, no Chinese take-out, no frisky, and so on. *Sometimes being me sucks*, he thought.

They had barely entered the war room when the phone on the desk began to ring. Jack turned to Garcia, and said, "See if we can get a trace."

She reminded him that the calls to the war room came in on a trunk line for the Civic Center because they hadn't budgeted to have caller ID. Jack threw his hands in the air at the stupidity of city government.

"Answer it," Liddell said.

Jack picked up the phone. "Murphy," he said.

The line was silent for thirty seconds and Jack thought maybe the caller had hung up, but then a familiar voice came on the line.

"Do you know why I killed my father?" Cody asked.

Jack's heartbeat picked up pace. He was straining to listen, hoping he would hear something that would tell him where Cody was.

"I'm tracing this call, asshole," Jack lied, trying to sound sincere. *It was worth a shot.*

"Don't mess with me, Detective Murphy," Cody said. "I know you don't even have a tape recorder on the line."

Or not, Jack thought.

Cody's voice became all business, and asked again, "Do you know why I killed my father?"

"Do you want *Reader's Digest,* or the long version?" Jack said, and was rewarded at hearing Cody's intake of breath.

"I warn you, *Jack.*" Cody spat Jack's name out. "I take my work very seriously."

The line was silent again; then Cody went on, his voice mellow now, thoughtful. "As do you. I've been a fan of your work, you know?"

"Great. Another fan. Just what I needed," Jack said.

Jack heard the heavy breathing again. "Okay, I'll play your game," Jack said. "Why did you kill your father? Hmmm? Let's see. Maybe it was because you were unloved. Or maybe because your mommy left you behind. Well, guess what, Cody? Life sucks. We all have a sad story, but not all of us become killers. Most of us don't kill our sisters and mothers and countless innocent people. Doesn't really matter. All that matters is that I have to stop you. So here's my offer to you. Are you listening?"

The line was quiet, but not dead, so Jack continued. "Come in," he said.

Cody chuckled. "You want me to come in? And why would I do that Detective Murphy?"

"If you do I'll let you live," Jack answered.

Cody's voice turned playful again, and he said, "Are your parents alive, Detective Murphy?"

"No," Jack said.

"Too bad," Cody responded. "I would have liked to kill them."

"I don't do phone sex," Jack said.

The line went dead.

CHAPTER NINETY-THREE

Cody closed the cell phone he'd stolen from his sister the night he murdered her. He'd have to dispose of the phone now because it was a piece of evidence that could link him to the murder. His years in reporting crime stories had allowed him to study his pursuers.

Another thing he'd learned was that the general public was like sheep. They weren't as aware as the police and media portrayed them. He could probably go anywhere he wanted to in Evansville and no one would notice.

He doubted that even half of the police department was aware that he, Cody Morse, was wanted by the other half. *Tomorrow will be a different story,* he reminded himself. But if he played his cards right, he could do what he had planned and be gone by then.

A change of scenery, maybe a new occupation, new hairstyle, gain a few pounds, and he could become someone else. Maybe darken his hair, get a deep tan, and pass for Hispanic.

"What are you doing, pod'na?" Liddell asked, when Jack got off the phone call. "Why do you always have to be the Lone Ranger?"

"He pissed me off," Jack answered. He hadn't really intended to make Cody angry, but it wasn't a bad backup strategy. Just in case what he was planning didn't work.

"We stick with the original idea, right?" Liddell said.

"We're in this together," Garcia said in agreement.

Jack looked at the two of them, trusted friends who loved him. All they were asking was that he not go out and get himself killed. But he knew that he had every intention of lying to them and going up against Cody alone. He couldn't risk one of them being hurt.

"Together," Jack said to his friends. "To the end."

CHAPTER NINETY-FOUR

Jack sent Angelina and Liddell home and sat down in the office to call Captain Franklin and report that Cody had called him. When he began dialing Franklin's number he had second thoughts. What was there to report? And if Franklin knew that Jack had punched Cody's buttons, he'd find a way to sit on Jack to prevent what Jack knew had to happen.

He dialed the number and waited for two rings before hanging up. *Well, I tried,* he thought and was about to leave the office when the desk phone rang and shocked him. It was probably Franklin, but he didn't have a choice now.

"Murphy," he growled into the receiver.

"I'm going to rock your world, cowboy," the voice on the phone said.

It wasn't Captain Franklin.

"Only my friends, or cross-dressers, have ever called me cowboy, Cody. You're not a friend so you must be a cross-dresser?"

Cody laughed out loud. "Jack. Can we start over? I don't want to fight. I'm not a bad guy. I'm doing the job you guys won't or can't do."

"What job is that, Cody?" Jack asked.

Cody sighed as if this was testing his patience. "I'm rid-ding the world of the scumbags that think they can bully anyone they want. I have never killed an innocent person."

"Well, now we can agree on something," Jack said. "Your mother definitely deserved to die for letting you out onto society like some flesh-eating slime. But I still can't see what your sister did to deserve what you did to her."

Cody said, "You haven't told anyone about my call, have you?" It wasn't stated like a question.

"No need," Jack answered coolly. "You'll be dead and cold before I'll have to tell. Why don't we meet?"

Cody laughed again. "Not so fast, sport. No wonder you can't keep a woman in your life. You're always in a hurry and definitely not a nice man."

Jack knew he should just hang up. The second part of the plan was to have Jansen leak the info to Claudine Setera that Lieutenant Johnson was still alive and under guard at Welborn Clinic downtown. The idea was to drive Cody into making a second attempt on JJ. The trick was that JJ was in Indianapolis and not in Evansville.

But Jack knew Cody would never fall for that. He had probably already figured out that JJ was alive. And JJ hadn't given the diary up even when Cody was pouring gasoline on him. Zimmer had men watching Cordelia and Samuels's old apartment on the off chance that Cody might turn up there looking for it.

"This is between us, Cody," Jack said. His best chance was to lure Cody out. Then take him out.

"You're right about that, Jack. It is between us, but I'm not going to make it easy for you. I know how devious you can be. We have to play a game first."

"If it's a game of minds you're basically unarmed, so what's the point?"

Cody seemed to be enjoying this repartee. "Good one, Jack. So here is the first test. What am I going to do next?" And with that, Cody broke the connection.

Jack hung up and swore like a sailor, cursing himself for being too anxious.

The phone rang again.

"Listen, asshole," Jack said, but then Captain Franklin broke in.

"You called me, remember?" Franklin said.

"Sorry, Captain," Jack said, and then filled Franklin in on the two phone calls from Cody, leaving out the parts where he had tried to lure Cody out with his smooth style.

"Get Garcia and Liddell back in there," Franklin said, when Jack had finished. "I'll call the chief and we'll meet you in the war room in twenty minutes."

Susan sat at the cabin, alone, the small kitchen table littered with containers of Chinese takeout from Two Brothers, her chopsticks poking into an eggroll that had lost its appeal an hour ago. Jack Murphy was definitely the most infuriating, juvenile, opinionated, interesting, lovely, sexy man she had ever met. She was sure he had gotten caught up in something to do with the cases he was working, and she really did understand how important his job was.

But why can't he pick up the phone and make a ten-second call?

She would give him another half hour. Then she was packing the remnants of this romantic dinner into his refrigerator and heading home. She didn't like staying in the cabin by herself, and especially at night.

Cinderella let out a whimper and Susan said to the dog, "Sorry, hon, I'm not mad at you. You're a good girl."

She picked a piece of chicken out of one of the containers and carried it to the makeshift bed she had prepared for the injured animal, who lapped it up and then licked Susan's fingers.

Susan patted the dog's neck, being careful not to touch

the long wound on top of Cinderella's head. She felt so sorry for the poor creature, who had been trying to protect her master. And that thought made her think again of Jack Murphy, who'd had the compassion to bring the dog to his home. *Maybe there's a real man under all that tough exterior after all.*

She knew Jack wasn't going to be happy that she had used his two extra bed pillows and one of his best blankets to make a bed for the dog. Well, it served him right for standing her up. If he'd been here he could have found his own bedding.

She sat on the floor beside the dog and stroked her neck until Cinderella began breathing softly. *The pain pill must be working,* Susan thought. *Poor baby.*

Cody borrowed an old Chevy pickup truck from the man who was staying in the room next to his at the Alpine Motel. The man must have been a traveling salesman because there were maps all over the front seat and the floor was littered with fast-food wrappers. The man wouldn't need the truck anymore, and had eaten his last chalupa from Taco Bell. Those things weren't good for him anyway.

He drove the truck southeast on New Harmony Road until he reached the Hill Top Restaurant, where he knew he would have to turn left and follow that street to Fulton Avenue. The lights were still on inside the Hill Top, but only one or two cars were parked in the front.

He turned sharply into the gravel lot and bounced over the potholes to the back of the building. He parked in the rear and went to the back door, which he found unlocked and propped open. The smell of ammonia competed with the smell of the day's cooking.

"We're closed," came a voice inside. Cody saw a large man in his mid-fifties, dressed in khaki pants, a T-shirt, and a stained apron, standing just inside the back door holding a mop.

"I'm in need of some food," Cody said, stepping inside.

A food-prep table held a rack of knives, along with various other cooking tools and pots and pans. "You missed a spot," Cody said, and pointed to the floor at the man's feet.

The man looked down and Cody's hand was a blur. He plucked a cleaver from the table and drove the blade into the side of the man's neck, just below his left ear. The heavy cleaver sliced through tendon and muscle and hit the carotid, causing the man's eyes to roll back in his head before he fell to the floor, hands grasping for the handle of the cleaver.

"Okay," Cody said. "Now let's get something to eat."

CHAPTER NINETY-FIVE

Susan finished the note for Jack, checked that Cinderella was comfortable, and locked the cabin door behind her. *No Jack. No call,* she thought, and sighed. It was late, and the moon was hidden behind heavy clouds. Tomorrow threatened rain and she needed to weatherproof a basement door where she had found a leak during the last downpour.

She got into her baby-blue Honda del Sol and adjusted the clips that held the hardtop in place. The car was about the size of a postage stamp, but had the speed and maneuverability of a race car. She started the engine.

She remembered how Jack had reacted the first time he had seen her tiny car. How he'd made a big show of trying to get into the car, like he was stuffing himself into a sardine can. But on the infrequent occasions that she wore a skirt, the car seat had a way of making it ride a little high on her legs. That was the only thing Jack liked about the car.

She backed out and turned toward Lynn Road, making her way west along the river road that would take her to downtown Evansville. Getting on Riverside Drive, she turned down the street that paralleled the river and then into the driveway of the three-story bed-and-breakfast that she had purchased and was restoring.

She was almost too tired to fight with the heavy door on the carriage house and thought about leaving the car in the driveway, but then remembered the coming storm. The latches on the car's hardtop were a little hinky at times and a high wind might blow the top off.

She pulled herself from the car and wrestled the heavy wooden door up.

As she started back to her car the rain came. It beat down with such ferocity that she stood in the doorway to the carriage house, thinking that she should not have left the keys in the car. She grabbed a heavy hooded jacket from a peg on the wall just inside the doorway and slid into it, then ran for the vehicle and dove inside.

Cody watched the car stop outside the building. A good-looking blonde got out and opened the overhead door. She was coming back out when the skies opened and a torrent of rain fell. Cody liked the rain. It would make this much easier. He could use the noise to cover his entry into the house. And then he'd gut the bitch like a catfish and leave her head in Murphy's cabin. Minus the face, of course. That was his. When Murphy came home and found her head, he would lose his . . . literally. Cody couldn't wait to collect Jack's face.

He leaned his head back and closed his eyes. The faces of his sister and mother came to him. They were together now—wherever they were—and they were happy. His father's face had ceased to come into his consciousness some years ago. *Too bad it was missing from my collection.* He reached across the seat, putting his right hand on top of the leather case that had been with him since his release from the asylum.

Inside the simple leather satchel that was held closed by a single strap were the faces of his enemies. He had fought

with evil, conquered it, and carried its faces to remind him
of how far he had come. "Veni, vidi, vici," he said softly. *"I
came, I saw, I conquered."* The words were written by Julius
Caesar in 47 B.C. as a comment on his short war with Phar-
naces II of Pontus in the city of Zela, which is in Turkey.
Cody had enjoyed reading about great military leaders during his imprisonment in the asylum. He admired their bold
campaigns.

He heard a noise and opened his eyes. Looking across the
children's park where he had parked the stolen truck, he saw
the little blue car backing out of the garage. *Where the hell is
she going?*

He shifted into drive and rolled forward. When the Honda
del Sol reached Riverside Drive he was less than fifty yards
behind it. She headed east on Riverside and turned south
onto Waterworks Road.

This is the way to Murphy's cabin, he thought. *Well, that
works for me.* He planned on leaving part of her there anyway, so maybe this would be more convenient. He wouldn't
have to risk driving to Murphy's with a head on the front
seat. He could kill her there and then wait for Murphy to
come home. "Honey, I'm home," he said out loud, and
chuckled.

The car picked up speed on Waterworks Road. Cody wasn't
expecting her to run from him. *She couldn't have seen me
watching her house.* He knew that Murphy was still at the
police station, where he would now have to have a meeting
with Liddell, Garcia, and the chief of police about the telephone calls he had made.

There's no way Murphy has this figured, he thought. But
just to be sure . . .

Cody took Cordelia's cell phone from his pocket and
punched in the number for the office at the police station.
The phone rang five times before Jack Murphy picked up.

"Murphy," the voice said angrily.

Cody closed the phone and broke the connection. He pressed the accelerator down and felt the truck hurtle forward in pursuit of the blue del Sol.

Waterworks Road runs between Riverside Drive, where it intersects with Veterans Parkway, and U.S. Highway 41. Two miles of straight road with no hills or turnoffs. Nothing on either side but dead cornfields. It reminded Cody of the pursuit he'd had earlier in the day with Lieutenant Johnson, but this time he had the advantage of having a bigger engine and no curves to deal with.

She poured on the speed as he came up close behind her and was pulling away, but he knew her flight was futile. In the end he would catch her and take her face.

About a quarter mile west of Highway 41, the little car veered off the roadway and seemed to disappear in the cornfield. Cody locked up the brakes, but the heavy truck slid on the rain-slickened blacktop, flying past where the small car had disappeared.

Cody put the truck in reverse and backed to where he found a small dirt road running between the fields. He had never seen it before, but then, he really didn't travel these roads all that much. Maybe it was a farm road to get into another part of the field?

He drove to the end of a row and came to a T-intersection. He pulled forward enough to see both directions, but it was pitch black. He turned the ignition off and rolled his window down. To his left he could hear the low throaty growl of the Honda. He cranked the starter and headed that direction.

About two hundred yards down that path he came to what looked like some kind of pumping station. The tall metal structure was a twist of green-painted pipes housed on a concrete base with a door set in the side. In his headlights he could see the back end of the Honda sticking out from behind the structure. He noticed there was exhaust coming from the Honda, and the door to the pumping station was ajar.

Cody shut off his engine and picked the bone axe from the passenger seat.

"Susan," he said in his television anchor reporter voice, "there's no place to hide, hon. Why don't you come out and talk to me? I just want to talk about Jack."

Something metallic clanked inside the structure. *Is she trying to find a weapon?* Cody wondered. *Well, I think mine is bigger than hers.*

He approached the door and shoved it open with his foot. "If you don't come out it's going to get messy."

There was no further noise from inside. No crying. No sounds of scurrying around trying to find a nonexistent hiding place. She didn't even have the good sense to beg for her life.

Time to end this, he thought, and moved into the opening.

The cell phone in his pocket rang. He stopped and felt for the phone. Plucking it from his pocket he saw the number displayed on the tiny LCD screen. It was Murphy. *Perfect,* he thought.

He flipped the phone open with one hand, the bone axe poised in the other, and said, "Guess where I am, Jack?"

The voice that came over the phone sounded funny. It was definitely Jack Murphy, but it almost sounded like he was on the phone and . . .

"I know where you are," Murphy said, and a deafening blast echoed around inside the concrete structure.

Cody's face registered surprise just before a red bloom of liquid trickled down the middle of his forehead. The back of his skull was blown into the cornfields, where it could later become a delicacy for the crows. Cody collapsed in the doorway of the pumping station, the phone still in one hand, the axe in the other.

"Game over," Jack Murphy said.

EPILOGUE

The FBI grilled Jack for five straight hours inside the Federal Building, which was conveniently located just across the street from the police station. Agent Frank Tunney remained mostly silent while three local special agents asked every question they could think of, but somehow skipped over the question of why Jack had driven Susan's car into the cornfield in the first place.

Captain Franklin followed procedure and had taken Jack's weapon and badge pending a full shooting board and Internal Affairs inquiry. Jack wasn't worried. It was a routine he'd been through before. And, unknown to anyone but Liddell, he still had two backup guns at home.

Liddell and Garcia had fawned over him like mother hens until Jack had threatened to shoot himself—or them—if they didn't stop.

All that remained was to face Susan, whom he had scared half to death when he had grabbed her inside her carriage house and hijacked her car. He'd explained that the man in the truck across the street was the killer they had been looking for and had further given her the bad news that the killer was there for her. She had insisted that he wait for backup and Jack had made some kind of excuse why he couldn't do that. He wished he could remember what lie he'd told her now. She had promised to meet him at his cabin that morning. That was where he was now headed, almost six hours later.

As he pulled up in his rear parking area he noticed two things. His personal vehicle—a 2010 Jeep Cherokee—was there, but Susan's Honda del Sol was not. *Maybe crime scene is still going over it,* he thought, but couldn't imagine what they expected to find. He'd been told that they had recovered a suitcase full of mummified faces from the front seat of the stolen truck. And that they had found the very much deceased owner of the truck—also missing his face— lying on the floor of a room at the Alpine Hotel. Apparently Cody wasn't as concerned about covering his tracks, or making an escape, as he was about getting to Jack Murphy.

He parked his unmarked vehicle next to his Jeep and walked around the side and up onto the front porch. The sun was barely up, and the cabin seemed unnaturally quiet. He reached into his pocket and pulled out the small velvet case. He flipped it open and looked at the two-carat princess-cut diamond solitaire. It had cost him more than he'd paid for his Jeep.

It was Susan's birthday, and he'd managed to buy the jogging suit for her. He found the front door locked, the cabin quiet and empty. Jack didn't know what he had expected. Maybe a welcome home from Susan, a big kiss, a "thank you for not letting him kill me," and then some Chinese takeout and sex. But what he found instead was Cinderella.

He remembered then that he had asked Susan to pick the dog up at Branson's Veterinary Clinic and take her to the cabin. The dog looked up from the couch and growled softly at him. He noticed on the living-room floor was what looked like a pillow that had been shredded and the batting was stuck to one of his favorite blankets.

On the small table near his recliner was a handwritten note from Susan that read:

Dear Jack,

*I'm sorry I couldn't stay. I hope you'll understand.
I fixed a bed up on the floor for Cinderella. There's
something about her that makes her the perfect
female presence in your life. I know she doesn't seem
to like you, but if you treat her like a lady I'm sure
she'll come around. (Me too.)*

*PS: I bought peanut butter and chicken breasts at the
store. The chicken is in the fridge. The vet said
Cinderella is to get the antibiotic twice a day and the
pain pill each morning. She took them fine for me, but if
she won't take them Brent said to put the pills in a little
peanut butter. She loves the peanut butter. If that doesn't
work boil a chicken breast and bury the pills in the
chicken.*

She's a very sweet girl. Good luck, hon.

*Xoxoxo
Susan*

Jack went to the kitchen table and found two amber-colored
plastic bottles from the vet's office and a large jar of peanut
butter.

He took one of each of the pills out of the bottles and then
opened the peanut butter. He scooped out a large dab on his
forefinger and buried both pills inside the glob.

"We get you well, then get you out of here," he said to the
dog, who cocked her head as if listening.

I'll give the dog the medicine and then call Susan, he
thought.

"You want some of this?" he said to Cinderella and held
out the peanut butter.

Cinderella cocked her head to the side, keeping her keen
eyes on him. He came a little closer and her ears perked up.

"Okay, you get a peanut-butter/pain-pill cocktail, and I'll have a couple of Guinnesses."

When his finger with the peanut butter came near her snout, Cinderella began to growl.

"Bite me and I'll shoot you myself," Jack muttered and continued pushing the peanut butter toward her.

She leaned forward and sniffed, then poked out her tongue and lapped the glob from his finger.

When she had eaten it all, Jack pulled his hand back slowly and then wiped it on his pants leg. "That wasn't so bad now, was it?" he said.

Cinderella's head moved up and down as if she were going to vomit, but instead she spit the pills out on the floor.

"Awwww," Jack said, and went into the kitchen to boil the chicken.

The box from Hibbett Sports lay on the table. He would buy a card after he got some sleep. It was a start.

ACKNOWLEDGMENTS

My heartfelt thanks to:

Michaela Hamilton, my editor, and her colleagues at Kensington Publishing Corp.

Dr. Brent Branson, DVM, and the staff at Vetview West Animal Hospital.

My friends at the New Harmony Coffee House in New Harmony, Indiana.

And of course my fans, for your continued support, suggestions, criticisms, e-mails, and friendship. Without you I would not be a writer.